The Outcast

Feridon Rashidi

A Bright Pen Book

British Library Cataloguing Publication Data.
A catalogue record for this book is available from the British Library

ISBN 978-0-7552-1666-6

Authors OnLine Ltd
19 The Cinques
Gamlingay, Sandy
Bedfordshire SG19 3NU
England

This book is also available in e-book format, details of which are available at
www.authorsonline.co.uk

To my mother and father

The Outcast

This life, whether auspicious or a vale of tears, will pass,
Whether we are in Bushehr, Mashhad, Tehran, Shemiran,
Or Qasr-e Qajar, our incarceration will soon be over.
We belong to that race of unblemished innocents,
Who bear no grudge against any soul.
We have a city full of enemies, and not a single friend.
We are among those rarest of victims,
Who are not afraid of being stoned by the mob.
We entered the church, they chased us out.
We declared that there is one God; they threw us out of the mosque;
When we professed that Mohammad and Ali are the truth,
Having made us a target, the rabble buried us under a hail of stones.

(A popular Persian poem)

1

It was on a Sunday morning in mid-August 1978 that Kazem stepped out of his cell in Tehran's Central Penitentiary. He had on a pair of grey, creased trousers, a black shirt with tobacco stains on the front, and a shabby pilot's jacket that was worn smooth at the elbows, frayed at the collar, and scaled off all over like the scabrous skin of a donkey. His black patent-leather shoes were chipped from toes to heels. A tangled mop of black hair crowned his head. His face was almost hidden by the coarse hairs of his beard. His fox-like, intelligent eyes darted around beneath his thick, dark eyebrows. With a cigarette dangling between his lips, he clutched his bundle of personal belongings and stared blankly into the void, like someone who has just woken from a bad dream. Suddenly, he became aware of the harsh voice of the prison guard issuing from the loudspeaker booming a brazen blast above his head, like the Seraph blowing its horn on Doomsday and echoing in the wide central corridor running along both sides of the prison cells.

"Kazem, known as Alaki, from Block Number Five, Cell Number Three, report at once to the prison office."

Over the years Kazem had been nicknamed Alaki by his friends and cellmates because he was a happy-go-lucky sort, always smiling and cracking jokes, making everybody laugh. Everything in his life happened for no rhyme and reason. His closest friend in prison, Nasser Sibil, a stubbly, middle-aged man with a grey-streaked, drooping moustache, came out of the cell and followed Kazem along the corridor, shouting to the convicts to throw whatever money they could spare into the spread-out blanket that was carried by a group of Kazem's closest friends. Some inmates had saved money, which they had hidden in various places such as holes in mattresses, inside cracked teacups, or sewed to the inside of their trousers. These men stuck their hands out through the iron bars and dropped some crumpled banknotes into the blanket.

At the end of the corridor, Nasser Sibil raked the banknotes off the blanket and handed them over to Kazem, who reluctantly accepted them. He then thrust the notes into the inside pocket of his jacket.

"Once again you took me completely by surprise, Agha Nasser," said Kazem, his eyes shining with gratitude. "I don't deserve this generous gesture from my friends. I'm in your debt, Agha Nasser."

Nasser Sibil listened thoughtfully, combing his moustache with his fingers and gazing at the floor. He then spoke in a fatherly voice, separating each phrase with a long and significant pause:

"These fellows here like you, Kazem. Anyway, listen, son: let's make no bones about it. You've been inside these four walls for two years. Many inmates will soon be let out and go about their lives out there in the wide world. If you ever wind up back here again, you'll most probably see strangers who'll not be as big-hearted and kind to you as this bunch. You're still young and have a future ahead of you. Don't throw away your life like this by smuggling, stealing and gambling. When you're out of here, try to mend your ways and live a decent life, otherwise you'll end up like me – spending the rest of your days here, slowly rotting away. I hope I'll not see you again here before the week is out."

"I'll do my best, Agha Nasser," said Kazem gruffly, bowing his head and struggling to suppress his emotions.

Two stone-faced prison guards came to take him away. The two friends shook hands and hugged one another. With his bundle, containing all he had in the world, tucked under his arm, Kazem walked briskly in the middle of the corridor, a guard on either side. He turned every so often and glanced at Nasser, who remained in the same spot, watching him go, as an old peasant watches his only son leaving him on his own in the village to go to the capital to seek his fortune.

After Kazem had signed some papers, the two guards accompanied him to the Penitentiary's interior iron gate behind which he stood as still as a bronze statue, waiting. An eternity passed before the huge, charcoal-grey gate slid along its rusty groove, making a dull clanking sound. The pale, early morning light flooded in from the outside world, hurting Kazem's eyes. Blinking, he shaded his eyes with his hand. Once the gate was wide open, he glanced back for the last time to see if Nasser Sibil was there, but he must have gone back to the block.

Kazem stepped outside into the vast, drab courtyard. The same clanking sounded behind him again, this time shutting the prisoners in. He strode to the main wooden prison gate, stood behind it, drew in a deep breath and looked up at it. As he raised his head, he heard the sounds of the city of Tehran, that most brutal of all cities, stirring from its slumber. Two sturdy-looking prison guards pushed the gate open from outside.

Kazem stepped out into the city a free man. Like a famished urban wolf, he stretched out his hands, thrust forward his chest, lifted his head up, looked at the blue sky, and sniffed the fresh, end-of-August air, ready to pounce on the waking city, a monster struggling to get on its feet.

* * * *

It took some time for Kazem to get used to the mayhem going on around him. He looked to his left. The tall brick wall of the prison stretched up to unknown, distant districts of Tehran. His eyes slowly glided back, taking in everything in the large Qasr Square. Finally, they came to rest on the tall wall to his right, stretching to far-off parts of the sprawling capital. He sauntered towards the middle of the square, stopped, turned on his heel, and stared at the colossal façade of the prison. High on top of the gate dangled a gigantic model of a crown – the symbol of the ruling Pahlavi Regime – decorated with garish, colourful light bulbs. Attached to the brickwork arch, just beneath the crown, was a huge, permanently lit projector that glared down on everyone like a one-eyed monster. The sentries were hidden from view inside their observation huts perched at regular intervals on top of the walls. The gate was flanked by two sentry-boxes, inside each of which stood a sentry with his rifle propped on his shoulder.

A motley crowd of visitors poured out of buses and joined in a long queue that ran along the wall on the left. They were all gripping bundles of food and necessities such as cigarettes, sugar and tea for their relatives and friends in the prison. The prison guards yelled, swore, shoved and pushed the subdued folk, who swarmed, like tiny insects, at the foot of the main gate that towered over them.

All kinds of street traders had established themselves along the wall to the right. They were all chanting at the tops of their lungs, praising their wares – boiled broad beans, lamb-liver kebab, shelled-and-salted walnuts in glass jars, lentil stew, hot milk, and roasted-and-salted watermelon seeds. Kazem walked to one of the stalls, conscious of the vendor looking him over. He bought a paper-cone filled with watermelon seeds, ambled to a bench in the middle of the square and flopped on it. He picked one seed at a time, popped it into his mouth, shelled it between his teeth as skilfully as a parrot, spat the husks out, and munched the soft core inside, looking around at the throng of people milling in and about the square.

Where should he go? Paper cone in hand, he stood up and wandered about the square, popping seeds into his mouth. Men and women crossed the space in a hurry to catch buses or taxis. Some long-necked, spindly-legged, tight-trousered adolescent boys with long, tangled hair stood idly here and there in small clusters, gaping at young girls in mini-skirts or tight-fitting trousers. Some of the boys, who considered themselves ladies' men and wanted to show off to others, hurled witty remarks at the girls, who haughtily ignored them.

I'll walk down Shemiran Street and decide what to do next, Kazem decided. He walked out of Qasr Square and strolled a while before coming to Shemiran Street. Every imaginable kind of vehicle, driven by men, pulled by donkeys or horses, trundled frenetically in the street. Horns blasted, brakes screeched, sirens wailed. Kazem, totally bemused and amused, wandered down the pavement, devouring everything he saw. As he walked, he stopped every now and then and gazed at the shop-windows, behind some of which glassy-eyed mannequins were dressed up in the latest European fashion. Goat-like, he poked his head into some lanes just for fun to see what was going on. Every so often, putting his life into grave danger, he crossed the street, hopping over the gutter on to the pavement, to see what novelties were to be found on the other side. He mingled with the pedestrians, who crossed the street singly or in droves, as if a herd of cattle was let loose, without paying the slightest attention to traffic lights or zebra-crossings. The angry drivers stuck their heads out of the windows of cars, buses, and trucks and swore at them. The pedestrians just glanced at the drivers nonchalantly, cursing and hurling the most colourful obscenities back at them.

As soon as he saw the first cinema, he stood with his hands clasped behind him and inspected the pictures. On the huge billboard, painted in the foreground, was the picture of an ill-tempered man with a handlebar moustache wearing a black suit, patent-leather shoes, and a black bowler hat that was pulled down over his frowning brow. A woman, painted in gaudy colours, stood in the background in dancing posture. The plumply pretty and heavily made-up woman had a very short skirt, barely covering the lower parts of her ample buttocks. She was touching, with one hand, the rim of a black bowler-hat, under which was tucked her jet-black hair, and with the other, she was waving a white handkerchief, raised aloft.

Kazem went on examining the billboard for some time, admiring the sulking actor who had been his hero since he was a little boy running around in the gutters of Najeebkhaneh Street in Shahr-e No in downtown Tehran. He then turned his attention to the dancing woman who brought back memories of his mother who had been a dancer in a small cabaret in Shahr-e No.

2

The cinema reminded him of his best friend Davood, who had grown up with him in Shahr-e No and with whom Kazem used to go and watch movies. When young, they'd had great hopes of becoming movie stars. I wonder what happened to Davood Jigool, Kazem thought. Last time I saw him he was into pushing drugs in the Citadel. Maybe he can lend me some cash till I sort myself out.

Kazem speeded up his pace. He wandered down Shemiran Street, his jacket flung over his shoulder, feeling like any Jack-the-lad who was out of place in those affluent parts of the city. Upon arriving at Naderi Avenue, he caught a bus to Gomrok Street. Once there, he got off the bus, found Jamshid Street and walked through the narrow Jamshid Walk and entered into the Citadel.

Hardly had he entered the Citadel than he felt that things were not the same. There were fewer people scurrying around. They all seemed as if afraid of something or someone. Kazem threaded his way through the crowd and entered one of the houses. There was no sound of the usual tape-recorder playing popular songs. A handful of anxious-looking young men were sitting politely on some rickety chairs near the *hauz* filled with murky water, on the surface of which floated a few dead fish. The men were all staring at the rooms, each waiting for the *khanum* of his desire to finish with her client and come out. Kazem walked straight to the *maman* who, sitting bolt upright on a chair behind a tin table, was fiddling with tokens.

"How many tokens do you want?" droned the *maman* without looking up at Kazem. "For half an hour with a *khanum* you need one token, for an hour you need…"

"Now you're selling me tokens, Zeenat Boshkeh!" said Kazem.

Zeenat, known in the Citadel as Boshkeh on account of being so fat, looked up and peered into Kazem's hairy face.

"*Bah, bah*, Kazem Agha!" exclaimed the old hag upon recognising Kazem. "Why do you look so hairy like a bear? I hope you've not joined those whoresons mollahs."

"What do you mean?"

"They send their hairy-faced thugs to the Citadel threatening us to raze it to the ground if we don't stop our trade."

"Why do they want to do that?"

"Because they say that we should prepare for the coming of the Ayatollah."

"Oh, yes, I've heard a bit about him."

"They've taken it upon themselves to clean up the land from all sinners before the second coming of the Imam."

"If you lose your profession," asked Kazem, dismayed, "how are you going to live?"

"The Devil only knows!" Zeenat grumbled. "What have you been up to these past two years?"

"You know, this and that," replied Kazem, perching on the wobbly desk.

"Would you like to see Zari Farangi?" Zeenat asked, lowering her voice.

"Not now," said Kazem, combing his hair with his hand. "I've come to see if you know where I can find Davood Jigool."

"His mistress, Shaheen Rashti, told me that he works in Cinema Tamaddon in Lalezar."

Leaving the house, Kazem came out of the Citadel and took a bus to Estanbol Street. Once there, he walked straight to Cinema Tamaddon, which was at the end of a short cul-de-sac in Melli Lane. Night had fallen by now and Melli Lane was teeming with people. The air was filled with the racket of a popular song coming from a loudspeaker fixed on top of a billboard embellished with gaudy pictures of actors and actresses in the film that was showing. Every ten seconds the singing abruptly stopped and the pathetic voice of a man could be heard droning:

"The programmes have just started. Tonight and every night you can watch all sorts of dramas, comedy-musicals, moral, and tear-jerking films. Tonight we're showing 'Saucy Housemaid' and 'The Day The Suitor Came', followed by the acrobatics of the Janbazaan Brothers, the magic tricks of Professor Shishaki, the singing of Afsaneh the Nightingale of the City, the dancing of Firoozeh, the renowned Lebanese star of radio and television, and Turkish and Indian dancing. At the end of the shows you'll have two hours of laughter till you split your sides watching the antics of the renowned *ruhauzi* comedian, Ebraam Siyah…"

All kinds of street pedlars had established themselves in the narrow pass and near the entrance, chanting at the tops of their voices. Long-haired skinny men in tight trousers, soldiers on leave, policemen, women in short skirts or in black chadors all stood in the long queue, devouring *piroshkis* wrapped in greasy papers, popping roasted-and-salted watermelon seeds into their mouths, hotly discussing the movie and the shows they were about to see.

Someone tapped Kazem on the shoulder, making him jump. He glanced back.

"I've lots of tickets for the film," a pale-faced, stooping young man, as thin as a straw, whispered into Kazem's ear, breathing down his neck, his eyes darting around like a hunted animal.

"No thanks, bro," said Kazem. "I'm just looking at the pictures."

The young man moved off, eyeing his likely victims like a pickpocket.

Kazem waited a while in the queue till he reached the little tin kiosk inside which a pock-marked, grumpy woman was sitting selling tickets, a cigarette butt dangling between her heavily rouged lips.

"How many tickets?" she muttered, without looking up.

"I don't want tickets, khanum," said Kazem.

"What do you want, then, love?" said she. "If a kiss and a cuddle is what you're after I can't give it you from here!"

"I was told I can find a tall man with the body of a wrestler called Davood who works here."

"I know nothing of a man with a wrestler's body," replied the woman, glancing up at Kazem. "If you mean Davood *Amali*, he's there in his cubbyhole talking into the microphone."

"Can I see him then?" said Kazem. "I'm an old friend."

"I've never seen any friends of his," said the woman, eyeing Kazem curiously. "All right then. Hang on a minute." She stuck her head out of the little opening and boomed at the ticket collector, "Hoy, Taghi Ghoozi, let this man in. He wants to see Davood Amali."

Taghi Ghoozi, a hunchback with a grotesque face, ordered his young assistant to look after the customers before limping towards a short corridor at the far corner of the hall, muttering curses at the woman as he went. Kazem followed the grumpy Quasimodo, who halted in front of a cubbyhole at the end of the corridor, pointed at it, and hobbled back to the hall. Kazem peered into the small opening through a cloud of thick smoke. He saw a dopy-looking man who was dragging hard at a cigarette butt, dozing off with his head about to fall any minute on the battered record-player placed on a counter in front of him. Remembering that he should talk into the microphone, he suddenly half-opened his eyes, lifted the needle off the record, and whimpered into the microphone:

"Hurry up, folks. By not watching the 'Saucy Housemaid' you'll regret it all your life."

Behind the wasted face, Kazem recognised good old Davood. He took a few steps towards the door of the cubbyhole, then stopped, thinking whether he should talk to Davood or not. Finally, he made up his mind, and stood just outside the door, staring at his friend. Davood lifted the needle, placed it at random on the turning record, and began to doze off. The singer resumed his singing from somewhere in the middle of his sorrowful song. Nothing was left of that handsome, athletic Davood Jigool he had once known but a scrawny man with shaggy hair, dressed in filthy rags.

Tears sprang to Kazem's eyes, distorting the dim glow of the light bulbs dangling from the ceiling.

The walls of the cubbyhole were adorned with pictures of Iranian and Western artists. Davood chucked his cigarette butt on the floor, lifted the needle and placed it on the record again. The music blared on while he dozed off. Becoming aware of someone's presence at the door, he slowly raised his head and gazed at Kazem with bleary eyes.

"Are you looking for someone, bro?" Davood asked in a feeble voice.

Kazem remained motionless, gazing at his friend.

"You look at me as if I've horns on my head!" Davood said.

"It's me, Kazem, your old friend," Kazem said finally, his voice trembling with emotion. "Don't you remember your old friend, you sonofabitch!"

"K-a-zem?" Davood muttered the name like a man talking in a dream, peering into Kazem's face.

"Yep, that's me," said Kazem.

Davood's face slowly lit up with a smile that cracked his bloodless visage into ghastly wrinkles.

"Yes, that's him, all right," Davood said, his eyes widening in surprise. He grinned broadly, revealing his rotten teeth and greyish gums. "Ah, look at his beard and mop of hair!"

Davood got up with great effort, his back bent like an aged man. He almost ran towards Kazem, nearly stumbling over before clutching Kazem in an affectionate bear hug.

"How happy I am to see you, mate!" Davood mumbled in Kazem's ear as he hugged him with his no longer strong arms.

"What's happened to you?" Kazem asked.

"That's a long story, mate," said Davood. "I'll tell you all about it later."

"Can you put me up for one night?" Kazem asked after a short pause. "I'll sort myself out tomorrow."

"You can stay as long as you like," said Davood. "I have a hovel somewhere in downtown. Shaheen would be very happy to see you."

"Is she still with you?"

"She's been a loyal companion to me all these years since you went to jail."

After convincing the hunchback and the woman that he would do some extra hours the following day, Davood took Kazem's arm and led him out of the passageway. They took a bus to Davood's place. On the way, Davood bought *sangak* bread, some salami, yoghurt and a few cucumbers. From the delicatessen of his Armenian friend he also bought a bottle of *arrack*.

Once in his room, Davood spread a cloth on the floor, and placed the food in the middle of it. With his flick-knife he chopped the cucumber and mixed the pieces in a bowl of yoghurt. He then opened the bottle, half-filled two small glasses and handed one to Kazem.

"Knock it back, mate," said Davood, "it'll warm you up like *hammam*."

Kazem shoved a spoonful of yoghurt and cucumber into his mouth and smacked his lips.

"So tell me," Davood asked, relaxing with the warmth of *arrack* in his achy bones, "when did you come out?"

"This morning."

"After I visited you in jail a year ago," Davood said, lighting up a cigarette, "I fell into this cursed opium. Opium not being enough to make me forget my sorrows, I started on heroin and all sorts of other drugs. As things got worse, I felt ashamed of seeing you in my state. I've been kicking myself for being so unmanly towards you who had been so good to me. But I never forgot you, mate, never."

"That's all right, Davood," Kazem said, lighting a cigarette for himself. "I'm not complaining, but I'm just wondering how you could end up like this, having seen all your life the state in which all our childhood friends ended up."

"Did I have any other options left to me, Kazem?" Davood whined, puffing away at his cigarette.

"You could leave that hell, Davood, as I did."

"I'm not like you, Kazem," said Davood, gazing at him. "You departed and I stayed, you passed, I remained. That's why I slowly rotted away. This is the way we were created."

"So what happened to the others?" Kazem asked.

"They're still pretty much the same," replied Davood. "Some of them just faded away and dropped into the gutters. As their corpses began to rot, some trucks came from outside the Citadel and took them away. The die-hard ones are still squatting on the edge of the gutters, holding heroin powder under one another's noses to get high before going about their daily task of selling drugs to prostitutes and pimps."

They knocked back a few more glasses of *arrack* and nibbled at salami wrapped in pieces of bread.

"I think you taught a good lesson to that sonofabitch Reza Zepeleshk who swaggered around Shahr-e No, extorting money from poor *mamans, khanums* and pimps," Davood said.

"Any idea what's he doing these days?" Kazem asked.

"You'd be surprised to know that he's joined the Ayatollah's camp, runs around in and around Shahr-e No, harassing the *khanums* and *mamans* to stop their sinful ways of living."

"What?" Kazem exclaimed. "That rogue has now become a good Muslim, converting sinners to Islam!"

"Yes, mate," Davood said calmly. "That's what these people are like. They sniff the air like hyenas and move in packs to wherever the feast is going to be."

"Do you know where he is now?" Kazem asked, lighting up another cigarette.

"I heard that he's gone to Mashhad to repent and reform in the holy shrine of Imam Reza." Davood's face clouded over with dark thoughts.

"But what do these poor souls do if they give up the game?" Kazem asked, dragging hard at his cigarette. "They'll all end up in the street, which is much worse. At least in Shahr-e No they belong to the Community of Sisterhood and are being looked after."

"That's where the ever benevolent mollahs come in," Davood pointed out, filling up the glasses. "Once the *khanums* are out of here, they'll be taken to mollahs who hang around in the holy shrines around Tehran. The mollahs will then pour a few bowlfuls of repentance water on their heads to make them as pure as virgin saints. The women, now chaste and clean, will then be forced to become *sieghehs*, first to mollahs for a while, and after that will be made to marry a good Muslim brother and live happily ever after, converting other sinners."

"What happened to the other knife-fighters and strongmen?" asked Kazem, becoming more and more amused.

"Pretty much the same story, mate," Davood went on like a man in the know. "They've all of a sudden changed their ways. Like carrion-eaters they've sniffed the auspicious wind blowing their way, so they're preparing themselves to feast on the future spoils that'll be brought in by the establishment of the Islamic State that the Ayatollah is going on about.

Unlike the likes of you and me, these guys are smart, I'm telling you. They know how to move with the times!"

There was a pause. Distant chants of '*Allahu akbar'* could be heard coming from the roofs in the neighbourhood, mingled with the sound of popular music from radios.

"I don't remember hearing so many people shouting 'Allahu akbar' at this time." Kazem spoke again.

"This has been going on for weeks," Davood explained. "In this way they're telling the Pahlavi regime that we're here now and we're not going to go away."

"When is Shaheen coming back, then?" Kazem put out his cigarette in the tin ashtray.

"Some nights she works until the small hours."

"That's very late, isn't it, Davood?"

"No, no. Don't worry," said Davood. "She's not on the game any more. She works in a cabaret, singing, dancing, and a does a spot of acting every now and then. I trust her. She brings in some cash that helps us to get by."

He topped up the glasses.

"So what're your plans now that you're out, Kazem?" he asked.

"I'll have to go to Mashhad tomorrow."

"Why Mashhad?" Davood said, alarmed. "I hope you're not thinking of repenting and joining those sons-of-bitches."

"You know, Davood, more than anybody else, that that's not my style," Kazem said.

"So what business do you have in Mashhad?"

"I made some good friends when I did some errands there years ago," Kazem said. "I want to find out if we can still get together and do some business."

He kept quiet about what he had in mind for Reza Zepeleshk.

"Whatever you've in mind, mate," Davood said, "just be careful. Times are changing and we don't know what's in store for us all."

Late the next morning, Kazem and Davood woke up and tiptoed out of the room, trying not to disturb Shaheen, who was deeply asleep. They caught a bus to Shams ol-Emareh Garage in downtown Tehran so that Kazem could catch a coach to the holy city of Mashhad.

3

The square in front of Shams ol-Emareh Garage was teeming with all kinds of people from all over Iran, speaking in innumerable dialects. This multitude consisted of uprooted peasants who had come to Tehran to seek easy fortune, leech-like beggars, street pedlars, wandering dervishes, and itinerant entertainers. Hairy, grim-faced *pahlavans* showed off their physical prowess by tearing large copper trays in two or breaking chains tied round their chests. Multi-coloured *chadored* women shrieked at their grubby, shabbily-clothed children, who howled non-stop, tugging at their mothers' clothing, demanding sweet-meats and baklavas heaped on large trays balanced on the heads of pedlars. The women stood before the stalls and bickered bitterly with the hawkers over the prices of the goods. They invoked the names of all the Islamic martyrs as witness to their misery; they swore on the graves of their parents who left them orphaned when only small babies.

Kazem and Davood squeezed their way through the seething mass and walked into the coach station. They manoeuvred through the passengers who had mobbed the coach. The travellers squabbled among themselves for the pettiest of reasons. The most bad-tempered ones hurled abuse at the bewildered young driver's mate, who had perched on the roof of the coach, sorting out the battered suitcases, rolls of dusty kilims, and bulky bundles of quilts and cushions. None of the passengers was satisfied with the efforts of this lad, who tried hard to please everybody. Once at the door of the coach, Kazem stopped and hugged Davood affectionately.

"Take care of yourself and Shaheen, mate," he said. "When I come back to Tehran I'll come and see you."

He climbed up, found the nearest available seat, and settled down. Happy to be unharmed so far, he placed his bundle on his lap, rested his hands on it, and looked outside. Davood was standing just under the window gazing up at him and smiling his kindly smile. Kazem gestured at him to go, but Davood did not budge.

The travellers, having survived the battlefield of the garage, had no sooner scrambled up into the coach – panting, sweating, and jostling each other with their shoulders – than the driver's mate sprang into action by snatching a plastic bucket to collect the fares. He waited until the brawling passengers, after some minor scuffles, managed to find a seat and settle down. Clutching the handle of the bucket and holding it high up, he began to walk through the aisle, cluttered with bundles and sacks among which sprawled many ragamuffins, to collect the cash, shouting above the furore of prayers, curses and swearing.

At long last, the coach began to rumble its way out of the garage, hooting incessantly to disperse the noisy bands of passengers' relatives, who besieged the coach, trying to give a send-off to their pilgrims. They held aloft the trays in which were placed copies of the Koran and burning incense for the safe journey of the voyagers. They cried last farewells to their loved ones, begging them to supplicate Imam Reza to intervene between them and Allah so that He would forgive their sins and help them out of their countless misfortunes.

Kazem tried to spot Davood in the mass of well-wishers to take a last look at his friend, but the swirling mass had devoured him in its belly.

A bullnecked passenger, who had taken upon himself the role of the pilgrims' bellwether, stood up and yelled in a coarse voice at the top of his lungs:

"All the lackeys of Imam Reza chant a very loud *salawat*."

"Blessed be Mohammad and the Clan of Mohammad," the pilgrims chanted discordantly, articulating each Arabic syllable and emphasising loudly the name of Mohammad. Ragged little tots, frightened out of their wits, burst into howling, adding to the din. Hiking up the pandemonium and terrifying the poor little devils further, another bearded, grotesque-looking zealot, who appeared to be more Shiite than Imam Ali, got up and roared over people's heads, demanding a few more *salawats* from the pilgrims for the health of the driver, the safe journey ahead, and for the salvation of the souls of the sinners in the coach. Most of the passengers, who had seen the Arab man – the saint Imam Reza, that is – in their dreams, beckoning them in the direction of his shrine in the holy city of Mashhad, chanted even louder *salawats* to be in both Imam Reza's and the driver's good graces.

Once the passengers had chanted several *salawats*, exhausting the stock of their well-wishing, Kazem heaved a sigh of relief. He leaned his head against the back of the seat to get some much-needed sleep. Its horn sounding relentlessly, the coach finally rolled out of the garage and crawled its way through the chaotic Tehran traffic to the highway leading to the holy tomb of Shah Abdolazim. Some overenthusiastic pilgrims believed that they could not possibly visit Imam Reza without first paying their due respects to his holiness' younger brother, Shah Abdolazim.

After a brief stopover near the holy shrine, the coach, amid a deafening din of *salawats*, moved on. Kazem rested his head against the backrest of his seat and looked out of the window. The vast cemetery that stretched out on both sides of the road shimmered under the hazy rays of the afternoon sun like the ruins of an ancient city. Black-chadored women, like ravens with tattered wings, walked among the gravestones, their veils fluttering in the slight breeze. Some others squatted beside the slabs, touching them with their fingers. The coach soon came to the limits of the cemetery and entered the autonomous territory of shantytowns – governed and managed exclusively by hordes of uprooted peasants, who crawled and crept upon each other like pests of all shapes, colours and sizes. The ramshackle, makeshift huts were created out of cardboard boxes, rusty corrugated sheets of tin, sooty tarpaulins, broken-down carts, bricks stolen from the nearby brickworks, large corrugated cement blocks, rusty old cars carried there from the junkyard, and rotten pieces of wooden planks. The warm air was filled with the foul stench of the decomposing corpses of blown-up dogs and cats, rats squashed by kids whose only games were to torment the animals and the offal of slaughtered sheep thrown there from the nearby abattoir. A dark swarm of gigantic gadflies, their colourful wings glistening in the slanting rays of the sun, hovered just over the trash heap, feeding not only on the decaying matter, but also on other creatures such as skinny dogs, cats, donkeys, and human beings. Appearing like black patches of cloud, flocks of carrion crows hung overhead, cawing raucously. At the first opportunity, they swooped down in small batches and snatched whatever they could get their beaks on from the other tireless scavengers.

The wretched inhabitants of this forgotten 'town', grown like a malignant pus-filled boil on the backside of the capital city, had emigrated from their villages and hamlets to that elusive Eldorado of Tehran in search of fortune. After interminable and hopeless wanderings in the streets of that cruellest of all cities, with their ideas of a better life shattered, they had ended up creating their own homes, resorting to any means and building materials and leading a precarious, day-to-day existence.

The men of these shantytowns roamed the streets of downtown and uptown Tehran doing all sorts of odd jobs to make ends meet. They did not shy away from any of those jobs considered shameful in their native villages, such as pimping or serving as underlings to the knife-fighters and strongmen in rough districts such as Shahr-e No and other whorehouses. The younger ones turned into hub-cap thieves, ticket touts who lurked around cinemas, or drug-pushers. Most of the women, with their swaddled babies wrapped tightly in rags to their backs with a pack of hungry children trailing behind them, roamed the vast courtyard of Shah Abdolazim, and hassled the pilgrims from dawn to dusk, begging for alms. The ones who were willing to work found jobs such as charwomen, maidservants, and washerwomen in filthy washhouses in the better-off districts of Tehran. All of these lost souls scavenged, whenever they had time, among the heaps of trash like famished mongrel dogs.

As the coach drove along a dusty unmade road that hugged the railway track, Kazem mused over the grotesque-looking men and women scuttling here and there among the heaps of garbage. At that moment a train that had just pulled out of the train station, crawling along the rail tracks, caught his attention. All of a sudden, upon hearing the roar of the locomotive engine, a swarm of ragamuffins, who were scavenging in the rubbish heap on the far side of the rail track, emerged from among the heap like masses of vermin. An army of raggedly-clad barbarians with grimy faces, they all scampered to the low embankment, howling and shrieking at the tops of their lungs. They crept down the embankment on all fours, leapt over the rails and stood up, facing the slow-moving locomotive with their hands stretched out, and running backwards, gambolling about between the rails like frisky calves let out of a barn. In an uproar of squealing, they challenged the driver to catch up with them. The approaching train, the booming sound of the horn, and constant cursing and swearing of the driver who stuck his head out of the window did not deter these intrepid young scavengers. Instead, their faces, caked with muck and filth, were cracked with broad, devilish grins.

This bizarre spectacle of foolhardiness brought back memories of Kazem's own wild childhood, making him smile.

The coach finally left all these spectacles behind and passed through the numerous hamlets and villages lying along the road that led to the holy city of Mashhad.

4

The following day around late afternoon the coach arrived at an ancient caravanserai, converted into a coach garage, in the outlying districts of Mashhad. Kazem had to go through the same scenario, if not worse, as that of the departure from Tehran. The same endless *salawats* came rolling one after another that roared like loud waves, crashing upon his head. Cattle-like, the passengers trampled over one another to get out of the coach. Dirt-covered women and children moaned and wallowed in the stench of their own vomit. Hungry, restless babies howled and screamed. Sleepless men hurled abuse at the driver's mate who, once again, took his position on the roof, chucking the dust-covered suitcases, trunks and bundles on the ground, raising a thick cloud of dust in the midst of which the pilgrims moved around like lost souls, cursing and tugging at their belongings which other pilgrims had wrongly snatched.

Glad to be still in one piece, Kazem stepped out of the coach and stood beside it as stiff as a poker, all his muscles and joints aching. Stretching and breathing in the familiar air, he walked over towards a crumbling arch that cast a patch of shade on a low stone platform beneath it. He sat on the platform, tossed his bundle in the corner, lit a cigarette, and surveyed the vast grounds of the caravanserai. The shadows of the tall, ancient mud-brick walls were slowly lengthening in the slanting golden rays of the sun. The shrill chirping of flocks of sparrows, nestled in the cracks between the bricks, mingled with the incessant, melancholy cawing of carrion crows that hovered overhead. The pilgrims, bent beneath their huge bundles and trunks, looked like large insects, scurrying here and there over a sun-scorched, barren land carrying tiny clods of earth on their backs. Upon spotting a *droshky*, a taxi, or a horse-drawn cart, they stuck their heads from under the bundles, glanced around and scuttled off to catch the vehicle to take them to the city centre in which was located the tomb of the holy Imam Reza.

Kazem fumbled in his jacket pocket, fished out the crumpled notes and counted them. Realising that he was not left with enough cash, he decided to hitchhike his way to the small town where he lived. His hometown was some kilometres to the east of Mashhad.

He walked out of the garage and wandered along the main road, lifting his thumb to the passing cars, trucks and heavy lorries, hoping that someone would give him a lift. Seeing his scruffy appearance and his shabby outfit, many drivers just drove past him without stopping. Finally, a truck pulled up a few paces away from him. Kazem ran up to it.

"Where are you going?" the driver yelled at him, pushing the door open.

"Hosseinabaad," Kazem shouted back, holding the open door.

"Hop in," cried the driver. "You're in luck, I'm driving there to do deliver my cargo of watermelons to the fruit and vegetable market."

"Thanks, bro," said Kazem, climbing up the step and sitting on the seat beside the driver

"It'll be quite a while before we get to Hosseinabaad," cried the driver, casting a quick glance at Kazem. "I'll have to stop at a few places to hand over some of these watermelons."

"That's all right with me," said Kazem, shutting the door, "I'm in no hurry to get there."

The driver was a middle-aged, good-natured man who soon began to tell stories about the adventures he'd had on the road. Kazem listened to him while gazing at the barren lands all around dotted with hamlets with adobe houses huddled together, baking under the harsh sun. The fallow lands, on which could be seen, now and again, heaps of the sun-bleached skeletons of starved cattle, stretched up to the horizon across which reclined purple mountains, shrouded in a pale haze. Every now and then, some dust-covered, bone-dry, lone trees loomed large by the roadside.

The droning voice of the driver, the monotonous humming of the engine, the jolting of the truck, the stale odour of cheap tobacco mingled with the strong smell of petrol and the steady, warm desert breeze that blew into the cabin from the open window combined to make Kazem doze off. The driver, wrapped-up in his stories and smoking one cigarette after another, carried on cheerfully, regardless of his sleeping passenger.

It was well after midnight that the truck pulled up beside a vacant lot in the main thoroughfare of Hosseinabaad.

"We've arrived, bro," said the driver in a loud voice, throwing a quick glance at Kazem.

Startled, Kazem opened his eyes, rubbed them, yawned loudly, snatched his bundle, thanked the driver, and hopped down from the truck.

He stood motionless on the edge of the road and watched the truck lurch off, trundling along the thoroughfare, dimly lit by pale-yellow light bulbs that hung at the top of the occasional wooden lampposts. The bulbs cast a murky light on the dusty leaves of a few inky trees that stood along the route.

The rumbling of the truck resounded in the silent neighbourhood, lingered in the distance and died down. An eerie silence began to reign again. As the truck moved down the thoroughfare, its headlights cast patches of light on the squat, ramshackle, clay-and-mud-brick houses with cave-like windows veiled in darkness and on the rusty corrugated tin shutters of shops.

His bundle flung on his shoulder, Kazem walked along the thoroughfare. From the vacant lot on the right rose the stench of rotting dead cats and dogs, mingled with the trash chucked there by the town's inhabitants. The subdued voices of phantom-like creatures rummaging among the refuse could be heard, as though in a nightmare. Every now and then, the screech of a hungry cat or howling of a mongrel dog rent the silence of the sleeping town. Kazem walked in and out of endless scruffy alleyways that twisted under pitch-dark arched passes. From time to time, a shadowy figure glided along a half-dark lane and disappeared into an alley. At the angle of each alleyway stood a weather-beaten lamppost, a pale-yellow bulb dangling from its top.

"I hope Nasrollah Kachal is still running his lodging house," Kazem mumbled to himself as he headed towards the house in which he had rented a room before his arrest. At the end of the lane, he stood before the main door hidden in the shadow cast by the overhead brickwork arch. He looked around, rapped a few times with his knuckles on the door, and waited. No sound. He rapped again. Shuffling footfalls punctuated with coughs could be heard approaching the door. The bolt clicked in its socket and the door was opened with a groan. A dishevelled sleepy face appeared in the doorway.

"If you're looking for a room, we're full," the stubbly middle-aged man muttered, a cigarette butt between his lips.

Kazem smiled.

"So you don't have a room for an old friend?

"Old friend?" the man repeated, peering into Kazem's face in the dim light of the lamppost.

"Yes," said Kazem. "It's me, Kazem Alaki."

"Bah, is that you, Kazem?" Nasrollah cried.

"That's me, all right."

"You sonofabitch!" exclaimed Nasrollah. "How do you expect me to recognise you if you look like a hairy highwayman who has come to rob me in the dead of night? Come in, come in."

"Did I wake you up?" asked Kazem.

"How can I get any sleep when jinns like you appear from nowhere, looking for a room!" Nasrollah grumbled. "You came just in time. I've just put some fresh tea in the pot."

He stepped down the two steps into the courtyard, which was shrouded in darkness. Kazem followed him. The cautious rhythm of their footfalls on the flagstones echoed in the silence, disturbing the creatures of the night. All around the courtyard were little matchbox rooms, their doors left open a crack like the mouths of dead men. All the lodgers were asleep, moaning while dreaming their chaotic dreams.

Nasrollah led Kazem to a small room at the far end of the courtyard. A samovar with a teapot roosting on top of it was whistling in the corner near the window ledge. He picked up the pot, poured some tea into two small glasses, filled them up with water from the samovar's tap, and placed them on a small table. Kazem sat on a chair, picked up his glass, popped a sugar cube into his mouth, poured some tea into the tiny saucer, and began to slurp his tea.

"Have you got somewhere for me to stay tonight?" he asked.

"For an old friend I always have a room," said Nasrollah, placing his glass in the saucer.

"Is Kal Abbasgholi still running his teahouse, Nasrollah?" Kazem asked, rifling in his pockets for his pack of cigarettes.

"He's still there all right," said Nasrollah. "We were talking about you the other day."

"I'll have to see him tomorrow."

"Till tomorrow God is great," said Nasrollah. "Tell me what you have been doing all this time."

Kazem recounted what had happened to him. Nasrollah listened thoughtfully, smoking and nodding his head. They went on talking till the small hours about old friends and the latest happenings in the country.

"Let me show you the spare room I keep for devils like you," said Nasrollah, yawning.

Kazem followed Nasrollah up the stairs on to the terrace. After showing him the room, Nasrollah shuffled back downstairs, muttering to himself.

Kazem inserted the key into the small lock hanging from a latch and turned it. He pulled the two leaves of the door towards him. No sooner had he opened the doors than a foul-smelling, warm draught of air assailed his nostrils, brushed against his cheeks with its cool, sickening caress, and wafted past. Gently, he pushed the door open, remaining for a moment stock-still on the threshold, then stepped inside, leaving the door open a crack behind him. He leaned against the wall near the door and peered into the darkened room. Groping for the light switch on the wall, he flicked it. The smudgy bulb threw a murky yellow light on the sparse pieces of furniture, covered in a thin film of cobweb and dust. The room smelt of squalor.

Kazem scanned the room, nodding. He tossed the bunch of keys on to a small rickety table that stood near the wall, kicked his shoes off one at a time, and sauntered, hands on hips, looking around, shaking his head and whistling a popular tune. He stood two paces away from a largish oval mirror placed on a ledge on the opposite wall. He took a step towards the mirror and peered into it, staring at his reflection in the clouded-over, chipped glass. Prepared to admire his muscular chest and biceps, he did not see, however, what he expected to see. Instead, from the depths of the foggy mirror, a hairy monkey-like creature sneered back at him. From beyond the muck and mist, his familiar features became more and more recognizable. Once fully aware that the creature in the mirror was none other than his own self, Kazem burst into loud laughter.

"You scared the hell out of me, you bastard!" he shouted at his image.

He went on examining himself further. All of a sudden, he saw the reflection of something in the mirror that made him anxious. He froze, gazing at the thing. As if stung by a wasp, he briskly turned back and looked at a birdcage that was suspended from the corner of the ceiling, as still as a hanged convict. He walked over to the cage and looked inside. A canary was lying lifeless on the floor of the cage. He lifted the tiny latch of the small door of the cage, pushed his hand inside, and picked up the dead bird. Gently, he took it out. The fluffy yellow head of the bird, its tiny eyes closed as if in a deep sleep, flopped limply on his index finger with its yellowish-green beak slightly open, as though frozen when singing its last song. Overcome by sadness, Kazem closed his eyes. Holding it up, he carefully unfurled one of the bright yellow wings and walked slowly towards the casement window with his eyes fixed on the dead bird.

Once beside the window, he unlatched it, and pushed it open. Kazem looked at the canary for the last time, stretched his hand out of the window, held it there for a moment and gently let go of it, as though he were setting it free to fly away, to find its own companions with whom, once again, it could sing joyful songs. The bird, instead of flying off, fell like a rotten fruit on the hard flagstones of the pitch-black backyard, making a muffled thud. In a matter of seconds, Kazem heard the screeching of some hungry cats, which jumped out of the shadows and fell upon the tiny corpse, fighting over it. Having snatched pieces of its body and carrying these to dark corners, the cats devoured their find and fell silent. The incessant trilling of beetles and crickets, silenced for a while by the fracas, resumed and filled the night air.

Kazem listened helplessly to the fiendish noises of the cats down there in the gloom. He looked at the feathers of the canary stuck to his sweaty hands. Slowly, he raised his hand high and blew the feathers off it. Fluttering quietly everywhere in the room like yellowish-bright butterflies, the feathers, one at a time, alighted noiselessly on the curtain beside the window and the tattered kilim on the floor, clinging to them and quivering in the slight breeze from the open window. All the while, Kazem followed the feathers with his eyes, as an enchanted little boy does when he sees butterflies flapping their wings around him. He gazed at them, all settling one by one on the kilim, remaining there motionless.

In order to freshen up a bit, he left the room, walked to the *hauz* in the middle of the courtyard, squatted beside it and gazed at it awhile. Some dead leaves, fallen from the weeping willow whose slender branches hung over the *hauz*, floated noiselessly on the smooth, shiny surface of the water. A gentle breeze, warm and reassuring as the breath of a young mother bending over her newborn baby, caressed the still surface, making it heave a sigh. Kazem rolled up his sleeves, scooped up handfuls of water and splashed it over his face. The ripples, after making the leaves bob up and down, assumed their former tranquillity. He got up, dabbed his face with the corner of his shirt, and walked back to the room.

The whirlwind of activity of the past two days had worn him out. He walked to the bed and flopped on it, making the wood creak. He lay on his back fully dressed, without covering himself with the threadbare quilt. He stared for a short moment at the ceiling, from which yellowish-brown scales of paint dangled, revealing geographical patterns in the dirty plaster beneath. Soon his eyelids became heavy and closed, and within a few minutes he was fast asleep.

5

Next morning, around midday, was Kazem startled out of his troubled sleep by the sounds coming from the outside world. He found himself curled up and hugging the bolster. He lazily rolled over and stared at the ceiling, imagining that he was still in his cell in Qasr Prison. He sat up in bed, yawned loudly, and listened to the noises from the courtyard. He jumped off the bed, opened the door and, leaning against the doorframe, watched the women and children. Three of the women, their sleeves rolled up to their elbows and with their chadors wrapped round their waists and knotted in front, sat near the *hauz* with large tin basins, filled with filthy greyish-blue water frothed over with soap suds, tucked between their legs. They were vigorously scrubbing the clothes and linens with huge chunky slabs of brownish-yellow soap. Large drops of sweat dripped down their brows to their cheeks that looked like ripe pomegranates. Two others squatted on the edge of the *hauz*. They dipped the already washed clothes in the water, pulled them out, shook them violently, examined them critically, and finally beat them forcefully against the lip of the *hauz*. If the rinsed clothes were light, such as shirts or vests, the women wrung them with their powerful hands to drain the last drop of water out of them. In order to wring the larger articles, they asked another woman's help to hold the other end of the twisted linen or a pair of trousers. They then piled the wrung items in tin basins and carried them to the clotheslines laden with washing and criss-crossing the courtyard.

While they were busy doing this, some of them jabbered at the tops of their lungs with the latest gossip in the neighbourhood. A young, rosy-cheeked woman with her baby swaddled in rags and wrapped tightly to her back was hanging the linens on the clotheslines and fastening them with wooden pegs. She hummed a popular song in her sweet Shirazi accent. Her melancholy voice mingled with the flapping sound of the washing in the fresh morning breeze:

You ravaged my heart and went away.
Though I'm perishing here without you,
At least I'm happy and comforting myself that,
Wherever you are, my love, you will not break my heart.

A clutch of puny little boys and girls with muck-smeared faces and dressed in rags, ran around, chased one another, and rolled on the flagstones, squealing with delight. A brood of tots, left to their own devices on the steps of the terrace, howled without let-up, while one of the women shrieked at a couple of the brats tormenting these abandoned victims.

"No, I'm definitely not in the prison," said Kazem to himself as he watched this scene of humdrum everyday life. His face lit up with a smile. He went back inside the room, grabbed his keys and put his shoes on. He stepped out on to the terrace and went down the steps. He greeted the lodgers, who stopped and froze in whatever they were doing, looking at him mutely. Kazem walked to the *hauz*, squatted beside it, put his cupped hand under the long-necked running tap and chucked a few handfuls of water over his face. He got up and pulled his handkerchief out of his trouser pocket and began drying his face. As he did so, he saw out of the corner of his eye Nasrollah, who had just emerged from the privy at the far end of the courtyard, clutching a ewer in his hand.

"*Bah, bah*, Nabi Agha!" Nasrollah cried out, shuffling towards a shabbily-dressed and terrified-looking young man who was about to sneak out of the courtyard. "Long time no see. What've you been up to these days, I wonder?"

"Doing this and that, Hajj Nasrollah," Nabi whimpered, freezing in his tracks.

Nasrollah Kachal placed the ewer down near the *hauz* and scratched his stubbly face, pulling down his sleeves as if getting ready to launch into his familiar litany about his unpaid rent.

"I know, I know, Hajj Nasrollah," said Nabi, turning round. "My rent is overdue. I'm a bit short of cash right now. As soon as I get my hands on some money, I'll pay all of it."

"You know, Nabi Agha," Nasrollah went on, putting on the smarmy mask of a wretched landlord who eternally chases after his lodgers for unpaid rent, "I've so many mouths to feed and soon I'm going to marry off my youngest daughter."

"Don't you worry, Hajji," said Nabi, becoming more and more anxious to run away. "I'll pay all my rent by the end of this month, promise." As he turned to escape, he added, "I wish all the happiness for your daughter, Hajji."

Amused, Kazem watched this all-too-familiar exchange between the landlord and one of his tenants. He then walked back to his room, picked up his jacket, and walked out of the house. Women, veiled from head to foot, scurried in and out of the alley, going about their daily chores. Urchins were scampering in the dust, hopping over the narrow gutter that ran along the middle of the alley. After wandering through a few twining alleys and lanes, Kazem ended up in the main thoroughfare. Hosseinabaad was humming all around him in the clear late August air. He walked straight to the barbershop just outside the marketplace. After being shorn and shaved, he regarded himself in the mirror, admiring his clean looks.

“Welcome back to the fold of human beings,” his barber friend said, chuckling.

Kazem paid the barber, and headed towards the grocers’. located a few paces away, where he bought a lump of cheese wrapped in a piece of greasy paper, and a half *sangak* bread. Clutching the packet of cheese in one hand, the bread hanging loose in the other arm, his jacket flung on his shoulders, he made his way towards Kal Abbasgholi’s Teahouse that was just round the corner, near the entrance to the market.

6

Kal Abbasgholi's Teahouse was at the end of a short arcade. Two brick columns stood in front of a small porch-like area that opened into the large room. Rickety, bentwood chairs were arranged round some wobbly wooden tables inside and outside the teahouse in the porch. Two daybeds, spread over with kilims, were placed against the wall just outside the teahouse for people who wanted to have meals sitting on them.

Kazem walked into the porch and looked around. He found a table beside the door and tossed the packet of cheese and bread on the table. He glanced back inside the teahouse. A few regulars were sitting around a table in the far corner, popping sugar lumps into their mouths, slurping their tea off saucers and talking animatedly. In another corner sat a solitary young worker who, deep in thought, drew hard at his cigarette, tossing his matchbox on the table to see which side it would land. The tea boy, a lanky lad of about seventeen, was running from one table to another, serving the customers.

The walls inside the teahouse were whitewashed. A large picture of the Shah, prim and clean-shaven in full military regalia, was stuck on the wall near the door, glaring down benignly, as the crowned father of the nation, at his subjects. His Majesty's picture had pride of place between of two prayer-mats hung on the wall, depicting the golden dome and tall minarets of the holy shrine of Imam Reza. Nestled in niches in the walls were a few oil lamps, some large cracked teapots that had seen better days, a massive, out-of-service brass samovar and a battered radio covered with black, greasy dust and ash. The melancholy voice of a man was issuing from the radio, singing a song cursing the cruel sweetheart who had broken the heart of her lover and run away with his undeserving rival. A teapot, rimmed with gold and glazed with vertical black-and-red lines, was roosting on a large tin samovar placed on a high brick platform, under which was the stove. Right on top of the stove, against the wall, tiny terracotta pots were piled up, upside-down, one on top of each other in the shape of a pyramid. On top of the stove, near the wall, were placed round tin trays, a few teapots, sugar bowls, piles of saucers and rows of tiny, gold-rimmed tea glasses. The gentle clucking sound of the lid of the teapot, the whistling sound made by the vapour coming out of its spout, mingled with the humming of the samovar, created a cosy atmosphere.

"*Salaam*, Kal Abbasgholi," Kazem called out, grabbing a chair and throwing his jacket on the back of it. Kal Abbasgholi, a tall, gaunt man with a swarthy complexion, with high cheekbones and a thick handlebar moustache and a tea towel flung over his shoulders, was about to grab the teapot when he heard someone calling him from the porch. He glanced back and saw Kazem, not sure whether the voice really belonged to his friend.

"Hey, Kazem!" cried Kal Abbasgholi, leaving the teapot on the samovar. "*Salaam, salaam*, you sonofabitch!" He rushed towards Kazem, giving him a bear hug. "Tell me, son. When did you come back?" He grabbed a chair and sat down facing Kazem.

"Last night," said Kazem, tearing off a piece of bread, wrapping it round a chunk of cheese, shoving it into his mouth and wolfing it down.

"I can see that you didn't have too bad a time while you were inside," remarked Kal Abbasgholi, regarding him with interest and puckering his dark-grey lips. "You're eating with appetite."

Kazem looked at him, smiling his devilish smile. He shovelled king-size wraps of cheese into his mouth and cracked a few jokes.

"You've not changed a bit!" exclaimed Kal Abbasgholi, chuckling. "You're the same Kazem Alaki as you've always been."

Kal Abbasgholi got up and ambled inside the teahouse. He picked up the teapot, half-filled a small glass with freshly brewed tea, added hot water to it from the samovar's tap, placed it in a saucer, grabbed a tiny tin sugar-bowl and shuffled towards Kazem. He put the tea things on the table in front of Kazem. "There you go." Then he sat down again. Kazem swallowed his last mouthful, picked up a sugar lump, blew hard at it to clear the dust, popped it into his mouth, and drank his tea.

"You know, son," said Kal Abbasgholi in a voice tinged with shame and guilt, looking away and fiddling with his rosary, "truth be told, I'm ashamed of myself. I ought to have come to Tehran to visit you while you were in jail."

"What are you talking about?" Kazem said.

"The truth of the matter is," said Kal Abbasgholi mournfully, glancing at Kazem, "it was all because of me that they arrested you."

"How so?" said Kazem getting up, saucer in hand. "Because of you? Don't even talk about it. Let bygone be bygones." He stood before Kal Abbasgholi drinking his tea. "Well, tell me how your life is going?" he asked, squatting down looking up into his friend's eyes.

"Not so good," sighed Kal Abbasgholi, playing with his rosary. "These are hard times. They've made our lives very hard."

Kazem gazed beyond his friend, nodding thoughtfully.

"You most probably have heard that they're hanging the smugglers in droves to prove that they've things under control," Kal Abbasgholi went on.

Kazem looked at him intently. He stood up, sat on the edge of the daybed, and poured the remaining tea into the saucer.

"I decided to give up selling drugs secretly at the teahouse," Kal Abbasgholi said.

"Tell me something," said Kazem, leaning forward, "Did you chicken out?"

"Yes, you may be right there, son," replied Kal Abbasgholi, glancing at him. "It's not worth the fear and trembling that go with such trade. What's more, all the time you were not here, they broke into the teahouse twice and turned the place upside-down." He sighed heavily. "So, what are you up to now?" he asked.

"Do you know where I can find Mohsen Chakhaan?" Kazem said.

"You can most likely find him in a garage down the thoroughfare."

"What's he doing there?"

"He now delivers fruit and vegetable in a truck to the grocers in the market."

"A truck?"

"Not his," Kal Abbasgholi explained. "His boss's."

"So he travels around?"

"Yes," said Kal Abbasgholi. "He drives to neighbouring towns and villages to get his stuff."

"Does he make enough to get by?"

"He seems content," said Kal Abbasgholi. "After running errands for shopkeepers in the marketplace and procuring opium for mollahs and rich merchants he seems to have settled down a little."

"Where does he live now?"

"In a hovel in an old lodging house near the holy shrine," said Kal Abbasgholi. "Luckily, he hasn't been kicked out of this one after a month. I think he manages to pay his rent all right."

Kal Abbasgholi stood up, picked up the tea glasses, and ambled inside the teahouse. Kazem grabbed his jacket, dusted it, and walked to the daybed that stood against one of the columns. He sat on its arm, put his feet on a chair, and watched the passers-by, thinking what to do and where to go.

7

The plaintive chanting of the muezzin perched on one of the minarets of the nearby mosque began to drift over the market place and the neighbourhood, calling the faithful to noon-prayers. The workers, in small groups, had begun to flock to the teahouse. Some were quiet, others chatting loudly about the events unfolding in the capital, fluttering their hands before them. Kazem stood up, looked around, and began to stroll at a leisurely pace.

Upon arrival at the garage, Kazem walked straight up to a young mechanic whose face and clothes were smudged in black grease. The young man was standing on the front of a truck with his head buried in the engine, fiddling with some wires.

"Where can I find Mohsen, bro?" Kazem asked.

The mechanic popped out his head, wiped his nose with his sleeve and pointed at a truck in the corner of the garage.

"Do you see that truck over there?"

"Yep," said Kazem, glancing in the direction he was pointing.

"He's fixing it."

Kazem, his hands clasped behind his back, strode over to where the truck stood, walked round it, inspecting it carefully. No sign of his friend. Thinking that he might be beneath the truck repairing something, Kazem was about to bend down to look when he heard someone humming a popular tune:

You're so cruel and you know it,
That loving you has deranged my mind.
Your magical pair of black eyes
Are as big as ripe plums...

This was definitely Mohsen. He always sang the lousy songs he had either picked up from the taverns in which he knocked about, or from the prostitutes he met in brothels in different towns and cities when he was off on his errands.

Bending down beside the truck, Kazem saw Mohsen lying on his back with the same old ragged cap, absorbed in his work, carefully turning a bolt with a spanner. Smeared all over with grease, he huffed and puffed, crooning his favourite tune.

"Still singing the same lousy songs," said Kazem, squatting and poking his head under the truck.

"*Bah, bah*, Dash Kazem!" yelled Mohsen. He at once dropped the spanner on the floor, crawled out, and leapt to his feet, saying over and over, "Good to see you!"

"Good to see you, too!" shouted Kazem.

"It's been a long time, Kazem," said Mohsen, leaping up and down like a dwarfish demon, trying to hug and kiss Kazem.

"Don't make my shirt black with your greasy hands and face," Kazem yelled at him.

"All right, all right, I'll not touch your shirt." Mohsen laughed, slapping Kazem's arm. Kazem grabbed his wrists and held them up in the air. They wrestled awhile, pulling, pushing, and tapping one another on the shoulders, laughing heartily.

"I wouldn't have been so happy even if I were given the prettiest women," said Mohsen, having eventually calmed down.

"You've only seen me a minute ago," said Kazem, smiling, "and you've started lying again."

"All right, all right," Mohsen said. "Maybe that was over the top."

They began to walk among the broken-down cars and trucks.

"I missed you a lot, Mohsen," declared Kazem as they walked.

"Me, too, mate," said Mohsen, smiling and looking at him affectionately. "Well, Kazem, I'm sure you've a lot to tell me."

"Nothing much to write home about." Kazem sighed loudly, stopping beside a dilapidated car and throwing his jacket on its bonnet.

"This one was far too long for me," he muttered.

"It was, mate, it was," said Mohsen, nodding. He then turned and hollered across the garage at the young mechanic. "Listen, boy. Nip off to the office and bring us two glasses of clean, freshly brewed tea." He turned back towards Kazem. "Well, Kazem, tell me all about it."

"You have more to tell than I do," Kazem chuckled, jumping on the bonnet of the car. "You know that nothing much happens while you're inside. Tell me now who's where and doing what."

"Nothing much is going on in the town, either," replied Mohsen, hopping on the bonnet of another car, facing that of Kazem. "All's as it has always been – the same things you do day in day out just to get by." He went on after a short pause, "Only lately Eshrat Ikbiri has recruited a first-class young beauty, as pretty as the full moon, just arrived from Mashhad."

"N-o-o!" Kazem said. "You don't say!"

"Oh yes," Mohsen said. "She's also educated, and, wonder of wonders, she sometimes even says '*merci*'."

They both let out guffaws, bending and slapping their thighs. Mohsen suddenly became quiet, looking down as if about to reveal something confidential.

"Between you and me, Dash Kazem," he said, "I think she definitely fancies me, yes. A few nights ago, she even gave me a few pairs of socks as gifts. Last night she made a divination for me by reciting Hafez to me..."

Kazem's smile slowly faded.

"I hope you're not making up fantastic stories again," he said, fixing his eyes on Mohsen's.

"What stories?" said Mohsen. "This is nothing but the truth. Anyway, let's go," he shouted.

Kazem frowned.

"Did you know that Reza Zepeleshk is back in town?" he asked, his voice gone strangely hoarse.

"Yes, I know," said Mohsen, contemplating his rosary with which he fiddled constantly. "I saw him in one of the gambling dens a few days ago. He was ringed with his usual mates. I just ignored them."

"I was told he came to Mashhad to repent and become a good Muslim," said Kazem.

"He's repented all right," said Mohsen. "I've seen him as drunk as a skunk in A-Sayyed Musa's tavern, braying like a mad donkey. He's also a regular at Eshrat Ikbiri's brothel."

"If you wash a mongrel dog one hundred times, it's still a dirty dog," Kazem observed.

"You haven't forgotten about that bastard, have you?" said Mohsen darkly, staring goggle-eyed at Kazem. "Everybody knows that he was the one who did the dirty on you when you were inside. Otherwise you wouldn't have stayed in jail for two years."

"That's the reason I want to get even with him," said Kazem, "because he grassed on me even when I was in jail."

Kazem leaped down the bonnet of the car and strode away rapidly. Mohsen followed, trying to catch up with him.

"Listen, Kazem," he said, "try to forgive and forget."

"Forgiveness is the job of saints," said Kazem. "I'm not a saint."

"Come on, let's forget about the past," said Mohsen, taking his cap off and scratching his head. "If you like, tonight we could go and see some *khanums* in Eshrat Ikbiri's house."

"There's still plenty of time left till night-time," said Kazem. "Tell me," he asked, putting his arm round Mohsen's shoulder, "where's the best place to find Reza Zepeleshk this time of day?"

"He and his men usually go to the roof of the tomb of the saint to play knucklebones," Mohsen replied reluctantly.

"All right then," said Kazem. "Let's go find them."

8

After hurriedly gulping down their teas, the two friends left the garage. Kazem strode forth, deep in thought. Mohsen, being short-legged and small, scampered at his heels. Once out of the town, they took a dusty road that led to the graveyard on high ground overlooking the town. At the end of the road, they turned right and climbed up a footpath that pitched steeply up the rise leading to the vast graveyard. By now gasping for air, they stopped a while to draw breath. They both surveyed the graveyard that sloped steadily up. With its tombstones – some rectangular slabs, others cuboid-like, and most of them just simple mounds of earth – the graveyard looked like the sun-baked ruins of an ancient city. The tomb of an unknown saint was perched on top of a tiny hillock at the end of the cemetery. Its blue-and-beige mosaicked, cone-shaped dome, flanked by two stocky round minarets, shimmered in the hazy heat of the late August sun.

The two men began to trudge silently in the oppressive heat. Shading their eyes against the blinding sun with their hands, they stepped over the gravestones, mopping, every so often, with their handkerchiefs the large drops of sweat pouring down their foreheads to their cheeks, obscuring their vision. Skinny little lizards, disturbed by the footfalls of the two men on the graves, stuck their tiny heads out of the holes around the gravestones and darted off among the stones with their tails raised high, vanishing into other crevices. Beside some of the graves sat solitary women, veiled in frayed black chadors, weeping noiselessly. Sitting cross-legged beside the other graves were other women who screeched like wounded ravens whose wings are covered in dust and wisps of straw. Added to all these lamentations was the mournful cawing of flocks of carrion crows circling overhead, the trilling of crickets hidden among the thorn branches and the humming of gadflies.

Upon arriving at the main building of the tomb, Kazem leapt on the first step of a tumbledown staircase at one corner that led to the tomb proper. He tore up the steps like a mountain goat, followed by Mohsen, who scrambled after him, wheezing loudly. At the top of the steps, they walked past the first minaret, climbed some more steps, walked briskly a short distance, jumped on a low, mud-brick wall and ended up on the roof of the building.

Once Kazem came to the second minaret, he saw a band of roguish-looking men squatting on the dusty floor in the shade of a small dome, playing a game of knucklebones. Kazem stood close to the base of the minaret, tossed his jacket on it, and leaned his left elbow against it. Unmoving, he fixed his eyes on his man – Reza Zepeleshk – like a hawk on a chicken. Mohsen took up his position beside Kazem. Striking a swaggering attitude like a loyal underling, he tilted his cap down over his brow, coolly eyeing the men, ready for any trouble. Small flocks of carrion crows hovered above the dome, clinging to gaps created by dislodged bricks and swirling around the minarets, squawking continually.

The gamblers carried on with their game, not aware that they were being watched.

"I read seven," said Reza Zepeleshk.

"I read five," one of the men said gruffly.

"Seven and five, bro," cut in Reza Zepeleshk. "You read it beautifully. My turn now." He went on tossing up the knucklebones and slapping his knee hard in hope that the knucklebones would land on the floor the way he wished.

"A stroke of bad luck, as always!" Kazem's loud and angry voice made Reza Zepeleshk look back over his shoulder. Kazem stood there with his cold gaze fixed on him, intent on doing him harm. He was conscious of the other men also looking at him.

"*Bah, bah,* Kazem Agha!" exclaimed Reza Zepeleshk, beckoning to him to go over. "What a pleasant surprise to see you here, of all places. It's good to see you out. Come and join us."

"I've come to settle a score with you," said Kazem, his voice hoarse with anger.

"If you're still thinking about that matter. . ." Reza Zepeleshk chuckled, waving his hand as if shooing off an annoying gadfly. He gathered the knucklebones from the floor and handed them over to one of the men, telling him to toss them. "How could I possibly betray you while you were inside, Kazem? Before you went to jail, we used to drink *arrack* together and you were a good mate for years. You still are."

Reza Zepeleshk stood up.

"But you betrayed me when I was helpless and condemned," said Kazem calmly, walking towards Reza. Sensing the looming danger, one of the gamblers got up. He took a few steps towards Kazem, put his hand on his shoulder and said in a friendly tone of voice, "Come on, Kazem. Say a *salawat*, and let bygones be bygones, bro."

Kazem grabbed his hands, glaring at him, and pushed them away. The man stood aside and watched.

"As for me, I've forgotten nothing," Kazem growled, walking menacingly towards Reza.

"I didn't betray you," said Reza, waving his hands.

"You did," Kazem insisted, scowling darkly.

"All right, I did," shouted Reza. "So what?"

Overcome with rage, Kazem head-butted Reza, who tumbled backwards, tripped over a low brick wall and sprawled on the floor.

"Now I'm going to teach you what it costs to grass on a friend!" Kazem cried out, leaping over the wall and pouncing on Reza like a wild cat. Reza struggled back on his feet, but Kazem swiped so hard at his jaw that he fell back on the floor. He snatched Reza's shirt, lifted him up, swung him round, and pushed him against a small dome. He lunged at him, delivering a blow to his chin that sent him reeling down some high steps. Leaping down the steps, he pounded Reza relentlessly. Reza staggered towards some more steps, trying to run off. Kazem caught up with him and went on raining hard blows on him.

"That's enough, Kazem!" yelled Mohsen who, with the other men, was watching the scene helplessly. "He'll remember this lesson by heart."

Deaf to Mohsen's imploring, Kazem fell upon Reza and clasped his hands round his neck. The two men rolled over in the dust, panting and sweating. Kazem managed to sit astride Reza's back, bashing his head against the floor. He then lifted Reza up, punching him hard until he staggered backwards and fell on his back on the edge of the roof. Kazem ran to him, grabbed his feet, and dangled him over the edge.

"Do you want me to throw you down?"

"N-o-o!" Reza croaked, paralysed by fear.

"That's enough. Cut it out, Kazem!" shouted Mohsen, running towards him. "You've just come out of jail. Do you want to go back inside for murder?"

"You're in luck this time," growled Kazem, "but only because I don't want to end up in that goddamned jail again."

Kazem left Reza Zepeleshk on the roof, spread-eagled, groaning and whimpering, his head dangling over the edge.

"Let's go," said Kazem, buttoning up his shirt and pushing Mohsen ahead of him.

Kazem walked swiftly a few paces ahead of Mohsen. He kept mopping his brow and neck with his handkerchief. It was now late afternoon and the graves were quivering in the hazy, saffron-tinted rays of the sun. The shadows of the tombstones were lengthening. The cawing of carrion crows could be heard from far off beyond the graveyard as they flew over the drowsy town whose inhabitants were waking up from their afternoon nap. The humming of the insects had died down a little, but the shrill trilling of crickets had become louder.

At the end of the graveyard Kazem stopped and looked back. A handful of black-chadored women sat cross-legged here and there at the edges of fresh mounds of earth, gazing numbly at them, touching them with pebbles in their hands, and weeping softly. From time to time, the warm breeze rustled their dusty chadors.

Both men turned and walked down the rise, raising dust behind them, each plunged in his own thoughts.

9

Soon after they arrived in town they went to Kal Abbasgholi's teahouse to drink tea and catch up with the latest news about the religious ceremony that was to take place late that evening in the mosque in the centre of the town. Instead of the usual bustle, the mood of the regulars was sombre. The workers drank their teas, dragging at their cigarettes and hotly debating the forthcoming ceremony. The older men sat bolt upright on the daybeds. They puffed away at their *chibouks*, pompously recounting stories of the courage and sacrifices of Imam Ali and the other Arab martyrs at the dawn of Islam. Thick smoke hung in the air, adding to the cheerless atmosphere of the place. From the battered radio the funereal, droning voice of a mollah was blasting out, braying the same old tales about Imam Ali – the son-in-law of the Prophet – who was martyred by infidels and the enemies of Islam fourteen centuries ago in Iraq so that the flag of Islam could remain aloft and fluttering all over the world. Kal Abbasgholi was busy pouring tea into rows of glasses on a tin tray. His enthusiastic tea boy, now dressed in a black shirt with a black scarf flung over his shoulders for the solemn occasion, carried the full trays to the customers, putting a glass in front of each one, yelling, "Your tea, bro, your tea, bro…"

The holy month of Ramadan having overlapped that year with the month of August, Hosseinabaad was getting ready to commemorate the martyrdom of Imam Ali. As the ceremony was supposed to start after sundown, Kazem and Mohsen left the teahouse; each went to his lodgings to change into long black shirts for the occasion.

Before going to the mosque, the two friends met in the marketplace, then sneaked into the tavern of their Armenian friend who secretly sold *arrack* to his special customers at all times, no matter what day, week or month of the Islamic calendar. Kazem and Mohsen walked straight to the counter behind which stood the shabbily-dressed Armenian, a rag thrown across his shoulders, with his elbows propped on the counter. He was having an intimate conversation with one of his drunken habitués who was leaning over, gazing stupidly as his glass was refilled by the Armenian.

"*Babam jaan*, I've to make a living to support seven hungry mouths," Kazem heard the Armenian drone in his heavy accent. "If I follow all these Islamic customs and rules and shut the tavern, I'll be ruined and who's going to look after my wife and kids then? Besides, some poor souls need to drown their cares in a few glasses of *arrack*. I don't see anything wrong with that."

Upon seeing Kazem and Mohsen, the Armenian cut his complaints short and warmly greeted the two friends. After rummaging under the counter, he produced a bottle of *arrack*, popped it open and placed it on the counter, flanked by two small glasses. Next, he cut slices of salami and arranged them on a plate beside which he put chunks of white baguettes and pickled gherkins. He then busied himself with the other regulars who were trickling in, two or three together, to fortify themselves before taking part in the religious ceremony. Grim-faced and scruffy and dressed in black shirts, they knocked back glass after glass of *arrack,* saying loudly, "*Yaa Ali madad.*"

Kazem and Mohsen drank the whole bottle, smoked several cigarettes, and talked about the fresh prostitutes just brought in by pimps from the holy cities of Qom and Mashhad to Eshrat Ikbiri's establishment where they were planning to go after the ceremony in the mosque.

Perked up after having drunk themselves silly, they were ready to fulfil their Islamic duties by taking part in the annual ritual of listening to Hosseinabaad's resident mollah, beat their foreheads and weep buckets of tears to wash away their unforgiveable sins.

Darkness had fallen when they arrived at the square around which surged a dark mass of people all dressed up in black, mostly Hosseinabaad's inhabitants and people from the neighbouring villages. A large crowd of men, young and old, all wearing long black shirts that hung over their trousers, were being herded by some other black-clad men inside the mosque. Most of these scruffy-looking men had moustaches and black beards grown long for the occasion. They consisted of day labourers, errand boys, shopkeepers, butchers, greengrocers, bakers, hawkers, artisans, stallholders, itinerant entertainers, wrestlers, pimps, smugglers, knife-fighters flanked by their underlings, strongmen who held sway over different patches of the town, junkies and gamblers of all kinds.

Kazem, followed by Mohsen, pushed and shoved his way through the mob, staggered into the mosque and joined the army of Islam. He had to cover his nose with his arm against the nauseating stench of sweat mingled with smelly socks. The stuffy air of the hall made him nearly tumble over on a seated old man who was lost in his communion with Imam Ali. The prayers hall was crammed with men who all sat cross-legged, listening with mournful faces to the ramblings of the mollah perched on top of the pulpit, wrapped in his *aba*. The mollah was yelling a dirge, praising Imam Ali, who, at that holiest of nights – Night of Destiny – was martyred by a whoreson infidel. All the men beat their chests and foreheads to the slow rhythm of the dirge, sobbing so noisily that their shoulders convulsed as if in the grip of incurable epilepsy. They took up the refrain and chanted at the tops of their lungs, weeping bitterly, sniffling and wiping their noses and eyes.

"I can't make head or tail of what they're singing," Kazem mumbled to himself. "I'm going to sing my own tune that has more rhythm in it and is more down-to-earth and homely and not so far-away in time." The sorrowful voice of the dirge singer, turning slowly into gibberish, faded away. Kazem began to hum with feeling the song he had, in all likelihood, picked up in a tavern, a gambling den or brothel:

As I was wandering one night under the marketplace of Galubandak,
My eyes fell upon a gorgeous woman veiled in her black chador.
A wink from her was enough to steal my heart forever.
On seeing her, I chased after her to declare my love.
Muddled, I stammered and garbled some poppycock
Without being able to tell her that I fancied her...

After a short while, Kazem felt so fed up that he turned to Mohsen and whispered in his ear, "Let's get out of here."

"Why?" Mohsen whispered back.

"I'm bored."

He got up and quietly slipped out. Mohsen had no choice but to do the same. Not being able to spot their shoes, hidden somewhere under a heap of others, they found some other pairs, put them on, and walked into the square, where they joined the grief-stricken crowd who were blubbering and shedding copious tears. Upon breathing in fresh air and thanks to the excitement around them, the two friends sobered up a little and were able to see and think more clearly. So they peered into the gloom to see whether they could spot some pretty young women among the dark mass of inconsolable female enthusiasts watching the men from behind the rim of their chadors, admiring the most zealous and handsome ones, hoping, if lucky, to spot an eligible future husband.

Having discreetly surveyed the crowd of women whose faces glowed in the pale light of the streetlamps, Kazem's eyes fell upon a young beauty whose lily-white face, framed in a black chador and surrounded by a sea of other dark figures, shone like the full moon in a dark sky. Her calm gaze was fixed at something beyond the crowd. She was not weeping or shrieking like the rest of the women. From time to time, she whispered something to her friends who had made a ring round her as if she were something precious to be protected from the prying eyes of the predatory mollahs and other men. Kazem went on staring at her. She was completely unaware of his gaze.

"Who's that girl?" he asked in a low voice, nudging Mohsen in the ribs.

"Which one?" Mohsen stopped his chanting of the dirge and peered into the dark mass of women.

"The pretty one with arched eyebrows who's so quiet," Kazem said, pointing discreetly.

"Oh, that one," Mohsen whispered back. "Don't you know her?"

"No, I don't," said Kazem.

"She's the daughter of Hajji Harirchi," said Mohsen under his breath. "Maryam the Beauty."

"Hmm, how she's grown!" muttered Kazem, gazing at Maryam, a faint smile fluttering on his lips.

"Girls are like little baby sparrows," observed Mohsen like a sage, looking at the other women. "In a blink of an eye they grow into fully-fledged birds."

Kazem went on gazing into the darkness, contemplating Maryam's ethereal beauty.

He felt a tap on his shoulder.

"Kazem! Kazem!" Mohsen's quiet voice sounded in his ears.

"What?"

"It's about time we went," Mohsen told him. "The ceremony is coming to an end."

Mohsen grabbed Kazem's arm, gently pulling him away. Kazem kept looking back at the spot where Maryam was hidden among the clutch of her friends.

The mass of people had begun to disperse in small bands, disappearing into shadowy lanes and alleyways.

10

Worn-out and having nothing better to do, the pair wandered aimlessly in and out of the dusky lanes and under archways, dimly lit here and there by the grimy light bulbs that dangled on worm-eaten lampposts. All the rusty tin shutters of shops were down and the stalls were packed away and left near the walls. Some inhabitants of Hosseinabaad, hands thrust in their trouser pockets, scurried about mutely, lost in their own worlds. Some of them were rushing to their dwellings, others to late night taverns, and yet others to gambling dens tucked away at the end of squalid-looking lanes. The usual murmurings of the town were dying one after another. The shrill trilling of insects pierced the calm night, mingling with the distant howling of the stray dogs that prowled in the graveyard and the vacant lot. From behind the shut doors, through the half-open windows of some houses, one could hear men and women arguing and shrieking.

The night was warm and the air still.

Mohsen, walking silently beside Kazem, all of a sudden began to sing the song he loved most:

You're so cruel and you know it,
Loving you has deranged my mind.
Your magical pair of black eyes,
Are as big as ripe plums.

"I feel like knocking back a few glasses of *arrack.*" He turned to Kazem.

"Bah," mumbled Kazem, shaking his head reproachfully, "you must have a belly like a bottomless pit. Only this afternoon you drank a whole bottle of rotgut."

"My heart is burdened with so much sorrow," muttered Mohsen and went on intoning his song again.

You're so cruel and you know it...

"Go on, Kazem," said Mohsen, stopping and squinting at Kazem. "Help me out with the rest of it. "You're not with it tonight," he added, struggling to remember the rest of the lyrics.

"I'm out of it," said Kazem wistfully.

"Maybe you left your heart in the square, hey?" said Mohsen, winking at him mischievously from under his cap that was pulled down to his brow.

"Who cares about such things?" Kazem drawled, chuckling.

"What else would you be thinking about?"

"Becoming an actor," he said, exasperated.

"An actor?"

"Yes, Mohsen, an actor. I've spent two years in jail and now I've galloped headlong back here – to see whom and to do what? Smuggling is no longer on. My old gambling pals aren't around any more. They have all gone off in different directions. Most of them are now workers in the car factories that have sprouted up everywhere like mushrooms. So what the devil am I doing here? Where am I supposed to go? Honestly, who am I, hey? When I was a little boy, I used to sneak into Shahr-e No Street and peep into the *cabaret* in which my mother sang and danced. Admiring her, I made up my mind to become an actor. Later on, a lot of film stars became my heroes and I wanted to be famous like them.

"But as kids we were imprisoned in the Citadel. Not ever having known or seen our fathers, we soon turned into young delinquents, roaming from dawn to dusk in the Citadel, pickpocketing the clients who poured into it to have the cheapest possible sex. I went on like this for a few years, sticking to the underpants of Tehran's society, living off the filthy skin flakes in the warmth of such places.

"I soon began to shine in my gang and took upon myself the role of ringleader. As the knife-fighters and the strongmen were always on the lookout to recruit fresh blood, one of them heard about my daring and foolhardiness. No sooner had he asked me to join his underworld circle, operating in Jamshid Street and its neighbourhood, than I was flung into the cruel, vice-infested whirlpool of Tehran's underworld and was soon transformed into an urban wolf, always on the look-out for fresh prey.

"To start with, I began smuggling and pushing small quantities of drugs in both streets in the Citadel. I was quick to learn the ropes and climbed the ladder of crime and became one of the closest confidants of the strongman. Before long, I was asked to leave the Citadel and travel further afield to organise the delivery of the assignments of contraband goods that were brought in secretly from Kuwait and Dubai, and opium that was smuggled into Iran from Afghanistan.

"Truth be told, Mohsen," he went on, "I never wanted to follow this path of winning my bread and onion by smuggling and pushing drugs. So, when I grew a bit older, I began hanging around the theatres and cabarets to do anything, anything at all, to become an actor. No one appreciated my enthusiasm. One day a friend of mine told me to go and try my luck at the film studios in Arbaab-Jamsheed Street. I jumped at the idea and joined an army of hopeless bastards like myself who hung around the studios all day long, desperately trying to get the attention of a producer. Every other month a producer spotted some of us and asked if we could take part in a scene as extras, acting as if we were the underlings of a strongman, to be beaten up by the main actor in a cabaret brawl. We would be herded into a real cabaret, asked to sit round the table on which were placed bottles of *arrack*, all provided free by the producer. The director would then tell us how to playact a fight with the famous actor's men over the pretty dancer who fancied the artist and not our strongman. Once the acting was over, the producer would fork out our cash and tell us to bugger off.

"When acting in scenes like this we'd settle on the chairs to drink, eat, and smoke and watch the small band of musicians play. Soon a gorgeous actress playing the role of a cabaret dancer would appear on the stage, dressed in a short skirt that revealed half of her buttocks, wriggling her knockers and bum to the rhythm of the music, and moving her lips following a song sung by a famous singer. Forgetting where we were and what we had been told to do, we guzzled down the *arrack*, devoured all the food, and began singing and dancing on the tables. The good old director thought that we were acting very well. As the filming went on we forgot all about our roles. The same thing happened to the men who were sitting around the star. The whole scenario soon turned sour. The rival gangs set upon each other, smashing bottles of *arrack* on one another's heads. All these men came from different districts and cities – the thugs from Tehran beat the Turks from Tabriz, the rogues from Mashhad bludgeoned the louts from Qom, the scoundrels from Esfahan tried to throttle the young enthusiasts from Arak. Upon realising that things had got out of hand, the director kept screaming 'Cut! Cut!" but no one listened. The actress, realising that things had gone seriously wrong, would shriek and run behind the stage. The funny thing was that the orchestra would go on playing, enjoying their own music and oblivious to what was going on around them. The famous actor would be hustled out by the backdoor by his minders. Once everything was smashed into pieces, the director would yell at the would-be actors and kick them out of the studio. Every time I tried to show my talents, these good-for-nothing louts spoiled my chances. All day long, from dawn to dusk, we hung around in teahouses and taverns in Arbaab-Jamsheed Street, drinking tea, smoking and talking about our favourite actors and actresses, discussing who was good, who was making the most money and who was sleeping with whom."

"But how long did you go on like this?" Mohsen interrupted.

"Not long," went on Kazem. "As all my efforts ended up in complete fiasco, I decided it wasn't worth the aggro and started looking for some other way to earn my living. But things never worked out the way I wanted them to. They kept asking me for my birth certificate, passport, election papers, party membership card, bank account, my father's name, my real mother's name, my friends' names, any bit of paper to show my identity on it. How could they find out about my credentials from whores, pimps, knife-fighters and strongmen who were given either different names or freaky nicknames that described their appearances, their origins or their jobs? As you know, some women were given names of the cities, towns or districts in which they were born – Shaheen Torkeh, Maheen Rashti, Shamsi Baboli and Akram Shemrooni. Others were given names that described their appearances or habits – Esmat Boshkeh, Vaji Charcheshm, Pari Bolandeh, Badri Bachebaaz and Zivar Gareh. All the men were given nicknames, too, according to how they looked, behaved, or what they did for a living – Asghar Sibil, Hossein Bighavareh, Mehdi Khalvat, Akbar Beeorzeh, Mammad Susul, Vali Kallehpaz, Gholaam Peshkelfuroosh and Safdar Dallehdozd."

Kazem stopped talking, his eyes fixed on the ground as if looking for something he had lost. Mohsen walked beside him quietly. They went on walking aimlessly. After traipsing around the marketplace, they came out, took the thoroughfare and continued walking in and out of several half-dark alleys. Glancing around, Kazem realised that they were heading towards Eshrat Ikbiri's establishment.

"Do you know where we are now, Mohsen?" Kazem asked, turning towards his friend.

"Sure I do," Mohsen replied.

"We've been trudging towards this place without knowing where we've been going, son," said Kazem, smiling.

"Old habits die hard, as they say!" Mohsen chuckled, glancing at him.

"What do we do now?"

"Well, that's flipping obvious, Dash Kazem," exclaimed Mohsen, "we're going to pay a visit to the *khanums* and drink some more *arrack*. I think you'll enjoy that after all the excitement of chest-beating and sobbing."

Kazem said nothing. He was too worn-out to argue for or against seeing the *khanums* during the holy month of Ramadan. They soon arrived at the outskirts of Hosseinabaad near the graveyard. Eshrat Ikbiri's house, tucked away at the end of a sordid-looking alleyway, was shrouded in darkness. Kazem stood beside the weather-beaten wooden door, shoehorned between two crumbling mud-brick walls in the shadow of a shabby, brickwork arch.

Mohsen, catching up, stepped beneath the arch, looking furtively around, like a thief about to break in. He lifted the rusty doorknocker, knocked on the door several times, and waited, leaning against the wall. Kazem heard him sing, punctuated with hiccups:

You're so cruel and you know it,
Loving you has deranged my mind...

Mohsen pushed his cap back, leaned forward, stuck his head against the door and peeped through a crack in the wood, reeling like an anchorless dinghy.

"Let's hope that they're working tonight," he said under his breath.

"I'm very doubtful." Kazem leaned back against the wall. "On a holy night like this many of the *khanums* go to the chest-beating ceremony near the mosque to listen to the mollahs in the hope of finding some rich merchants to make them *siegehehs* to escape their wretched lives for a short while."

"You're right there, Dash Kazem," Mohsen's muffled voice came from beneath the arch, "but let's see, anyway. Who knows? The Almighty, being compassionate and merciful, might feel sorry for poor devils like us and let us see some of His lovely creatures on earth tonight."

He knocked harder. The dull sound echoed in the silence of the alleyway, drowning the other noises of the night. After a moment, the sound of dragging footsteps was heard approaching the door. Keys jangled in the rusty old lock. Hearing this, Mohsen swiftly doffed his cap, tucked it under his left arm and stood to attention with his back to the wall, as if a high-ranking army officer was about to emerge from the house.

The door was opened a crack and the head of an old hag veiled in a black chador with tiny flowery patterns appeared. Peeking from behind the door, she recognised Mohsen. She opened the door wide.

"Atten-tion," cried out Mohsen with a resounding emphasis on '-tion', stiffening like a dutiful soldier who faces his superior by raising his hand in salute.

"*Bah, bah,* Agha Mohsen," she croaked from behind the chador. "Welcome, welcome, tonight of all nights!"

"I've dragged an old friend here tonight, Eshrat Khanum," said Mohsen, grinning.

On seeing Kazem, a ghastly smile spread over Eshrat Ikbiri's wizened, pockmarked face, daubed with powder, blusher and mascara. In the half-dark her face looked like the skin of a rotten, withered walnut with dark-brown and yellowish blotches.

"Well, well, Kazem Agha," she squawked, "fancy seeing you here again. Maybe you lost your way. What happened that you remembered unworthy folk like us?

"I was having lots of fun in jail, gorgeous," said Kazem, smiling.

"Come in, come in, please," squeaked Eshrat, turning round and leading the way. "You've lit up our wretched dwelling with your presence."

"You go in first, Dash Kazem," said Mohsen, touching Kazem's elbow politely.

No sooner did Kazem step into the dark passageway than a foul-smelling current of air swung the door and hit it against the doorframe, making it rattle. Kazem watched Eshrat Ikbiri's head sunk into her stooping shoulders like that of a sorceress as she shambled along the gloomy passageway, muttering to herself. The hem of her chador trailed on the uneven flagstones. The courtyard was lit by pale light bulbs that dangled from a few sickly-looking trees, throwing a yellowish glow on the surface of the murky water in the *hauz*. Around the courtyard were a number of small rooms with worm-eaten doors, behind the cracked windowpanes of which hung shabby curtains, smeared with large patches of stains. On the rough cobblestones at the left side of the courtyard were placed several shaky bentwood chairs. A handful of unsmiling, bearded clients in black shirts sat politely on some of the chairs. They looked like the faithful who sit reverently in a mosque. Mutely, they ogled the *khanums*, deliberating hard as if over the most agonizing decision they had to make in their entire lives: which *khanum* to select to give them the maximum pleasure for the smallest amount of cash. Worn-out after going through so much religious ecstasy, weeping, chest beating, and self-flagellation earlier that night, they needed something to soothe their frazzled nerves. What better than quick, cheap sex?

Near the *hauz* were placed three unsteady daybeds, spread over with tattered kilims. Seated cross-legged on one of these were two *khanums*. They were humming along with a melancholy song that was pouring out of a battered gramophone that stood on the corner of the daybed. In the middle of the other daybed stood a cooking stove on top of which was placed a cauldron, surrounded by three *khanums*, dressed in gaudy short skirts. One of the *khanums* was hugging a large, dented tin pot between her almond-coloured legs, vigorously plucking a headless chicken soaked in warm water which had turned the colour of blood. The other two *khanums* picked up aubergines, potatoes, tomatoes and onions from a wicker basket, peeling and slicing them with large knives, and tossing them into the cauldron with a plop. Once the chicken was thoroughly featherless, it was submerged in the cauldron. One of the *khanums* then took a ladle and began to stir the stew. They also joined in humming the song, looking like the three witches in a Sabbath. Every now and then, they threw mischievous glances at the bemused clients, whispered to one another, and giggled noiselessly. On the third daybed sat a beautiful, meek-looking creature in a long dress, idly flipping through a women's magazine, looking at the pictures.

Eshrat Ikbiri directed her guests to two chairs in the front row, shuffled across the courtyard and flopped into a large chair placed on the other side of the *hauz*. She dropped her chador on the back of the chair, hoisted herself upright and remained silent.

Not having seen her for a long time, Kazem eyed Eshrat surreptitiously. As he studied her, memories of long ago invaded his mind. Her ravaged face glowed in the gleam of the light bulbs that peeped out of the dusty branches of a tree beside which she sat, gruesome-looking and betraying no emotion, an old monarch who had ruled over her wretched subjects for an eternity. She had fallen into deep reflection, gazing intently at the still surface of the water in the *hauz* as if searching for something she had lost long, long ago that was lurking at its slimy bottom. Years of selling her body to strangers and pimping had made of her an empty shell.

The soft crooning of a tune by one of the *khanums* stirring the cauldron brought Kazem back to the real world. She winked at him, and nodded familiarly as if to an old habitué of the establishment. Kazem glanced at Mohsen who was looking, goggle-eyed like a lovesick adolescent, at his beautiful Mashhadi sweetheart. Lost in her own world, the pretty creature went on leafing through the magazine, wholly unconcerned with the tormented young man.

"Is this the educated newcomer you were talking about?" Kazem nodded in the direction of the young lady.

"Yep," mumbled Mohsen mechanically, not taking his eyes off the Mashhadi beauty.

"What are you waiting for, then?" said Kazem under his breath. "You go with her and I'll take my good old friend, Faati Komando."

Kazem walked over to Eshrat Ikbiri, thrust his hands into his jacket pocket, took out a few crumpled five-tomans, and handed them to her.

"Ohoy, Faati," Eshrat squawked across the courtyard, "will you go with Kazem Agha? Make sure you look after him well."

The job done, Faati Komando got up, slipped into her clothes, and left the room. Kazem dressed and stepped outside, buttoning up his shirt.

He then sat on one of the chairs, waiting for Mohsen to come out of his sweetheart's room. He surveyed the courtyard. Most of the men were now in the rooms with *khanums*.

By the time Mohsen showed up, most of the *khanums* had come out and taken up their positions on the daybeds. At that moment, a thunderbolt flashed across the night sky, lighting up the courtyard, revealing every detail of its squalor. A crash of thunder followed, bringing a downpour. As the clients and the women ran for cover, Kazem and Mohsen got up and left Eshrat Ikbiri's establishment. Rainwater, mixed with filth and dirt, streamed down the drainpipes sticking out from the edges of the roofs.

Kazem covered his head with his jacket.

"Did you see that, Agh Kazem?" Mohsen shouted.

"See what?" cried Kazem.

"My sweetheart, of course," Mohsen said. "Did you see how she was looking at me?"

"Will you cut it out, Mohsen!"

"You were not in the room, were you?" Mohsen said, fluttering his hands in front of Kazem. "She went down on her hands and knees, crying and begging me not to abandon her there in that place."

Kazem, preoccupied, didn't pay much attention to him.

"What's the matter with you, for God's sake?" Mohsen shouted, throwing up his hands in despair.

"I'm not in the right mood, Mohsen."

"You and your moodiness!" cried Mohsen.

"I'm completely shattered," Kazem said.

They walked through the mud and streaming puddles.

"Never mind all that, Agh Kazem," Mohsen said in a consoling tone. "Let me sing you a song to cheer you up."

You're so cruel and you know it,

Loving you has deranged my mind...

"For heaven's sake, man," muttered Kazem as they walked through the dark alleys in the rain. "You're driving me nuts with your lousy song."

11

The following day, around midmorning, Kazem was sitting on his usual chair in the porch in Kal Abbasgholi's teahouse drinking tea when he saw Maryam pass by.

As she was trying to hold an empty bowl and a plate she was carrying, her chador accidentally slipped off her head and fell down to her waist, revealing her jet-black hair which rolled down in cascades on her shoulders and breasts that peeped from under her blouse like a pair of ripe lemons. She hurriedly grabbed the edge of her chador, pulling it up to her head, and gathered it round her.

Kazem sat frozen for a few seconds, holding the saucer close to his lips, but not drinking. Eventually, he put the saucer on the table, stood up, and watched Maryam walking down the lane.

After a while, he made to go back inside the teahouse, but then turned on his heel and decided to shadow her just for the joy of looking at her. He ran after her a short distance, then slowed down, keeping a good distance behind her. She entered a passage, on both sides of which were small shops with awnings. Maryam walked at a leisurely pace, absorbed in her own world, every now and then pulling her chador back to her head.

Kazem stood at the bend of an archway, bracing his elbow against a corner of the wall. Maryam was gracefully gliding past the shops, her chador flapping in the slight breeze.

At that moment two youths cycled into the street from a lane, manoeuvring and going round in circles, creating havoc among the passers-by and knocking down the fruit stalls laid out in the shop fronts. One shopkeeper ran out of his shop, raising his hand to heaven and cursing the unruly lads, who went on riding, laughing and playing pranks on the passers-by. All of a sudden, they spotted Maryam. They rode towards her, circling her, and yelling rude remarks.

"I love your chador!" one of them cried out, going round and round her. "Will you, only for my sake, open up and close your chador once more. You're so lovely."

Kazem glared at the youth, thinking that he should intervene. The other youth joined in, circling Maryam and harassing her.

"Where're you going in such a hurry, my gorgeous bride?" he jeered. "I die for you, my lovely."

They carried on cycling round her, taking turns in making amorous remarks.

"What a lovely-looking doll. I'll die for you if you want. Come on, hop on the bike and I'll take you anywhere you like."

Maryam walked on unconcerned, clutching the bowl and the plate in one hand, holding the hem of her chador with the other, not even once glancing at them. As one of them came too close to her, putting his fingers to his lips to blow a kiss to her, he lost his balance and fell on the ground, laughing like an idiot. Kazem, overcome with anger, ran towards the young rogue.

"Oopsa-daisy!" said the youth. "Bloody hell, I fell. Not to worry, I'll be on my feet and after you in a second." The youth stood up, dusted his backside, and tried to hoist up his bike. As he grabbed the handlebar and lifted his foot to mount the machine, Kazem caught up with him.

"Wait a minute," Kazem growled, grabbing the saddle.

"Who the hell are you?" said the youth, turning towards Kazem.

"Count me in, too, pretty boy," Kazem said.

"Don't mention it." The youth's mouth cracked open in a silly smile. "You can join in the fun, too. It's free for all."

Kazem, without warning, delivered a resounding slap to the youth's face that sent him staggering off his bike.

"Aye, why are you hitting me?" the youth cried out, reeling backwards.

As he fell, Kazem kicked his backside.

"You sonofabitch!" he said. "How dare you go clowning around in the lanes bothering decent folk? Come on, get up and beat it. Run off home and do your homework, instead of fooling around like this."

The youth crawled on all fours, whimpering like a beaten dog. Then he struggled up to his feet and took to his heels, hollering loudly like a spoilt brat and soon disappeared into an alleyway at the end of the narrow street.

"Oh my god!" shouted the other youth, petrified after seeing his accomplice being thrashed by Kazem. He rode into Maryam from behind, pushing her into a lamppost. He tumbled down from his bike, dragging it down with him.

"Watch out, young lady!" he shouted, before lifting his bike and pedalling off in a holy panic.

Maryam balanced herself on her feet, pulling her chador back to her head. She entered the same alleyway down which the youth had ridden. Kazem picked up the bike abandoned by the first youth, leapt on it and pedalled fast, riding after the second culprit who cycled like a demon, his bike wobbling this way and that. He rode past Maryam, who stopped to watch the chase.

"Where're you running to, you sissy?" yelled Kazem. "Stop, if you're a man. I'll teach you how to treat decent women."

The youth rode as fast as he could towards the end of the lane. Kazem stopped in the middle of the lane, dismounted, and followed him with his eyes as he rode off.

"Look at him," mumbled Kazem, holding the handlebar with one hand. "The brat is escaping like a frightened dog."

He squatted beside the bike and began to deflate the tyre.

"I'll let the tyre down so that he'll never again think of chasing decent girls in this neighbourhood," he muttered.

Maryam had started walking towards him. Once at a level with the bike, she stopped and looked at Kazem.

"Thank you," she said quietly, pulling her chador to her face. She then carried on walking.

Kazem looked up at her. He sat there as if turned into stone, letting go of the handlebars in slow motion. The bike dropped to the ground. He remained squatted, watching her gliding off towards the end of the alleyway.

"She said thank you to me!" Kazem mumbled, dazed. "Oh, I love the way she said that!"

He got up and began to walk like a sleepwalker in and out of the alleyways and lanes, ending up finally in the marketplace. He went back to Kal Abbasgholi's teahouse, where he sat in a quiet corner in the porch, and asked for a glass of tea. He lit a cigarette and took a long drag, gazing at the floor. The teahouse was filled with workers, shopkeepers and pilgrims going to or coming from the tomb of the saint. Kal Abbasgholi was too preoccupied with the customers to talk to Kazem, so he sat there, smoking and brooding over what had just happened.

12

Have I fallen in love without even knowing it? Kazem wondered. Was this what they called falling in love? The blow was so sudden that he was stunned. He had never known anything like this before in his life. He had known many women, flirted with them, chased them, and teased them like those two youths. The only intimate relationships he had known were his numerous encounters with prostitutes in various cabarets, taverns and establishments such as Eshrat Ikbiri's. These encounters lasted not more than half an hour, depending on how much he had to pay. The women were, most of the time, older than he was.

He looked around. Only a few customers were sitting at the tables, smoking, drinking and talking in low voices. Kal Abbasgholi was busy washing the tea glasses and drying them with his teacloth that made a scratchy sound. The distant din of the marketplace, like a noisy carnival, could be heard.

Kazem sat there lost in thought, not knowing what to do or where to go. The thought of going back to his room in that god-forsaken lodging-house was unbearable. He had already wandered around enough and was sick and tired of going through the same rituals.

How about popping in to A-Sayyed Musa's tavern, he thought. Maybe a few swigs of rot-gut accompanied by the music and singing of the musicians would help him to sort out his thoughts a little. But he needed the company of a good friend. And who better than Mohsen Chakhaan at a moment like this? Following the age-old custom of inveterate tipplers, he would then pour his heart out to him,

Mohsen Chakhaan was not difficult to find; all you had to do was to burn his hair and he would pop out before you! Kazem located him in the garage sitting on a tin cask, drinking tea and smoking. Mohsen, being always ready for a few glasses of rot-gut, was more than willing to be his friend's companion in trying times.

The two friends arrived at A-Sayyed Musa's tavern around sundown. The tavern was built on a small, flattened patch of land on a hill overlooking the town. Colourful light bulbs hung on electric wires that stretched from tree to tree like washing lines. A small spring passed through the garden, making a gurgling sound over the pebbles. A number of rickety daybeds were placed under the trees. On each daybed was spread a kilim. On each daybed sat two men, cross-legged and facing one another. All of these men were regulars. Between each pair, on a piece of cloth, were placed one folded *sangak* bread, a small bowl of yoghurt mixed with chopped cucumber and a bottle of *arrack*. All the men sat quietly, lolling and swilling down glass after glass of *arrack*. They smacked their lips, wiped their moustaches with the palms of their hands and offered one another spoonfuls of yoghurt and cucumber, saying "cheers" and talking in low voices. Two scrawny musicians in shabby coats and trousers sat under a mulberry tree decorated with two pale neon lights. One of them was strumming at an old *kamancheh* and the other was drumming on a raggedy *tonbak*. Every now and then, the musicians, as if suddenly coming back to life from their opium-induced slumber, burst out into a mournful croak, singing in unison a popular folk song:

You drove a hundred secret arrows into my heart,
Yet you ask me why my skin has turned as yellow as turmeric.
You, who know all about me, why feign ignorance?

Having become the best friends in the world, the cronies vowed eternal promises of loyalty to one another, shaking their heads from time to time to the rhythm of the musicians, who were singing their hearts out. Every now and then, a gentle evening breeze rustled the leaves of the trees, making them heave a subdued sigh. The trilling of crickets and the distant noises of the town were drowned by the doleful music and plaintive voices of the musicians.

Kazem and Mohsen were welcomed by the owner of the tavern, A-Sayyed Musa, who cheerfully led them to a vacant daybed, turned to the tavern-boy and commanded him to come along and look after his favourite clients. As he shuffled in front of them, he chuckled, repeating words of greeting, his shoulders bobbing up and down. A-Sayyed Musa was a good-natured old man who wore an oversized grey coat, with a large, patterned handkerchief flung over one rounded shoulder. Having made sure his two friends were settled comfortably, he shambled from one daybed to another. He stopped beside each, asking the regulars if everything was to their satisfaction. He fingered some yoghurt from one daybed, picked up a slice of cucumber from another, held his hands high up in the air, snapped his fingers loudly and sang and wriggled his bum to the musicians' tune. From time to time, he yelled at the tavern-boy – an enthusiastic country bumpkin – and asked him to place one more bottle of *arrack* on one daybed, replenish the yoghurt on another, or run and fetch some more *sangak* bread for others.

The two friends, after knocking back a few glasses of *arrack*, became a little tipsy. Kazem, however, did not feel like his usual self. He cast a wistful glance at the musicians, listening with a preoccupied expression.

"You look very thoughtful," said Mohsen, peeling a cucumber, "as if your ships were drowned."

"I'm thinking of her," muttered Kazem, turning his head and gazing at the patterns on the kilim.

"Of whom?" Mohsen stopped peeling the cucumber and gaped at his friend.

"I think I've fallen in love, Mohsen." Kazem heaved a sigh, looking up at Mohsen.

"*Ey baba*!" said Mohsen. "It doesn't mean that you should look like a man whose mother has just died."

"Kazem Alaki with the daughter of Hajji Harirchi," said Kazem desolately. "There are oceans between us, Mohsen. Do you understand? Oceans."

"I must find a way of helping you two to get together," said Mohsen, taking a swig of his *arrack* and wiping his moustache with the back of his hand. "That's what friends are for."

"To your health," said Kazem, picking up his glass and knocking back the fiery liquid.

"Cheers," said Mohsen, looking straight at Kazem. "Drink up. It'll make you warm like *hammam*."

Kazem picked up a cucumber slice, bit it, and looked absentmindedly at the musicians who, with their eyes closed, were drumming, strumming and singing mournfully, oblivious to the hubbub around them.

"Is it really possible that one day a miracle will happen and I'll settle down to a decent life?" Kazem asked.

"You never know what God has up his sleeve," said Mohsen, shoving a spoonful of yoghurt into his mouth. "Wait till I get my driving licence," he went on proudly. "You see, mate, I swear to our friendship, this time I drove the truck up the winding mountain passes of Kermanshah."

"Are you telling lies again?" Kazem stared intently at Mohsen.

"What lies?" said Mohsen. "I swear on your life, I'm telling the absolute truth."

"Now it's as clear as daylight that all of what you're saying is a hundred per cent lies," said Kazem.

"As someone or other put it," said Mohsen, laughing heartily, "you could even say a hundred and fifty per cent."

A long silence ensued. The two friends sat there motionless, listening to the musicians. The drinking folk had all become drunk by now, chatting and laughing cheerfully.

"What do you plan to do with the girl now?" Mohsen broke the silence.

"Not a clue." Kazem sighed, gazing at the gurgling spring that passed near the daybed.

"*Ey baba*," Mohsen droned on, "forget about it. Falling in love has nothing to do with our lives, Agh Kazem. Besides, as you yourself rightly said, you're worlds apart and don't match."

Mohsen, fiddling with his rosary, went on recounting, with a combination of relish and wistfulness, one of his unlikely tales of brief romantic adventures. He gesticulated, acting out the scenes of anguish and ecstasy and changing his tone of voice when describing his sweetheart and her final self-sacrifice on the altar of unfulfilled promise of a happy marriage.

"When I was in Tehran recently, a woman was dancing in the Shemshaad Café-Restaurant. She was not only gorgeous but had pots of money, too. Her face was as fresh and beautiful as a spring blossom, the skin of her hands and legs were as white as snow. She was as tall as a poplar. One glance at me, she fell head over heels in love with me. I met her outside the café and we spent some time together. She was all over me, not giving me a moment of peace. She kept crying day and night that I should marry her. Finally, I agreed to take her as my wife and make an honest woman of her. Well, to cut a long story short, I jilted the poor soul at the altar, as they say, in the registry office, that is. Last time I was in Tehran, I found out that she had swallowed two rolls of opium and had departed this base world. I heard later when she was in the throes of death she kept mumbling my name, asking for me..."

Kazem went on gazing at Mohsen, hearing his story, but not really listening. He knew that Mohsen was at it again. As he was too preoccupied with his own troubles, he had to cut him short.

"For the sake of your mother's soul, Mohsen," said Kazem, "cut it out now! Don't you ever get tired of telling so many lousy tales? Don't your screws get loose making up these stories all the time?"

Open-mouthed, Mohsen stared at Kazem, not comprehending why he had snapped at him. They sat there throughout the rest of the night, going through a few more bottles of *arrack*. They nibbled at the bread, offered spoons of cucumber and yoghurt to one another, and listened to the musicians.

Just before daybreak, Kazem, now completely drunk, surveyed the garden. Only two diehard clients, out and out drunk by now, sat on one daybed, swaying to and fro, muttering incoherent phrases to one another. From time to time, they accompanied the musicians by croaking whatever song they were able to remember. The musicians played on, singing a cheerful folk song to keep themselves and the two men awake. Kazem snatched up his jacket, mumbled goodbye to Mohsen and struggled down from the daybed. Digging his hand into his trouser pocket, he found a few crumpled *tomans*. He walked unsteadily to the musicians and shoved the notes into the breast pocket of the older one, who blessed him profusely. Kazem walked out of the tavern, pausing to listen to the tune.

Dawn is peeping out from behind the horizon,
Defeating the dark night by chasing it away.
No one has ever seen, oh my heart,
Such a beautifully wondrous image!
The moment that the old magician of nature
Casts light on the dark night,
It's as if an invisible hairdresser is washing
The jet-black hair of the night with liquid silver.
What do you know about the glory of the daybreak?
You, who are slumbering, wrapped up in sweet sleep.
Oh, how joyful and lucky are the folk like us,
Who rejoice watching the rising of the sun!
The dawn whispers softly to my ear that another day flits past me,
Without me knowing how my life came to be, and how it will end.
A new and different dawn is what I need now,
The kind of dawn that puts an end to all my solitary nights.
Darkness, like a mute flock of ravens,
Has flown away from the roof of the world,
Welcoming a milky-white, fresh daylight, as heavenly as your face.

13

Kazem took the well-trodden path down the hillside. Midway down the path, he stopped and looked with bleary eyes at the streak of pale, milky-hued light across the horizon. Day was dawning over sleeping Hosseinabaad. The squat, mud-brick houses of the small town were being slowly revealed from behind the hazy, ashen-blue light. A few cocks crowed in some distant courtyards on the outskirts of the town. The baying of stray dogs pierced the silence before the daybreak.

Kazem, now sobered up by the fresh breeze, groped his way down the narrow path. Reaching the first few houses, he lumbered along by the leprous walls. He sauntered in and out of sombre alleys and lanes flanked with run-down, squalid-looking houses. He hummed the songs he had picked up in the tavern, muddling them up. He walked on till he reached the thoroughfare and entered the deserted marketplace. He wandered past the shops with their rusty tin shutters down, passed under the half-dark archways, and emerged into the lanes on the other side of the marketplace.

Kazem felt his life had changed. The sense of emotional freedom he had enjoyed so far had abandoned him. He felt as if a thief who had suddenly jumped out from an obscure corner in a deserted bazaar had snatched his carefree lifestyle from him, and then vanished into the shadowy lanes, running off with his booty, never to be found again. He was in serious trouble and he knew it. He sensed he was going through some feelings hitherto unknown to him. It was as if a tiger had fastened on him, digging his claws into his feeble, inexperienced heart. Everywhere he looked he saw Maryam's image.

Bodily and emotionally drained, he found a platform under an arch in front of a closed shop and sat down. He cast furtive glances around and began the most painful soul-searching soliloquy, trying hard, after his own fashion, to have a debate with himself:

"I'm now well and truly in a pretty pickle. I can neither go forward nor backwards. I did my best to sham ignorance, but it didn't work. I've definitely lost my worthless heart to this young lady. This is not a manly deed by your own heart to track you down like this, confuse your mind and start playing scandalous tricks on you. If your own very heart acts like this, whom can you trust in this life? It will make me an object of ridicule for everyone to laugh at. Now, this little heart of mine has become the master of my life. I had no idea that this was coming. What's this new thing happening to me? Don't ask me. Don't have the faintest clue, I tell you. Why should a big boy like me be turned into a slave to a small thing like that? Why should this happen? Who has decreed this? Who am I, hey? Who has said that a little heart the size of a fist should bully a grown-up man like me? I tell you what, mate. Forget about what *we* want. We've to see what that cursed *thing* wants. This is not right; I'm telling you. Something somewhere has gone wrong. Where can we spot that unfairness? Now, that's something that a wretched man like me can't puzzle out. This is, no doubt, the task of the Devil himself. Did I want this to happen? No. Was I warned about it? No. I was happily minding my own business, getting along with my few trustworthy buddies, drinking the odd glass of *arrack* in A-Sayyed Musa's tavern, sometimes sleeping with gorgeous *khanums* in Eshrat Ikbiri's whorehouse, having my breakfast and drinking my tea in Kal Abbasgholi's teahouse. All in all, I was enjoying my life. I was a happy man."

He peered out, thief-like, from behind the angle of the wall, making sure that no one was around, and began to hum a song, blaming his sweetheart for having brought him to this pitiful pass:

Oh, beautiful Khorasani girl, you have stolen my heart,
You've plundered my heart with no regard to my feelings.

He stopped singing and clasped his head in his hands. The town had begun to stir outside the marketplace. The muffled voices of a few street vendors began to ring in the early morning air. The chanting of a muezzin from the minaret of the local mosque floated over the rooftops. The rattling wheels of a cart on the uneven flagstones made Kazem jump out of his confused reveries. He stood up and resumed his wandering. In the thoroughfare stallholders were setting up their stalls, shopkeepers were pulling up the tin shutters and a milk vendor was pushing his bicycle laden with two large tin casks full of fresh hot milk.

Worn out and fed up, Kazem decided to head for the lodging-house to get a few hours of sleep. Upon arriving at the house, he kicked the door open. He stepped down into the courtyard. A profound silence reigned in the house. Some of the lodgers were either out in gambling or opium dens, some still in taverns, others in the mosque, and the rest, mostly women and children, were slumbering quietly in their rooms. Kazem crossed the courtyard, climbed the steps, staggered along the terrace, and came to the door of his room. He fumbled in his pocket for his keys, mumbling, "Where have I put the damned things?" Finally finding them, he glanced over his shoulder, located the keyhole with difficulty, inserted his key into it, and pushed the door open. The rusty hinges made a squeaking sound, making a lodger in a neighbouring room stir, groan sleepily, and go back to sleep again.

No sooner was Kazem in the room than he tossed his jacket on the corner of the bed and plonked himself on the moth-eaten mattress, making the wooden frame creak. He grabbed the bolster and hugged it tightly like a lover squeezing his sweetheart in a passionate embrace. A vague drunken smile spread over his face. Ghost-like images began to invade his head. His eyelids became heavy and began to close, though he struggled to keep them open. Half-asleep, he fell into vague musings about himself and Maryam in some far-distant future.

Kazem soon passed the threshold of reality and stepped into the magical land of fantasy.

In that hazy future, he saw himself walking briskly in the alleys of Hosseinabaad, baking under the blazing midday sun. He, looking more mature with a black moustache, his long, jet-black hair combed back, and dressed in a nicely cut black suit, was returning home from work for lunch. He was carrying in one hand a bundle of grapes wrapped in white cloth, two *sangak* breads flung across his arm, and in the other hand he held a bowl of fresh yoghurt. He pushed open the door of a large house and stepped down into the courtyard, crisscrossed with washing lines on which hung linens and clothes to dry.

Maryam, dressed in a white, short-sleeved blouse showing her soft-skinned arms, with her flowery-patterned chador wrapped round her waist, rushed towards her husband smiling blissfully, embraced him, and showered him with fond kisses. He told her to be careful not to knock the bowl of yoghurt from his hand. He then walked towards the steps leading to the terrace on which two little boys were sitting. Kazem put the bundle and the bowl down on the step. He walked towards a baby girl who was sitting on a platform near the terrace, picked her up, and kissed her affectionately, dandling her. Maryam, who was squatting on the edge of the *hauz*, dipping some clothes in the water, looked at him lovingly, beaming with the contented smile of a happily married woman.

Kazem put the baby down, sneaked behind his wife, and grabbed her suddenly from behind. Maryam stood up and told him to be careful, as she was pregnant. Not believing her, he put his ear against her belly and listened carefully. Smiling affectionately, she ran her fingers through his thick hair.

He looked at her, biting his knuckles as a sign of surprise, and asked her when it had happened. She laughed and said she did not have a slightest clue. On hearing the little boys giggling behind him, he looked back at them. They had put the yoghurt bowl between them and were digging their fingers in it, licking the yoghurt, and smearing their faces with it. Kazem slapped the back of one hand with the other, laughed, and told Maryam to look at the boys. He and his wife laughed heartily. He caught her by the waist, trying to kiss her. As she wriggled, trying to set herself free from his embrace, they both lost their balance and tumbled into the *hauz* with a loud splash. When they were both up to the waist in the water, he seized hold of her and tried to kiss her again. She struggled, laughing loudly.

The splashing and Maryam's laughing gave Kazem a start. He opened his eyes wide and looked around, confused, thinking that he was still in his own house with Maryam and his children. His lips were squashed against the bolster he was hugging. Realising that it was all but a sweet dream, a sad smile flitted across his face. He closed his eyes, yawned loudly, and dug his chin back in the bolster. He stretched out his hand to grab the dented tin bowl on a small wooden plank placed across the top of a vat of water that stood close to the bed. He dipped the bowl into the water, filled it, put it to his parched lips, and drank it all in one draught, making loud gulping sounds. His thirst gratified, his eyes grew dim. He smacked his lips with pleasure, placed the bowl back on the plank, hugged the bolster again, and arranged his head comfortably on it. In a minute, he was fast asleep.

14

Around midmorning, Kazem opened his eyes and stared at the ceiling, bewildered. Everyday sounds were pouring in from the courtyard and the lane outside. Women were making a rumpus, babies were howling, and the ragamuffins were chasing one another in the alleyway, squealing with delight as they played in the dust and dirt. The street vendors and hawkers were chanting.

Kazem sat up in bed and listened. He clasped his head in both hands to calm his headache. He then jumped out of the bed, put on his shoes and ran to the courtyard, where he greeted some of the other lodgers. Squatting beside the *hauz*, he splashed handfuls of water on his face and left the lodging house. He needed to drink some tea and smoke a few cigarettes to get rid of his headache.

Kal Abbasgholi's teahouse was quiet. Kazem greeted him gruffly. He climbed on a daybed near a column in the far corner of the porch, sat against its backrest, and began to fiddle with his rosary. Kal Abbasgholi soon brought a tray on which was placed a glass of tea in a saucer, a small bowl of sugar lumps, a lump of cheese, and a half *sangak* bread. After exchanging a few words with Kazem, he left to attend the other customers. Kazem drank his tea, lit a cigarette, and drew hard at it a few times, staring at the geometrical patterns on the kilim. The townsfolk scurried by, talking loudly and gesticulating, going about their daily lives. Kazem sat there, thinking.

Kal Abbasgholi, a cigarette between his lips, shuffled out of the teahouse again, bringing Kazem another glass of tea.

"What's wrong, son?" he asked. "Why haven't you touched your breakfast, hey?"

Kazem did not even look at him. Kal Abbasgholi shambled back inside the teahouse.

At the same moment, Kazem saw Laylan the Gypsy walk into the porch. Passing Kazem by, she took her large bundle off her head and plonked it on a table near the door. She pressed her palms to her back, stretched herself, and heaved a loud painful sigh, invoking a holy saint.

"Give us a nice glass of tea, Kal Abbasgholi?" she called out.

"Right away." Kal Abbasgholi's voice came from inside the teahouse.

"*Salaam*, Kazem." Kazem gave a start as someone grabbed his arm. He looked to his left. Laylan was sitting on the edge of the daybed, grinning at him. Kazem glanced at her vacantly.

"What's up?" she asked. "You look like an old sparrow that dozes off in the shade of a wall."

She flung one flap of her kerchief over her shoulder, tore a piece of bread from Kazem's breakfast tray, wrapped it round a lump of cheese, and shoved it in her mouth.

"You've been so quiet since you've come out of jail," she said, noisily munching the bread and cheese. "Don't tell me that you've lost your plumage and given up your unholy ways."

Kazem glanced at her distractedly and looked away.

"Tell me something," she went on, sliding closer to him. "Maybe you're in love."

"Leave us alone, will you?" muttered Kazem moodily, scowling at her. She gave him an uncomprehending look, got up, and walked in a huff to other end of the porch.

"Ohoy, Kal Abbasgholi," she cried out, dropping heavily on a chair, "make sure the tea's freshly-brewed." She went on casting furtive glances at Kazem.

"My tea always is freshly-brewed," said Kal Abbasgholi, putting a glass of tea on the table. He then grabbed a chair and sat on it, facing Laylan.

"So what's the latest news, Madam Matchmaker?" he asked.

"Nothing much," replied Laylan, dipping a lump of sugar in the tea, "except that everyone is all right, thanks to God."

"Only the devil knows what would happen to the youth of this town if you were not here." Kal Abbasgholi sighed. "Tell me, Laylan, honestly, how many love messages do you pass each day among the youngsters here?"

"Will you let me drink my tea in peace?" said Laylan, pouring her tea into the saucer. "They can't help it. They're in the bloom of youth."

"If you manage to pass so many letters among those boys and girls," Kal Abbasgholi said, winking mischievously at her, "why don't you find a young lady for me?"

"Your dancing days are over," said Laylan. "You and I both have one foot in the grave."

"Where have *you* been, pretty lady, when I was having one carry-on after another with beauties in the South?"

"All right, all right," Laylan said, slurping her tea. "Don't get puffed up. I know all about your youth, too."

During the course of this conversation, Kazem sat on the daybed, brooding. Upon hearing about the love messages, he pricked up his ears. An idea had flashed through his head. Once Kal Abbasgholi got up and walked off to attend to a customer, Kazem leapt to his feet and walked briskly over to Laylan.

"Laylan, Laylan," he whispered into her ear, grabbing her arm, "come over here a minute."

"What happened?" cried Laylan, looking alarmed. "Am I worthy of your friendship now?" She popped another sugar lump into her mouth, drained her tea to the dregs, put the glass down, and jumped to her feet, snatching up her bundle.

"What is it? What are you pulling me like that for?" Laylan protested as Kazem pulled her arm, hustling her off to a far corner of the porch.

"Tell me something," he asked, facing her and keeping his voice down, "do you happen to know Hajji Harirchi's daughter?"

"Sure I do," said she, grinning broadly, revealing her row of rotten teeth. "I raised her myself. Praise the God! She's become as beautiful as the full moon!"

"Can you pass a message from me to her?" Kazem asked, putting his arm round her shoulder. She looked at him, rolling her eyes meaningfully. Kazem understood at once the meaning of that look. He quickly thrust his hand inside his trouser pocket, pulled out a few crumpled *tomans*, counted them quickly, and handed them over one by one to Laylan, who stretched her palm upwards, looking at the money greedily, swaying her head sideways like a barn owl following the movements of a frightened mouse.

"I'll grease your palm again," said Kazem hurriedly. "Will you tell her I'll be waiting for her just after midday outside the ruins of the ancient caravanserai just under the tomb of the saint? Tell her that I must talk to her about a very important matter."

"If her father finds out," said Laylan quietly, clutching the banknotes in her claw-like fingers, "he'll get his thugs to scalp you alive."

"Never mind about her father," said Kazem, throwing his hand up in a show of bravado.

"Well, I have to warn you first," Laylan reminded him with a shrug.

"And I have to ignore it," Kazem chuckled.

Laylan laughed heartily. She opened her sweaty palm and began counting the notes. The pleasure was so intense that she completely forgot that Kazem was still standing there.

"Five tomans, two tomans, and another two tomans will make nine tomans. May God give us more," she mumbled. She folded the notes and thrust them inside the fold of her long, black veil that was tightly wrapped round her waist. She then hefted her bundle on to her head, and lumbered off to fulfil her side of the bargain.

15

In order to kill time till after noon, Kazem wandered around aimlessly in the marketplace, drank tea in a teahouse, and played a few rounds of knucklebones in the vacant lot.

Just after midday, he hurried to his place of rendezvous in the ruins of the caravanserai and stood in the shade of a crumbling archway. The small stream that passed nearby gurgled cheerfully. Flocks of sparrows hopped here and there on the edges of the crumbling walls, chased tiny insects in the air and bickered noisily among themselves. In order to calm his nerves, Kazem lit a cigarette, drew hard at it and started pacing up and down the ruins. He began to rehearse how he was going to declare his love to Maryam and what to say to her.

"I'll tell her," Kazem said to himself, looking at an imaginary Maryam standing before him, "I want you. I love you, Maryam. If you don't believe me, ask Mohsen Chakhaan, who knows all about this."

"No!" cried Kazem, throwing his hands up in despair, "that doesn't sound right."

He turned and paced up and down again.

"I'll tell her I'm the very ground on which you tread," he said, after a short pause.

"Pah, it doesn't make sense, does it?" That sounded ridiculous. "She'll think that I'm talking gibberish and will laugh at me. I must tell her something big, something lovely, high-sounding and romantic so that she'll enjoy hearing it."

He paced and hopped on the stones like a cat on hot bricks.

"Aha, I found it!" he exclaimed. "I'll tell her, 'I'm your slave. You see me standing here. I'm your slave, body and soul.'"

"If I talk like this right from the word go," he decided, "she'll soon start to ride on my back forever. Oh God, I don't know what to tell her."

Casting anxious glances around, he walked to a wall, propped his elbows against some broken bricks, clutched his head in his hands and talked to himself in a voice choked with anguish. "She'll show up any minute and I haven't been able to come up with anything nice to say to her."

Having thought of a new idea, he turned round and stood still for a second, posing like a lovesick man proposing to his sweetheart for the first time. He knelt slowly down, lifted both hands in supplication and said in a fervent tone, “I’ll tell her: Maryam, I want to marry you. Will you be my wife? Will you be part of my life?” He froze suddenly and went on as if addressing an imaginary friend: “Say she rejected my offer, then what?”

He picked up his jacket, hitting it hard against a rock as if trying to swat an insect. “Oh god, why didn’t I become literate like others? Why didn’t I learn to read and write so that today I wouldn’t be stuck in the mud like a stupid ass?”

Exactly at that moment, Kazem heard a loud guffaw. He looked in the direction of the laughter. He saw Mohsen Chakhaan leaning against a broken-down column, laughing loudly and slapping his thighs.

“Have you gone off your head, man?” Mohsen managed to say, choking with mirth.

“*Na baba*,” said Kazem loudly, his voice hoarse. “I’m waiting here for Maryam to come.”

“What? Waiting for her?” Mohsen cried out, walking towards Kazem. “I saw her going to the public bathhouse.”

“Not making up stories, I hope?” Kazem remarked, looking hard at him.

“May they wrap me in a shroud if I lie to you,” Mohsen insisted, fiddling with his rosary. “She’s gone to the bathhouse. Don’t sit here wasting your time.”

“She didn’t consider me worthy enough to pay me a short visit,” Kazem said, gazing blankly at the ground.

“Maybe she wasn’t able to,” said Mohsen. “Besides, maybe Laylan didn’t pass her your message.”

Kazem got up, put his finger on his lips and froze, thinking.

“Go and wait outside the bathhouse,” Mohsen advised, pointing in the direction of the bathhouse.

“What are we standing here for?” Kazem put his hand on his shoulder. “Let’s go, then.”

Kazem pushed Mohsen ahead. Both disappeared under the narrow, crumbling archway, and re-emerged from the other side into an opening cluttered with large blocks of stones and half-demolished brick walls. Kazem ran in front with Mohsen on his heels.

“We’re going there,” said Kazem, looking back at Mohsen who was hurtling behind him, “but I can’t pluck up enough courage to talk to her. I swear to Imam Reza that I’ve been struggling with myself for an hour and I couldn’t cobble any words together to make a decent sentence to say to her.”

“Two glasses of *arrack* will make you twitter like a nightingale for her," Mohsen suggested, raising his hand and wiggling two of his fingers.

"Despite being a cabbage-head most of the time," said Kazem, chuckling, "this time you've said something sensible." He thrust his hand into his pockets to find some cash to give to Mohsen.

"Hey, listen, be back by the time I reach the door of the bathhouse. Run along and get a bottle of *arrack*."

"All right then," cried Mohsen, ready to dash off while fumbling in his own pocket for some money.

"Wait a minute," Kazem shouted after him, "we've a long way to go. Let's walk some of the way together. Here, take this cash first."

Mohsen, not finding a single *gheran* in his pockets, slowed down and grabbed the cash offered by Kazem.

"Listen, I don't know what to say to her, Mohsen," Kazem went on. "Don't you reckon she's deliberately making a fool of me?"

"Who am I to tell?" replied Mohsen, stopping and staring at Kazem. "You know better than I do."

"I swear to you she smiled at me," said Kazem with conviction. "How lovely she was. She even said 'thank you' to me in her sweet voice."

Kazem laughed aloud, pleased with himself. Mohsen just stood there, gazing silently at him.

"Why have you gone dumb all of a sudden?" cried Kazem, prodding Mohsen's chest. "Don't just stand there and stare at me like a goat! Why don't you say something?"

"You keep telling me that all I say is nothing but lousy tales," answered Mohsen.

"Never mind," said Kazem cheerfully, "just tell us one of your fantastic stories. Go on, hurry up."

Mohsen began at once to spin one of his yarns as they walked through the narrow alleyways and lanes.

"One day I was sitting on a kerb in Pahlavi Street in Tehran, enjoying my shelled walnuts with a bottle of *arrack* beside me. I was completely hammered. All of a sudden, a red convertible stopped right in front of me. The screeching of brakes made me jump out of my skin. I wish you had been there to see, Kazem. Behind the wheel sat one of those gorgeous rich women who kept staring at me. She then winked at me. Being very drunk, I thought maybe I was seeing pink elephants. I rubbed my eyes and looked again. She winked again, leant over, opened the door, and shouted, asking me if I'd like to go with her. I said to myself, 'Mohsen, what are you waiting for? This is a godsend.'"

"Did you get into the car?" Kazem cut in.

"I leapt to my feet, looked around, slipped into the car and sat beside her. Guess where we went, Dash Kazem?"

"Where?" asked Kazem, laughing, eager to know.

"Straight to her beautiful villa, right up on the hills overlooking Tehran. We swam and fooled around a while in the large pool, drank plenty of whisky, and made love till I collapsed..."

"All right, son," Kazem cut him short, "leave it there for the moment. You can tell me the rest of the story later. Now run off, and get the bottle and come to the bathhouse. I'll be waiting there for you."

16

Kazem found a low wall facing the bathhouse that was perched on a patch of high ground. He squatted beside the wall and, leaning against it, stared at the door of the bathhouse. Mohsen soon appeared clutching a bottle of *arrack* which he handed over to Kazem. He then ran off and hid behind a wall at the bottom of the narrow path.

Kazem went on gazing at the door of the bathhouse tucked under an imposing arch with brickwork patterns that shimmered in the blazing sun. He took swig after swig from the bottle. He soon became tipsy. A loud whistle made him start. He glanced back over his shoulder. Mohsen's head stuck out from the angle of the wall, like a lost sheep checking whether a pathway is familiar or not.

"Are you all right?" Mohsen cried out in a muffled voice, winking at Kazem.

"Smashing," mumbled Kazem, after taking a long swig at the bottle.

By now in a state of stupor, Kazem began to gaze into the void. He started to sing in a melancholy voice a ditty, hiccupping between every other word:

Your lovely eyes have made me drunk, babe,
I'm head over heels in love with you, babe.
Your eyes have made me…

All of a sudden, he stopped singing. He struggled to keep his eyes open to see when Maryam emerged from the bathhouse.

"Oh, my darling Maryam," he began to address an imaginary Maryam in a mawkishly sentimental voice, "I want you so much. Tell me what I should do so that you believe me. I want to come and ask your hand in marriage from your father. I want you to become my wife, my missis."

He chuckled tipsily. He cast a glance over his shoulder to see if Mohsen was still there. Mohsen, at his post, was peeking out from behind the wall, keeping an eye on things.

"I'm beginning to get the hang of it, son," Kazem yelled gleefully to him. "Don't you worry. I'll tell her all about my secret passion. Oh, yes, I will. You just wait and see."

His eyes soon clouded over, though, and in a sombre mood, he stared at the dusty ground. He raised his head with difficulty and looked at the sky. The blinding sun hurt his eyes, making him blink several times. The incessant cawing of a flock of crows gliding overhead echoed in his befuddled brain, becoming magnified out of proportions. The dazzling light and the heat were too much to bear. In slow motion, he folded his knees and hugged them with both hands. His head drooped slowly, like a worn-out marionette whose strings are loosened by an invisible puppeteer, and rested on his knees. He felt he must look like one of those junkies in the narrow alleyways in Shahr-e No, abandoned and forgotten by the whole world. In a matter of seconds, he was claimed by the fanciful world of oblivion.

But not all was lost. Thankfully, he was a young man in love and for the first time at that, and he was capable of dreaming beautiful dreams, despite all the odds ganged up against him. Whom else could he dream of but Maryam?

In that magical land of dreams, Maryam came out of the bathhouse, looking as fresh as the lilies in the meadows. Her head was wrapped up in a white scarf and her body veiled in a brightly patterned chador. She stood like a proud peacock under the high arch, in front of which were criss-crossed washing-lines on which hung bathhouse loincloths that flapped in the gentle breeze. She looked around anxiously, trying to find Kazem. Once she spotted him squatting down there beside the opposite wall, her face flowered like cherry blossom in springtime. She quickly dropped her bath-bundle on the steps, letting her chador slip down her shapely body, revealing her short white dress. Her hands and legs, as white as marble, gleamed in the bright sun. Beaming with delight, she ran down a few steps to meet Kazem.

Upon seeing Maryam, he leapt to his feet. No longer drunk, he stood there upright with his head high and looking as proud as an ancient Persian prince smiling at his beautiful damsel who has just escaped from an enchanted castle around which enemy flags were fluttering in the fresh breeze. Instead of the cawing of crows, the cheerful cries of hundreds of swallows now rang in the blue sky. The joyful noises of children playing in the neighbouring lanes filled the air. Kazem rushed headlong towards the door of the bathhouse, dashing up the steps to meet his sweetheart. Full of thoughts of holding her in his arms, as bad luck would have it, he forgot to leave the bottle of *arrack* behind near the low wall. The lovers met each other in the middle of the steps. Maryam threw herself on Kazem's neck and began to kiss and cuddle him lovingly. Pearls of sweat, as dewdrops on fresh rose petals in a rose-garden on an early summer morning, appeared on her flushed face. Her deliciously warm breasts made him quiver with untold delight. They went on whispering sweet words of love, as young lovers do. As she was chattering away cheerfully, Maryam noticed that Kazem was hiding something behind his back. Thinking that he was hiding a surprise gift for her, she, after teasing him playfully, spotted the bottle of *arrack* in his hand. Snatching it from him, she smashed it angrily on the floor.

The loud shattering of the bottle on the steps of the bathhouse jerked Kazem rudely out of his heavenly dream. He raised his head from his knees, blinked a few times and looked in a daze at the deserted door of the bathhouse. No sign of Maryam there. The same loincloths, no longer looking like enemy flags, flapped melancholically in the warm breeze. He looked around, picked up his bottle of *arrack*, and, recollecting his wonderful reverie, a smile spread across his face. He took a swig at the bottle.

"Pssst, pssst…" He heard a voice.

Kazem looked drowsily over his shoulder and saw Mohsen's head sticking out from the same spot below him.

"Did she come?"

"Nope," mumbled Kazem, throwing his hand up in despair.

Mohsen made a grimace, like one who is utterly baffled by an incomprehensible problem.

"Come on, catch this bottle," said Kazem, throwing the bottle to Mohsen. "You made me flipping drunk."

Mohsen caught the bottle, unscrewed it, took a gulp, and laughed, unable to conceal his untimely amusement.

Kazem lit up a cigarette and took a deep drag. With his brain now all muddled up, his eyelids as heavy as lead, he propped his hands on his folded knees, took another puff, and fell into thinking. It did not take him long to sink, once again, back into the marvellous land of dreams.

This time he saw Maryam and her friends stepping out from the bathhouse into the glaring light. Their brightly coloured, flowery chadors flapped in the breeze like the wings of a small flock of turtledoves, revealing their shapely bodies and lovely legs. They were all laughing loudly and chatting cheerfully as young women do when they come out of a bathhouse. All of a sudden, Maryam saw Kazem and smiled at him, revealing a row of milk-white teeth. He leapt to his feet once more, stood upright with his chest thrust forward, a joyous grin on his lips, unconsciously acting the part of a mythological Persian prince. He prepared himself to meet his beautiful damsel who was surrounded this time by her charming maidservants. In front of the enemy castle, the bathhouse that is, the same flags still fluttered. Kazem, once again completely sobered up, mounted the steps in the dignified and proud manner of a princely hero. Maryam, seeing him coming up towards her, rushed to him and jumped, yet again, on his neck, nearly knocking him over. As the happy lovers locked in a tender embrace, kissing and caressing one another, the maidservants clustered round them, giggling and laughing, warning them of the possible dangers lurking in the neighbourhood of the bathhouse. But the lovers, being young and wrapped in the pleasure of each other's company, did not heed the warnings. All of a sudden, something like the roar of a wild beast came from the alleyways behind the bathhouse. In the blink of an eye, a stocky fat man with a nightcap on his head appeared from nowhere in front of the girls. Upon seeing this monster, Maryam's companions scurried inside the bathhouse for safety, cackling like a flock of frightened hens. The rough-looking man, who was none other than Hajji Harirchi, strode clumsily towards the embracing couple. He brayed harshly, demanding to know what was going on. He then shoved Maryam to one side, and delivered a resounding slap to Kazem's cheek.

The painful slap made Kazem jump out of his reveries, yet again. He touched his cheek involuntarily and looked around. In front of the door of the bathhouse the dull-coloured loincloths fluttered in the breeze, making a dismal flapping sound.

"Did she come?" Mohsen's voice, coming from his hideout, startled him.

"Leave us alone, will you?" Kazem snapped back at him dispiritedly, flicking his cigarette stub.

Kazem slouched there against the wall, his hands across his chest, gazing at the floor. He felt groggy, like a hopeless drunkard, or a junkie in desperate need of his fix.

17

Exactly at that moment Maryam emerged from the bathhouse, her bath-bundle hidden under the chador and tucked under her arm. She clutched the hem of her chador with one hand to make sure that it would not flap in the breeze to reveal her body. Seeing her coming carefully down the steep steps, Kazem leapt to his feet, his face lit up with a joyful smile.

"*Salaam*, Maryam," he stammered in a polite, stiff manner, standing there like a peasant greeting an ill-tempered mollah in the mosque first thing in the morning.

At the foot of the steps, Maryam turned left and carried on walking, not casting so much as a glance at Kazem, as if he did not exist. Baffled, Kazem stood there blinking repeatedly in absolute disbelief that she had treated him like this. He followed her with his dreamy eyes. Maryam walked up a steep, bumpy pathway, turned left into an alleyway, and disappeared from view. Kazem, rooted to the spot, lingered a while, not knowing what to make of her behaviour. He sat down slowly and leaned against the wall. The distant, muffled sounds of the town and the mournful cawing of the crows mingled with the flapping of the loincloths on the washing lines.

The rapid sound of someone running up towards him startled Kazem out of his confused thoughts. He looked back. Like a bat out of hell, Mohsen was racing up the steps, panting heavily, gripping his jacket in one hand and his rosary in the other. No sooner had he planted himself before Kazem than he yelled at him at close range, slapping Kazem's knee.

"Why are you sitting here like this?" cried Mohsen, pointing in the direction of the alleyway into which Maryam had walked. "Stand up and go after her, man!"

"Knock it off, will you?" Kazem grumbled, waving his hand like one who is fed up with everything.

"I saw her coming out of the bathhouse," said Mohsen, digging Kazem in the shoulder. "Come on, do something about it!"

As Kazem was unwilling to budge, Mohsen grabbed his arm and pulled him up.

"Stand up, for heaven's sake!" Mohsen commanded. "What a hopeless, clumsy man you are."

"Get off me," whined Kazem, like a sulking brat. "I don't want to, and I don't want her."

"Just listen to me and come along," insisted Mohsen. "Never mind what I'm doing. Just leave it all to Mohsen Chakhaan and he'll sort you out."

Mohsen dragged Kazem along up to the top of the pathway and stood at the angle of the alley into which Maryam had walked.

"Go on!" shouted Mohsen, egging Kazem on to follow her. "Look, she's walking down the alley. Go on, hurry up and say something to her."

"I don't know what to say," mumbled Kazem, rocking back and forth in anguish.

"Anything you like, mate, anything!" Mohsen cried.

Kazem stepped into the alley, glancing, every so often, over his shoulder at Mohsen.

"But if," he kept repeating.

"No more buts and ifs," yelled Mohsen. "Just go after her."

As Kazem quickened his pace to catch up with Maryam, Mohsen looked at him with a wistful smile – the wistful smile of a proud man who regards his best friend taking the first, albeit faltering, steps on the road to conjugal bliss. He looked around, hoisted up his pants, and chuckled, swinging his rosary round his finger. He then stepped into the alley, shadowing his lovelorn friend.

Meanwhile, Maryam, oblivious to all the drama going on behind her, glided along like a peacock in the dusty alley, staying in the shade of the mud-brick walls. Every now and then, she pulled her chador back to her head, adjusting it so that it would not slip down on her shoulders.

In a shaded archway, hearing the sound of hurried footsteps behind her, she glanced back to see who it was. Kazem, casting anxious glances around every so often, walked briskly behind her. As soon as she came out of the archway and into the dazzling light, he drew closer to her.

"Maryam, Maryam…" Kazem called after her.

Maryam carried on walking, not paying the slightest attention to his fervent calls. He drew abreast of her and walked a little alongside her, trying to pluck up the courage to speak.

"I'm fond of you, Maryam," he managed to say at last in a voice hoarse with emotion. "I intend to come to your house and ask for your hand in marriage."

Maryam glanced at him timidly. At that very moment, her chador slipped down her head a little, revealing a jet-black lock of her hair that glistened in the bright light. She blushed, and, as she moved to adjust her chador, the bath-bundle slipped from under her arm and fell on the ground. Embarrassed, she squatted to pick it up. Kazem did the same, picking up the bundle for her. As he handed it to her she looked into his eyes with a bewildered innocence. Kazem, thrown into confusion by her ethereal beauty, gazed at her. They regarded one another in silence, each trying to fathom the other's soul. Kazem, for the first time in his life, realised the painful inadequacy of his intellectual faculties. He struggled desperately to put together some decent words to express his feelings. Having found nothing in his limited stock, he resorted to some hackneyed expressions he had picked up from popular films.

"I know that you and I don't match," he stammered finally. "You can read and write. I don't even know what a school looks like. Your father is a *hajji* and wealthy. I don't know who my father is or whether he's alive or dead. I lost my mother when I was a little kid. Despite all these misfortunes and failures of my life, I'm still fond of you."

Maryam listened patiently, gazing timidly at Kazem as he went on pouring out his soul to her. She then lowered her eyes.

"Thank you," she murmured at long last, tucking her bath-bundle under her arm. She arranged her chador on her head and began to walk. Kazem waited a little, following her with his eyes and calling after her a few times in a low voice. He began to shadow her, then caught up with her and managed to speak to her again.

"If you consent," said Kazem, "I'll come to your house to ask for your hand in marriage. I'll bring along my friend Kal Abbasgholi, too, if you like, that is. I have known him for years. He's a good man, he is."

"This is not possible," Maryam said, throwing a brief glance back at him as she quickened her pace.

"Well," Kazem took on a defiant tone of voice. "I'll make it possible."

"I've no say in these matters," replied Maryam meekly. "My father decides everything in my life."

"If you wish, I'll make them agree," Kazem went on, throwing his hands up to the air, as if marriage could be achieved by mere brute force. "I'll finish them off, all of them."

"So this was the important matter you wanted to talk to me about when you sent that note through Laylan the Gypsy?" Maryam said suddenly, stopping and looking at him with sad, disapproving eyes.

"Yes, it was." He lowered his eyes, looking up at Maryam like a little boy ashamed of his silly outburst. "Think about what I said."

"I've nothing to think about," said Maryam in a resigned voice. "I can't even say a word about this to my mother. If my father finds out that I've talked to you in the alley, he'll skin me alive. Goodbye now."

She began to walk briskly. Kazem took a few steps in her direction, then stood still and watched her gliding away. Before she reached to the end of the alley, Kazem, worked up now by despair, cried out in a sudden burst of bravado so that she could hear him:

"Kazem Alaki has always got what he wanted. I haven't been in jail for two years for nothing. I'm telling you, Maryam: you must become my wife. Think carefully about what I told you. I want an answer from you by tomorrow."

He followed Maryam with anxious eyes till she turned out of the narrow alley and vanished from sight. He heard the hurried clatter of footsteps approaching from behind. Mohsen was hurtling towards him, his rosary beads swinging. Planting himself beside Kazem, he looked at him questioningly, waiting for some kind of response. Without uttering a word, Kazem turned his head and fixed his eyes on the end of the alley. Mohsen did the same. They stood beside one another, as mute as two statues. After a moment they turned on their heels, walking in silence without looking back.

It was now four o'clock in the afternoon. After knocking around in the marketplace, they ended up once again in the ruins of the ancient caravanserai. They sat on the remains of a low platform. Kazem lit a cigarette and drew hard on it, musing over the events of the past few hours. He gazed at the broken mud-bricks and large stones scattered here and there that cast long shadows on the copper-coloured earth. Mohsen, his head bowed, sat beside him, fiddling quietly with his rosary. Sparrows hopped on the edges of the broken walls, chirping noisily, creating an untimely racket. From time to time, a lone crow appeared from nowhere, perched on top of a wall, flapped its wings, stretched its bony neck, and screeched, as if calling the others to come and look at these two lonely men. On its pebbly bed, the nearby spring flowed drowsily by.

"What do you want to do now, Agh Kazem?" Mohsen spoke all of a sudden, yawning loudly.

"Not a clue." Kazem heaved a rueful sigh, staring vacantly at the lengthening shadows on the ground.

"I've an idea." Mohsen's loud cry rang in the air, startling a small flock of sparrows pecking at insects crawling among the stones. "Why don't you go and see Laylan the Gypsy? She might be able to do something for you."

"What can she do?" said Kazem, sounding as if he had abandoned all hope. “She’s already passed my message to Maryam, who just told me to my face that it is hopeless.”

“Why don’t you ask Laylan to pass her another note?” suggested Mohsen. “So that you can see Maryam once more. Maybe she’s now brooding on your proposal and will have changed her mind by the time she gets your second message.”

“Hmm, not a bad idea, Mohsen,” Kazem muttered a little more hopefully, despite knowing still that it was all pointless. “Maybe this time I’ll be able to find better ways of putting my thoughts into words. I think I flew off the handle this time and said things that I shouldn’t have said. All that scared her off.”

“Maybe you did, Kazem,” Mohsen agreed. “When you propose to your future missus, who will be one day the mother of your children, you’ve to learn to be a little tactful and as cool as a cucumber in order to get your feelings and intentions across. Being in love is not a simple matter.” After a short pause he went on, “Once I fell in love with a prostitute in Shahr-e No…”

“All right, Mohsen,” said Kazem, cutting him short, “I think I grasped the point you’re making. I’m honestly not in a mood to hear one of your wretched stories. There’s a time and a place for them.”

“All right, all right, Agh Kazem,” said Mohsen. “I have to go to the garage. You go and find Laylan and see what she can do for you this time.”

Kazem found Laylan the Gypsy sitting on a daybed in Kal Abbasgholi’s teahouse, drinking tea and chatting to one of the regulars. Kazem dragged out a chair and sat down.

“You look down in the dumps, Kazem!” yelled Laylan across the porch. She drank the rest of her tea in a single draught, got up, lumbered towards Kazem, and sat on a chair beside him.

“What happened? Did you manage to see Maryam?” she asked in a whisper, leaning towards him.

“I saw her, all right,” said Kazem, “but she said she cannot become my wife because her father will kill her.”

“I knew it, Kazem,” said Laylan. “Listen, Hajji Harirchi is a very rich man and is well-respected and feared in this town. He’s not going to give his daughter to a ne’er-do-well, down-and-out fellow like you who roams the streets from cockcrow to sundown and drinks himself cockeyed in dodgy pothouses such as A-Sayyed Musa’s. Someone who’s a regular visitor to Eshrat Ikbiri’s den of vice, and haunts gaming dens in hidden corners in the marketplace or the vacant lot to play knucklebones with a bunch of hopeless rascals like himself."

"Never mind about me and my friends, Laylan," cut in Kazem, annoyed at this picture of himself. "I want to see Maryam again tomorrow to find out if she's thought over my proposal."

"If you want me to pass her a note tonight or tomorrow morning," said Laylan, "it's out of the question. But I know for sure that tomorrow afternoon she and her friends will go to visit the tomb of the saint. If you go and hang about there, you might be able, if lucky, to catch her and talk to her. Be careful, though: walls have eyes and ears and someone might spot you talking to her and inform her father. I hope you know that he is a violent old fanatic and can have you skinned alive for that."

"I know Laylan, I know," said Kazem impatiently, standing up. "I'll go with my friend Mohsen Chakhaan. He can stand at a distance and give me a warning if he sees anything suspicious."

Kazem left the teahouse and went to find Mohsen.

18

Kazem found Mohsen perched on the bonnet of a broken-down car drinking tea, swinging his rosary, and chatting away to the young mechanic. On seeing Kazem, Mohsen gulped down the last of his tea, leapt down, and ran towards him.

"Did you see Laylan?" he asked.

"Sure I did," answered Kazem. "Maryam and her friends are going to visit the tomb of the saint before sundown. We've to be quick before they arrive there so that I can talk to her."

"Let's go right away," cried Mohsen, always happy to play his part in any romantic adventure.

The two friends arrived at the gate of the tomb of the saint late afternoon. The two huge wooden leaves of the gate were wide open, each leaning from inside against the wall of a short, shaded passageway that led to a small courtyard at the end of which could be seen the entrance to the tomb, sunk in gloom. The tomb was crowned with an egg-like, pointed dome, adorned with patterns created with golden-brown and turquoise-coloured bricks that gleamed in the afternoon sun. On either side of the gateway, tucked under a decorative brickwork arch, were two high platforms made of rough-cut flagstones.

Mohsen leapt on one platform and sat down, dangling a leg and swinging his rosary. The graveyard, which stretched to the edge of the town, shimmered hazily in the heat. Kazem paced back and forth in front of the gate like a caged animal, muttering to himself and, every so often, throwing anxious glances inside the courtyard of the tomb. Finally, he sat on the other platform, brooding over what he was going to say to Maryam.

"I hope Laylan the Gypsy didn't put the bite on you again," Mohsen said.

"Nope," replied Kazem, glancing at him. "She was sure that Maryam and her friends were going to come to do their weekly devotions in the tomb. Maryam's supposed to give me her final answer today."

"You know what," Mohsen suggested, jumping down from the platform, "let's forget about all this love business and drop by Eshrat Ikbiri's and see some *khanums*."

"That would be a shameful thing to do on the eve of my becoming a family man!" Kazem laughed, but shook his head disapprovingly.

"No worries." Mohsen shrugged. "Truth be told," he said, "I'm thinking to join you soon by marrying my Mashhadi sweetheart."

"How the hell are you going to do that?" Kazem looked at Mohsen as if he had taken leave of his senses. "She's on the game, Mohsen."

"It's as easy as winking, Agh Kazem." Mohsen outlined his plan in his usual care-free, self-confident manner. "I'll take her to the holy shrine of Imam Reza in Mashhad, light a couple of votive candles for her, ask her to pray to the saint who can intervene, asking God to forgive her. She'll then repent on the spot by mumbling some prayers and mend her unholy ways. I'll at once take her to one of the mollahs who are always on hand in the courtyard of the shrine and ask him to marry us right away."

"Remember only," said Kazem, wanting to sound like an understanding friend, "a whore is like a loincloth they rent out in a public bathhouse; every day a different man wraps it round his body. She'll not settle down; she's not tamed. Sooner or later, she'll fly away from the nest."

"I've heard that many rich merchants and mollahs marry these whores and make decent wives out of them."

"Do you reckon?" asked Kazem, trying to tell Mohsen some hard home truths. "These mollahs and merchants make short-term *siegehehs* out of these wretched creatures, give them food and shelter for a while and make them pregnant after gratifying their insatiable lust. Once tired of the women, these men kick them in the backside and chuck them out into the gutter. Not being able to bring up the children left on their hands, these women end up, sooner or later, in whorehouses all over this country."

They continued to discuss women, love, and marital bliss. Not coming to any meaningful conclusion on these topics, they got up and walked to one of the graves closest to the entrance of the tomb, squatting beside it. The grave was a small mound of earth on top of which was laid a nameless slab which had been smashed into several pieces. It was covered with fine dust.

"One day we'll be lying in the earth under a mound like this," Mohsen sighed, gazing at the slab.

"For the moment we're on the surface of this earth," said Kazem in the manner of a more pragmatic philosopher. "When you're standing on the surface, don't think about what'll happen when you are buried under it."

"You're right there, Dash Kazem." Mohsen nodded pensively. "Whoever we are, whatever we do, wherever we live, this is the end of the journey, bro."

After a moment Kazem raised his head. A woman, veiled from head to foot in a black chador, was walking silently towards them, the hem of her chador trailing over the graves, raising dust and dirt. Seeing that she was holding a bowl of votive dates in her hand, Kazem got up. Mohsen also stood up and took his cap off. They waited respectfully for the woman to come to them. Once beside the grave, she stopped and stretched out the bowl clutched in her bony gnarled hand. Kazem took a date and mumbled some commonplace blessings for the soul of her departed. Mohsen parroted roughly the same words. The woman then turned and walked to a freshly dug mound of earth a few paces away and sat down cross-legged beside it, remaining there like a tired old raven. Her bent back began to shake convulsively under her chador. Her smothered weeping was gradually drowned by other muffled sounds in the graveyard.

"Look, Mohsen," said Kazem under his breath, digging him in the ribs and pointing to the middle of the graveyard, "I think they're coming."

"Who's coming?" replied Mohsen, alarmed.

"Maryam and her friends, of course."

"Aaah, yes," said Mohsen, putting on his cap and looking down between the graves.

A small flock of women, all veiled in black chadors, was scurrying among and over the graves, coming towards the tomb of the saint. Upon recognising Maryam among the women, Kazem nudged Mohsen and pushed him down to sit beside the grave. Kazem also sat down. Picking up two pebbles, he gave one to Mohsen, and the two friends fell into praying fervently for the soul of the unknown dead person, tapping the pieces of the broken slab with their pebbles and mumbling some muddled-up prayers in Arabic which they had picked up from here and there without knowing what the words meant. They bowed their heads as a sign of respect so as not to be noticed by the approaching women.

Kazem watched the women out of the corner of his eye. Ignoring the two men, the women passed them by, stepped into the gateway, and entered the passage one at a time. Kazem kept throwing furtive glances over his shoulder trying to spot Maryam among them. Mohsen just kept looking at them.

"Don't make it so obvious that we're spying on them by looking at them," Kazem told him under his breath, his eyes darting right and left.

Maryam was the last woman to step under the arch.

"Maryam, Maryam…," he whispered loudly.

Not taking any notice of him, Maryam carried on walking and entered the passageway. Cat-like, Kazem leapt to his feet. He rushed to the gate, where he stood beside the platform and stuck his head out from behind the angle of the gate.

"Hey, hey, Maryam…," Kazem whispered loudly to get her attention.

Maryam turned round reluctantly. She heaved a sigh of gentle annoyance, as if she did not want to hurt the feelings of her admirer. She regarded him questioningly, then unveiled herself, revealing her brightly-coloured, flowery mini-skirt, before arranging the chador carefully on her body again, veiling it completely.

"Did you think about my proposal?" Kazem asked, eagerly awaiting her response.

Maryam stared at him for a moment. The shadow of a faint smile flitted on her shapely lips, then she turned on her heel and followed the other women into the courtyard of the tomb. Kazem, taking Maryam's smile as a signal of her agreement, stood rooted to the spot, his face lit up with rapture and grinning like an idiot.

"Did you see that?" Kazem asked, turning to Mohsen, still grinning blissfully.

"See what?"

"The smile," Kazem said. "She smiled at me. What do you think she means by that?"

Mohsen shrugged his shoulders. He glanced back into the courtyard. Kazem, all of a sudden, strode into the passageway and made as if to go inside the tomb.

"Don't go inside!" Mohsen cried out. "It's sinful to go in when women are praying there."

They had no choice but to sit and wait until the women came out. The tomb of the saint was completely silent. All that could be heard was the occasional sigh of the pilgrims lost in their devotions. Before an hour had passed, the group of young women emerged from the tomb, all completely wrapped up in their chadors and looking serious as pilgrims do after visiting a holy place.

Watching them walking towards the gate, Kazem shoved Mohsen out of the way, leapt back to the platform by the gate and turned his head against the wall, pretending that he was saying his prayers. Mohsen walked back to the grave and sat on his haunches, as if praying for the soul of the unknown dead person. The women sauntered past the two men, chattering among themselves and paying no heed to Kazem. Once the women were a few paces off, Kazem glanced back into the tomb and saw Maryam coming out.

She crossed the courtyard and walked into the passageway, still in a trance-like state. She had just reached the gate when Kazem jumped up and planted himself in front of her. Startled, she gazed at him like a child taken by surprise.

"So what's your answer, Maryam?" he asked miserably.

"I didn't even dare mention it." Maryam spoke calmly, looking kindly into Kazem's eyes.

"But, why not?" exclaimed Kazem, baffled. "I know you don't believe me, but I really love you so much."

"No use talking like this, Kazem," Maryam said in a melancholy tone, her eyes darting around. "My cousin was chosen as my future husband when they cut my umbilical cord. I'll be engaged to my cousin this Thursday." She then went on walking.

This was an unexpected blow. Utterly downcast, Kazem stood motionless under the gateway. He turned and gazed after Maryam, who was running over the graves to catch up with her friends, who were now some way off down the graveyard, their chadors fluttering and flapping in the rising warm breeze.

Kazem continued watching the small flock of women until they turned into tiny, flickering black patches at the end of the graveyard. He felt weak in the knees. He stepped back to the platform, sat down in slow motion, and slouched against it, staring vacantly at the spot where the black patches had disappeared, the last flicker of hope snuffed out in the ruins of his life.

A handful of men and women, scattered all over the graveyard, sat cross-legged beside some of the graves, tapping the slabs or the mounds of earth with pebbles, gazing vaguely at the incomprehensible things that lurked below those scorched clods of soil. A few dust-covered gravediggers, like large ants working diligently beside gigantic anthills, half of their bodies hidden in freshly dug holes, were throwing out spadefuls of earth. One or two professional prayer-readers, wrapped up in their tattered black *abas*, sat on the edges of some of the graves, rocking back and forth like dung beetles, reading litanies from moth-eaten prayer-books and small volumes of the Koran to console the souls of the departed. From the town below, at the bottom of the graveyard, a dark patch of black-clad mourners appeared, moving sluggishly like a bristly caterpillar towards the centre of the graveyard. Soon it became clear to Kazem that they were following a ladder placed on the shoulders of a few men, on top of which was stretched a corpse wrapped up in a dusty kilim. The lamentations of the chest-beating and head-slapping mourners chanting "There is no God but Allah" became louder and louder until it drowned the other noises. On the edge of the graveyard, some families were shaking out their wretched food cloths, raising a lot of dust, packing up to go home after having had a day out under a few dust-laden, withering trees in the company of the mourners and the dead.

The shadows of the larger gravestones were becoming longer and longer, creeping on the earth in the slanting, saffron-hued rays of the setting sun that poured, like a curse from heaven, over the living and the dead. The cawing of the crows, the howling of the mourners, the croaking of the Koran-readers, the sounds coming from the town down below, all were slowly dying down.

Kazem folded his hands on his knees, rested his chin on them, and slowly closed his eyes. He imagined that the hope of possible future happiness, shone like a ray of light for an instant in his life – as dank and cold as one of those cells in Qasr Prison – had revealed all the squalor of his existence. With that ray of light gone, he found himself freezing in the wilderness. He was now left with nothing but a handful of memories of that sudden love, unprepared to face the melancholy autumn days and icy evenings of the coming winter. Self-doubt and painful soul-searchings had begun to gnaw at his soul like vermin. All hope had gone from his life. It was as if the very sun were dying out, leaving his body as cold as that corpse the mourners were carrying on the ladder. How happy those short-lived moments of hope had been, he thought. He imagined himself as one of those Persian merchants in ancient times, who travelled along the Silk Route to far-off lands to bring back exotic goods, only to be ambushed on the way back home by highwaymen who seized all his merchandise, leaving him empty-handed and bankrupt.

All of a sudden, he heard a piercing scream behind him. Scraps of chaotic thoughts, images without order or connection, flickered in his head. The faces of people he had seen when a child, the shrieking of a woman in agony, someone singing a lullaby, thugs brawling, black-clad men flagellating themselves in a pitch-dark alleyway, black-chadored women wailing, a pregnant woman giving birth to a dead baby, a muezzin's chanting in his ass's voice, the howling of stray dogs or screeching of hungry cats, all these crowded his feverish brain. One followed another, spinning like a whirlwind in his head. Like echoes of ghosts in an empty house that one is about to leave forever, he heard those noises of the past.

The babel in his head grew louder and louder until it became unbearable, drowning out the other sounds. Unable to stand them, he raised his head and looked around wild-eyed. He listened harder. The shrieks were coming from inside the tomb. He bent forward and peered inside the courtyard.

At that moment an eerie silence fell on the tomb.

As he peered, straining his eyes, into the sombre passageway, he saw a long dark mass like a reptile appearing on the threshold of the inner shrine, crawling slowly out of the tomb. It began to move towards the passageway. The creature crept towards Kazem and stopped dead at his feet. It looked like a leper wrapped in torn, many-coloured filthy rags. A most hideous face peeked out from under the heap and stared at Kazem with bleary blood-shot eyes. The face cracked into wrinkles like the skin of a rotten walnut and a dried-up, claw-like hand came out from among the rags, stretching itself tremblingly towards Kazem.

"May God bless you, young man," she spluttered, "give us some alms. I'll pray for you so that the saint here will bless your youth and fulfil all your wishes."

Kazem fumbled in his shirt pocket and unthinkingly took out a *one-toman* note, which he chucked at the crippled woman, who at once snatched it up from the soil and stuffed it into the folds of her rags. She then crawled down the steps of the gateway, dragging her dusty legs behind her. They made a sickly thud on the ground. She then crept among the graves like a crippled dog, evoking the name of the saint and muttering prayers for Kazem.

"Hey, hey, Agh Kazem!" Mohsen's familiar voice gave Kazem a start. "What did she say?"

"Who?" Kazem looked up at Mohsen, perplexed.

"Maryam, of course," Mohsen said.

As if unaware of Mohsen's presence, Kazem went on gazing after the crippled woman as she dragged herself among the graves, turning gradually into a tiny dark spot. Mohsen followed Kazem's gaze.

"Poor Soghra the Cripple." Mohsen heaved a wistful sigh. "They say she's been crawling here every single day of her life, taking refuge in the tomb the whole day, repeating the same prayers, and begging the saint to ask God to cure her handicap. Every day she's the first to settle in the shrine, no matter who's here, and she's the last to leave the place and crawl back to her hole down there at the bottom of the graveyard. So far, both the saint and God the Compassionate have been deaf to her unending prayers and begging. Well, I wonder how long will she go on like this."

Mohsen stopped and glanced at Kazem, who was still fixed in the same pose.

"Come on, Agh Kazem, let's go to A-Sayyed Musa's," Mohsen suggested resignedly. He grabbed Kazem's arm and pulled him up. "Maybe a couple of glasses of *arrack* will cheer you up and will make you talk."

Kazem followed Mohsen mechanically, his hands dangling beside him. The two friends walked silently among and over the graves. The sun, like a burnished copper disk, hung above the crimson-hued horizon. On reaching the end of the graveyard, Kazem stopped and glanced back. The dome of the tomb, the minarets, the graves and the gigantic anthills looked as if they were all on fire.

19

The sun had gone down when they arrived at A-Sayyed Musa's tavern. A-Sayyed Musa, who was busy as usual shambling about and bossing the tavern-boy around to make the place ready for the long night ahead, greeted Kazem and Mohsen cheerfully, leading them to a daybed overlooking the town.

Once they were settled, A-Sayyed Musa asked the tavern-boy to look after his best regulars. The boy disappeared into the scullery, reappearing with a large tray of the usual things that go with *arrack*, and placed it on the kilim. A-Sayyed Musa ran over to the musicians, who had just taken their place on the daybed under the mulberry tree, and urged them to play something to cheer the place up a little. After tuning their instruments, they struck up a cheery tune.

Mohsen poured some *arrack* into two glasses, grabbed one for himself, and handed the other to Kazem.

"To your health," said Mohsen, raising his glass and drinking slowly with obvious relish.

Kazem knocked back his glass, then poured a few more glasses for himself and drank them one after another. Instead of cheering up, as in his happier days, his face clouded over. Down below Hosseinabaad was slowly becoming tinted in a bluish-grey haze.

"She'll be engaged to her cousin on Thursday." Kazem sighed. He then looked at Mohsen with blank unseeing eyes and added, "I'm left with no other choice but to kidnap her, Mohsen."

"Are you serious, Kazem?" Mohsen looked aghast.

"Y-e-s!" Kazem cried, "I swear to Imam Reza that I'll kidnap her." He looked sharply at Mohsen. "Can you nick your boss's truck for one night?"

Mohsen, a slice of cucumber between his teeth, stared at him with eyes popping out of his head.

"Are you sure you haven't gone nuts, Kazem?"

"If you could do that for me," Kazem went on, fiddling distractedly with his box of matches, "all will be sorted. Otherwise I'll lose Maryam forever."

"Drink up your *arrack* now," said Mohsen, shoving a piece of bread soaked in yoghurt into his mouth.

"If you promise," Kazem pleaded, "half of the job is done." He continued in a melodramatic tone, as if he were looking at a future scene of his happy life with Maryam, "We'll leave this town. I'll take her to Tehran and we'll get married there. After that, I'll mend my ways, find a regular job and settle into a decent family life." He shook his head. "I'm desperately fond of her, Mohsen."

The musicians had now taken up a doleful tune.

"Cheers," said Mohsen tipsily after a short silence, draining his glass in one draught and biting into a piece of cucumber. Tossing his rosary from one hand to the other, he started telling one of his cock-and-bull stories:

"One day as I was busy loading up the truck in a street near Soraya Square, I looked around and saw one of those gorgeous young women in a mini-skirt standing in the doorway of her house, secretly eyeing me up and down. No sooner had our eyes met than she winked at me. I said to myself, 'Mohsen, this is your chance; you'll regret it later if you don't take it.' I asked my mate to get on with the loading up and walked up to her. She at once asked me in for a glass of tea, which was, of course, a ploy to lure me in."

Mohsen became silent for a moment, gazing fixedly at a far distant point over the horizon. He then went on, sounding and looking as tragic as a romantic hero, accompanied by the mournful melodies of the musicians, who were still at it.

"You can't imagine what magical moments I spent with her. Her body was as white as marble. It smelt of rosewater and was so soft and fresh, as if she had washed herself in a pond of warm milk. Her long black hair was scented with the jasmine perfume of Kashan. I was driven insane with passion. She told me that her father was one of the richest merchants in Tehran's Bazaar. After we made love a couple of times, she fell head over heels in love with me and began to beg me to marry her…"

"Don't you get tired of making up these lies about yourself, man?" Kazem spoke suddenly in a loud voice.

"Hey, Dash Kazem, I can't help it." Mohsen heaved a sigh and went on in a rueful tone, "You know, my life has been nothing but a heap of lies. From the moment that I was born, I was told nothing but lies. I, too, was left to fend for myself in the gutter. I've never known what loving a woman means. I've always led a life of dissipation by spending my wages on *khanums* in Eshrat Ikbiri's house. I live on a day-to-day basis. Like you, I don't know what a school looks like. I've no ambitions in life, no plans, no hopes, no future; n-nothing. So, the only joy left me is to go on making up these stories to make my life more colourful and tolerable, rather like a prisoner who imagines lovely things to get him through his solitary days..."

"Come on, now," Kazem cut him short, getting ready to move. "Get up and let's go."

"Where to?" said Mohsen, grabbing Kazem's hand.

"We've to find a truck or a car," said Kazem purposefully.

"What am I here for then, Kazem?" said Mohsen. "If I kept silent about my boss's truck, it was because I did not want you to leave. Truth be told, I was hoping you might forget her. But now that it's clear to me that you love her so much, a big cheers to you and your sweetheart." He downed his glass of *arrack.*

"Cheers," said Kazem, doing the same and feeling more hopeful. He looked at the musicians.

"A-Sayyed Musa," he called out across the tavern, "can you ask your musicians to play a more cheerful tune?"

A-Sayyed Musa shuffled over to the musicians, who were strumming, banging, and singing with feeling.

"*Baba*, enough of these mournful songs!" he yelled at them. "You play and sing as if your mothers had just died. Come on, play something more joyful to cheer up these poor devils."

The musicians stopped their singing and playing, whispered to one another, and began to play a lively piece. One of them acted like a lovesick man and the other acted the part of his sweetheart.

Oh, my gorgeous Golpari!
Yes, what do you want?
Would you become my wife?
Oh, no; I will not!
Why not?
Because I can't.
Why, why, why...?

Hearing the song, A-Sayyed Musa at once began clicking his fingers loudly, wiggling his bum to the lively tune and singing the refrain: "why, why, why..."

Hosseinabaad was now plunged into a ghostly twilight, getting ready to go to sleep. Like a rusty old coin, the full moon was suspended over the outskirts of the town. Only some dim lights hanging on the lampposts flickered through the darkness. All the lights in the tavern were now on. The other habitués had already settled on the other daybeds – drinking, smoking, talking in hushed voices and gesticulating. A-Sayyed Musa bustled here and there, shuffling from one daybed to another, and performed his familiar antics, bullying the tavern boy to look after the customers.

Kazem's face darkened once again.

"What are you thinking of now?" Mohsen asked him, noticing his change of mood.

"I'm racking my brains as to how we're going to kidnap Maryam," said Kazem. "We can't do it when she's outside her house because people will see and it's too dangerous. She's never alone at home. So what are we going to do?"

Mohsen rubbed his chin thoughtfully, trying to think of a plan.

"Hmm, how do we find out if she's alone at home?" Mohsen said, as if talking to himself.

Kazem lit a cigarette, ruminating over this problem. Mohsen also fell into deep thought, running his fingers through his hair from time to time.

"I have it!" Mohsen suddenly yelled as if stung by a wasp. "Laylan the Gypsy might be of use to us here. She always hangs around in Hajji Harirchi's house. She must know a lot about what's going on in there. Maybe she can provide us with some useful information."

"I think you're right there," Kazem said. "She knows a lot about people in this town."

"What are you waiting for, then?" cried out Mohsen. "You'll have to go and find Laylan tomorrow and see what she can do for you."

20

Kazem spent the whole night imagining his future with Maryam in Tehran. He woke up late and at once dashed to the market place, in the hope of finding Laylan the Gypsy there. After some wanderings, he finally tracked her down. She was sitting cross-legged on a tattered kilim surrounded by a jumble of amulets, talismans and small teacups to help her tell people's fortunes. A small bunch of idle onlookers made a ring around her, huddling together and craning their necks. A skinny young man with a sunburnt complexion and a thick mop of hair squatted politely on the kilim, stretching out his palm which was clutched in Laylan's claw-like left hand. With the index finger of her right hand, she traced the lines of his palm, mumbling some magic formulae, and telling him all about his future. Bemused, the young man listened attentively to her mumbo-jumbo and all the wonderful things awaiting him. Upon hearing promising news about his future with his sweetheart, a big grin cracked his face, revealing his yellowish-brown teeth.

Kazem pushed his way through the crowd, stepped on the kilim and squatted beside Laylan.

"Can I talk to you for a minute?" he whispered in her ear.

"Can't you see I'm busy working?" said Laylan under her breath, casting an annoyed glance at him. She then went on murmuring some gibberish, wished her satisfied client all the happiness in his future life with his sweetheart and snatched a five-toman note from him, shoving into the folds of her chador and ignoring Kazem completely.

"This is urgent, Laylan," Kazem whispered, slyly thrusting a five-toman note into her claw. "It's about Maryam's family."

"All right then, come and see me later in Kal Abbasgholi's teahouse," she whispered back, sounding friendlier.

"I'll have to speak to you in private," Kazem muttered. "No one should hear about this. Can you meet me in the ruins of the caravanserai at noon?"

"Well, that's possible." Laylan threw a meaningful glance at him. "That'll cost you a bit more."

Kazem was at the ruins around noon. He found a crumbling arch with a patch of shade and sat on the remains of the platform beneath it, lighting a cigarette. Broken bricks were scattered everywhere. An army of insects buzzed and hummed among the tall brambles and nettles that had grown in a thick tangle around the rubble. The ruins of the ancient caravanserai were shimmering in the blazing midday sun. Kazem sat there waiting anxiously for a good hour.

A muffled jingling sound gave him a start. He scanned the ruins. A dark blob, flickering in the quivering heat, appeared in the distance, moving rapidly towards him. Kazem soon recognised Laylan by the way she was ambling, swinging one bracelet-laden arm and holding her bundle under the other. He jumped down from the platform and walked to meet her.

"All right, Kazem," said Laylan, clasping his arm, "what's all this private business of yours?"

"Listen, Laylan," said Kazem, flicking his cigarette butt, "I want you to find out when Maryam is going to be left alone in her house."

"How should I know when she's going to be alone in the house?" Laylan exclaimed.

"You go a lot to Hajji Harirchi's house, don't you?"

"Some days I do, yes."

"So, you should know what's going on there most of the time."

"I suppose I do."

"So you might be able to find out when Maryam will be left alone in the house, won't you?"

"How do I find out if she's going to be left alone in the house?"

"It's very easy," Kazem explained. "All you've got to do is hang around the house and see when she's going to be alone."

"Nope, don't even mention it," Laylan said. "You think it's easy, but it's not. I can't do it."

"For heaven's sake, woman," Kazem said, exasperated, "don't say you can't do it. You're my only hope. Only *you* can help me now."

"I'm terrified of someone finding out what I'm up to loitering around Hajji's house."

"No need to be afraid, Laylan," Kazem soothed her. "All you've to do is let me know when Maryam is alone. The rest will be my affair."

"Imagine that she'll not be left alone till doomsday. Then what?"

"You never know," said Kazem, flinging his jacket over his shoulder, "she might be alone tomorrow."

"You talk as if it's written on the door of the house that she'll be left alone at this time or that."

"I'm sure you're capable of thinking up a plan so that she'll be by herself in the house."

Laylan snapped a bramble stalk and began to pluck its tiny leaves as if an idea had just flashed through her scheming mind.

"Truth be told, Kazem," she said, "such risky tactics need a lot of planning and thinking and can be very costly."

"How much are you thinking of?"

"Let me see . . ." Laylan put her index finger to her lips and rolled her eyes upwards, counting. "I reckon each day will be nearly…"

"All right, all right, I'm with you," Kazem cut in. He thrust his hand into his jacket pocket, pulled out a few crumpled five-tomans, and handed them to Laylan. "There, take this advance payment for the moment."

Looking at the notes with her hawk's eyes, Laylan snatched them one by one, nearly scratching Kazem's hand with her blackened sharp nails.

"I'll grease your palms once the job's done," said Kazem.

"I hope you're not giving me empty promises again." Laylan cast a suspicious glance at Kazem.

"I'll keep to my side of the bargain; promise," he said. "I hope you'll come back to me with some good news."

"With the help of God," Laylan said, raising her hands heavenwards. "I'll find you this afternoon and hopefully give you some good news." She walked off, humming a tune to herself. The jingling of her bracelets and necklaces slowly faded, drowned by the trilling of crickets and the humming of insects.

Kazem stood looking after her till she disappeared at the end of the ruins. He then turned on his heel and headed straight to Kal Abbasgholi's teahouse to consult him over his risky plan to kidnap Maryam.

He found Kal Abbasgholi inside the teahouse. He was sitting on a chair beside a table around which sat a few of his regulars. Kazem strode to the table and greeted everyone. He whispered to Kal Abbasgholi that he had to talk to him in private. Kal Abbasgholi excused himself, stood up at once and followed Kazem outside. They stood beside a column at the far end of the porch.

"Kal Abbasgholi," said Kazem under his breath, "I'm in serious trouble."

"What, trouble again, Kazem?" Kal Abbasgholi asked. "You've only just come out of jail a few days ago."

"No, no, no," Kazem hastened to reassure his friend, "not that kind of trouble. You know too well that I've learnt my lesson the hard way not to go anywhere near smuggling."

"What kind of trouble, then?" asked Kal Abbasgholi, looking at Kazem searchingly.

"Trouble of the heart, my friend," said Kazem.

"You don't mean you've fallen in love!" Kal Abbasgholi exclaimed. "Wonder of wonders. Kazem Alaki has fallen in love! The man who always laughed such things off, has now has fallen into the same trap himself."

"What's wrong with that?" Kazem grumbled. "You think I don't have a heart?"

"You have a heart all right, and a very large one at that, but…"

"But, what?"

"Never mind…" Kal Abbasgholi decided not to go on. "Tell me who the unfortunate girl is."

"Promise me you'll not laugh at me." Kazem looked down at the floor, embarrassed.

"You've my word."

"She's the daughter of Hajji Harirchi."

"Hajji Harirchi!" Kal Abbasgholi could not help crying out. "I hope you've not taken leave of your senses. Hajji Harirchi is the richest man in this town. Do you honestly believe that he's going to put his daughter on a golden plate and offer her to a young man like you?"

"What's wrong with me, Kal Abbas?" Kazem said, hurt.

"As my good friend, there's nothing wrong with you." Kal Abbasgholi put his hand on Kazem's shoulder. "But, when it comes to Hajji Harirchi and his pretty daughter, everything about you becomes wrong. Has it never crossed your mind by any chance that you're a happy-go-lucky young man with no steady job, no education, no skills, no parents, not even a family name to tell people who you are and where you sprout from and who your father was? A good-for-nothing loafer who has just come out of jail with no future …"

"All right, all right," Kazem muttered, "I know exactly what I am. Still, I want to marry this girl, mend my ways, and settle into a quiet life, just like everyone else."

"Marry this girl!" Kal Abbasgholi repeated. "Take my friendly word and forget about it, son, before it's too late."

"It's indeed too late, Kal Abbas."

"What do you mean?"

"She's going to be engaged to her cousin next Thursday."

"So, end of story."

"Well, not for me."

"What?"

"I'm thinking to kidnap her and take her with me to Tehran," Kazem said.

"You've to be bonkers to think up such a thing, son," Kal Abbasgholi said, looking at Kazem in the same way a sane man looks at a maniac. "If Hajji Harirchi gets wind of this, he'll send his thuggish henchmen to slit your throat and throw your body into a vacant lot. Don't mess with him, son. You've no idea how nasty he can be."

"Don't you worry about him and his roughnecks," said Kazem with the self-confidence of a man who has made up his mind. "Once we're in Tehran, we'll melt into the crowd in that vast city and no one can easily track us down. Moreover, with all this chaos going on at the moment over there, a kidnapped girl who's married to her lover wouldn't interest the police."

Some men walked inside the teahouse and Kal Abbasgholi got up to attend to them, urging Kazem not to be so hotheaded.

Kazem stood there for a while, deep in thought. His soul being agitated, he decided to wander around the market place for a while, sorting out things in his mind and hoping that Laylan would come to him with some good news.

21

Around four o'clock in the afternoon, not seeing any sign of Laylan anywhere, Kazem thought he might find her in the ruins of caravanserai. He sat on a small rock, gazing at the spring. An hour passed and Laylan did not show up. Eventually, someone yelling his name in the distance made him start. It was Mohsen, riding on a bicycle.

"Kazem! Kazem!" Mohsen went on yelling till he reached him. He got off the bicycle, letting it drop on the ground.

"Where the heck have you been?" Mohsen said, sitting down on the rock beside Kazem. "I've been looking for you all over town."

"What's up?" said Kazem wearily, tapping his shirt pockets to find his box of matches to light the cigarette he was holding between his fingers.

"Laylan came to see me," said Mohsen, panting and wheezing. "As she couldn't find you anywhere, she came to see me."

"What did she say?"

"She told me that Maryam's mother and her younger sister are going tonight to Ozrah the Dressmaker's."

"S-o-o?" Kazem put the cigarette between his lips.

"Maryam and her father will be alone at home."

"Do you think we can carry out our plan if Hajji Harirchi's at home?" Kazem replied with heavy sarcasm.

"We'll find a way to get rid of Hajji," Mohsen declared.

"But how?" Kazem cried. Sometimes Mohsen just didn't think.

"You're right there," agreed Mohsen, rubbing his hands. "How's it to be done?"

Kazem, the cigarette wedged between his fingers, fell into brooding. Mohsen pushed his hat far back on his head. He ran his fingers through his cropped hair, mulling over the problem, as if trying to undo a tangled skein.

"I know!" he shouted all of a sudden, clapping his hands. "How about beating Hajji into a pulp!"

"*Aye zeki!*" Kazem glanced at Mohsen in vexation. "Well done for the brilliant idea!" He got up, and began to walk. Mohsen stood up and followed him.

"You're right, Agh Kazem," he said sheepishly, "that would make a lot of noise." He paused briefly. "What about…?"

“Let me think a minute, man,” said Kazem, cutting him short and throwing up his hands in despair. Mohsen hung his head, like a child who has been told off. Kazem looked away, contemplating the ruins. He then turned to Mohsen, a smile slowly lighting up his face. “I have the answer. Come on, I’ll tell you all about my plan.”

He put his hand on Mohsen’s shoulder and they began to stroll along by the spring.

“Listen to what I’m going to say carefully,” Kazem said. “Tonight you’ll bring the truck and park it somewhere a short distance away from Hajji Harirchi’s house. We’ll then hide in the corner of a dark alleyway near the house, keeping an eye on it to see who’s coming and who’s going. When we’re sure that Maryam’s alone with her father, I’ll wait in the alleyway watching. Once her sister and mother have left the house, you’ll walk up to the door, knock it, and tell Hajji that the shutter of his shop in the marketplace has been left unlocked. He’ll leave Maryam alone in the house to go out to check. You’ll then dash to the truck, sit in it, and wait for me. I’ll find a way to enter the house, kidnap Maryam, and, once out of the house, we’ll come to you, and you’ll drive us out of town.”

Mohsen nodded his head like an obedient errand boy, twiddling his hat in his hands.

Once out of the ruins, Kazem asked Mohsen to meet him after dusk in the narrow lane beside of Hajji Harirchi’s house. Mohsen was instructed to park the truck in a side street a short distance away and wait for Kazem. They then parted, each taking a different direction.

Darkness had not yet fallen when Kazem went to wander about in the neighbourhood of Hajji Harirchi’s house to see when Maryam’s mother and sister left the house. Some shopkeepers were taking their wares inside the shops, putting the lights out, pulling the shutters down and getting ready to go home. The dusky streets and lanes were slowly becoming deserted. Every now and again, a figure emerged from the shadows, holding *sangak* bread in one hand and carrying bundles of grapes in a packet in the other, hurrying home to his family.

When it was completely dark, Kazem entered the alleyway next to Hajji Harirchi’s house and positioned himself in the angle of the walls of the lane and the alleyway under an arch, watching the door of the house like an assassin waiting for his victim to show up. It did not take long before the door of the house opened with a groan and Maryam’s mother and sister emerged from the dark passageway behind the door into the dimly-lit lane. They turned right and soon faded into the depths of the lane.

Mohsen joined Kazem at the agreed time. As planned, Mohsen walked to the door of the house, looking over his shoulder to make sure that no one was watching him. He stood in front of the huge door, half-lit by a pale street lamp. After a few seconds, he lifted the heavy knocker, knocked a few times, and waited, swinging his rosary on his fingers. Meanwhile, Kazem, hidden in the shadows, kept sticking his head out to see who would open the door. Mohsen knocked again. The door opened a crack and a woman's head, wrapped up in a chador, appeared behind the door. Kazem was relieved to hear that the voice as the woman spoke belonged to Maryam.

"*Salaam*, khanum," Mohsen greeted Maryam respectfully. "Is Hajji at home?"

"Whom shall I tell him it is?" Maryam asked politely.

"Hajji has left the shutter of his shop unlocked," Mohsen said rapidly, fluttering his hands in the direction of the marketplace. "The policeman on duty has sent me to inform Hajji about this. Can I speak to Hajji myself? I can explain it to him better. Excuse me, please," he added, stepping inside the passageway, not waiting to be asked. Once he was inside, the door remained ajar.

Kazem looked around and dashed to the door, poked his head inside a little, and listened, at the same time keeping an eye on the quiet lane. He picked up snatches of the exchange between Hajji, Maryam and Mohsen.

"What's going on, Maryam?" he heard Hajji grunting.

"This man…," Maryam was about to explain everything to her father when Mohsen chimed in hurriedly.

"*Salaam,* Hajj Agha," Mohsen called out. "The shutter of your shop is unlocked. The policeman on duty has sent me to let you know."

"That half-wit Moraad has forgotten to lock up." Hajji Harirchi's angry growl rang across the silent courtyard. "Listen, fellow, have they stolen anything?"

"Not a clue, Hajji."

"I hope they've not stolen anything. I always lock…" Hajji's voice faded away, as he hurried inside the house, most probably to get the keys.

Kazem heard the rapid sound of footsteps in the passageway behind the door. He turned, ran quickly back, and stood against the wall of the shadowy recess. Soon the door of the house opened. Mohsen slipped through, looked around like a thief, and shut the door behind him. He stood there, wiped the sweat off his brow, acting out some parts of the scene he had just played, mimicking his own actions, and thinking aloud about the story he had concocted. He seemed very pleased with himself for having accomplished another part of his daring mission.

"Phew!" Kazem heard him say. "The lock on your shutter is not locked, the policeman on duty... Pah, what a lot of monkey business!" He scurried towards Kazem and stood before him, gaping like an imbecile.

"Why are you standing there and looking at me like a goat? Say something." Kazem stepped out of the recess. "Is it done?"

"Y-e-s!" cried Mohsen, punching the air. "All is sorted."

"Come on, then," said Kazem, leaping into a narrow alleyway near the recess. "Let's wait here till Hajji shows up." Mohsen followed him. They stood in a dark corner of the alleyway, keeping their eyes on the door. After a minute it creaked open and Hajji Harirchi stepped out of the house. He shut the door firmly behind him, and walked briskly, putting his coat on as he went and growling like an angry bear.

"Oh, God in heaven! What could've possibly happened?" Kazem heard Hajji's voice fading away in the quiet lane as he walked towards the marketplace. "I always lock…"

As soon as the sound of Hajji's footsteps and voice sank into the silence, Kazem stepped gingerly out into the lane, casting cautious glances around. Mohsen tiptoed out, too, looking about him.

"We only have half-an-hour to do the job," said Kazem in half-whisper. "Hurry up."

They ran up the lane to the narrow street where the truck was parked. They climbed in and sat in the cab, panting.

"Start it up quick," said Kazem.

"All right," Mohsen said, losing his cool a little.

Mohsen tried to turn the engine on. As it was taking some time to start, Kazem lost his patience.

"Make it quick," he urged Mohsen.

"All right, man," Mohsen muttered. "I'm doing what I can."

The engine took a while to start. Finally, Mohsen, after tinkering with the switch and the pedals, managed to get it going. He rested his hands on the wheel and stared at Kazem, grinning triumphantly.

"Go on then. Move!" Kazem ordered.

Mohsen drove the truck closer to Hajji's house, and parked it there. They got out and ran to a narrow alleyway at the back of the house. At the foot of a tall, roughcast wall, they looked around. The alleyway was plunged into half-darkness, with not a soul in sight. Mohsen stood with his back flat against the wall, cupped his hands in front of him and whispered to Kazem,

"Up you go." Kazem placed a foot in Mohsen's clasped hands, grabbed his shoulders and hefted himself up, clutching at a brick sticking out of the wall and climbing on Mohsen's shoulders. He then grabbed another brick, put his feet into some crevices, and clambered up the wall, clinging to it like a lizard.

"Don't look up," Kazem whispered, looking down at Mohsen who had tilted his head backwards, watching him anxiously like a devilish little urchin. "The dust will fall into your eyes."

Kazem climbed up to the top of the wall, where, clutching two sharp stones, he hitched himself up and crouched on top of the wall.

"Be careful," whispered Mohsen loudly, backing away from the wall and looking up at Kazem.

"Listen, Mohsen," Kazem whispered back, "you go back to the truck and wait there for me."

Mohsen obeyed and scurried off, vanishing into the shadows.

Kazem looked fixedly at the roof half a metre below him, then dropped down, landing there noiselessly on all fours. Raising himself to his full height, he swept his gaze over the roofs of the neighbourhood houses from amongst which, here and there, the bleakly yellowish gleams of street lamps glowed through the cracks like dim flames from the underworld.

Bending down, Kazem tiptoed to the *kharposhteh* at the far end of the roof. Casting rapid glances about once more, he gently pushed open the two leaves of the wooden door and stepped inside the half-dark, narrow staircase. The cool smell of clay and bricks hit his nostrils. He groped his way down the worn steps, stretching his hands wide to feel the walls. In the middle of the staircase, he stopped. Aided by the dim light at its foot, he climbed down and came to the wide-open door of the staircase which led straight into the vast twilight zone of the courtyard.

In the doorway, he hesitated for a moment, and peered into the silent courtyard. From the latticed windows of three basements and a privy nearby, the pale gleam of a few light bulbs cast a patterned light on the flagstones, while the light coming from the windows of rooms under the high-ceilinged vaulted portico at the end of the long terrace also threw a pallid glow on the flower bushes, in the middle of which stood some short oleander trees. The colossal walls that enclosed the courtyard were covered with thick ivies. The scent of honeysuckle and roses filled the air. The still water of the *hauz* beside the weeping willow glistened from among the geranium pots, reflecting the dull light pouring out from the portico. The shadowy passageway that led to the door of the house gaped like the mouth of a cave.

Crouching and keeping close to the windows of the privy and the basements, Kazem ran on tiptoe and came to the staircase leading to the terrace. He stopped, listened, and glanced about him. He could hear only the humming of the creatures of the night, stirring among the bushes and trees. Panther-like, he leapt on the first step, raised his head high, sniffed the air, and, creeping on all fours, ended up on the terrace. Once on top of the steps, a few paces took him to the shut doors of three rooms to the side of the portico. He stopped in front of the doors and pawed them like a curious cat to see if they were open. The doors were all locked from behind. He then walked gingerly to the portico. After peering inside the portico, he stepped on to its raised floor. A faint light lit up the niches in the walls and the vaulted ceiling. Imagining that he heard someone heaving a sigh somewhere in the house, Kazem stiffened on the spot, arched his back, and glanced quickly behind him. He saw no one and heard no one, only the trilling of crickets and beetles. His elongated, slender shadow crept away from under his feet and was lost at the bottom of the steps, merging into the half-darkness of the courtyard.

He inspected the portico and peeped inside the rooms through the windows. The rooms were all quiet. Noiselessly, he tiptoed out of the portico and looked along the terrace. Immediately attached to the portico were three rooms, all the windows of which were shut. After carefully examining all three doors, Kazem found the middle door unlocked from behind. Gently, he pulled one leaf of the door open a crack and peeked inside.

Maryam was lying on her bed. She was resting her head on her hand that was propped up on a pillow, looking at a magazine. Kazem opened the door wide, stepped inside, shut the door behind him and stood there, looking at her. Hearing the noise, Maryam looked up and saw Kazem smiling at her. She looked at him as if she had seen an apparition which had all of a sudden materialised in her room.

"I was talking of kidnapping you," said Kazem in a low voice, gazing at her, "but now I've made up my mind to actually do it."

He took two steps towards the bed. She screamed and sat up. In her panic, she jumped off the bed, dropping both her chador and her magazine on the floor. Now in her short dress, she ran to the door of the drawing-room and opened it to escape. Like a predator, Kazem leapt a few paces forward, and caught her from behind, pulling her inside the room.

"No! No!" screamed Maryam. "Let me go!"

As Kazem dragged her inside the room, she managed to free herself from his grasp, screaming all the time: "Let me go! Let me go!"

Catching her, Kazem put one hand round her waist, bent down, grabbed her chador off the carpet with his free hand, and flung it round her body. In her frantic struggle, she reeled backwards and fell on the bed. As he tried to cover her with the chador, she got up, slipped through his hands like a sparrow from the claws of a hawk, and tried once again to run to the door. Kazem leapt behind her, swinging the chador over her head. Finally, after an exhausting cat and mouse game, Kazem managed to capture her. Gagging her with his handkerchief, he wrapped the chador round her head and upper body. He then hoisted her on his shoulders. By the door, he looked around with his priceless treasure struggling on his shoulder. Maryam, however, did not abandon herself to Kazem's unchivalrous conduct. She kicked the air with her bare feet and waved her hands about behind Kazem, punching him as hard as she could with her feeble fists. Kazem ignored the muffled protestations that came non-stop from under the chador and carried on with his perilous mission.

Kazem trotted along the terrace and descended the stairs. Cutting across the courtyard, he entered the dark passageway, and came out, leaving the door gaping open behind him. He pulled back the chador on Maryam's face, looking both ways. Once the coast was clear, Kazem ran as fast as he could. Maryam's muffled shrieks were lost in the silence of the lane.

Like a thief who has stolen a rug, rolled up and balanced on his shoulder, Kazem stumbled along the lane. Finally, he arrived at the side street in the middle of which Mohsen, sitting behind the wheel of the truck, was waiting for him, headlights on and engine running. Kazem rushed towards the truck and opened its door. He took Maryam down from his shoulder, set her down carefully on the seat like a precious object and hoisted himself up to sit beside her.

"Let's go," he said.

Mohsen, cigarette in one hand, drove the truck out of the side street, coming to the thoroughfare along both sides of which the closed shops shone in the headlights of the truck. Eventually, they arrived at the main highway, lit up every fifty metres by tall neon lampposts. Maryam threw a furtive glance at Mohsen, who had fixed his eyes on the road ahead, and pulled up her chador to cover her head. Kazem began unbinding the handkerchief from her mouth, talking to her meanwhile to justify his foolhardy actions.

"I never wanted to take you to our future home like this," said Kazem. "But I had no choice, even when Kal Abbasgholi warned me about the risk."

"Where are you taking me?" Maryam protested as soon as she could speak. "This is a very foolish thing to do."

"I love you, Maryam," Kazem said wretchedly, looking into her eyes.

"Please take me back," pleaded Maryam. "I beg you. I'm terrified."

"What are you terrified of?" Kazem asked her. "I promise I'll not touch you. I'm head over heels in love with you. I want to marry you. I was left with no other option. Was I, Mohsen?"

Mohsen glanced quickly at him and nodded. Realising that her beseeching had no effect on her captor, Maryam abandoned all resistance and fell silent. Helpless, she sat there, whimpering quietly.

The truck soon left the highway and turned into an unlit road. Kazem gazed at the road as it disappeared under the truck like a fast-moving murky river, glistening under the headlights. Mohsen, grasping the wheel like a peasant at the shafts of a handplough, was peering forward through the windscreen. The only sound was the humming of the engine. The dark road stretched out before them, illuminated now and again by the distant lights of trucks and lorries.

After nearly two hours, Mohsen pulled off the road in front of an obscure, sordid-looking roadside teahouse, hidden away in the shadows behind a few dusty mulberry and almond trees, in the middle of nowhere.

"Listen, Mohsen," Kazem said, "we can stay in this teahouse till we find a coach or another truck. You go back before your boss finds out."

"Not on your life!" Mohsen insisted. "I don't give a monkey's about him. I can drive you up to Tehran and then I'll return."

"Don't be such a fool!" said Kazem. "You've done enough for me. It's better this way for both of us. We'll spend the night here, if need be, and first thing in the morning we'll find something to take us to Tehran." Kazem grabbed his jacket and opened the door. Taking Maryam's arm, he said, "Come on, let's get off."

"Where are you taking me?" protested Maryam. "Please let me go back to my home in this truck." She kept repeating the same request. Kazem, not paying any attention to her, pulled her gently out and shut the door, telling her not to make a scene. He told Mohsen to go back. Realising that it was no use arguing with Kazem, Mohsen slid to the window and stuck his head out of it.

"I wish all the happiness in the world for both of you," he said.

The two friends kissed one another's cheeks affectionately. Mohsen then slid back behind the wheel, drove off a short distance and made a U-turn in the road. Kazem put his arm round Maryam's shoulders and followed the truck with his eyes. All of a sudden, he let out a heart-rending cry, the cry of a man who has just lost his closest friend.

"Mohsen Chakhaan, I'll always think of you as my best friend," he cried, but his scream was lost in the darkness.

The two beams of light coming from the headlights of the truck pierced the night and shone into Kazem and Maryam's faces. Kazem's eyes glistened with tears as he gazed at the approaching truck. Slowly, he closed his eyes, as if not wanting to see Mohsen's departure. They stood there side by side on the roadside watching the truck pass by. Kazem half raised his hand to wave a last farewell, but changed his mind, and let his hand fall.

With Mohsen gone, Kazem was now left with the only companion he had in this world – Maryam.

22

Bewildered and disorientated, Kazem stood beside the road for a moment, as if not aware of Maryam's existence beside him. Maryam stood motionless, clutching the hem of her chador.

Kazem peered through the trees and spotted the door of the teahouse, nestled at the back beneath a tumbledown wooden arbour around which coiled withered ivies and crooked, sickly-looking vine branches. A faint light gleamed through the cracked windows of the door, casting a glow on the twining plants on the arbour.

Kazem struck out towards the door and rapped on one of the windowpanes. The sound echoed dully in the deathly silence. Hearing nothing from within, he stuck his face to the grubby window and peeped inside. As he waited by the door, hoping that someone would open it, Maryam walked towards him and began to assail him with questions.

"What are you planning to do with me?" she asked. "If you think you can do whatever you like, you're wrong."

Kazem, taken by surprise like an innocent child accused of a wrongdoing, turned to look at her. "Nothing," he mumbled. "I'm not going to harm you in any way. We'll go together to Tehran. I want to marry you."

"Bah, as simple as that!" said Maryam mockingly. "Tomorrow, before the day's out, my father and the rest of my relatives will come after us. Do you think they'll forget what a terrible thing you've done – kidnapping an innocent girl and running off with her? You've no idea what a mess you've got yourself into! Right now, they will have not only informed the police but also sent some rough friends of my father after you." She crossed her arms on her chest. "Yes, they'll come and find you."

Amused, Kazem listened to Maryam's threats, not without some admiration. He smiled the smile of a man of the world who knew exactly what he was doing.

"Come on, wear this jacket," said Kazem, not paying the slightest attention to her outburst and trying to put his jacket round her shoulders.

"No, I don't want to," protested Maryam, holding on to her chador and wriggling like an obstinate little girl being asked to wear something she doesn't like. "Just leave me alone, will you."

"You'll catch a chill," insisted Kazem, like an exasperated father dealing with a headstrong daughter. "Wear this and don't kick up a fuss."

Maryam, feeling the chill in the air and exhausted, abandoned her struggle and let Kazem wrap her up in his jacket. Pulling the front of the jacket together, he looked intently into her eyes, repeating reassuringly, "You've no reason to fear me. I swear to God, I'm not going to do you any harm."

At that moment a rasping cough was heard coming from inside the teahouse. Kazem gazed at the door. A grotesque-looking shadow with two pointed horns was cast from behind the door on the windowpanes. The phantom, groaning and muttering, unlatched the door, pulled open the two leaves and stepped outside. The spectre belonged to a stooping, middle-aged man with a yellow, stubbly face, like that of an old waxwork. His head was crowned with a pointed fedora with a high, turned-up brim – the kind of hat worn normally by Turkmens. He wore a grubby white shirt, buttoned up to his neck, and a shabby, black waistcoat. He stood before the door, puffing at his cigarette and yawning noisily. Rubbing his heavy-lidded eyes, he then vigorously scratched his chest, armpits and the greasy flaxen hair that hung out from the edge of his hat. A feeble light from behind him cast his long shadow on the ground under the arbour.

"Is there a coach passing this way tonight that could take us to Tehran?" Kazem asked.

"I don't think you'll find a coach this time of night, yes," croaked the man in a ghastly gurgling voice.

"Do you have a room to let us for tonight?"

"Of course I have," answered the man, yawning loudly. "Please come in. You're most welcome. Plenty of coaches usually pass this way in the morning, yes."

Kazem turned round and caught sight of Maryam's terrified face. He pulled her towards him, put his arm round her shoulders, and walked with her to the door. They passed the man and entered the teahouse. The man drew hard at his cigarette stub and tossed it away, then followed the couple inside and latched the door.

A putrid smell, like that of a corpse-washing room tucked away at the far end of a graveyard, hung in the air. Kazem took in with a circling gaze everything in the dank room. An unshaded smudgy light bulb dangled from the ceiling. The dirty, yellowish paint was flaked in places, revealing blotches that looked like the underbelly of a diseased animal. On top of a rickety counter, under which was the cold stove, stood a rusty samovar surrounded by ranks of chipped teapots, scratched tea glasses, and piles of saucers gone yellow. The recesses under the platform were cluttered with cracked terracotta pots and small jars. Around a few clapped-out wooden tables stood some shabby bentwood chairs. Along the wall beside the counter gasoline drums and crates of bottles were heaped on top of each other. On all the walls were stuck gaudily-painted pictures of serene-looking, immaculately-clothed Muslim saints, holy shrines and grave-looking wrestling champions of past and present, alongside the Shah in full military regalia and the First Lady with perfect hair and dressed in a magnificent, pearl-studded robe. Some Koranic verses and prayers in Arabic, written in decorative calligraphy, adorned whatever gaps remained.

With his back bent, the man shambled towards the far end of the room, beckoning Kazem to follow. Like an overburdened sick mule, he snorted, continually scratching himself all over. Kazem looked at Maryam and followed him closely. The man came to a doorless, closet-like room and stepped inside it. Kazem followed him in, looking quickly around, inspecting all the objects in a swift glance. There's no room to swing a cat in this cubbyhole, he thought, throwing a glance at Maryam who stood by the entrance, looking around with a worried expression.

The man bent down in slow motion over an unmade, mangy bed tucked in the right corner of the room, spread over with a threadbare, stained blanket. He grabbed a large, lumpy bolster, chucked it to one side, pulled the blanket off the bed, and began to smooth out the rumpled sheet that covered a knobbly mattress with his hands, muttering, "I only have this one bed in my establishment."

"Not a problem," Kazem mumbled.

"But it's very comfortable and cosy, yes" spluttered the man. He sniggered meaningfully, revealing a mouth like the inside of a rotten pomegranate. "Don't worry about anything. This place is very quiet indeed." After a short pause, he asked, "Have you eaten anything?"

"Yes," said Kazem.

"All right then," said the man, waddling out of the room. As he walked past Maryam, he mumbled, "Excuse me, khanum," spun round on his heel and said, "If you needed a morsel to eat, let me know, yes?"

"All right, all right," Kazem snarled. The man was getting under his skin the way he crept at their feet like a hungry reptile. Maryam stepped inside the room, throwing a covert glance at the man. He drew himself to his full height, grabbed the edge of a large piece of moth-eaten cloth nailed to the top corners of the opening, and let it drop, unfurling like the sail of an old boat. With the fall of the cloth setting up a cloud of dust, the cubbyhole was curtained off from the rest of the teahouse. The man lingered outside for a few seconds, muttering and tittering, his bent shadow trembling on the cloth. The shadow turned round and moved away, the sound of his shuffling footfalls gradually fading into nothing.

Kazem, now alone with Maryam, looked around. Suspended from the low ceiling of the cubbyhole a grimy light bulb threw a gleam on everything, revealing the squalor. With no windows, the room had a neglected, musty air. The bare walls were streaked all over with rust-coloured patches that had oozed and dried out around cracks in the plaster. The only other piece of furniture in the room besides the bed was a bulky wooden trunk, spread over with an old rug with faded colours. Kazem stood against the wall beside the curtain. Becoming aware of Maryam's gaze, he looked at her. She regarded him with reproachful eyes. He walked over to the foot of the bed and sat down on the floor, staring at the fraying kilim. Maryam sat on the edge of the bed.

For a moment neither of them spoke. Kazem was the first to break the heavy silence.

"Are you still afraid of me?" he asked, gazing with downcast eyes at the kilim.

"For the sake of whomever you love most, take me back home," Maryam said softly.

"I'm not the kind of man you think I am," Kazem went on as if he had not heard her.

"Why did you do this, then?" She looked at him uncomprehendingly.

"What do you mean?" Kazem asked.

"Kidnapping an innocent girl," replied Maryam, sniffling and wiping her tears with the hem of her chador. Kazem lowered his eyes. A shadow of a wry smile passed over his lips.

"You'll be the last thing I've stolen," Kazem said musingly.

"How can I believe that you'll not do any harm to me?"

"I'm a changed man, Maryam." Kazem sighed, stood up slowly, and walked to the wall. "I know that I was a drinking, gambling, good-for-nothing rogue, and the most notorious scoundrel in Hosseinabaad. But I'm no more like that.

"As soon as we arrive at Tehran," he said, "I'll take you straight away to a registry office and have you engaged to me. Then I'll start looking for a job." He leaned against the wall and went on talking wistfully, as if to himself. "I'll work hard like a decent man. Then we will live a happy life. We'll have children, many of them. At noontime, after you've washed a pile of clothes, hung them on the washing line and cooked some lunch, I'll be returning home from my work with a bowl of yogurt in one hand and some bread in the other. We'll talk, joke about things, laugh and play with the kids, who'll soon grow up." He paused, his eyes wide open. "We'll get old together, and then..."

The peaceful, rhythmical breathing of Maryam brought Kazem back to reality. With her head leaning against the wall, her hands crossed over her chest and with her chador slipped down on her shoulders, she had gone to sleep. Kazem tiptoed towards her. Gently, he rested her head on the bolster, lifted her legs up and placed them on the bed, before covering them with the chador. He spread the blanket over her.

This done, Kazem walked up to the trunk and sat down beside it, facing away from the bed. Hugging his knees to his chest, he rested his head on his folded arms and fell into an uneasy slumber. His short bouts of stupor were continually disturbed by vague, chaotic dreams. Then the high-pitched squeal of the brakes of a truck coming to a stop somewhere close-by startled him awake. Someone began to talk, sniggering loudly at intervals. The door of the teahouse was opened and some heavy footsteps approached from the outside. Two men greeted each other in a familiar manner, talking and laughing loudly.

Kazem drifted briefly into deep sleep. The voices of the men grew more and more indistinct. But then he heard footsteps, one stumping and the other shuffling, getting louder and louder as they approached the cubbyhole. Mindful of protecting Maryam and anxious as to what was going on out there, he struggled to keep his eyes open. But being utterly worn out, his eyelids became heavy and soon closed. Hovering between sleep and wakefulness, he vaguely made out the shadows of two figures cast on the curtain, like those of marionettes held up behind a thin cloth. One belonged to a tall, stout, threatening-looking man that towered over a dwarfish figure with a bowed back. They whispered and laughed between themselves, like two conspirators about to execute a foul deed.

Kazem then made out, as if through a thick fog, the shadow of the little bent man coming closer to the curtain. An eye, lustreless as that of a corpse, peeped through a tear high up in the curtain. The shadow retreated and there was a confused conversation. Then the large, barrel-chested shadow approached the curtain. Hairy fingers appeared from behind the curtain, clutched its edge and pulled it back a little. The head of a thuggish-looking man with a black handlebar moustache and thick sideburns poked in. His large eyes rolled as he scanned the room. As soon as he saw Maryam, his eyes opened wide with lustful pleasure and an evil smile cracked his broad face. The face soon disappeared behind the curtain, leaving behind it a pungent smell that wafted towards Kazem. The stink of *arrack* mixed with bad breath filled the cubbyhole. The shadows put their heads together and spoke in undertones with the bent one fluttering his hands before him as if reassuring the other of possible eventualities that he would take care of. The small figure retreated, leaving the big one standing behind the curtain.

After a moment's hesitation, the large figure pulled the curtain aside, stepped gingerly into the room and tiptoed towards Maryam, who was curled up under the blanket. As he began to pull the blanket off her body, she whimpered. Kazem awoke fully to see a man stooping over her. He vigorously rubbed his eyes and looked again. Maryam's sudden scream confirmed that he was not dreaming; someone was really trying to pull the chador off Maryam's body. In the blink of an eye, Kazem sprang up and pounced on the man's back in a single bound. Maryam, now wide awake, kicked out violently and scratched at her assailant's face. The man grabbed her shoulders, trying to pin her down on the bed.

"Who are you? Get off me!" Maryam yelled. Taken by surprise, the man swung round violently and shook Kazem off his back. Grabbing Kazem with his powerful hands, he hurled him out of the cubbyhole before falling upon Maryam like a wild beast on defenceless prey. Having fallen flat on his back on top of a table, Kazem bounced back on his feet. He leapt into the room and jumped up on the man's broad back from behind. Arms locked round his neck like iron clamps, Kazem tried to push him away from Maryam. In order to tackle Kazem, the man let go of her. He flailed his arms in the air, bumping Kazem around furiously. Managing to clasp his hands around Kazem's head, he banged him hard against the wall beside the curtain. Kazem, his feet pushed behind him against the wall, shoved the man forward with all his might, sending him staggering so that he fell flat on his face on the trunk. Before he knew it, Kazem had set upon him like a wild cat. The man threw a punch, but Kazem parried, swiped him back on his right cheek, grabbed his shirt, lifted him, and threw him on the bed. Maryam sat up on the bed, her knees drawn up and clasping her legs. Cringing in fear, she leant back against the wall, covering herself with the blanket and crying feebly. Kazem head-butted the big man on his nose so hard that he had to cover his face with his hands, groaning like a wounded bear. Kazem then delivered a heavy kick with the flat of his foot to his belly, which sent him lurching backwards. As the man floundered out of the room, he became entangled in the curtain, pulling it down off the nails. He then bumped into a chair, fell against a table, and lay spread-eagled on the floor. Kazem leapt out of the cubbyhole. He sat astride the man's chest, raining punch after punch on his face in uncontrollable rage. The man struggled in vain to shield his face from Kazem's blows.

But, inflamed by lust for Maryam, he was not going to give up easily. He pulled his hands down his face as if tearing way his already ghastly mask to reveal a more sinister, blood-drenched one. Dark blood gushed from his smashed nose. As he let out a groan, blood spurted from his mouth. Yet he mustered all his strength and kicked Kazem hard in the groin, throwing him to one side. After knocking over crates of bottles, gasoline drums and chairs, and smashing some teapots, Kazem finally grabbed a chair and smashed it over the head of his opponent. The sturdy intruder fell on the floor with a thud, like a sack of rotten potatoes. Streaks of dark-red blood oozed out of his scalp, glistening in his bushy black hair. He ceased to struggle. His body twitched and, blood-shot eyes fixed on the ceiling, he lay groaning in agony. Breathing hard, Kazem glanced up and saw Maryam at the threshold of the cubbyhole with her chador slid down on her shoulders, watching him. Her cheeks had gone chalk-white.

The teahouse keeper, who was hiding behind a tattered cloth hanging in front of an alcove, all of a sudden showed up. He shuffled towards Kazem and planted himself beside the half-dead intruder, who was grunting like a dying boar. He looked at Kazem with terrified eyes.

"You killed Safdar Farmun," he spluttered.

Seeing Kazem glaring at him and too scared to think straight, he scurried, like a rat, back to the alcove. Kazem ran after him, pulled the cloth off the wall, disappeared behind the curtain, and beat the man until he was silenced. He emerged from the alcove and looked at Maryam, who was leaning against the wall, shivering. He dashed to the door and, looking out of the windows, saw a truck parked outside the teahouse. Guessing that the truck belonged to the intruder, he ran back and squatted beside the man, patting his pockets, where he found a bunch of keys. In a sink, he let the tap run on his bloodstained hands, and dried them by rubbing them on his shirt. After dusting the dirt off his trousers, he grabbed Maryam's trembling hand, and dragged her to the door. Pushing her out first, he stepped outside, shut the door, and began to walk calmly towards the truck with hand round Maryam's waist.

Exactly at that moment, another truck pulled up in front of the parked one and two men got out. They strode towards the door of the teahouse, swinging their arms as truck-drivers do. As they got closer to Kazem and

Maryam, the older man glanced at her and poked his half-wit-looking mate in the ribs, muttering something about her. Kazem glowered at him.

"Did you say something?" Kazem growled.

"No, no, nothing," gabbled the fellow, unnerved by Kazem's tone of voice. "I was just telling my mate that what a lovely night it is."

"Well, I bloody don't think so," Kazem snapped. To stop the men from going into the teahouse, he added, "Don't waste your time; there's nothing to eat in this place."

"Whatever you say, bro," the man stammered. He grabbed his mate's arm and pulled him towards their truck, into which they climbed and at once took themselves off.

Kazem led Maryam gently to the truck, opened the door and helped her up into the cabin. Climbing into the driver's seat, he sat himself behind the wheel, turned on the engine, and drove off.

23

The road was dark, occasionally lit up by the headlights of vehicles coming towards them. Kazem had his headlights on full and did not bother to dip them. He drove roughly, leaning forward, his elbows almost on the wheel. From time to time he glanced at Maryam whose eyes were fixed on the road. At a safe distance from the teahouse, Kazem turned into an unmade by-road. The road was pitted and bumpy and the headlights shone on thick bracken, nettles and overgrown reeds that straggled on either side of the road.

After a while, he found a spot far away from the main road. He stopped, turned off the engine, and switched off the headlights, leaving the small cabin light on. He propped his elbows on the wheel, placed his chin on them, and fell into deep thought. He kept looking at the rear-view mirror, as if he expected somebody to spring out from the shadows at any moment. Feeling Maryam's furtive glances like heat on his cheek, Kazem turned and regarded her. They both sat there perfectly still. The unearthly serenity of the world outside the truck was disturbed only by the gentlest of breezes that caressed the desolate-looking wild plants, making them rustle and sigh.

Kazem rested his head on the wheel.

"Why did it all end like this, Maryam?" He leaned his head against the back of the seat and fell silent once again.

"I'm done for now," he said after a pause. "I've beaten two men up and I don't know if they're alive or dead. As soon as we arrive in Tehran, the police will come after me. When I'm caught, I'll have to go back to that cursed jail again for the devil knows how long this time. And if the two men are dead, they'll definitely hang me." He glanced at Maryam. "You're free to go, as I'm now in serious trouble. First thing in the morning, I'll find a safe coach and send you back to your parents." After another pause he added wistfully, "I wanted to marry you and start a decent life. But it wasn't to be."

He gently pushed away a lock of hair which had fallen over Maryam's eye. She regarded him kindly.

"I'm not going to leave you, Kazem," she said softly, tears starting to her eyes. "I'll stay with you forever."

"Do you really mean it, Maryam?" said Kazem in disbelief, gazing into her eyes.

"Yes, I do."

"I worship the ground you walk on," Kazem murmured rapturously. Then his expression darkened.

"But it's too late now, Maryam," he said. "I don't want you to get into trouble for me. I had different plans in mind. I wanted to make you happy." He shook his head ruefully. "Well, this was my lot. There is no chance I can make you happy. We can't be together. You'll go back to your home."

"I'll never go back without you, Kazem," Maryam said, looking at him directly. "I'll not leave you alone. I love you, Kazem."

"I think the world of you," Kazem said. "These could be the last hours we spend together."

"Don't say anything, Kazem." Maryam put two fingers on his lips. Kazem, grasping her hand, kissed them. He then buried his head in Maryam's neck, kissed her cheek, and finally their lips touched. Kazem put his arm round Maryam's shoulder. Like a trusting child, she nestled her head against his neck, closed her eyes, and soon fell into a peaceful sleep. Kazem remained awake for some time, listening to her soft and rhythmical breathing. Then he, too, was overcome with sleep.

* * * *

Kazem opened his eyes, blinked several times, and looked around. The pale, slanting rays of the sun, now up on the horizon, were pouring into the cabin. The distant, muffled roar of traffic could be heard on the main highway. He looked around, taking everything in. Barren fields stretched out to the horizon, across which lay hills and mountains veiled in a purplish haze.

"Maryam, Maryam," he whispered gently in her ear, "wake up. We've to crack on. Sooner or later somebody might come this way."

Maryam quivered against his arm. She sat up and pulled her chador up over her head. Kazem started the engine, and, after a few jolts, moved forward in the hope of finding a main road that could lead to Tehran. After a short while, he hit another road and began to drive along it. Soon he found himself driving beside a railway track.

After an hour, the traffic in front gradually slowed down and finally came to a standstill. Kazem pulled up behind a car in front of which was a very long trailer carrying a huge cargo of tyres stacked on top of each other. Anxiety spread inside him like a drop of ink in clear water. He looked at Maryam and laid his forehead on the wheel. Looking up again, he opened the door, stuck his head out, and saw a long line of vehicles on the road ahead. Some of them had pulled off the road and among these hustled a swarm of military men with rifles slung across their shoulders. They strode around the vehicles, poking their heads into them. The roadblocks were too massive in order to catch an amateur kidnapper like him, Kazem thought. What were the military doing there in full force? What was going on? Why were they in such huge numbers?

Kazem shut the door and waited. Some gendarmes walked towards the front of the trailer. One gendarme, following his officer's order, tapped the window with the muzzle of his rifle, gesturing to the driver to step outside. Another climbed up into the cabin, emerged after a few seconds, and said something to the officer, who then asked another gendarme to inspect the rest of the trailer. This man sauntered calmly round the whole length of the vehicle, examining the sides. He bent down to look under it and tapped the tyres. Kazem shut the door and stared vacantly at Maryam, who sat there looking worried. The throbbing of the truck's engine made the decorative tassels, hung in a row on the top edge of the windscreen, shiver like baby canaries perched on a branch.

Kazem opened the door of the truck. Leaping down, he slammed the door shut, ran round to the passenger door, and asked Maryam to step down. Once outside, she threw anxious glances right and left and arranged her chador round her body and head. By now, she had put her trust wholeheartedly in Kazem. The gendarmes could be heard ordering the trailer's driver to get into his vehicle. Kazem swiftly opened the large tool box just behind the cabin. Taking Maryam's hand, he whispered to her to get into the box. Trustingly, she crawled in and curled up on her side in the box, pulling in her chador. Kazem clicked the hatch in its catch, and locked the door, checking the lock with trembling hands to see if it was secure.

"You're not afraid?" Kazem whispered against the box, peeking inside it through a slit.

"No, no, I'm not," came Maryam's muffled voice.

Kazem climbed back to the cabin and settled himself behind the wheel. As he lit a cigarette, he peered over his cupped hands, keeping his eyes on the gendarmes, following their every movement. He went on smoking in a composed manner. Led by the stocky morose-looking officer with a thick moustache, the gendarmes marched towards the truck, clutching their riffles. No sooner had they reached the truck than Kazem opened the door, climbed down and stood upright, as if standing at attention.

"Is there anyone else in the truck?" the officer asked gruffly as he opened the door and climbed up into the cabin, not so much as glancing at Kazem.

"No, Captain," Kazem said, "only myself."

The officer shut the door behind him. His head bobbed up and down as he searched all the nooks and crannies under the dashboard. Kazem stood, puffing away coolly at his cigarette. As he waited, he kept casting oblique glances at the two young gendarmes who stood there motionless, eyeballing him with fed-up expressions. Once the search was over, the officer opened the door, stepped down, and shut the door. He then motioned Kazem to get in the cabin.

"Forgive me, Captain," Kazem dared to ask before opening the door, "may I ask what you're looking for?

"Smuggled opium," replied the ill-tempered officer, beckoning the two gendarmes to follow him as he walked round the front of the truck to the passenger door. Kazem sat behind the wheel, smoking and watching them out of the corner of his eye. He felt his heart beating against his chest. He heard the officer ordering the two gendarmes to look at the other vehicles queuing up behind the truck. An ominous silence ensued. Kazem heard the faint clinking of the padlock on the toolbox. The clinking stopped, and the passenger door opened wide. Yet again the officer stood there.

"Open the toolbox so that I can take a look at it," he ordered.

Kazem glanced at him silently, took out the keys from the ignition, twirled them a bit, and opened the door, playing for time. He sauntered round the bonnet to stand before the officer, his eyes darting from the officer to the toolbox and back.

"Hurry up," grunted the officer, "we've a lot of vehicles to search."

"Whatever you say, Captain."

"We searched the truck carefully, Captain," one of the gendarmes shouted, "and there's nothing there."

"Go ahead and take a look at the lorry behind this one," the captain yelled back at him. He stood waiting for Kazem to open the toolbox. With his heart in his mouth, Kazem took his time finding the right key, looking, from time to time, out of the corner of his eye at the officer and trying to appear at ease. Upon finding the key, he inserted it into the padlock, turned it slowly, and opened the lock. As the padlock dangled on the latch, he heard the two gendarmes yell, "We found the goods, Captain."

"Never mind about the box," the captain said. "You can drive off now."

Like a general who has won another battle, the officer marched off triumphantly towards the lorry, swinging his arms. Kazem followed him with his eyes, smiling. He looked about him, stuck his head close to the box, and said in a low voice, “Stay there, Maryam. Everything’s all right.” He then locked the box, shaking the padlock to make sure it was secure. In the cab, he looked into the rear-view mirrors, before pulling out of the restricted space, and trundling off until he reached the front of the long line of vehicles. Once on the open road, he pressed down on the accelerator.

Making sure he had driven far enough from the roadblocks, Kazem stopped the truck. He leapt out, ran to the toolbox, opened it, and helped Maryam to get out. As he drove off once again, he kept glancing at her.

“We were so lucky,” Kazem said. “That was the luckiest escape in my life.”

“I hope you’ll be lucky from now on,” Maryam said.

“I’m terrified, Maryam,” he said. “Never in my life have I been so frightened.”

“Everything will be all right, Kazem,” said Maryam, looking at him reassuringly.

24

After half-an-hour, they turned into a road that ran parallel to a railway track. They had barely driven for ten minutes when the engine began to groan, making the truck jolt forward. After a short distance it stopped. Kazem's efforts to restart the engine were hopeless.

"Damn it!" He slapped the wheel with both hands. "I think we've run out of petrol."

"What do we do now?" said Maryam.

"Don't know," replied Kazem, looking around in the hope of finding a solution. All of a sudden, the whistling of a train coming from behind the truck could be heard. Kazem peered into the rear-view mirror and saw in it the reflection of a train crawling along the tracks like a black caterpillar at a distance, belching greyish smoke into the hazy air.

"A train's coming this way," he said. "Let's get out." Maryam jumped down and joined Kazem, who was peering in the direction from which the train was approaching. He had already planned another reckless action – that they should jump with on that train, come what may.

In order to reach the track they had to cross some scrubland.

"We must catch that train," said Kazem, looking Maryam up and down. "You can't run across here with that chador wrapped round your body. Let me carry it." He snatched the chador off her, grabbed her hand, and they began to run as fast as they could, jumping over clods of earth baked under the cruel sun.

Kazem helped Maryam to manoeuvre her way through the small bushes with needle-like thorns. He was surprised to find out how agile she had become without her chador, leaping over the obstacles like a gazelle. With her long hair fluttering, her brow glistening with beads of sweat, her wide-open eyes, her lemon-like breasts bobbing up and down under her frilly dress, her fast breathing, and her shapely marble thighs revealed at every jump from under the short flowery dress, she had indeed turned into a beautiful gazelle.

The train was drawing closer by the minute, its muffled whistle ringing in the still air.

"We must run faster to reach the tracks before the train gets here," shouted Kazem, quickening his pace and tightening his clasp on Maryam's hand.

As the train drew close, Kazem could see that it was a freight train. He felt reassured by this, as freight trains move more slowly than passenger trains. They reached the track at the same time as the train passed. Kazem thought it would be best to run along beside the train until he could find an empty section which they could climb on to.

As soon as he spotted one, Kazem ran closer to it, dragging Maryam behind him. To free his other hand, he chucked the troublesome chador on to it. It blew off, but caught on a nail on the edge of the carriage, flapping in the strong current of air. Kazem finally managed to grab a piece of metal that stuck out at an angle at the end of the section. With something to hold on to, they both began to run alongside the train, nearly stumbling. Kazem leapt and put one foot on a small step. He dangled there precariously for a moment. Lifting the other foot, he tightened his clutch on Maryam's hand. Maryam struggled to fasten her sweaty hand on Kazem's. Her dainty little hand could easily slip off any second, he thought.

"Grab my arm with your other hand," he yelled, his voice distorted by the horrible thought of losing Maryam.

With a mighty effort, she jumped as high as she could and grabbed Kazem's forearm with her free hand. Kazem felt in that delicate hand a powerful upsurge of life and hope that kept her clinging to him.

Gathering all his strength, Kazem heaved Maryam up. Her feet were now off the ground, gliding along the track. With her feet dangling in the air, she looked like a delicate little doll held out of the window of a moving coach by a child. Finally, after a desperate struggle, Kazem hoisted Maryam up to the step, then pulled her up on to the section and climbed up on it himself. Drained of energy, they collapsed flat on their backs, panting and breathing hard. They remained there, gazing at the clear sky that was darkened every now and then by puffs of the locomotive's greyish smoke as it was blown towards the back of the train.

Looking towards the back of the section, Kazem realised they could lean against it and be safer that way. They crawled there and sat up against the low back. Kazem leaned over, grabbed the fluttering chador, and covered Maryam's body with it. He put his arm round her shoulder and she nestled against his chest.

When the cargo train slowed down near a small town, they jumped down, running across some rusty rail tracks, before arriving in the backyard of the railway station. They wandered through narrow streets and found the market-place. Kazem bought a pair of cheap shoes for Maryam to wear as her feet were bruised and scratched. He then found a small garage in front of which a coach was parked, about to depart. The ill-tempered driver sat behind the wheel puffing away at his cigarette, sticking his head out from time to time, yelling at his mate and some of the passengers. Kazem asked if the coach was heading for Tehran.

"Yes, yes, bro," shouted the driver irritably.

"When are you leaving?" Kazem asked politely.

"In twenty minutes flat."

Kazem rushed back to Maryam, who was standing a few paces away, covering herself carefully in her chador. They walked over to a nearby grocer and bought some cheese and fresh grapes. From the baker beside the grocers' they bought a freshly baked *sangak* bread. They then walked over to the coach, found a seat, and settled down. The coach soon started amidst loud *salawats* and the all-too-familiar racket. Once the coach left the town, hitting the open road, Kazem and Maryam began to eat some of the food in silence. They now looked like those young peasants who, just married, have decided to leave their native village to seek their fortune in the capital city.

25

It was just after midnight when they arrived at Sepah Square. As the coach slowly drove round it, the enormous old buildings bordering the sides of the square came into view. The driver manoeuvred his way into the large garage at the far corner of the square. Amidst the howling of children, being shaken like ragdolls by their parents to wake up, and the barrage of *salawats*, the sleep-ridden passengers began to scramble over one another in the half-darkness of the coach to get off. Kazem, worried about inexperienced Maryam being trampled underfoot in that barbaric rush towards the door, asked her to wait till everybody had left the coach.

Once out of the coach, Kazem, holding Maryam's hand, pushed his way through the throng of passengers who were frantically groping around the coach to get their hands on their belongings wrapped in large bundles of cloth or stuffed into suitcases. Whenever they got hold of the poor driver's mate, they kept blaming him for not being able to find their bundles.

Upon leaving the garage, Kazem and Maryam stood side by side outside the gate and looked around. Street pedlars of lamb's liver and kidney kebabs, roasted corn, boiled beetroot and lentil stew stood behind their carts, lit by small pressurized lanterns. Around each stall stood a clutch of hungry, newly arrived travellers either munching hot kebabs or noisily slurping their lentil stews. Kazem and Maryam walked to a lamb's-liver kebab stall, bought two skewers wrapped in *taftoon* bread, crossed the roundabout and sat on one of the benches.

The monolithic, symmetrical facade of the Town Hall, crowned by a gigantic, helmet-shaped, dull-grey cupola, the point of its dome peeping out from behind the pediment, flanked by two smaller ones on each end of the long building, sprawled in the gloom along the north side of the square. Smack in the middle of the square stood a cuboid-shaped monument on each angle of which were attached bulky, cylindrical stone columns. On top of each column sat bronze statues of two bulls, attached to one another by their torsos, each glowering in opposite directions. The monument was set on a massive block of granite on each corner of which stood bronze statues of royal guards in front of the columns, attired in the style of soldiers of another Persian emperor of faraway times, their heads bowed in respect and gripping their long, sharply pointed spears held upright. The equestrian statue of the Reza Khan the Cossack, the founder of the Pahlavi Dynasty, in full military regalia, perched on top of the monument. The awesome, thickly moustached father of the ruling Shah sat erect and proud as an all-powerful monarch on his magnificent mount, calmly gripping the reins with his left hand and clutching a riding crop in the other. He scowled piercingly from under his bushy eyebrows, shadowed by the brim of his military hat, to far distant horizons beyond the roofs of the capital city, trailing the motley backward Iranian peoples behind him on the relentless march towards modernity.

Some bored-looking policemen marched wearily around the monument, guarding it out of fear of displeasing the present king. The other colossal buildings such as the Police Department, Criminal Investigation Department, and Telecommunications stood, bleak and uninviting, on either side of the square. The large rectangular pond in the middle of the square, surrounded by a wooden fence and occasional ornate lampposts, glistened as still and dark as tar. Around the square strutted policemen, suspiciously eyeing the idle folk who, having nowhere to go, lingered here. Some peasants, forced to leave their native villages and hamlets to come to the city in a mad rush, wrapped up in their rags, sprawled along the outer edge of the square, their heads resting on their cloth bundles. They all seemed worn-out and weary, thought Kazem, dreaming no doubt of a better future in that glittering brothel of a capital city, of their wretched lives in their native villages, and of the loved ones left behind.

Kazem lit up a cigarette and drew hard at it, looking around in the hope of finding one of those men who knock about, day and night, around the garages to find newcomers to the city who do not know where to go and where to stay.

As he puffed away, Kazem became aware of a seedy-looking, powerfully built middle-aged man with a thick moustache who was eyeing them from a short distance. Constantly looking around over him, the man wandered towards them and stood beside Kazem.

"Looking somewhere to stay for the night?" said the man in a low voice, throwing a sideways glance at Kazem.

"Yes," replied Kazem, giving him a questioning look and automatically putting his arm round Maryam's shoulders.

"I've got just the room for you." The man stroked his moustache with the palm of his hand.

"We want something cheap and comfortable enough to stay in for a while," Kazem said.

"That can be done, too."

"If it's somewhere down in these neighbourhoods, it would be perfect."

"That's not a problem," the man answered. "I've got somewhere traditional and nice down in the neighbourhood of Execution Square if you're willing to share the courtyard, water, and the privy with the other lodgers."

"We can live with that," agreed Kazem, glancing at Maryam who sat beside him, silently listening to the conversation.

"Let's get cracking, then," said the man, gesturing to them to follow him.

He led the way and Kazem, holding Maryam's arm, followed. Once out of Sepah Square, the man walked briskly down the deserted Khayyam Avenue at the end of which he arrived at Galubandak Crossroad. He entered one of the streets and guided them through a labyrinth of dimly lit, quiet alleys and lanes. After a long trek through another set of alleys, they arrived at Execution Square. From there they took a narrow street, turning into yet more winding alleys.

Finally, they entered a sombre-looking, dead-end alley, lit by a bulb dangling from the top of a lone lamppost. As Kazem walked along the slime-choked gutter that ran in the middle of the alley, he glanced at the wooden doors of the houses wedged into the cracked walls from which half-smashed bricks stuck out. The man stood in front of the worm-eaten door of a house tucked away at the end of the alley.

"Finally, we arrived," he said.

He thrust his hand into his coat pocket, took out a bundle of keys, inserted one into the keyhole, and pushed the door open. He pulled aside a thick black cloth that hung behind the door, stepped down three steps and beckoned to the couple to follow him. Kazem peered into the large, gloomy courtyard, filled with a foul odour coming from a dented gasoline barrel choked with decaying trash, placed near the door. Barely had he taken a few steps when another powerful stench wafting out of the privy on the other side assailed his nostrils. In the middle of the courtyard was a round *hauz* with its still water gleaming through the dark leaves on a number of pots placed on its edge. As he carefully trod his way on the uneven cobblestones, his head brushed against tattered pieces of plastic and the remains of kite tails that dangled from the sooty branches of two short trees. Before reaching the flight of steps that led to the terrace, he had to negotiate washing lines that criss-crossed the courtyard. The doors of the rooms along the terrace were left open a crack. Straw blinds were rolled on top of the doors. At the back of each door hung a filthy cloth, billowing gently in the warm night breeze. Set in the wall in front of casement windows, raised a little above the floor, was rusty metallic latticework with arabesque patterns. The drawn muslin curtains behind the latticework ballooned languidly. The fitful, heavy breathing of the sleeping lodgers, interrupted now and then by groans, could be heard.

The man stood in front of a door of a room at the end of the terrace. He opened it, stepped in, and pulled the curtain aside. After flicking on the light switch, he motioned the couple in.

"This is the room," he said in a low voice.

No sooner had Kazem, followed by Maryam, stepped inside the room, than a musty odour mingled with the smells of paraffin, dust, cheap tobacco, mouldy raisins, roasted peas and stale bread hit his nostrils. Kazem took in the sparse furniture in the anaemic light of a naked light bulb hanging limply from the ceiling. Rust-coloured patches adorned the whitewashed walls. The floor was covered with a large rug whose rich, flowery patterns had faded due to age and overuse by countless lodgers. Close to the angle of the walls nestled a bulky commode, with one of its doors gaping open, revealing some objects inside. Two large backrests, encased in shabby, wine-coloured rug cases, were propped against a wall. Leaned against the opposite wall in the far corner were the bedclothes, wrapped up in a chequered black-and-white cloth, across the top of which lay two bolsters. A large, tarnished mirror, set in a dark-brown wooden frame, was placed on the ledge of the opposite wall. Beside the mirror sat a chunky, battered radio, left there as if from the age that the invention first appeared in Tehran. A yellowed and cracked electric wire snaked out of the radio and vanished into an outlet in the wall. A grimy piece of fabric with faded floral patterns hung from two nails concealed the alcove at the far left corner. A rusty, dirty-green Aladdin paraffin heater stood beside the alcove. An old tin samovar stood upright in a narrow window recess in the wall. An overused teapot, tea glasses, saucers, and a sugar bowl were placed, all upside-down, on a piece of teacloth beside the samovar. A hefty tin carafe, flanked by two tin tumblers, stood beside the tea things. The wooden doors of the casement were shut.

"How much for each night?" asked Kazem.

"Only ten tomans a night, including electricity and water bills," came the reply quickly.

"All right then," Kazem agreed, fishing out a crumpled twenty-toman note from his jacket pocket and handing it over to the man. Snatching the note, he handed the keys to Kazem, wished them a happy stay, walked out of the room, and vanished into the night.

Kazem shut the door, took off his shoes and stepped on the carpet. Maryam did the same. He then walked to the alcove, pushed aside the cloth, and peeped inside. Cool air smelling of damp chalk and clay hit his nostrils. Barely visible in the half-darkness of the alcove, some dented grubby pots and pans heaped on the corner of a wooden table gleamed, all nestled against an upturned, hefty copper cauldron. He wandered back to one of the large cushions, sat down, and rested one hand on his knee and gazed at Maryam, who was standing before the mirror, contemplating herself. She let her chador slip down over her shoulders, gently pushing aside a lock of stray hair from her brow. She walked to the window and sat beside the recess, gazing at the tea things. A languid smile flitted on Kazem's lips.

"You've never lived in a lodging house before," Kazem said, breaking the heavy silence. "I know this will not be easy for you."

"I don't mind," said Maryam in a low voice, looking at him. "I'll soon get used to it."

Kazem got up and went to sit beside her.

"As soon as you become my legitimate wife and I find a decent job, we'll leave this place and find somewhere better," he said.

"Good job that man didn't ask us about our personal details," said Maryam, smiling like a little girl who has managed to get away with something naughty.

"This lodging house is so out-of-the-way that I don't reckon your dad and his men will be able to find us here," Kazem reassured her, looking back at the door.

Maryam smiled.

"You ought to be very careful when looking for a job," she said, putting her hand on his and looking him intently in the eye.

"Don't worry about that," Kazem said, meeting her eyes. "Tehran is like a jungle in which no one knows who you are and where you've come from. With a cap and a pair of dark glasses, not a soul would recognise me."

They spread the bedclothes on the floor and slept like two exhausted children.

26

The noise of women bawling at one another or singing loudly, children whining nonstop, and the chanting of street vendors woke Kazem up. He listened, wondering for a moment where he was. Through the chinks of the shut doors of the window slanting rays of sunlight cut across the room like sharp blades. He got up, walked to the window, opened it, and pulled the string of the straw blind, rolling it up. Dazzling bright light flooded into the room. He then put on his clothes and shoes and stepped out of the room onto the terrace. He blinked, scanning the courtyard with sleepy eyes. Some women lodgers were squatting around the *hauz*, washing clothes and chattering at the tops of their voices. Others were lumbering among the washing lines, carrying the washed clothes in large tin trays. Kazem climbed down the steps and walked to the *hauz.* He greeted the women, then squatted down beside the long-necked tap, put his hand under the running water, and chucked handfuls of water to his face, not so much as glancing at any of the women who were eyeing him on the sly as if he were a rare animal. Pulling his handkerchief from his jacket pocket, he vigorously dried his hands and face and hurried back to the room. Maryam had woken up and was folding and piling up the bedclothes in the cloth cover. Kazem helped her to knot the cloth and push it against the corner.

"While I nip out to get some bread, cheese, tea and sugar, you set up the samovar," said Kazem. "The lodgers are very noisy here. If they ask about us, just tell them we're married and have come to Tehran to work." Maryam nodded, picking up her chador from the floor.

* * * *

The first thing in Kazem's mind was to make Maryam his legal wife so that if her people came after them their status would be legally watertight. Just after midmorning, Kazem, with Maryam, set off to find the nearest mosque to see if he could find a mollah to marry them according to Islamic custom. As it was the holy month of Ramadan, the lanes and streets in the neighbourhood were deserted.

After some wandering about and asking some passers-by as to the whereabouts of the nearest mosque, Kazem finally found one. As they approached the mosque, the mournful chants of the muezzin could be heard, announcing noon prayers to the faithful. Kazem and Maryam followed the men from the neighbourhood who were rushing towards the mosque. He asked Maryam to wait outside while he went in to see if he could find a mollah who could do the job. He asked a pale-looking seminary student with a downy black beard and bulging eyes if he could find a qualified mollah who was an expert in marrying people.

"I think Mollah Hossein has got all the necessary expertise and know-how to help you, brother," said the fledgling mollah, gathering his newly made *aba* round his scrawny body.

"Excuse me, Agha," asked Kazem, "where can I find this Mollah Hossein?"

"He's standing at the bottom of the pulpit leading the prayers as an imam," replied the student. "He's got a black turban and wears spectacles. You won't miss him."

After thanking the young man, Kazem strode into the small courtyard. He stood beside the wide-open door of the prayers hall, took off his shoes and entered. A miasma of foul odours, given off by unwashed bare feet and bad breath due to hunger and sweat, made his nostrils flare. Although the noon prayers had already finished, many of the men, being overenthusiastic, were performing extra prayers formulated for them by all sorts of dead and dying ayatollahs. The dull murmur of the Arabic words and phrases filled the hall, making it echo like a nest of wasps. Others, who looked starving from self-inflicted hunger, were sitting cross-legged in small clutches chatting quietly, idling the time away for want of nothing better to do until they broke their fast after dusk. The air in the hall was stifling. The sound of Kazem's footsteps was deadened by the tattered kilims spread upon chipped straw mats, trodden upon by countless pious folk.

Kazem spotted the mullah sitting cross-legged facing the pulpit nestled in an arched niche. The man of god was hunched over a copy of the Koran placed open on his lap. Cloaked in his well-worn camelhair *aba* and with his frayed black turban bobbing up and down, he reminded Kazem of a large yellowish-brown dung-beetle crouching over bits of manure, its legs tucked under it, noisily munching away at juicy rotten matter. That had to be Mollah Hossein.

Kazem tiptoed towards the mollah. Once close enough, he could hear the guttural voice mumbling some verses in Arabic. Upon reaching him, Kazem bent down and asked politely if he was Mollah Hossein. The man of god nodded while carrying on mournfully with the recitation of the holy verses. Kazem whispered his request into the large hairy ears of the pious man, who motioned to Kazem to sit beside him. Kazem sat on his haunches with his hands rested on his knees, as a child sits respectfully beside a great-uncle to whom he has been introduced for the first time.

Kazem went on looking at Mollah Hossein out of the corner of his eye. It was not difficult for a man like Kazem to read this clergyman like an open book, as he did the others of his type. Through his own experiences and what he had heard about these mollahs who crawled in every hamlet, village, town and obscure places of the big cities looking for half-witted victims, Kazem saw before him another typical small-time mollah from the poor quarters of Tehran. Like others of his profession, he was a vicious predator who sponged off the uprooted, hard-working, hopelessly superstitious peasants by spouting all kinds of Arabic gibberish.

Smelling the sweet scent of ready cash, Mollah Hossein's nose twitched like the snout of a starved rat spotting scraps of offal in the gutter. He quickened his recitation, ended it, and shut the holy book. He then raised his head sluggishly, rubbed his face with the palms of his hands, and stroke his hennaed beard with his fleshy fingers. He picked up his *Shahmaghsood* rosary and began telling his beads, mumbling some more prayers. Finally, he turned his head and peered over the rim of his spectacles at Kazem, eyeing him quizzically with his prying eyes like a pair of burning charcoals. He was a well-built man with dark, arched eyebrows, aquiline nose, and lustful, shapely lips, above which grew a scanty moustache. On his chin a well-combed black beard flourished. From under his bushy eyebrows, unsmiling, he fixed his penetrating gaze on Kazem.

He began to speak in a monotonous voice as if he were preaching to an invisible devout audience seated in front of him, meanwhile beading his rosary with his flabby red fingers.

"How fortunate we all are, my son, that our all-encompassing Sharia Law and the sayings of the Prophet in *Hadith* have prescribed all the solutions for every aspect of human life and condition from cradle to grave. These laws and commandments have made available to humanity all the remedies for all the possible ills that can afflict Muslims in all societies – past, present, and future generations to come. According to Sharia Law, and the strict decrees of the Messenger of Allah, every Muslim *must* find a wife or a husband. Our glorious religion can be likened, if you like, to a monumental edifice built on two sturdy pillars, half of it supported by marriage and the other by a strict regime of piety and absolute devotion to Allah. Matrimony, my son, keeps a man and a woman from the temptations of Satan who has vowed, since he was kicked out of paradise by the Almighty Himself for tempting our mother, Eve, to lead good people astray from the path of virtue and righteousness. The almighty Allah, in His infinite wisdom, has created men and women not only to keep the human race going, but also to procreate more Muslims to populate the whole earth to keep the victorious flag of Islam fluttering in every land. The delicate female sex, with all her secret charms, is an extra bonus for the faithful men with whom to calm their carnal needs in their hours of tormented loneliness. When two Muslims join in holy matrimony, the angels of seven heavens begin at once to pray for the happy newlyweds. At the summit of heaven the celestial cherubim, while carrying the majestic throne of Allah on their dainty winged shoulders, become ecstatic for the couple down here in this base world of ours. These ethereal creatures cannot help dancing, joyfully chanting forever the tunes of "Hosanna, hosanna…" followed by "Halleluiah, halleluiah…" for bringing two good human beings together to live and love one another forever. As they go on…"

His head lowered as a sign of humility, his eyes downcast in respect, Kazem listened with some impatience. He could not help wondering about all those goings-on up there in heaven.

Crikey, thought Kazem, I never knew that angels would take the marriage of two fugitive lovers so seriously and have a big party up there!

The droning voice of Mollah Hossein went on, harping on with gusto on the subject of the sacredness of marriage and the merry-making in heaven by the angles. At some points, his voice choked with emotion of thinking that the Almighty's creatures cared so much for two wretched young lovers such as this man and his future wife. Mollah Hossein's jaws had become warm; he was enjoying the sound of his own voice, and there was no way of stopping him.

Kazem began to scratch his head, fidgeting restlessly. He was by now more worried about Maryam whom he had left waiting outside than the merry bunch of winged angels capering around up in heaven, celebrating his union with his sweetheart. Knowing the predatory nature of mollahs and their novices, he was worried that any minute one of them might spot Maryam, approach her and ask her to be his *siegheh*. As the mollah's unending string of poppycock was beginning to get on his nerves, Kazem was compelled to butt in, letting him know that he was in a mortal hurry to get over and done with the formalities.

"Forgive me agha mullah, to interrupt you in your wonderful sermons," he chipped in apologetically, “but we’re in a rush and have to get on with our engagement.”

Mollah Hossein was so wrapped up in his harangue that he failed to hear Kazem.

“Excuse me, agha mollah,” called out Kazem, as if trying to wake him from a trance.

“Yes, my son?” Mollah Hossein gave a start and looked at Kazem, bewildered. “Did you say something?”

“Yes, I did,” Kazem said. “If you don’t mind, could you please kindly sort us out because we’re in a terrible rush.”

“Oh, yes, my son, of course,” Mollah Hossein muttered. “The youthful impatience we all suffer from, as soon as we set our heart on a young lady. There’s nothing wrong with that; nothing at all.” His eyes misted over. “Oh, where are those joyful, carefree days of youth?”

Mollah Hossein became motionless, his unblinking eyes fixed on a faded pattern on the kilim, and soon forgot all about Kazem. He looked like a man sunk in bittersweet reveries, wandering aimlessly in the scorched ruins of his life, looking for scraps of memories of his youth, buried under the mounds of earth and rubble of smashed mud-bricks. His lips began to move imperceptibly, like those of a man talking in a dream. He waxed lyrical, declaiming nostalgically in a singsong voice:

Youth, like a magic bird, has flown away.
He sang a little morning-hour in May,
Sang to the Rose, his love, that, too, is gone –
Whither is more than you or I can say.

There was something in his aspect and the sound of his voice that forced Kazem to sit there still and think before deciding to interrupt him again. He went on gazing at the mollah. Hearing him declaiming the poem in the melancholy voice of a man who was once in love with a sweetheart of his own made Kazem sad. The memory of the mollah’s far-off youth when he was in love with his beautiful Rose was now as faded as those patterns on this kilim, thought Kazem. Maybe too many disappointments in his life had brought him to this pass.

27

Mollah Hossein raised his head and looked at Kazem as if he had seen him for the first time.

"So, you're thinking of marrying?" said he, with a faraway look in his eyes.

"Yes." Kazem repeated his request. "And as soon as possible, too."

"What's your name, son?"

"Yours truly, Kazem."

"Where's the young lady, Agha Kazem?"

"She's waiting outside."

"Are her father and the two witnesses here?"

"Her father's not here," replied Kazem. "I don't know what you mean by witnesses."

"In order to marry a woman you need the consent of her father and two adult witnesses."

"We've none of them with us."

"And why not, may I ask?" Mollah Hossein asked, clearly sensing something fishy going on.

"Because we love one another and her father is not willing to give her hand to me in marriage," explained Kazem. "We had to escape from our town near Mashhad."

"Has she got her birth certificate with her?" Mollah Hossein asked. "I'll have to see her age."

"No, she hasn't."

"How old is she?"

"She'll be eighteen in a few months' time."

"In that case I cannot marry you to that young lady."

"Why not?"

"Because she's not eighteen yet," said Mollah Hossein. "The Civil Law stipulates that a girl must be eighteen to be married."

"Can't you just bend the law a little in this case?" Kazem suggested.

"No, my son."

"Are you sure?" said Kazem, searching his eyes for a glimmer of hope.

"Positive."

"I'm sure there *must* be a way," said Kazem.

Mollah Hossein put his hand under his *aba* and pulled out a crumpled handkerchief from a pocket in his long robe. Pushing his turban back, he began to mop the large beads of sweat on his forehead. A round scar like a bruise glistened sickly in the middle of his brow – a sign of long years of devotion by pressing his forehead on a small wafer of dried-up clay signifying the earth. He pulled his *aba* round his shoulders, deliberating over a way to help this eager young man.

"Don't despair, my son." Mollah Hossein spoke in the mournful voice peculiar to men of his trade. "Help is always at hand. Luckily, we're all born Muslims, and being doubly fortunate, we're blessed by being Shiite Muslims. According to our holy Sharia Law formulated by our sinless imams and virtuous ayatollahs over the centuries, it is perfectly possible, over and above the usual law that permits us to possess four wives, we're allowed an unlimited number of *siegheh*s, for a period ranging from one hour to ninety-nine years. You'll be pleased to know, my son, that these *sieghehs* have no inheritance rights, and are not officially registered with the registry office or even the mosque, and don't require the consent of their fathers. Therefore, we have absolute freedom to do whatever we like with them. I myself have one wife and several *sieghehs*, all from around this neighbourhood. Mind you, I can afford these temporary wives because my business, with the help of Allah, is booming these days. Thankfully, many womenfolk in these parts are poor and desperate and in need of an honest hard-working man to marry them, to have a breadwinner for themselves and their kids. All this keeps me so occupied that I don't even have time to scratch my head."

Kazem listened with downcast eyes, waiting for the mollah to conclude his bright new idea. Mollah Hossein, however, looking self-satisfied and content with his way of life and his solutions to all the problems facing humankind, carried on like a man of god who is resigned to bearing the burden of responsibilities loaded on his shoulders by Providence.

"After all, we're only donkeys of Allah the Almighty to carry out his plans in this mean world of ours. All this hectic life keeping the holy faith alive and kicking among these folk sometimes makes me feel a little world-weary and down in the dumps. In my moments of solitude, of which very few are left to me these days, I sometimes say to myself, "Mollah Hossein, pull the reins of your horses in a little, slow down and take it easy. With the way you're galloping, you will soon kill the horses and yourself with them. It's time to give yourself a treat by finding a fresh young woman to make your *siegheh* for a while to refresh and rejuvenate yourself so that you can get on with the more serious religious duties Allah the Merciful and the Compassionate has lumbered you with. From then on when I'm solemnising a marriage ceremony, preaching in a mosque, or saying prayers to the ears of a newborn baby, I keep my eyes open to see if I can spot the right young woman to become my *siegheh* for a while.

"Once I spot her, one who is young enough to keep up with my legitimate human needs, I launch myself into action to make her my *siegheh* without even asking who her family is or where she comes from. All I care about is her youth, beauty, manners and how pious she is. I then propose to her. Upon the young lady agreeing to my proposal, I then read on the spot the formula for temporary betrothal, asking her to be my wife for a specific period of time. This obligation is even mentioned in *Hadith*, that whenever we men are in need of another woman other than the mother of our children, we should marry her, albeit temporarily, to not only make her happy but also to gratify our own natural needs bestowed upon us by Allah. This is indeed a charitable act, mind you. Some women have lost their breadwinners, some are not happy within their marriage, some of them don't get enough gratification from their husbands, who can be feeble, decrepit, or simply not up to it, if you get my drift!"

How can he talk about women like this? Kazem thought, flabbergasted. If only I could smash his jaws in. On second thoughts, I should rein in my anger until I've finished with him. Anyhow, one is not supposed to strangle a man of the cloth! As the old saying goes: mollahs are like rugs; the more you trample on them, the more precious they become in the eyes of the people! This sonofabitch has got the wrong end of the stick by not comprehending the gravity of my predicament and how much I love and respect Maryam. She's not going to be my wife just to gratify my needs, cook for me, and bear me kids. She's all I have. With her presence beside me, I can put my past life behind me, bury it deep under the ground, escape the squalor of my life and become a decent man. She's Maryam, my only soul mate in this world, the world that has abandoned me to my own devices since my childhood.

"Listen, agha mollah," Kazem spoke in carefully measured tones, "I want a legitimate wife, not a *siegheh*."

Mollah Hossein listened with his head lowered, twirling his prayer beads between his fleshy fingers.

"It's possible to make her your legally legitimate wife without the presence of her father or having any witnesses *only* after you've made her your *siegheh* for a while," murmured Mollah Hossein, throwing a meaningful glance at Kazem. "She can be your *siegheh* for a few months until she reaches the legal age. As soon as she's eighteen, come back to me. I know some people who can make a duplicate birth certificate and find the necessary witnesses for a small sum of money. According to the law, you can get married and ask for her father's consent later. Once she's your legitimate wife, her father will have no choice but to agree, because the marriage contract cannot be annulled." He shifted position. "So, if you decide to make her your *siegheh*, you can give me a small amount of cash as charity for a good deed."

Kazem thought hard. He was beginning to realise he had no choice but to agree for Maryam to become his *siegheh* for a few months. In this way, at least she could be seen as his wife according to the accepted norms.

However shameful this business of *siegheh* is to me, thought Kazem, I've no option but to go ahead with it.

"So be it, Mollah Hossein," he muttered. "How much do you ask for this *siegheh* business?"

"Being a good Muslim brother," said Mollah Hossein, not looking up from his prayer beads, "it will be round about twenty tomans."

"It's a deal," said Kazem. "I can only give you ten beforehand and when you keep your side of the bargain I'll give you the rest." He thrust his hand into his pocket, pulled out a ten-toman note and gave it to Mollah Hossein, who snatched it and shoved it into his robe pocket under his *aba*.

"May Allah bless your father and mother," he said. "You now nip off outside and meet me with the young lady in the courtyard near the pond. From there we'll go to my humble little chamber at the end of the courtyard and perform the *siegheh* ceremony."

Kazem got up, walked out of the mosque and joined Maryam who was very happy to see him again.

"I was getting fed up of leaning against a lamppost being ogled by the men," she said. "Some men kept hurling obscene remarks at me and others kept asking me whether I was a solo-worker. That I didn't understand."

"Never mind them," said Kazem, "I'm here now. When they see a woman on her own, the men in Tehran always try it on with her." He kept quiet about the meaning of solo-worker.

"Why did you take so long?" Maryam asked.

"You know how mollahs are," replied Kazem. "Once they find a willing listener, they just go on and on with their religious hogwash."

"What hogwash?"

"He says we can't become proper man and wife because you're not eighteen."

"What do we do then?"

"He says he can make you my *siegheh* for a while until you reach the legal age and only then will we be able to get married to one another."

"But I hate the idea of becoming your *siegheh*."

"I hate it too, Maryam," said Kazem. "But we've no choice. It only lasts for a few months and then I'll marry you."

Maryam fell silent.

"Don't worry, Maryam," said Kazem, looking reassuringly at her. "You know how serious I am about this. Let's go now."

"Where to?"

"To the mollah, of course," replied Kazem, gently pushing Maryam ahead.

After joining Mollah Hossein in the courtyard, the couple followed him to the tiny chamber, a dank little room with bare walls and a few threadbare kilims on the floor.

"Welcome to my humble office," said Mollah Hossein, entering the room. "Please sit down while I find the right formulae for *siegheh* in my prayer book." He ambled to a niche in the wall heaped with dog-eared copies of the Koran and prayer books. From among the pile, he pulled out a copy of the Koran and a book containing the formulae for a variety of occasions. He then sat down cross-legged on the kilim in the middle of the room, put the copy of the Koran on the floor beside him, opened the book of formulae, and placed it on his lap. Raising his eyebrows, he adjusted his glasses and leafed through the pages, licking his fingers every so often with his slimy tongue. Once he had found the right phrases, he looked up at the couple who were sitting politely facing him like well-behaved children.

"There we are, my brother and sister," Mollah Hossein muttered, "I have found them." He raised his head and said to Kazem, "Repeat these words after me, looking at the young lady: *Ankahtu wa zawagto*."

"*Ankahtu wa zawagto.*" Kazem managed to pronounce the Arabic words successfully, looking Maryam in the eye.

"Now it is your turn, young lady," said Mollah Hossein, turning to Maryam. "Say *Qabilto*, looking at Kazem Agha."

"*Qabilto*," murmured Maryam shyly, gripping the hem of her chador with her hand.

"You're now wedded to one another according to Sharia Law," Mollah Hossein declared in a solemn tone of voice. He picked up the copy of the

Koran, placed it on his lap, opened the back cover and scribbled the names of Kazem and Maryam on the back page in order for the couple to be blessed and to keep a record of the duration of their *siegheh*. He asked them to put their signatures on the page, signed it himself and shut the book.

As they stood up to go, Kazem, when he came to shake Mollah Hossein's hand, secretly thrust a ten-toman note into his sweaty palm.

28

It was late afternoon when Kazem and Maryam left the mosque. People were hurrying along the pavements, running after buses to go to their homes. Once near home, they stopped at a grocer's and baker's in the main street, where Kazem bought some grapes, a lump of cheese, and fresh *sangak* bread.

Following their age-old custom, some of the neighbours were out in the lane. Many of them stood on front doorsteps, chattering and laughing at the tops of their voices. A troop of scrawny boys, wearing tattered shoes and dressed in rags, were running after a deflated plastic ball, yelling at one another. Little girls with grimy, spindly legs in shabby dresses were sitting along the slimy gutter, talking and giggling, or playing hopscotch. Two hawkers pushed their carts, one loaded with grapes and the other with gherkins, chanting loudly. Every so often one of the mothers stopped in the middle of her conversation and shrieked at her children to get inside as it was getting late. A hush fell upon the clusters of women as Kazem and Maryam passed them by. They silently eyed the newcomers till they reached the door of the lodging house at the end of the lane.

A commotion was going on in the courtyard. Kazem, being cautious, waited a bit behind the door and listened. He was relieved to find that the lodgers were having their usual petty bickering, with which he was all too familiar.

He opened the door, pulled the curtain aside, and stepped down, followed by Maryam. All the lodgers were out in full force. Some stood on the terrace, leaning against the banister, some strolled around the courtyard, and others squatted around the *hauz*, watching two of the lodgers shrieking raucously and hurling the most colourful obscenities at one another. Both had wrapped their chadors round their waists and tied them in front, ready for the inevitable tussle.

"May you burn in the fire of your jealousy, Mohtaram Torkeh," bellowed the burly woman with a pockmarked, hairy face who stood near the privy, blocking its entrance with her body and waving a plastic ewer in her hand.

"You're the one who should burn in hellfire for your sins, not me, Shamsi Antar," bawled the buxom woman with a ruddy complexion who stood on the terrace with her fists pressed against her side.

"Al least I sleep with one handsome man," retorted Shamsi Khanum. "Not like you, opening your fat legs for all sorts of street hawkers who happen to visit our lane."

"I tell you what, love," yelled Mohtaram Khanum, "I'm enjoying them a lot, if you want to know. I'm pretty and can still turn heads." She then added with gusto, "At least I don't look like a baboon dressed like a woman. One ought to do penance for just looking at your ugly face."

"Bah!" mocked Shamsi Khanum, waving her hand as if shooing away some obstinate gadfly. "Pot calling the kettle black."

"All the men in the neighbourhood remember you in your young days in Shahr-e No," Mohtaram Khanum smirked.

Hearing this piece of information about her murky past, Shamsi Khanum was transformed into a monster. In a paroxysm of rage, she flung the ewer on the floor and charged towards the terrace. Unafraid, Mohtaram Khanum ran towards her. The two women came to blows in the middle of the stairs. They grabbed each other's hair, tugging and plucking fistfuls. As they grappled, they both tumbled down the steps and ended up on the cobblestones. They rose and set upon one another like two fighting cocks, screeching, spluttering and fuming with rage, their hair sticking up. They soon found that hair-pulling was not effective, so resorted to spitting at each other. They then snatched each other's chador, tearing them off their bodies. Once the chadors came off flying around them, they were left with their short dresses. By this time, their faces had turned as white as corpses, spittle hanging from their mop-like hair. Not yet done, they grabbed hold of each other's dresses, pulling hard at them. In a matter of seconds, their dress buttons were shooting in all directions, revealing their ivory-coloured skin. They soon found themselves covered only in the soiled shreds of their dresses. Once these were torn off their bodies, they were left in just their knickers and bras.

To bring this clash to a final and bitter end, Shamsi Khanum, being the one who was outraged and more versed in single combat due to her wild life in Shahr-e No, got the upper hand by seizing Mohtaram Khanum's bra and knickers and pulling them off her body. She held them aloft, waving them above her head as a token of her victory for all to see, to set an example so that no one else would dare meddle with her. Upright and proud, she stood beside her fallen adversary, her dishevelled hair ruffling in the slight breeze. Her face glowed in the pale golden light of the autumnal sun. She then turned and glowered at the lodgers who slithered quietly a few paces back, not daring to meet her medusa-like stare for fear of inflaming her anger.

Mohtaram Khanum, defeated and shamed, remained there at the bottom of the steps as naked as God made her. She curled herself into a ball, hopelessly trying to cover her bits, a flabby mass of white flesh blotched with bruises and streaked all over with scratches.

During the whole spectacle, the lodgers had stood back and watched, like those mute spectators who watch a *ta'ziyeh* in a village square. Meanwhile, the little boys and girls, familiar with these daily rituals, just capered around, clapping their hands with excitement and giggling. Even the sickly-looking canary, dozing off in the corner of its cage, did not bother to so much as flap around or peep out at them.

Kazem, not being able to bear seeing the wretched woman in that state, snatched a sheet from the washing line, walked to the naked woman, and covered her up. She raised her head and looked at him with gratitude.

"May God bless you, agha," she whimpered, wrapping the sheet around herself.

Kazem then beckoned to Maryam and they walked to their room, followed by the silent gaze of the lodgers.

Once in the room, Kazem took off his shoes, walked to the casement window and peered out at the courtyard through the slits of the straw blind. The oblique rays of the sun cast long shadows of the walls on the cobblestones. The lodgers lingered a little longer, doing nothing in particular. The older children, who had been playing out in the lane, trickled into the courtyard in twos and threes, teasing the little ones by kicking the old tyres with which they were playing. The women began to yell at the older children to go inside, dragging the tiny ones behind them. The muffled noises of the neighbourhood were slowly dying down. From a distant roof a muezzin started to chant, calling the faithful to the dusk prayers. The door of the courtyard was slowly pushed open and a rough-looking man pulled the curtain aside, stepped in, strode across the deserted courtyard, and disappeared in Shamsi Khanum's room at the far end of the terrace.

Kazem turned away from the window, thoughtful. Maryam emerged from the alcove, carrying a bowl of grapes. She put on her chador, left the room, and came back with the washed grapes. She spread a piece of clean cloth in the middle of the room and placed the bread on it, along with the grapes and cheese. They began to eat in silence.

"What are you thinking of, Maryam?" Kazem asked.

"Why do they behave like that, Kazem?" she replied, nibbling at a piece of bread.

"They've nothing better to do." Kazem tried to explain, biting into some grapes in a bunch. "This is the only entertainment they have. You see, almost all of these people can't read or write. They're just poisoning themselves and others in their own venom. They gossip and laugh at others to spice up their empty, idle lives."

"Why can't they read and write?" asked Maryam timidly.

"All of them have come from villages all over Iran in which schools don't exist," explained Kazem. "Even if there were schools of some sort, they were for boys. I've seen some of these villages with my own eyes, Maryam."

"They could go to schools here in Tehran," Maryam said.

"With all the worries and troubles they have to deal with day in day out," Kazem said, "their lives are eaten up by trying to make ends meet. Where would they find the time to become literate?

"During the day most of them melt into this godless and gateless city, doing odd jobs as day labourers. Depending on the season of the year, they do different jobs: backbreaking labour in the brickworks near Shah Abdolazim, on building sites uptown, peddle around in the neighbourhood, clean offices, become gardeners in posh houses, or, when there's thick snow, they go round shovelling the snow off the roofs and yards. At sundown they crawl from different parts of Tehran into their hovels, and shut themselves inside the four walls of their rooms. How they pass their evenings, only the devil knows! The lucky ones might have a battered old radio that they turn on without really listening to it, as the programmes have nothing to do with their lives. If the music played on the radio reminds them of their native villages, they become quiet, shedding silent tears. After a meagre supper of bread and onion, they are dead to the world, exhausted. Only the gambling veterans among them, after having their supper, creep out of the house and go to gambling dens in the ruins outside Tehran to play knucklebones, to return home before daybreak, worn-out and having lost everything they had earned during the day. The ones who are students or bachelors, some evenings, pop into the Shahr-e No up the road and spend whatever they have on prostitutes and have a good time there in the cheap taverns and cabarets."

"They must have some spare time to learn how to read and write," said Maryam.

"They use the little time they have for scandalmongering and gossiping about the other lodgers and neighbours."

Maryam went on nibbling at a piece of bread.

"First thing in the morning I'll have to go out to look for some sort of job," Kazem announced, changing the subject.

"I'm sure you'll find something," said Maryam. "I can work, too, Kazem. We'll manage."

Kazem gazed at her for a few seconds.

"What can you do in Tehran, Maryam?"

"I've got my National Diploma," said Maryam. "I can teach some illiterate women in the neighbourhood a few basic reading and writing skills."

Kazem listened to her attentively, thinking that she seemed to be very brave and was serious about things.

After some talk about their plans for the future, they spread the mattress on the floor and slept.

Next day, very early, Kazem went out in search of a job. From two street hawkers he bought a pair of dark glasses and a black cap. He then roamed the main streets of the neighbourhood, walking into different shops and offices to see if anybody could offer him work. They all asked for identity papers such as passport, birth certificate, or exemption certificate from military service. He had none of those. Exhausted and disheartened, he returned home around noontime.

Seeing him down in the mouth, Maryam tried to cheer him up by saying that it would all turn out well because he had changed and really wanted to work. She made an omelette over the Aladdin heater using the eggs she had bought that morning. They ate in silence. Kazem left home again to resume his search. Not being successful, he went back home worn-out.

"I think tomorrow I'll go to the bazaar," said he, hitting upon an idea. "I used to know some people over there. They might be able to help me."

The following day he wandered around Tehran's bazaar until midday, walking in and out of merchant cells without any luck. At midday, he returned home, had a meagre lunch and a short afternoon nap, and left home again.

He wandered around Heshmatodoleh Avenue looking at the stalls and shops. Not finding anything, he walked through Shahpur Street asking numerous shopkeepers if they could offer him anything. Not being successful, he walked aimlessly until he ended up in Ghazvin Square. By this time, dusk had fallen and all the stallholders and shops were bustling with people who were buying bread, fruit and vegetables to go home to break their fast.

Kazem joined a horde of idlers who had not been fasting and had never fasted in their entire lives. Lost in the throng of uprooted peasants, he gazed around looking for a familiar face. Street pedlars of lamb's liver and kidney kebabs, roasted corn and boiled beetroot stood behind their carts which were lit by small, pressurized lanterns. Street entertainers of all kinds were standing or squatting beside their equipment, inviting the idle folk to step closer and watch the greatest spectacles in Tehran.

Kazem stood in front of a cart behind which was standing a thickset, morose-looking man, fanning the red-hot charcoals in a brazier. The glow of the charcoals brought into relief his stubbly face, making him look like a hairy blacksmith. Every other minute, he turned over the skewers of lamb, kidneys, and liver, chanting:

"*Bah, bah; bah, bah.* What lovely kebabs! Each skewer for only five *gherans*."

Kazem walked up to the cart and asked for two skewers of liver kebab, staring at the man from behind his dark glasses. The kebab vendor looked up.

"Bah!" yelled the man, slapping his forehead. "Is that you, Kazem?" A broad grin cracked open his face that had become as red as a pomegranate.

"Yes, it's me, the very same Kazem Alaki," said Kazem, peering into the man's face, now recognising his old friend, Ali Khalifeh.

"Ah, look at his cap and glasses!" Ali cried, grinning broadly. "Who do you think you are? Alain Delon?" He ran round the cart, grabbed Kazem with his strong hands, and planted two smacking kisses on his cheeks.

"What happened that you remembered an old mate, Kazem Agha?" Ali shouted. He then looked into Kazem's eyes and said, "You never came to pay us a visit. That wasn't a manly thing to do, mate."

"I had to go back to Mashhad, Ali," replied Kazem, looking away.

"I know, I know." Ali nodded. "So why are you back here in Tehran, then?"

"To look for a job."

"When did you come out of jail?" asked Ali, now back behind his cart, preparing the kebabs.

"Last week," replied Kazem, glancing at a clutch of customers munching away at their kebabs and talking at the same time.

"What did you do in Mashhad?" asked Ali, placing the skewers on the brazier.

"Nothing much," said Kazem. "I was only there for a few days, met some old mates, and settled a few scores."

Ali Khalifeh stopped and looked up at Kazem, remembering what he had heard in jail about him being betrayed by some of his old mates and accomplices.

"What brings you to Tehran?" Ali vigorously fanned the kebabs with a tattered, soot-covered straw fan.

"To find a decent job," explained Kazem. "Hosseinabaad was becoming too small for me and I was as well known to everyone there, like a cow with a white patch on its forehead. Moreover, you can walk in Tehran streets without being recognised or pointed out by people."

"Mmm, a decent job!" repeated Ali. After a short pause he asked, "What have you been doing all this week?"

"Found a place round here and, as I said, I've been looking for a job," said Kazem. "I can see that you have changed your profession, Ali!"

Ali lifted the two skewers of kebab dripping with sizzling blood, placed them in the middle of a piece of *taftoon* bread that he folded over them, pressed one hand on them, pulled the skewers out, made a neat wrap, and handed it over to Kazem. Kazem pinched some salt from a dented tin bowl beside the brazier, sprinkled it over the kebabs, and asked how much he had to pay.

"No, no, don't mention it," said Ali. "Be my guest this time."

Kazem thanked him and stood beside the cart. He bit big chunks off his wrap and munched with appetite, his cheeks bulging.

"When I left the jail before you," Ali said in a measured voice, "I met a few old friends to start it all over again. It soon became clear to me that things had changed a lot during my stay in jail. They were arresting everyone left, right, and centre. Some of my old mates had turned into snouts, sniffing out their former friends and handing them over to the police. You know what people are like here in Tehran, Kazem. Like chameleons they change colour and side with the ones who wield the largest bludgeons. Things are changing, though. Now the people are stirring and dare to talk openly. They're becoming bolder by the day. They're now after more important things than opium and drugs."

"So what did you do for a living before selling kebabs?" asked Kazem.

"I had some old friends in a few cabarets up in Lalezar. I became a bouncer in the Cleopatra Café-Restaurant for a while. I was soon kicked out from there because I slept with the pretty dancer who was the mistress of the boss. After doing some odd jobs here and there I managed to buy this cart from a melon hawker and set up my own trade."

"I can see that you're doing well, Ali," said Kazem, looking around at the customers.

Ali went on gazing at Kazem, as if thinking.

"Listen, Kazem," he said all of a sudden, "why don't you work for me?

I don't know what the devil got into the head of my clownish assistant. One day he just vanished. I heard that he had run off with the young wife of a *Hajji* from the bazaar!"

"I would be very happy to work for you, bro," said Kazem, tired of knocking about in the streets.

"You can start right away," said Ali. "Come and stand behind the cart and serve the customers while I watch and tell you what to do."

Kazem did what he was told. Soon two young women, both wrapped up in black chadors, stood in front of the cart.

"Excuse me, Agha, can we have four skewers of kidney kebabs?" one of the women asked. Kazem prepared the kidney kebabs neatly and handed them over.

"You did very well, Kazem," said Ali, giving him a nudge of encouragement.

Kazem settled into his job and worked hard to make the money necessary to pay for Maryam's duplicate birth certificate. Every day he made frequent trips to the bazaar and slaughterhouse to buy bread, charcoal and meat. By and by, he came to know many people and made many contacts.

29

Less than a week into the job, the political unrest in some parts of Iran had become so widespread that the Shah, in a broadcast to the nation, made some concessions by pledging free elections. Having for more than two decades known the Shah's empty promises, people voiced their anger louder and louder to the point that the Prime Minister, Jamshid Amouzegar, imposed military curfew. That meant that Tehran's folk had to return to their homes before sundown and stay there until six in the morning.

Every day before dusk Kazem's stall was mobbed by hungry people. As he hurriedly prepared the kebabs, he listened to the many customers who stood around the stall debating politics for the first time without being afraid or looking over their shoulders to see who was spying on them. News of a huge demonstration in Isfahan that had ended in bloodshed had started to circulate in the area. The media, of course, did not report the ensuing unrest in various parts of Tehran. It was around the twentieth of August that Kazem heard people talking about a big fire in the Rex Cinema in Abadan, in which many people were burned alive. The media had to report this because it was the work of zealous Muslim agitators.

Whenever Kazem went to the bazaar to get the necessary provisions, there, too, the shopkeepers held open discussions about politics. Small groups of people gathered everywhere to discuss the political and social events. Teahouses, public baths, buses, bakers', grocers', cinemas and cabarets had all turned into political forums.

One early morning as Kazem was sitting at a table in a teahouse, listening to the regulars who were hotly debating the issues of the day, he saw a bearded, scruffy young man walk into the teahouse and glance around like a hunted animal, before throwing some pamphlets on each table and dashing out. One of Kazem's friends with a smattering of reading skill, picked up the pamphlet and read it out in a low voice. The message urged the people of Iran to rise up and fight for their legitimate rights. Kazem and the rest listened, smoking and nodding thoughtfully.

At the end of August, Amouzegar's cabinet was forced to resign and the veteran politician Sharif-Emami was asked to form a new cabinet. Despite these rapid changes, things got worse to the extent that the army opened fire on a large number of demonstrators in Jaleh Square in downtown Tehran, killing many people. From then on the people's protests began to gather momentum all over Iran. At the end of September, the regime had to put an end to one party system to calm down the people's anger.

By the end of October, massive strikes, prominent among them the newspaper and oil industries, set terror into the heart of the ruling regime. At the beginning of November, the army was sent to take control of the oil refineries. A few days later, a large number of students from the University of Tehran staged a demonstration against the regime. The army moved in at once, injuring many of the students. The following day, the Shah, increasingly fearful of losing his grip on events that were beginning seriously to threaten his very existence, once again addressed the nation in an emotional broadcast tinged with remorse and fear.

"Dear Nation of Iran. In the open political atmosphere that gradually began two years ago, you, the Iranian nation, rose up against tyranny. As the Shah of Iran and an Iranian citizen, I cannot but approve of the revolution of the people of Iran. Unfortunately, all through this revolution, other conspirators have taken advantage of your just sentiments of anger and outrage and have managed to create chaos and disturbance. The recent wave of strikes, most of them justified, has begun to change from the original goals and direction in order to prevent the wheels of the economy from turning. The consequences of such unwise actions will only cripple the daily lives of the ordinary people. I am well aware that, in the name of preventing chaos and mayhem, it's possible that the suppressions and mistakes of the past could be repeated again. I am also aware that some people might be mindful that, under the guise of keeping economic affairs running smoothly and getting on with the business of progress of the nation, the danger of an unholy alliance between material and political suppression, accompanied by corruption, will be repeated. I, however, as the king of the Iranian nation, reiterate my oath and commitment so that not only past mistakes, corruption, and tyranny will not be repeated, but also they will be put right at once. I will therefore undertake to form, in the first instance, a new national government after some measure of peace is established. My government will get democracy and freedom off the ground so that the constitution, for the creation of which the blood of so many heroes was spilt in the not-so-distant past, may be put in full practice. The message of your revolution was so loud and clear that I also heard it. I am the guardian of the constitutional monarchy that is a God-given gift put on my shoulders by my people. I am entirely behind you for what you have sacrificed to acquire. I guarantee that in the future the Iranian government will be based on the constitutional law, social justice and national autonomy free from tyranny and corruption."

This emotional speech fell on deaf ears and hearts hardened by years of hatred. In the first week of November, the Shah resorted to another tactic and arrested thirteen loyal members of his government in order to placate the people's anger. But the people just laughed at the last efforts of an absolute monarch flapping around to save his skin.

From then on bits and pieces of news began to trickle into Iran that a famous religious firebrand and rabble-rouser by the name of Khomeini, exiled from Iran fifteen years earlier, had left Iraq and gone to France. From the comfort of his little home in the suburbs of Paris, this Khomeini fellow kept sending taped messages and pamphlets, inflaming people's anger, urging them to rise and get rid of the corrupt Pahlavi Regime.

Kazem, though, had only one thing on his mind: to work as hard as possible and get some money together in order to make Maryam his legitimate wife, so that if the police came after him there would be no problem. Strangely, the chaotic turn of events was favourable for the two young fugitives. Everybody was busy sticking their own flag on top of the haystack and, luckily for Kazem, all the gendarmerie and the police force were called on to deal with the overwhelming number of troublemakers who wanted to topple the regime. They had no time and resources to spare for catching a delinquent fellow man who had kidnapped a young woman because he loved her. In reality, even if they'd had time, they would not have cared. So many young lovers were escaping from all parts of the country to settle in Tehran that the police, unable to tackle all these runaway Romeos and Juliets, had almost abandoned the effort of chasing them. On top of that, the law-enforcement agencies were so corrupt that a few hundred tomans, an offer of a few opium rolls, or a bottle of smuggled whisky would make them turn a blind eye to the whole affair.

As the ancient, deeply-rooted system of monarchy desperately tried to cling to power by resorting to fanciful stratagems, something far more sinister had already begun to creep in, insidiously taking its place. The hideous monster of religion and superstition, hidden deep down in the rotten history and culture of Iranian society, had begun to stir. This ghoul, having been temporarily tamed and put down nearly seventy years ago by the Constitutional Revolution, was beginning to grunt and growl, reminding people of its presence. Kazem, among many in downtown Tehran, was one of the first people to hear the ghastly growling of this slumbering ugly creature, which showed itself in the form of its age-old underlings: religious thugs of all sizes and colours.

Whenever Kazem stood behind his stall selling his kebabs or frequented shops or teahouses, he saw mysterious bands of Muslim fanatics who roamed everywhere, hyena-like, in packs, standing at the corners of crossroads, or by mosques and in the marketplaces, howling noisily about the next system of government, ruled completely by Sharia Law. Sometimes Kazem came across these rough-looking, bearded individuals, shrieking 'Allahu Akbar, Khomeini *Rahbar*'. Wherever there was a congregation of students, day labourers, or stallholders to talk about the political events and the possibility of finally having some semblance of democracy and freedom, these rowdy Muslim yobbos would mingle among them. They would then butt in, divert the subject of the conversation to Islamic laws, and if other liberal-minded and level-headed folk happened to disagree, they would accuse them of being treacherous and not true revolutionaries. If they were faced with resistance, they would smash up the groups, bullying them to talk only about the coming of the great saviour, meaning the Grand Ayatollah, and the establishment of Islamic ideology all over Iran.

Kazem had heard the name of this *saviour* before. He had first heard about a cleric called Khomeini when he was around fifteen years of age. At that time, he was too preoccupied with smuggling drugs and selling them to people in downtown Tehran to be concerned about this religious agitator. But he still remembered the demonstrations staged in central Tehran, soon after which the Shah kicked Khomeini out of the country. He had even heard from the notorious knife-fighter and thug called Teyyeb, who wielded a lot of power in poor districts, that the Shah's Prime Minister, Hassan-Ali Mansour, had slapped Khomeini's face for insulting the king and the Americans.

As the curfew remained in force, Kazem had to return home just around sundown every day. The lodging house was not exempt from the on-going political upheavals. Each evening the menfolk would gather on the terrace, smoking and hotly discussing events. The womenfolk would sit around the *hauz* talking about the Grand Ayatollah who was sending messages full of hope about a better life to come for all of them.

Kazem, most of the time, stayed in the room and rarely took part in these heated conversations. His attention was focussed somewhere else. Owing to his natural shrewdness and common sense, he knew that no good would ever come out of these mollahs, no matter how honest-looking they were and what promises they made. Anyway, in order to put the long evenings to good use, Maryam had begun to teach him to read and write. Eager to improve his lot in the future, he took the lessons very seriously.

However, he found it difficult to concentrate in the evenings as the folk in the neighbourhood had taken into their heads new ways of showing their discontent with the imposition of the curfew by going up to the roofs of their houses each evening and continually chanting "Allahu Akbar". After nightfall, the tumultuous yelling coming from near and distant roofs filled the air. The mingling of all these anguished voices suggested the wailing of wandering souls of sinners in purgatory. Kazem found this grim nightly chorus of unhappy voices disturbing. Being still young and thrown all of a sudden into this social and political maelstrom, he thought Maryam might not be well prepared to comprehend all this. He had noticed that whenever the other women showed some political fervour, she just listened quietly without making much comment.

* * * *

One day, just before sundown, towards the end of November, Kazem, returning home, stopped by the grocer's. A crowd of men and women stood in a long queue, loudly discussing an extraordinary phenomenon. As he waited, he could not help hearing some of them talking about the miracle on the moon.

"Did you see the image of the Ayatollah on the moon last night?" one woman asked her friend.

"Sure I did," her friend answered, pulling her chador back over her head. "Oh my God, what a divine light was shining through his face!"

"I've heard the mollahs say the holy men, having committed no sins in their whole lives, are all sources of light." The smothered voice of another woman came from behind the hem of her chador.

After buying his salami, gherkins, tomatoes and a packet of cigarettes, Kazem walked up to the baker's where huddles of men of all ages, hugging their freshly baked *sangak* breads to keep warm, were also debating the miracle. Some of them gesticulated, noisily swearing on the Koran and on the most beloved in their lives, dead or living, to convince the others that they had witnessed the wondrous happening. Others, eyebrows raised and goggle-eyed, listened quietly, nibbling at their breads.

"I swear on the grave of my mother that I saw with my own eyes the hallowed image of the Ayatollah on the moon last night," insisted a lanky, scantily-bearded young devotee of the holy man.

"May they wrap me in a shroud if I lie!" chimed in a middle-aged man. "I saw his haloed face on the moon as you see your own reflection on water."

"In my lifetime I've seen with my own eyes and heard about lots of miracles in hundreds of holy shrines in this country," a doddering old man declared, raising his stick aloft and pompously addressing some skinny youths, who stretched their necks like famished lizards, listening to him, shivering, "but I don't remember anything like this."

Kazem moved on from one group to another, stopping at the back of each to listen a while to a range of opinions, until he had to go home as the soldiers were urging people to hurry up.

No sooner had he stepped down into the courtyard than he saw all the women of the house, wrapped up in their black chadors, flocking around the *hauz* like ravens and jabbering loudly about the miraculous apparition on the moon. Kazem saw none of the men who would normally be standing on the long terrace, smoking, and talking about the latest events.

As he strode across the courtyard Akram Khanum, the most notorious busybody among the lodgers, looked at his direction and shrieked, "Kazem Agha, aren't you going up to the roof?"

"What for?" asked Kazem.

"Well, it's flipping obvious!" she yelled. "To see the Ayatollah's face on the moon. All the men have gone up to the roof to take a look."

"They say you'll be blessed if you look at his sacred face." Showkat Khanum added her thoughts on the matter.

"No, thanks," Kazem replied firmly. "I'm knackered and I want to rest. Besides, I've committed too many sins to be redeemed by the Ayatollah's benediction to save me from hellfire. I've neither faith to be grabbed by Satan, nor wealth to be snatched by the king."

"Don't you ever say that," Mohtaram Khanum said. "Your sins will be all written off if you so much as glance at his image, honestly."

"No, no, Mohtaram Khanum," Kazem said. "My sins are what the mollahs call cardinal sins, meaning that I'm condemned even if I mend my wicked ways."

"Why don't you repent and just be like the others here?" Mohtaram Khanum asked.

"I can't," said Kazem. "Even if I renounce my personal beliefs and correct my immoral deeds, I'm still a condemned man till God himself decides my fate while I'm waiting in purgatory."

"I think that heathen student is to blame." Molook Khanum aired her views, shrieking. "He reads all those bleeding books written by infidels that have curdled his brains. You should stop listening to him, Kazem Agha."

"Will you leave Mahmud alone, Molook Khanum," Kazem said, turning to her. "He's not the one who has made me infidel. I was born this way."

"So it was the devil himself who planted all these dodgy ideas into your head," cut in Showkat Khanum.

"If you really wish to know, Showkat Khanum, it was not only one devil but a troop of them where I was born and grew up," Kazem said, chuckling. "Come on, Showkat Khanum, honestly, every person with a smattering of knowledge knows that the moon is a lump of earth, sand and stone, just like our blessed earth on which we're crawling on top of each other like vermin." Kazem paused a little and added, "The Ayatollah's head must be as big as the moon itself to be seen from here. The Ayatollah, as far as I know, is in France right now, isn't he? He can't be in two places at the same time, can he?"

Speechless, the women stood stock-still, clutching the hems of their chadors, staring at Kazem as if he had all of a sudden grown horns and a long, pointed tail.

"If you ask me, Kazem Agha," Showkat Khanum mumbled, "with that black cap, those dark glasses and thick beard, if I ever saw you in a dark alley I would think you're the devil himself." All the women laughed heartily.

"Well I must inform you, khanums, as far as I can tell, each of us sees a different image on the moon, depending on who and what we are. Some of us might see a huge face, others an old hag sitting on a chair feeding a dog, and yet others the profile of a lovely-looking young woman, or even a rusty coin. I personally see nothing on the moon but a gorgeous young woman with her jet-black hair tucked up on her head."

Kazem walked to the steps, climbed them and reached the terrace. As he was about to open the door of the room he heard yelling from the rooftops:

"The Ayatollah is on the moon. Allahu Akbar."

"Allahu Akbar, Allahu Akbar…" The other moon-gazers on the rooftops in the neighbourhood took up the refrain, screaming like lunatics.

Kazem looked up and saw some men standing on the opposite rooftops with their hands lifted up, silhouetted against the dark sky in which hung the full moon, supplicating like those beggars who hang around the holy shrines. They then prostrated themselves, like marionettes whose strings are loosened, as if worshipping the moon. Kazem looked at the milky-blue sphere that was hanging up there, as impassive and cold as ever.

30

To keep the guileless populace entertained, for several days and nights the Muslim enthusiasts speedily organised festivals and celebrations in mosques and makeshift *tekiehs* in every city, town and remote village. Charity *halva*, dates, sweets, fruit and tea were handed out to the poor and the hungry who, upon hearing the news of the hand-outs, crawled out of their holes and hovels and thronged around the mosques, holy shrines and graveyards, scrambling to get as much alms as possible to last them for weeks till the advent of other miracles. The mollahs, being true to their old ways and always on the lookout for godsent opportunities like this to earn extra tomans, sprang into action. They buried their heads into old religious texts in the schools of theology to dig out every possible indication in the Koran and the *Hadith* about the coming of the 'Deputy of the *Mahdi*' – the person of the Grand Ayatollah, that is. Upon gathering their authentic evidence and convinced of the genuineness of the 'miracle on the moon', they donned their turbans, put on their camel-hair *abas*, and strode to the nearest mosque or *tekieh*, their *abas* ballooning in the wintry west wind. Upon entering a mosque or a *tekieh,* several *salawats* were chanted in honour of the "Man of God' on the moon by the zealous hoi-polloi, who had already taken up their positions on the kilims. The mollahs, after being hurriedly hustled to the pulpits, climbed up them as light-footed as monkeys, settled themselves comfortably, wrapped their *abas* round their plump bodies, pushed back their turbans, and brayed exactly the same sermon, as if devils had hastily put together the text of their preaching for them beforehand. All the discourses on the miracle ran something along these lines:

"My faithful Muslim brothers and sisters, you have all been very fortunate and blessed by Allah to have seen the holy face of the Grand Ayatollah on the moon. I have not yet been graced with that blissful experience, since I have been busy running from this mosque to that *tekieh*, spreading the glad tidings among believers. But, I promise, I'll soon join you in looking at the moon once I have fulfilled my duties. According to the verdicts of all the ayatollahs in the Shiite world, who are the true founts of all knowledge on all subjects from time immemorial, this is a sure divine signal to mankind that the Grand Ayatollah is now, beyond any conceivable doubt, the 'Deputy of the *Mahdi*'. As is clearly stated in the *Hadith*, the Sun, the Grand Ayatollah, that is, will rise, contrary to all expectations, in the West and his face will shine like a beacon of hope on the moon. The West, as you are well aware, is France, where our dearly loved Ayatollah has temporarily taken up residence and will soon join us like the archangels who descended upon the Prophet in the Harrah Mountains around Mecca. By that time we will have kicked out this Shah, who is the devil incarnate."

Emboldened by the anarchic atmosphere and the crumbling regime of the Shah, who had lost all control over the running of the country, many newspapers reported the mass ecstasy and mood of jubilation. Even secular intellectuals, writers, poets, scientists and philosophers, could not escape the populist mania that had engulfed the land and joined in affirming this unprecedented collective delusion. If any poor soul was foolish enough to question or doubt any of these fanciful sightings, he or she would be mocked at or even, in some cases, beaten up by gangs of loutish 'face-on-the-moon' vigilantes. All day long these idle zealots roamed the streets and alleyways, bullying the people of Tehran to climb up to their roofs, look at the holy man's image and spread the good news of the imminent coming of the long-absent saviour.

* * * *

One Friday afternoon, Kazem was sitting in the recess of the casement window with his head buried in a magazine, sounding out the words as a child does. All of a sudden, Mahmud the Scholar appeared outside, stuck his forehead close to the latticework, said jokingly, "Enough of reading, Kazem Agha. You'll become a scholar, the way you're studying."

"I wouldn't even dream of being a scholar like you," said Kazem, raising his head and looking at Mahmud.

"Don't say that, Kazem Agha," said Mahmud humbly. "I just like studying and reading and don't want to remain ignorant." He looked wistfully at the women, who were squatting around the *hauz* clacking like hens around a water trough and sighed.

"Let's go out and have a few glasses of *arrack,*"he suggested.

Kazem, tired and fed up, jumped at the offer. He told Maryam, who was sitting beside the samovar, that he would be back just before the curfew.

After a short bus ride, they arrived in Lalezar Avenue in central Tehran. Mahmud knew all the drinking dens there as well as he knew his pockets. They found a small tavern tucked away at the end of a narrow passage and settled down on two rickety chairs at a table spread over with a greasy oilcloth. A few other men who sat at another table were drinking, smoking, and talking quietly. Mahmud ordered a bottle of *arrack*, salami, pickled gherkins, a bowl of yoghurt mixed with chopped cucumber and mint, a baguette and tomatoes.

Mahmud poured some *arrack* into two small glasses, which they picked up and clinked.

"Knock it back to fill your heart with joy," Mahmud said, tilting his head backwards and gulping the contents of his glass in one go. Making a grimace, he shovelled a spoonful of yoghurt into his mouth.

"Cheers," Kazem said and did the same.

Downing a few glasses perked them up and they became a little tipsy.

"So, tell me, Kazem," Mahmud asked, a shadow of a smile flitting across his face, "have you managed to see the eighth wonder of the world yet?"

"The eighth wonder?" repeated Kazem, puzzled. "What? Have they discovered another one?"

"Oh yes, my friend," Mahmud said mischievously.

"What's that then?"

"The very image of the Grand Ayatollah on the moon!"

"Which ayatollah?" Kazem asked. "They come in so many different shapes and sizes. I don't know which one you have in mind."

"Don't be daft," said Mahmud. "The Ayatollah about whom everyone is talking these days. The one whose taped sermons are smuggled in and folk are scrambling over one another to get hold of in order to listen to them."

"Oh, I know," said Kazem, "the one who's in France and going on about setting up an Islamic State and shoving Sharia Law down the throats of hard-working people."

"Spot on," said Mahmud. "That's the one!"

"Is this the one who says the people should kick the Shah's backside and send him to hell, so that we become free and live in dignity and happiness forever?"

"That's him all right."

"What's he doing on the moon then?"

"Don't ask me," Mahmud said, rummaging in his pockets to find his packet of cigarettes. "Ask the people who have gone crazy about him."

"Why are these people behaving like this, Mahmud?" Kazem asked.

"Believe me, I'm racking my brains to understand all this odd behaviour," said Mahmud, offering the pack of cigarettes to his friend.

"I can only think of the Ayatollah turning into such a holy and mysterious being because of his years of banishment in Iraq," said Kazem, taking a cigarette and putting it to his lips.

"You have a point there," Mahmud said, lighting up Kazem's cigarette and then his own. "I vividly remember that hot summer day when the Shah told his henchmen to kick him out of Iran. The students of theology in Qom and the mollahs in Tehran went berserk and started beating themselves as a sign of protest."

"I remember it, too," agreed Kazem. "I was about fifteen when I heard the news. I was running some errands around here in Lalezar when I saw with my own eyes the troops pouring into the streets, arresting and beating up the protesters."

They both went on puffing away quietly, gazing at the patterns on the oilcloth.

After some moments Mahmud spoke.

"You see, Kazem, since the shameful Anglo-American coup d'état of the nineteenth of August 1953 that put an end to Dr Mosaddegh's democratically elected government and brought the Shah back to power, the people have been feeling deeply insulted and humiliated. The regime of the Shah didn't give a damn about their human dignity. For centuries, blows raining from all directions on their heads have stunned these people. Not knowing where the next blow would come from, they have had to resort to extravagant myths and the many superstitions brought to them as souvenirs by a host of barbaric invaders. All of these archaic beliefs and customs have come down to us, in the course of the centuries, from past generations without us ever questioning them. These beliefs were brought to us in the dark ages by countless foreign invaders and settlers such as Babylonians, Assyrians, Chaldeans, Greeks, Romans, Jews, Arabs, Turks and Mongols. The Chaldeans and Assyrians were the source of magic and superstitions with their bloodthirsty gods, sacrifices, auspiciousness or inauspiciousness of hours or days and the influence of malevolent stars on the destiny of human beings. The Greek invaders brought their fortune-tellers, little and large vengeful gods, demigods and goddesses, who had nothing better to do than fiddle with human affairs, siding with this king, revenging that prince or raping a pretty princess they were infatuated with. The constant wars with the Roman Empire made familiar to the Persians the role of a bunch of rogue astronomers, charlatan dream-interpreters and opportunist astrologists."

After this speech, Mahmud gulped down a glass of *arrack*, wiped his moustache with the palm of his hand, and went on, "The Jewish immigrants, who long ago were invited by Cyrus the Great to settle in Persia, brought with them as gifts the age-old wizardry from the Egyptian and Saudi Arabian deserts. Finally, the invasion of Arabs crowned this monumental misery in Persia. The Jewish people, being blood-relatives of the Arabs and of the same race, took the opportunity to spread these barbaric practices. Troops of Jewish and Arab *Hadith*-writers, chroniclers, and a bunch of superstition-manufacturers joined them in propagating mountains of meaningless absurdities in the minds of hard-working, tolerably rational Persian folk. Before all these invasions, the good old Persians went about their daily lives, working hard to create and maintain one of the oldest civilisations on this planet and minding their own business. They were a happy people and took great pride in enjoying what life offered them in this world, leaving the other one to fantasists and a load of good-for-nothing idlers who lived off the toils of poor peasants and labourers.

"The invasion of the Arabs not only confirmed the earlier superstitions but also added a completely new range to them. Among the infinite number of absurdities one can only count but some – the doctrine of one God who created Satan to tempt Adam and Eve in the Garden of Eden, the Fall from Heaven, life after death, Hell, Purgatory, Paradise, Doomsday, the idea that this world is just a passage leading to another one in which one can live forever with *houris* and *ghilmans*, the predominance of death over life, the superiority of torment over joy of life, the profanity of the human body, the existence of all manner of winged angels, the influence of fate in human affairs, leaving things to destiny, Sharia Law, fasting, unending prayers, prophecy, countless miracles attributed to Islamic saints, the dominance of men over women, being able to have many wives and an infinite number of *siegheh*s. These laws and rules have been infecting our lives from cradle to grave. All in all, they were too much for ordinary Persians to handle.

"When the Persians rebelled against the Arabs in order to get rid of them and their irrational faith, they were crushed so mercilessly that they could never even dream of asserting their own customs and traditions again. The defeat was so severe, so absolute and painful that they ended up being even more fatalistic than ever. In the course of the centuries, these primitive beliefs have paralysed their mental faculties. They try to explain everything by falling back upon superstitious balderdash."

Mahmud paused looked around him with glazed eyes.

"Add to all this the stinking cesspool of religion and ignorance and the frightening lack of real enlightenment that we never had, as happened in Europe after the Renaissance. If ever anyone, like Omar Khayyam, Zakariya Razi or Hafez, were brave enough to criticise the established ways of thinking, he'd be threatened with assassination, silenced in some way, or endlessly persecuted. Many books written by these courageous men were burnt in public to teach other freethinkers a lesson. Our tortured history shows that when people are oppressed for long periods and are not allowed to think freely for themselves, they hark back to primitive ways of behaviour, bringing back to life the ghosts of ancient superstitions and supernatural powers to seek explanations for events. After his expulsion, the Ayatollah was turned, overnight, into an unbelievable hero. He remained the only real hope of opposing the Shah's regime."

"I vaguely remember even many big-headed scholars thought of him as a holy man and pinned their hopes on him," Kazem put in.

"That's right," agreed Mahmud. "A group of them even took the trouble of travelling to Iraq as pilgrims to kiss his hands." Mahmud stubbed out his cigarette butt in the ashtray. "Now, after fifteen years in the wilderness, the holy man is coming back home, transformed into a saint."

"Hmm, a saint!" Kazem shook his head.

"A saint whose image has already appeared on the moon," Mahmud observed. "The Ayatollah has not even landed here and all sorts of farcical beliefs are already being fabricated, paving the way for yet another period of catastrophe in the history of our nation."

"You're right, Mahmud," Kazem agreed. "The signs are really worrying. Every day I witness more evidence of a new sort of oppression, far more sinister than the one we've been living with so far. Gangs of 'face-on-the-moon' vigilantes are stopping ordinary folk everywhere, asking them if they have seen the image of the Ayatollah on the moon. If some are foolish enough to say that they haven't, the gangs threaten to remember their faces and give them a good thrashing upon the return of the Ayatollah."

"Mark my words, Kazem Agha," Mahmud sighed, "the turn of events is definitely ominous. The other day, some books tucked under my arm, I was about to enter the university grounds when a bunch of bearded, rough-looking vigilantes barred my way and asked me if I had seen the holy face on the moon. I thought I'd better make up a story to keep these lunatics happy. I cried out enthusiastically that I'd seen it all. I even told them that every night I climb up to the roof, look at the moon, fall on the floor and pray in order to be blessed. Upon hearing me, they tapped my shoulder as if I were a sensible little boy who knew exactly what to do."

"Maybe I'll have to do the same one of these days," Kazem said.

"Good idea, Kazem Agha," Mahmud agreed. "Lies, lies, and more lies. It has become our second nature in order to survive. We're prepared to put on sale what's left of our humanity in order to lug these bodies of ours through this wretched existence we call living."

Kazem looked around with unfocused eyes. The tavern was now packed with men. They sat in small groups at the tables, clinked their glasses, knocked their drinks back, and puffed away at their cigarettes, talking quietly but animatedly. Every so often they vowed to remain truehearted to one another, whatever fate might throw at them. A few solitary figures were sitting on high stools at the bar counter, gulping down glass after glass, smoking, completely stoned. A cloud of thick smoke hung still in the air. Mournful tunes sung by a popular singer drifted out of a battered record player placed on the corner of the counter:

The night is falling and my heart is making excuses,
Longing to go to the tavern for a few cups of wine.
The folk who go to the tavern are not double-dealers,
They don't hide things from one another.
Tonight I'll take my heart with me there,
Where, at the end of the night, I'll abandon my woes.
We'll then wander in and out of alleyways in Shemroon,
Breathing the fresh air of Tehran after midnight.
I'll then whisper in your ear, "Forget the cares of this life,
Let's drink, sing, and dance, you and I, in the silent night.
Oh, my restless heart is fluttering, about to fly off,
To stay beside its sweetheart forever.

"Well, no more midnight wanderings with the sweetheart these days," said Mahmud tipsily, glancing around.

"That's right, mate." Kazem nodded ruefully.

It was getting late. Upon Kazem's insistence, Mahmud agreed that Kazem could pay the bill this time.

"Can we have the bill for our sins, bro?" Kazem called out to the waiter.

The two friends, both now quite drunk, stood up and staggered out of the tavern. The icy air lashed their faces, sobering them up a little as they wandered in the busy streets of Lalezar.

It was around dusk when they arrived at the lodging house. After saying goodnight to Mahmud, who staggered to his room beside the steps, Kazem shuffled up to the terrace. Hearing some noises coming from the roofs, he stopped and listened. He looked up. Overtaken by curiosity, he walked to the staircase that led up to the roof. He groped his way up the steps in the dark and into the *kharposhteh.* The whispers grew louder and louder, turning into wailing and lamentation.

He stepped out onto the roof. For a moment, he thought he had landed in a lost alien world. He rubbed his eyes, thinking that maybe he was still drunk and was hallucinating. He peered out at the moonlit rooftops around him.

Shadowy forms were prostrating themselves on all the surrounding rooftops. All of a sudden they all sat up and raised their hands towards the sky. The night air was filled with murmurs. Kazem looked up. The full moon, bathed in a murky whitish haze, was hanging in the black night sky.

Kazem gazed at the full moon, straining his eyes to see if he could see the face of the holy man. Alas, all he saw was the beautiful face of a woman, as he had always seen.

31

Kazem went on paying his rent regularly for the first few weeks. As he worked hard to save some money to make Maryam his legitimate wife, he found himself unable to pay his rent at the end of each week. So when the landlord appeared Kazem found himself making up all sorts of excuses, just like the other lodgers.

Every Friday morning, the landlord made his routine visit to the lodging house to collect his rents.

Kazem was well aware that most of the lodgers in those lodging houses were perpetually in arrears. Poverty and hunger had turned them into adept rent-dodgers. Throughout the years, generations of lodgers had devised their own tactics to put off paying their rents as long as possible until Providence dragged them, by some sort of miracle, out of an unholy difficulty not of their own making.

Every Friday morning Kazem would open the casement window wide and stand behind it, peeking through the slits in the straw blind, and watch the everyday tragi-comedy unfold in the courtyard.

Before the landlord's arrival, some lodgers would drag a few of their older and cleverer children out of their beds and tell them to go and sit near to the doorway of the house to keep an eye on the lane. The still-sleepy children would keep themselves occupied by playing games such as knucklebones while glancing from time to time at the end of the lane. These children were instructed to give early warnings to the lodgers of the approach of the much-hated landlord.

As soon as the landlord turned the corner at the end of the lane, these young scouts would get up, dash back to the courtyard and howl as loudly as they could, whereupon the courtyard would turn into a veritable bedlam. The women would snatch their babies, grab the hands of the toddlers, and dash helter-skelter to their rooms, slamming the doors shut behind them. They would then pull down the blinds, draw the curtains, and smother their babies and young kids under whatever cushions and rags were at hand, forcing them not to utter a sound. They would then sit in the window recesses and peep out from behind the curtains like terrified animals, holding their breaths.

The landlord would kick the shaky door open, almost tearing down the cloth precariously suspended behind it, and burst down into the courtyard. His powerfully built figure, dressed in a black suit, would come to a standstill at the bottom of the steps. He would then survey the courtyard from under his thick eyebrows, twiddle his handlebar moustache and snort like a bull, slowly shaking his head like the chief of a band of bandits. A puny little ragamuffin, blissfully enjoying his rest in the privy and unaware of the events about to happen, would usually emerge and look in abject terror around the deserted courtyard. Upon seeing the frightful figure of the landlord, he would then scurry across the courtyard, tying up the rubber strings around his trousers that kept falling down his dusty bottom. Ignoring the little devil, the landlord would shamble to the dented trash barrel and kick the mangy cat greedily lapping up the black slime oozing from under the barrel, sending it somersaulting on the paving stones. The screeching of the famished cat before it climbed over the wall and vanished would shatter the silence of the courtyard.

After sticking his thick snout into the barrel, choked with rotting garbage and darkened by swarms of flies, the landlord would shuffle here and there, dragging his patent-leather shoes, the heels of which were studded with nails, on the paving stones. He would manoeuvre through trash littered everywhere, lift the washing hung on the lines, examine carefully the rusty bikes with twisted wheels, and kick a few gasoline drums, sending them rattling across the floor. He would then walk to the privy, pull the cloth aside, stick his head inside, and sniff the air like a reptile. Finally, he would walk to the *hauz*, plant himself beside it, and glare at the rooms one at a time.

"I know you've all crawled into your rooms like rats!" His voice would thunder across the courtyard. "I'll stand here the whole day, if necessary, till you come out of your rooms and settle your rents. You know that it's no use hiding like this."

Kazem could hear only the stifled whimpering of a baby coming from one room or the smothered howling of a scared little child from another. He knew that the lodgers, just like himself, were standing behind their windows and watching the landlord's one-man act as he strutted about like a turkey cock, his heavy footfalls echoing in the quiet courtyard.

"This house is not a poorhouse, you know," the landlord would bellow. "I haven't opened a luxury hotel here for you to stay scot-free and have a good time. I've to earn a living, too. Who in heaven's name is going to support my large family if you don't pay your rents? So, be reasonable and come out and settle your arrears."

He would amble up and down the courtyard, gesticulating wildly, vigorously driving away the flies buzzing persistently around him, and talk, as if to himself, like an actor performing his often-repeated monologues for an uninterested audience. Not hearing a sound coming out of the rooms, he would gradually lose his temper and raise his voice to thunder-pitch, threatening to throw all the lodgers and their belongings out into the lane any minute.

As in a well-practised farce, the first lodger to appear on the terrace would be Ghanbar Vafuri, a one-time most formidable and feared strongman and knife-fighter in the area. He was a lanky, middle-aged man with a bent back. His hollow cheeks were permanently covered with greying stubble. His sparse, greasy hair made a few streaks on his balding head, enhancing the pallor of his face. Dressed in his sleeveless vest and frayed loose trousers, he would stand behind the banister rail and manfully challenge the landlord, brandishing the only faithful companion and weapon left from his days of glory – his opium pipe!

"Mashallah Khan," he would cry out feebly, "what's all this kerfuffle first thing in the morning again?"

"I want my overdue rents, Mash Ghanbar," Mashallah Khan would snort at the junky. "I'm not doing anything against the civil and Sharia law. You and the others give me my money and I'll go away this minute."

"All right, Mashallah Khan, all right, will do, honest," Ghanbar Vafuri would whine, quivering in the fresh air and waving his opium pipe about in the manner of a mythological champion swinging his mace to warn the enemy. "As soon as I get hold of some cash I'll sort you out. That's a gentleman's promise I'm making to you."

"I've had enough of your *gentleman's* promises, thank you," Mashallah Khan would yell. "I want hard cash, Mash Ghanbar. Do you get it, hard cash?"

Ignoring the junky contemptuously, Mashallah Khan would begin to stomp angrily up and down at the bottom of the terrace in front of the hovels, repeating his usual threats.

"Those of you whose rents are in arrears of one week to one month," he would say, "must settle your dues tomorrow without further delay, otherwise I'll come back with my men and chuck all your belongings out into the lane."

He would then fall silent and fix his eyes on one of the hovels. Next, he would advance towards the unfortunate family who had taken cover behind the curtained-off door. He would all of a sudden charge ahead, fuming and snorting like an enraged wild boar. Once in front of the door, he would call out the name of the man hiding in the hovel. Hearing no response, he would hammer on the door, kicking it open, and storming into the room

Then muffled bellowing of the landlord mingled with the heartrending screeches of the lodger, his wife and their kids. Next, various objects could be seen flying out of the room as the landlord grabbed hold of whatever he could lay his hands on and threw it out, working as diligently as if clearing a cellar choked with junk. This sorry collection of items was always the same, no matter from which room they were thrown out: blackened kettles, cracked pots, ancient samovars, dented braziers, tattered bundles of blankets, filthy and lumpy cushions, tin trays, saucers, cups, tin bowls and plates. They would all land on the paving stones, making a fearful clatter and joining the shambles of other junk in the courtyard.

Having accomplished his task, Mashallah Khan would storm out of the room, kicking whatever he could trample upon, swearing and cursing angrily. The husband and wife would then follow him out, howling hysterically. They would beseech him not to smash their wretched things. All their begging, hair-pulling, head-slapping and the invocation of all the martyrs of Karbala would fall on deaf ears. Mashallah Khan, without getting a *gheran* out of the hovel-dwellers beneath the terrace, would strut around again, addressing the ones on the terrace, roaring even louder.

"Come on out, everyone!" he would bawl. "If any of you can't afford your rent, just clear off. I've had enough of your excuses. I must repeat, I'll no more accept guarantors."

He would then go from door to door, reminding the lodgers of their overdue rents: "Hassan Agha, your rent is overdue for three months. Nayeb Agha, you haven't paid your rent for three weeks…"

The only person exempt from his angry outbursts was Shamsi Khanum. It was common knowledge that she stayed there free in exchange for her favours.

The lodgers, one at a time, would open their doors, stand on the threshold and repeat their well-worn excuses:

"I've lost my job again, Mashallah Khan. As soon as I find something, I'll pay," Hassan Ghorazeh would say.

"I had to spend all my money on my sick child last week. I had become so desperate that I had to sell my blood to a blood-dealer to earn some cash," Mehdi Kharaki would moan.

"My man has vanished, the devil knows where, and no one supports me any more. As soon as I find someone, I'll squeeze some cash out of him and settle your rent," Showkat Dallaak would shriek.

Fed up and exhausted, the landlord would then take himself off, threatening the lodgers with legal action against all of them, which he never got round to carrying out.

32

As the curfew remained in force, the social and political unrest gathered momentum. Many people had become so bold that they ignored the rules altogether. Going out after dark, they bought goods from the black-marketeers lurking in shadowy corners, and, if daring, carried on with their secret propagandist activities such as writing slogans on the walls and distributing pamphlets. The ruling Pahlavi regime was in its last death throes. Tehran's inhabitants were receiving Khomeini's messages through foreign radios. Towards the end of November, the Shah appeared on national television, addressing the nation in an emotional tone; he had heard their grievances, admitted that mistakes had been made, and he would do his utmost to improve things. He grovelled for forgiveness. He promised his subjects to sort things out by establishing true democracy if given another chance. People all over the land just laughed and cracked jokes at his farcical show of regret and crocodile tears.

Kazem, by now, had managed to dodge the rent one way or another and put some cash together. As Maryam had come of age, he thought that it was time they went to find Mollah Hossein.

It was on a cold morning towards the end of December that Kazem set off with Maryam to the local mosque. Downtown Tehran was as chaotic as everywhere else. The worn-out soldiers, who had had enough of all this mayhem, were patrolling the major avenues, squares and government buildings.

The local mosque was under siege from a large throng of people who had come to see the mollahs for various reasons. Kazem, followed by Maryam, found his way through the crowd in the small courtyard.

"You wait here and I'll go inside to see if I can find Mollah Hossein," Kazem said to Maryam, who stood near a pillar, veiled in her chador.

Kazem walked into the main hall. As it was noon, the place was packed with all kinds of workers, stallholders and shopkeepers doing their prayers. Kazem stood at the back of the rows of men and pretended that he was praying. Their devotions over, everybody sat down to listen to the brief sermon from the imam, whom Kazem soon recognised as none other than Mollah Hossein. He was talking without fear about the regime and its imminent downfall. Kazem's only interest, however, was in asking the mollah to marry him to Maryam as soon as possible.

Once his ranting against the regime of the Shah had finished, the crowd got up, shook one another's hands, and left the mosque, noisily discussing recent political events. Kazem waited until the hall was quiet. He then walked towards Mollah Hossein who was sorting out his turban and gathering his *aba* round him, preparing to rush to attend another religious function.

"*Salaam*, Agha," said Kazem, respectfully putting his hand on his chest.

"Oh, it's you, my son," replied Mollah Hossein. "So, I suppose you've come back to ask me to carry out the marriage formalities?"

"Yes, Agha, that's right."

"Can you remind me of your name?" asked Mollah Hossein. "It's been a while since I saw you last."

"Yours truly, Kazem Alaki."

"That's right, Kazem Agha." Mollah Hossein nodded. "As this is a legal matter, the formalities this time will take place in the registry office down the road not far from here. You go and wait outside the mosque and when I come out, follow me at a short distance with the young lady."

Kazem went out and found Maryam quietly waiting for him. After a few minutes, Mollah Hossein joined them, motioning to them to follow him. He walked briskly along the pavement, every now and then wrapping his unruly *aba* round him to keep warm.

Several men and women, bundles of papers tucked under their arms, crowded outside the main building of the registry, arguing in subdued voices and fluttering their hands before them. Upon seeing Mollah Hossein, the people parted to let him pass, bowing and greeting him profusely by putting their hands on their chests. Mollah Hossein, while nodding right and left to everyone, walked straight into the building, beckoning to Kazem to follow him. At the end of the narrow corridor, he stood in front of the office proper and asked Kazem and Maryam to wait just outside the door until they were called in. He then disappeared behind the door. A number of people were sitting on chairs ranged along the corridor, on each side of which there were two rooms. Every so often, the door of one of these rooms opened and a busy-looking clerk dashed out, scurried across the corridor, and vanished into another room, slamming the door behind him.

Kazem told Maryam to sit on the only available chair. Standing beside her, he began surreptitiously eyeing the others, all sitting there grim-faced.

Directly opposite him sat a timid young man with a dreary expression, soft black beard and well-combed hair and wearing a white shirt buttoned up to his throat for the occasion. He remained motionless with his hands on his knees. Beside him sat his tongue-tied wife-to-be enveloped from head to ankles in her black chador. Another couple sat on the chairs near the entrance. About thirty, the man was lanky with a bony face and a drooping moustache. His very long, neatly combed hair cascaded over his shoulders. The top buttons of his bile-coloured shirt were undone, revealing his bony hairy chest. The woman, who wore a short skirt, had put on heavy make-up with the latest fashionable hair-do and an abundance of tacky jewellery. Directly across from Maryam were a harassed-looking middle-aged man and a pale-faced young woman, both gazing mutely at a bundle of certificates held in their hands.

The religious-looking young pair was the first to go in. Ten minutes were not out before the door of the office opened and the couple emerged, no doubt now married. They both looked bewildered and as gloomy as before, as if something terrible had happened to them. The middle-aged man and his doom-stricken wife were next. The door had scarcely shut when Kazem heard swearing and mutual recriminations from both sides. After a short hush and some whispering, the door was opened and the angry-looking couple stormed out of the office, muttering a profusion of curses and threats. The fashionable couple were then asked to go in. This time the office echoed with joyful laughter and jokes. The happy couple soon emerged, holding hands. As they breezed past those waiting, they did not throw so much as a glance at anybody.

Finally, Mollah Hossein showed up, looking cheerful for some reason. By this time, the corridor was deserted, except for one man who kept pacing up and down, mumbling to himself. Mollah Hossein gathered his *aba* round him, walked over to Kazem and Maryam, and asked them in a low voice to follow him to the office.

The office was a small room with bare walls on which hung only pictures of the Shah, the Queen and some Arabic verses in frames about the absolute necessity of marriage in Islam. A podgy, middle-aged man in his fifties sat behind a bulky table on which sprawled an enormous open book. From behind a pair of antique spectacles, resting on the arc of his big nose, he was scrutinising some records in the book. A young man in a black suit frayed at the sleeves and collar sat behind another smaller table in the right corner, diligently copying from some papers into a voluminous book.

The middle-aged man raised his head from the register and peered at

Kazem and Maryam with his lacklustre eyes. He then greeted them, eyeing Maryam with interest..

"Most welcome," he said mechanically, sitting up a little on his chair and addressing Kazem. "Our devout friend Mollah Hossein here has been singing your praises to us as being a God-fearing good Muslim. We're always more than happy to help our brothers." He pointed to two chairs near the door, "Please be seated." Kazem smiled politely, amused at someone calling him a good Muslim for the first time in his life.

"Ahmad Agha." The registrar turned to his clerk. "Could you nip off to the *abdarkhaneh* and ask Mash Ghazanfar to bring glasses of tea for our guests? Don't forget to tell him to make sure the tea is freshly-brewed."

The young clerk dropped his pen on the book, sprang to his feet, threw a simpering glance at Maryam, and disappeared into another room that must have been the *abdarkhaneh*. Kazem could hear him talking to Mash Ghazanfar. Within a minute, he reappeared, followed by Mash Ghazanfar, who was balancing a tray of tea things on his hand. The ill-humoured old man, half-smoked cigarette between his lips and a teacloth thrown over his shoulder, deposited the tray on the corner of the bulky table and ambled off behind the door of the *abdarkhaneh* without looking at anyone. The clerk handed tea glasses to the guests and put one on his own table. He then sat on his chair, noisily slurped the whole of his tea in two saucerfuls, and carried on with his scribbling.

"Let's get down to the ceremony of sorting out the marriage certificate for our brother and sister," began the registrar in a solemn tone. "Your witnesses, Brother Kazem, are my clerk, Ahmad Agha, here and Mash Ghazanfar. They will sign the marriage certificate and Mollah Hossein, being like a father to you both, will forge a signature on behalf of the father of the young lady." He paused a little and added, "No need to emphasise the fact that none of this should escape this office."

"Understood, Agha," Kazem mumbled.

"What's your name, brother?" asked the registrar.

"Yours truly, Kazem Alaki," Kazem said.

"Is Alaki your patronymic?"

"Yes, Agha."

"And that's the patronymic of your father?"

"My father died before I was born," said Kazem, ill at ease. "No one has ever told me who he was."

"So where did you get that nickname from?"

"Everyone has called me Alaki since I was a little kid."

The registrar nodded his head, as if he understood it all.

"What is the name of the young lady, brother?" he asked.

"Maryam Harirchi, agha," replied Kazem.

The registrar then turned to Maryam and asked her the question he asked of all brides-to-be.

"Khanum-e Maryam-e Harirchi, do I have your permission to marry you to Jenab-e Agha-e Kazem, known as Alaki?"

As Maryam was not sure what to do or say, Kazem, panicking a bit, had to give her a gentle nudge.

"You're supposed to say *yes*," he said under his breath, half turning towards her.

"Yes," murmured Maryam.

"Louder please, Maryam Khanum," the registrar demanded.

"Yes," Maryam repeated loudly.

He then turned to Kazem, repeating the same question.

"Agha Kazem, known as Alaki, are you willing to accept Maryam Khanum-e Harirchi as your legal wife for ever?"

"Yes, yes," Kazem said loudly.

"I now declare you man and wife," the registrar stated.

All of a sudden, Mollah Hossein got up and started to hold forth solemnly with an oration in praise of the constitution of marriage:

"Praise be to Allah Most High, who keeps all life going by mixing and mingling men and women from all races. He makes sure that humanity survives due to His erecting the firm foundations of the institution of marriage. Eternal greetings and praise are also due to Prophet Mohammad (blessings of Allah be upon him and his descendants) the greatest prophet of all times, who has encouraged and emphasised the importance of this time-honoured, commendable tradition."

He then produced a small dog-eared volume of the Holy Book from under his *aba*, put it on the table and asked Kazem to stand up, put his hand on the Book, and repeat after him:

"I swear to this word of Allah that I'll be a good husband for my wife till I die."

Kazem repeated the phrase, kissed the Book, and sat down again.

Mollah Hossein then asked Maryam to do the same.

"I swear I'll be a good wife for my husband till I'm carried out of his home on a ladder wrapped in a shroud."

He then urged everyone to chant a few *salawats* so that the happy couple would be protected by the blessings of the Prophet and his clan. With unsmiling faces, everyone intoned the Arabic formula with feeling, as if they were sitting in a mosque listening to a mollah chanting a dirge to the martyrs of Karbala.

"If you don't have a ring, don't worry about it, brother," the registrar said after the *salawats* were over. "Find a ring as soon as you can and put it on your wife's finger so that other men know that she belongs to you."

The couple were then asked to sign their names on the marriage certificate. The first witness, Mash Ghazanfar, was called in. After planting his illegible, made-up signature at the bottom of the certificate, he got his share of a few tomans, muttered a "God bless" and walked back into the *abdarkhaneh*. Next was the clerk, who also knew exactly what to do. He took his cash, grinned broadly, pocketed it, and went back to his desk.

It was around five o'clock in the afternoon when the couple, now legally married, stood outside the registry office. Kazem glanced around. A few men and women lingered on the pavement, hugging themselves against the bitter cold. The sky was downcast.

"We should go and find a ring as soon as possible so that everyone knows that we're married," said Kazem.

They walked to the bazaar and found a cheap ring for Maryam, who wore it there and then.

33

The cauldron of Tehran's society continued to seethe with unrest. Having run through all the familiar tricks at his disposal, the monarch and his cronies kept trying desperately to come up with some new tricks. The masses, like a gigantic river that has overflown its banks, were now on the move and no power on earth was able to stop them. The media began timidly to touch upon taboo subjects, up to then unmentionable. The news from Paris was easily accessible to the populace through foreign radio stations and secretly distributed pamphlets.

As martial law remained in force, albeit in a farcical manner, every evening the menfolk of the lodging house gathered on the terrace to debate the events of the day.

To confound it all, that year, the holy month of Moharram happened to coincide with the beginning of December. According to an age-old superstition, Moharram announces itself by rotten weather. December started off with an icy north wind that blowing in the streets and lanes of Tehran, swirling dust and dirt along the pavements and carrying with it the stench of slimy gutters, choked with the rotting refuse that ran along the streets. The timing of Moharram was auspicious to religious zealots. Social and political discontent, poverty, the swelling Tehran's population with rootless peasants turned into lumpen hoi polloi, Ayatollah mania, the second coming of Mahdi, all these made fertile ground in which the lunacy of Moharram would hammer the final nail into the coffin of the Pahlavi regime. The inhabitants of Tehran were bracing themselves for the decisive showdown – the day of *Ashura* that occurs on the tenth day of Moharram when, many centuries ago, some Arab despots martyred the grandson of the Prophet, Imam Hossein, in Karbala.

Traditionally, the whole country comes to a complete standstill on the day of *Ashura*. If you went out on the morning of the day of *Ashura*, you would feel as if you had entered a city ravaged by plague. All the government institutions, shops, Tehran's Bazaar, transport system, teahouses, restaurants, taverns, cabarets, cinemas, stallholders, whorehouses in Shahr-e No – all stop working on this day.

On the day of *Ashura,* a mixture of clinking, banging and rattling noises coming from the courtyard woke Kazem. He sat up in bed and listened.

"This blooming *Ashura* again," he muttered, rubbing his eyes. "Year in year out they have to go through this charade, beating and flagellating themselves with chains, only the devil knows why." He looked at Maryam, who was sound asleep. "They don't even let one have a good sleep."

Kazem walked to the casement, opened it wide, and peered into the courtyard through the gaps in the straw blind. He went out of the room and looked up. Dark, menacing clouds were gathering over the sky above the shantytowns in the south of Tehran. An ice-cold wind blew down to the courtyard from the roofs, whirling around like a gypsy in a trance. It whipped, shrieking, around the courtyard, snatching the washing off the lines and sending it fluttering in the air like rags torn from the bodies of beggars. It knocked over the empty gasoline barrels, making them rattle mournfully. It spun round the trash barrel, grabbed handfuls of the rubbish covered in sweepings, and hurled them in the air. Turning round, it swirled round the terrace, making the straw blinds flap against the lattices.

The womenfolk, all wearing black scarves and wrapped up in black chadors, emerged from their rooms and hovels and ran about the courtyard, trying to catch the flying rags like kids chasing after low-flying kites. Some sleepy-faced ragamuffins, excited by the commotion, pursued the gasoline barrels, amusing themselves by kicking them. As the women ran around, their chadors flapped in the wind, like the feathers of ravens. The menfolk, dressed in black shirts and trousers, appeared from different corners of the courtyard, all dishevelled and with their faces darkened with stubble. They then sat in twos and threes, whispering to one another. Grave and thoughtful, it was as if awaiting the funeral of someone known to all of them. The stench of the garbage mingled with the foul odour of the privy was so strong that Kazem had to go back to the room.

It was impossible for Kazem and Maryam not to join the events of *Ashura*. After a quiet breakfast, they both, rather reluctantly, got ready to join the others to go out to a *tekieh* set up in the house of a devout bazaar merchant in one of the neighbouring lanes. Maryam, like the other women of the house, wrapped some lumps of cheese, grapes and *sangak* bread in a cloth bundle to take with them. Kazem joined the other men in the courtyard to smoke and chat about the coming chest-beating and self-flagellating processions that were going to take place in the afternoon. All the men, except Mahmud and Karim Darvish, were wearing black shirts, the backs of which were torn so that they could flagellate themselves in empathy with the martyred Imam Hossein.

It was around midmorning that all the women, their dinner bundles tucked under their chadors, left the house, heading noisily towards the *tekieh* to find suitable places with a good view of the spectacle, where they could settle down comfortably to chat and catch up with the latest scandals in the neighbourhood.

Most of the men left the house to take part in the procession that was to start from the *tekieh* well before noon. Kazem stayed behind for a little while to chat with Mahmud and Karim Darvish. As the wind had died down a bit, they sat on the steps to smoke.

"Aren't you both going to see what's going on?" Kazem asked.

"Nope," Mahmud said.

"Why not, Mahmud Khan?" inquired Kazem. "It's great fun."

"Fun!" repeated Mahmud, looking at Kazem suspiciously.

"Yes," declared Kazem. "I've taken part in *Ashura*, only because I always found it quite amusing to watch people doing such silly things." He laughed. "Over and above that, they give you votive sherbet, dates, halva and the most tasty *gheymeh khorosht*."

"You may be right, Kazem Agha," said Mahmud. "But I can't stand the sight of these imbeciles beating and lacerating themselves for an Arab man who, so the story goes, was killed by some other Arab bastards."

"I agree with you, Mahmud Khan," Kazem said. "Since I was a child I've been taking part in these ceremonies for the wrong reasons. I remember when I was growing up in Shahr-e No, the Citadel would be shut to all the clients during *Ashura* and the prostitutes would stop working to show their respects to the martyrs. They would get together and each put whatever money they could afford in a tin that would go towards setting up a *tekieh* that would take place in a converted cabaret. The strong-men and pimps would invite a small-time mollah from the local mosque to give a sermon about the martyrs of Karbala and chant some dirges in their praise. Once the preaching was over, all the pimps and knife-fighters, all wearing black shirts and black trousers, would organize a small procession, chant, beat and flagellate themselves till many of them fainted. The good old prostitutes would come out and stand outside the whorehouses, screeching and pulling their hair for the martyred Imam Hossein and his clan. We kids were in heaven during that day. Larking around the Shahr-e No from dawn to dusk, we were always as starved as the rats that lived and died in the stinking gutters. Nothing was more welcome than the votive dates, halva, and *gheymeh khorosht* carted into the place in large cauldrons by some rich, kindly men. We never understood what all that beating, weeping and chanting were about. Truth be told, we didn't give a monkey's about the martyrs of Karbala. We just amused ourselves by joining in the fun. Once our bellies were full, we just laughed at the whole thing, as if we were watching one of those hilarious farces the prostitutes staged in the cabaret."

"*Hey, hey*, Kazem Agha," said Mahmud, "if only we were all smart enough to learn a few lessons from those kids, not taking religion so seriously, the destiny of this nation would've been different."

"So you're not coming, then?" Kazem asked.

"Nope," was the emphatic reply. "I'll stay in my room and read a bit."

Kazem got up, tapped his friend's shoulder in a friendly manner, and walked out of the house.

The lane was deserted. The usual sounds of everyday life were absent. As Kazem walked past the front of one house, its door opened a crack and the wrinkled face of an old woman, framed in a black chador, appeared behind the door.

"May God bless you, my son," the old woman whimpered. "Can you take me to the *tekieh*?"

Kazem stopped. "Sure, mother."

He took the woman's hand, and helped her out of the door.

"You don't have anyone to take you there, mother?" he asked.

"No, my son," replied the woman, holding on to Kazem's arm.

"Some of the lodgers could have helped you," he said.

"They were all in a hurry to go," she said. "These folk only think of themselves these days and don't have patience to drag me along."

"Why are you going to *tekieh* instead of staying at home and having a rest?"

"I want to pay my respect to Imam Hossein and beg him to cure all my pains."

"Do you think he can do that, mother?"

"Oh, yes, my son," exclaimed the old woman with absolute certainty. "His martyred great-grandson, Imam Reza, performed a miracle on one of the old women in the neighbourhood. After years of being crippled, she made up her mind to go as a pilgrim to the holy city of Mashhad, take refuge in the holy sanctuary, and pray the whole day long till the Imam granted her wishes. After she had stayed inside the shrine for a few months, living only on votive dates and charity food, the Imam himself visited her in person and granted her wish. Once the Imam had vanished into a halo of light, she all of a sudden jumped to her feet and began dancing with joy like a young woman. If that is not a miracle, what else is?"

As she clung to Kazem's arm, they walked slowly. She went on rambling about all sorts of miracles performed by these holy men whose shrines were scattered all over Iran. Kazem just nodded his head, looking around every now and then. All the streets, lanes, and alleyways were deserted. From time to time one or two cripples in rags emerged from a lane and crawled along the gutters. They crept behind some beggars, who ran briskly towards different mosques and *tekiehs* to be the first to collect as much halva and votive dates as possible in their empty bags. Apart from these experienced hangers-on who benefited from *Ashura*, small bands of ragamuffins congregated to join the others to get their share of votive delicacies and food. Noisily capering here and there, they tormented, at every opportunity, the packs of skinny stray dogs and cats that roamed in the empty streets, sniffing the trash-choked gutters.

As Kazem, holding the old woman's arm, approached the *tekieh*, more people poured into the streets, hurrying in the same direction. Once they had turned into a long and wide lane at the end of which was the *tekieh*, Kazem saw a procession being formed by a dark mass of men surging out of the *tekieh* into the lane. He directed the old woman towards the entrance and asked another woman to help her to settle down. The old woman blessed Kazem effusively and became lost among the gaggle of black-chadored women behind a black curtain. He then turned and observed the crowd of men for a while before joining them.

The throng, all dressed in long black shirts that hung over their trousers, were being herded by some other black-clad men out of the *tekieh*. Most of these scruffy-looking men had moustaches and black beards grown long for the occasion. From the way they looked and behaved, Kazem guessed that this motley bunch consisted of day labourers, errand boys, shopkeepers, street pedlars, artisans, stallholders and all manner of low-life.

He walked to the front of the procession to see who the *alamdar* was. All his life he had been fascinated by those athletic-looking young men who would do anything to have the honour of carrying the *alam* in front of a procession. The *alam* was a long steel rod to which were fixed a number of different-sized, flat iron plates, tapering towards the top. At the tip of each plate was a stylized hand signifying the chopped-off hands of Abbas, the brother of Imam Hossein. The *alam* was lavishly decorated with brightly coloured green shawls – the colour of the Prophet's clan – on which were embroidered verses of the Koran and sayings of the martyrs. The young *alamdar* wore a thick leather baldric flung over one shoulder and reaching down to the opposite hip. Attached to the bottom of the baldric was a small cast-iron cup into which was inserted the vertical rod that supported the *alam*.

Kazem found a place right in front, close to the *alamdar.* The young man, sweating and panting, was struggling to lift the *alam* in the midst of *salawat* after *salawat* being chanted to spur him on. This must be his first time lifting the *alam*, Kazem thought. The bearded young *alamdar* was keen to show that he was up to the job.

Some morose-looking men were handing over bundles of chains made of small oblong rings attached to a handle, made to order by ironsmiths, to be used for self-flagellation. Each man hooked the handle to his belt and joined the procession of two parallel lines of men who marched solemnly out of the *tekieh.* In the middle of the procession stood a stocky, bearded man with a microphone in one hand, yelling into it with all his might, while raising the other hand as high as possible and bringing it down with terrifying force, in the same manner as a butcher lifts his cleaver to chop a lamb shoulder. A young man with a downy beard, as thin as straw, with a loudspeaker balanced on his head, followed the dirge-singer. The dirge issued from the loudspeaker at full blast.

Oh, beloved of Fatimah, I beseech you,
Do not go to the battlefield,
I implore you do not go.

As the two lines of men stepped out of the *tekieh*, they took up the last verse as a refrain, chanting, moving in step to the beat, and lashing their backs.

With the rhythmic rise and fall of the chains, the tail end of the procession, mostly children and women, trickled out of the *tekieh.* It then snaked out of the lane into the street. As the men moved in step to the rhythm of the refrain, they bawled louder and louder. In a frenzy of maniacal ecstasy, they speeded up the flagellation, slashing their backs as hard as possible, and tore the backs of their shirts into tatters, lacerating their flesh. The more zealous ones were keen on outshining the others by mutilating themselves. As this went on, the women, who had followed the procession with jars of water in their hands, broke into hysterical shrieks. The babies and children, terrified out of their wits, burst into non-stop howling and clung to their mothers' chadors, shivering and trembling in the cold air.

Filling up the whole of the street, the procession crawled slowly in the direction of Galubandak junction. More people from the neighbouring lanes and alleys emerged and walked parallel to it, weeping noisily and slapping their foreheads. The young men in the procession became even more excited and flagellated themselves even harder when they noticed that some young women were watching them with admiring eyes from the edge of their chadors.

Other processions from the neighbouring lanes and streets joined the main procession, swelling it to gigantic proportions. When the procession met another head on, they both came to a halt and faced one another. The two *alamdars* lowered their *alams* a few times as a sign of respect in the manner of generals of two allied armies who salute each other before sending their soldiers into a joint battle against a common enemy. Who was the friend and who the foe for this mishmash army of mourners? Kazem pondered the question.

By the time the procession reached the Galubandak junction it had become quite large. With others joining from the nearby streets, it now looked colossal. At the junction, the multitude stopped to listen to a famous mollah who was to give a sermon about the tragic events of the day of *Ashura*. The loudspeakers fitted outside a mosque amplified the mollah's braying. All the men, worn out and bathed in sweat running down their bruised and blood-drenched backs, stood with their heads bowed, their hands clasped in front of them, listening in respectful pose to the mournful voice of the mollah.

After going through his stock of fables, the mollah began to chant a sorrowful dirge in praise of the Prince of the Martyrs. His voice choked with emotion. Grief-stricken, all the men listened to the mollah as if they had lost beloved members of their own families. They sobbed so noisily that their shoulders convulsed like those in the grip of an epileptic seizure. The throng of people on the pavements took up the refrain and chanted at the tops of their lungs, weeping bitterly, sniffling, and wiping their noses and eyes.

All of a sudden, Kazem heard the voices of a few young men singing a different tune. He listened carefully. He could not believe his ears. "The Shah must go and Khomeini must return."

They must've gone mad shouting something like that, he thought. To his astonishment, not only did the others not rush to silence the young men, but they, too, began to chant the unthinkable slogan. In a matter of minutes, the whole place was shaking with the frenetic screaming of the multitude repeating the chant over and over. Upon hearing this madness, the mollah had no choice but to adopt a new direction, following the crowd. He, too, began yelling feverishly, "The Shah must go and Khomeini must return!"

Soon a veritable pandemonium ensued. Everybody by now had taken up the slogan, screaming as loudly as they possibly could for the Shah to step down. I'd better do as they do, Kazem thought, otherwise these blockheads will set upon me like rabid dogs, so he screamed even louder than others.

The mollahs soon threw their lot in with the angry multitude. With their *abas* wrapped round their bodies, they walked out of the mosque, surrounded by several rough-looking men. They began to lead the massive procession towards Baharestan Square in central Tehran. Kazem was shocked to see the sea of black-clad figures that had filled up such a large square. Everybody was shouting one single slogan. Kazem saw one of the mollahs leap, as agile as a monkey, on the bonnet of a car and begin to egg the mob on. He looks so familiar, Kazem thought. It was Mollah Hossein himself. The way he's screaming his head off, Kazem reflected, he'll climb to the top after the Shah's departure.

That evening Kazem joined a handful of the menfolk of the lodging house to talk about the day's events. Worn-out after a day of screeching and self-flagellation, they squatted around the *hauz*, smoking. Ghanbar Vafuri, his mangy sheepskin waistcoat flung over his shoulders, was the first to speak.

"After what happened today," said he in his pompous manner, dragging hard at his cigarette, "the Shah's a goner. Just mark my word, brothers."

"I think you're right, Mash Ghanbar," agreed Hassan Ghorazeh, blue with cold and shivering. "The soldiers just stood around the processions and did not even raise a finger to stop the people."

"The Shah's a goner, for sure," said Mehdi Kharaki, assuming the air of a sceptic, "but who's going to replace him? That's the worry."

Kazem listened without comment.

The men went on thrashing out every possible social, political and religious subject till late. Feeling the chill in their bones, they got up one at a time and shuffled to their rooms. Once in his room, Kazem sat in the window recess, smoking and thinking about the day. In the black wintry night faint murmurs could be heard as distant chants of "Allahu Akbar" drifted down from the neighbouring roofs.

34

During the rest of the month of Muharram Tehran was thrown into even more turmoil. By the end of the month, the people's anger had reached a tipping point. All that was needed was a pretext to ignite the revolution proper. This occurred on the seventh of January, 1979. On that day the daily paper *Ettela'at* published an insulting article about Khomeini.

The following day in the bazaar Kazem heard the news of big riots in the holy city of Qom in support of the Ayatollah. By now, he had found it impossible to remain indifferent to the rapid sequence of events engulfing all aspects of Tehran's life. Every evening after doing some literacy homework with Maryam, he would crouch over the radio, tune into foreign broadcasts in Persian, and listen to the latest news of yet more events unfolding in France. After the thirteenth of January, all the people in the lodging house had learned that Khomeini had formed a Revolutionary Council in Paris and it was only a matter of weeks before he would return to Iran.

Now familiar with the menfolk of the lodging house, Kazem had come to know more about the peculiarities of each, their habits and the intrigues in their private lives. Every late afternoon, just before the curfew came into effect, Kazem and Ali Khalifeh would pack up the kebab stall and go to Sayyed Vali's teahouse in the bazaar to drink, smoke, and catch up with the latest rumours. At that hour of the day, the teahouse would be jammed with workers and small-time merchants. The teahouse was also a favourite hangout for the men from the lodging house after they had finished work.

On the sixteenth of January, around four o'clock in the afternoon, as Kazem was busy spitting the pieces of meat and fanning them on the brazier, he heard the hooting of cars mingled with people yelling. Some hotheads must be demonstrating again against the regime of the Shah, he thought. But as the hooting coming down Shahpur Avenue grew louder, he saw lots of vehicles hurtling down towards the square. Rough-looking, bearded men were perched on the bonnets of cars, on the luggage racks, or hanging dangerously out of the windows. Most waved or held aloft pictures of the Shah on which were scrawled in bold letters "Shah Fled". Upon seeing the crowd of jubilant folk, Kazem's customers also began to leap up and down, yelling with their mouths full, hugging and kissing each other. Euphoria being infectious, Kazem and Ali Khalifeh joined in the merriment and started to jump up and down, brandishing the half-done kebab skewers and waving the straw fans at the exuberant people, who were stampeding by like an overexcited herd of wildebeest.

As they poured into the square from the backstreets, singing and dancing, hugging and congratulating one another, Kazem found it impossible to carry on with his job. Everybody had forgotten to eat.

"Just look at them, Ali Agha!" Kazem cried out, smiling. "I've never seen Tehran's folk so happy like this in my life."

"I don't blame them, Kazem," Ali Khalifeh shouted back at him. "I know what they've been through under that bastard Shah!"

"I wonder if this news is really true," Kazem said.

"I tell you what," said Ali Khalifeh, "let's go to Sayyed Vali's teahouse and find out for ourselves. To hell with selling kebabs today!"

After packing up the stall, the two partners pushed through the crowd and headed towards the bazaar. Everybody was out in the middle of the narrow passes chanting, dancing, and arguing about the Shah's unexpected departure. Sayyed Vali's teahouse was jam-packed with customers, who were sitting around the tables and on the daybeds, hurriedly slurping their teas, smoking cigarettes that they kept offering to one another, and discussing the shocking news. A cheerful song pouring out of the battered tape-recorder added to the joyful mood. Sayyed Vali stood beside the samovar, hands held high, keeping up with the beat of the tune by snapping his fingers. At the same time he filled up the tea glasses, piled them on trays and passed them over to the tea boy, who ran from table to table, handing the teas to the joyous customers. The teahouse, with its steamed up grimy windows, looked like an ancient bathhouse filled with *chibouk* smoke and vapour through which the dishevelled aspects of men appeared like demons, now popping up, now fading away in the dim light of the smudgy bulbs.

As the curfew hour was approaching, the clamour of voices gradually died down and all the customers, in small groups, began to trickle out of the teahouse. Tired, they walked in small bands in the now silent passageways of the bazaar. Once out in the street, they all scattered in different directions, vanishing into the darkening shadows of lanes, alleys, and back streets. Kazem, on parting from Ali Khalifeh, headed towards the lodging house, his head sunk into his hunched shoulders, his hands thrust into his trouser pockets, warm vapour streaming out of his nostrils.

Upon entering the lodging house, Kazem caught sight of the womenfolk who had gathered around the *hauz*, noisily discussing the news of the day.

After greeting them, Kazem strode towards his room. As he passed in front of Ghanbar Vafuri's casement, he peered through the latticework and saw all the menfolk sitting on the kilim in a ring around an Aladdin heater on which a dented tin kettle was whistling away, spouting vapour through its nozzle.

As Kazem turned to walk on, he heard Ghanbar Vafuri say, "You're very welcome to join us, Kazem Agha."

Hesitantly, Kazem opened the door and stepped inside the room. No one raised his head. Mahmud the Scholar was crouched over Kazem's radio fiddling with the knobs. The crackling noises of innumerable foreign tongues floated into the smoke-filled room.

"What's my radio doing here?" Kazem asked.

"Never mind about your radio," Ghanbar Vafuri said. "Sit down a while and listen to the Shah. He's going to talk in a minute."

"But I heard that he escaped from the country today," said Kazem, looking round at the group.

"The sonofabitch cleared off this morning like a mongrel dog as soon as he sniffed trouble brewing," chipped in Hassan Ghorazeh, his devilish black eyes twinkling in the gloom of the room.

"Before he ran off he was interviewed by someone and now they're going to broadcast the whole interview," said Mehdi Kharaki, rubbing his hands together.

Curious as to what trumped-up reasons the Shah had been given by his advisors to put out this time, Kazem joined the men on the kilim. As they all sat in total silence awaiting the familiar voice of the broadcaster, the door of the room was gently pushed open and Ghanbar Vafuri's wife, wrapped in a black chador, stepped inside, carrying a brazier on a tray. Her ravaged face was lit up from beneath by the glow of the red-hot charcoals in the brazier, making her look like an old witch. As mute as a deaf and dumb servant, she carefully handed the brazier to her husband and slipped out, noiseless as a cat. With great care, Ghanbar placed the tray on the kilim in front of him. He then took out from his shirt pocket what was left of an opium roll from which he sliced off with his old flick-knife a tiny piece the size of a chickpea. He grabbed the opium pipe from the tray, stuck the piece of opium near the pinhole in the headpiece of the pipe, took a burning coal by a pair of long tongs, blew hard at it, and stuck it near the opium piece. He then shoved the tip of the pipe between his dark lips and inhaled so hard that his cheeks sank in like those of a mummy. Two coils of white smoke streamed out of his nostrils. He went through the same ritual until his eyes became glazed over. High and happy, he was now ready to listen to the Shah's parting speech.

All of a sudden the crackles mingled with the jumble of voices from radio stopped. A woman's polite voice announced the sad news of the departure of His Majesty for health reasons, for the foreseeable future.

"Dear listeners, now we are going to broadcast the full interview with His Majesty, the King of Kings and Sun of the Aryans, that took place in Mehrabad Airport this morning." Her voice shook with emotion.

All the men's heads, like those of marionettes on a darkened stage, jerked towards the radio.

"What is the reason for His Majesty's sudden departure?" the reporter asked respectfully.

"I've not been feeling well recently and the time has come for me to have some rest," replied His Majesty in a weak voice. "I had already said that I would wait till the new government settled and then I would travel."

"For how long is His Majesty planning to stay abroad?"

"I can only say that it all depends on my health," declared His Majesty.

"Where would be the first port of call for His Majesty to stay?"

"I think we'll stay in Aswan in Egypt for a while so that I can rest."

"Do you have anything to say to the nation before your departure, Your Majesty?"

"I've nothing more to say," said the Shah with an air of finality. "May I add that a great deal of responsibility weighs upon my shoulders to fulfil my duties to my people and my homeland."

"Thank you very much, Your Majesty," said the reporter, wishing the Shah a safe journey and good health.

The interview stopped abruptly. Mahmud turned off the radio. A heavy hush fell upon the room. Kazem peered at everyone from under his eyebrows. Overwhelmed, the men sat there in the dim light like a bunch of dishevelled convicts gathered round the ashes of a fire in a labour camp to warm up their chilled bones, wondering about their uncertain fate. Ghanbar Vafuri, sunk in thought, was gazing at the glowing charcoals smothered under the ashes. Mehdi Kharaki was staring dumbly at his big toe which stuck out of a hole in his filthy sock, Hassan Ghorazeh, a cigarette butt hanging between his thin lips, was hugging his knees like an orphan. Karim Darvish cradled his *tar* on his lap and mumbling all the time, "Alas, alas…", and Mahmud the Scholar's eyes were glued to the radio.

The bafflement painted on their faces was so plain that Kazem was able to read what was going on in their minds. A cruel struggle between believing the news and what had really happened had stunned them. Most of them had lived through the harsh years of the tyrant. All of them without exception had suffered untold hardship just to earn their daily bread and onion. On the one hand, they wanted to believe, and on the other, years of suppression had robbed them off their ability to think clearly, to make their own decisions, to be free men. They had all left their native villages to find a better life in Tehran. But they had soon become caught up in that vicious circle of humiliating poverty and living in the cesspool of lodging houses like this one.

"All this fancy talk is just balls to the likes of me." Hassan Ghorazeh broke the silence, rubbing his bony shoulders to keep warm, "He not only flees at the first sign of trouble, but also talks of responsibility and the love of homeland. I still remember what happened in the last days of Dr Mosaddegh when this son-of-a-whore buggered off first to Iraq and then to Italy…"

"…and then was brought back again by the Americans and the British spies," broke in Ghanbar Vafuri in the manner of a veteran man-of-the-world. "He was even imbecile enough to say he was protected by Imam Reza and his returning to his *homeland* was destined by Providence."

"Providence in that case was the British and the Americans, of course!" Hassan Ghorazeh announced with a cynical laugh.

"No doubt the British and the Americans had a hand in getting rid of Dr Mosaddegh." Mahmud the Scholar decided to elaborate a bit more on the subject. "But don't lose the sight of the fact that many of us willingly helped them to carry out their dirty work."

"That's right, bro," Hassan Ghorazeh said, his reedy voice choked with rage. "At the time I had just arrived at Tehran and was working as an errand boy in a tavern in Lalezar. I saw with my own eyes how a troop of demonstrators in the morning shouted slogans in support of Dr Mosaddegh and in the afternoon, after being given a few dollars, shouted against him. I also saw the strongmen like Sha'aban the Brainless, his knife-fighter underlings, pimps and prostitutes from the Shahr-e No rounded up in trucks and doled out sacks full of dollars to shout slogans against Dr Mosaddegh's government."

"That's right, Hassan Agha," Mahmud agreed. "The monarchy and the mollahs, acting as mortal enemies on the surface to fool folk like you and me, had always had a secret love affair and stood up for one another in times when their grip on people's destinies was threatened. One has never survived without the other. Remember those highwaymen who, in olden times, always kept a mollah with them, fattened like a cow so that he, the mollah, that is, by having his share of the booty, would legitimise the plunder. The Pahlavi regime used a lot of these mollahs who licked their boots to legitimise their daylight robbery of the people. I've heard from reliable sources that the grand Ayatollah Kashani got thousands of dirty dollars from the Americans to change camps and organise his thugs against Dr Mosaddegh."

"True, bro, true." Hassan Ghorazeh vigorously scratched his head. "These bastards are all moulded from the same dough."

"When the horde of hoodlums attacked and ransacked the Prime Minister's house," said Mahmud, remembering a shameful treachery committed by one of his relatives who took part in the raid, "a close relative of mine, who was a policeman at the time, was among the looters. He just stood by and let the lunatics get away with it. He himself stole an expensive rug from the house and sold it the next day to a second-hand dealer in the bazaar."

At this point Kazem noticed that Ghanbar Vafuri had put the opium pipe in the corner of the brazier and his face was clouded over with dark thoughts.

"To my shame, I remember it all very well," Ghanbar said. "I was young and didn't have the faintest clue about politics. I had arrived in Tehran a few years earlier and was doing all sorts of odd jobs just to survive and, if I could, send some cash to my wife and child back in the village. Life was harsh and I needed money desperately. As I began to hang around the various unsavoury places in the city, I inevitably bumped into the notorious strongmen of the time, each one of whom ruled a district in downtown Tehran. Because of my strength and wrestling skills, I was soon spotted by one of the best known and most feared knife-fighters of the time called Haftkachaloon, who took me under his wing. I became his hireling, running round the passes and marketplaces, collecting protection money from the stallholders and small merchants.

"During the holy months of Ramadan and Moharram, I joined the other underlings like myself in self-flagellating, and weeping for Imam Hossein without understanding what all that was about. The usual wailings for the martyrs over, the mollahs ranted for hours about the dangers of communists who did not believe in God and were scheming to set up an immoral society. They cried out against Dr Mosaddegh, who had sympathies with the communist Tudeh Party. Being young, illiterate and filled with superstitious claptrap, I was convinced that the Prime Minister and his cabinet were a bunch of treacherous infidels who were planning to get rid of Islam by establishing a communist government. So on the day of the *coup d'état*, when all the strongmen and prostitutes were herded like cattle into trucks, I readily joined in. I remember how a group of mysterious-looking men were distributing American dollars in Amin-al Soltan Square, to persuade everyone to scream against Mosaddegh…"

"Yes, that's right," said Kazem, shaking his head. "I was still a youth, but I was myself in Lalezar and witnessed some of these events."

"…It was in the afternoon that the army jeeps, full of soldiers, surrounded Dr Mosaddegh's house and began to shell it," Ghanbar carried on, sucking hard at his opium pipe. "The mobsters then set to work, diligently ransacking and looting everything in the place. I myself managed to grab some good rugs and pots and pans."

Ghanbar paused, gazing at the dying glow of the charcoals.

"So what did you do after that day, Mash Ghanbar?" Hassan Ghorazeh asked.

"Nothing much," mumbled Ghanbar, like a man talking to himself. "They rounded up all the cabinet ministers, accused them of betraying their homeland, and executed them after mock trials. Dr Mosaddegh was put under house arrest. The Shah returned from his picnic in Italy and a new era of his iron-fisted rule began. The Shah handsomely rewarded Sha'aban the Brainless by making him a national hero overnight. The others who were on the side of Mosaddegh were rounded up, put into jail, or secretly assassinated.

"It didn't take me long to find out that the Shah was just another bastard king, just like the others. Many of my friends soon became disillusioned and ended up in poverty. I tried all sorts of jobs simply to survive. Unluckily, I was surrounded by rootless men like myself, for whom the only pleasures left were gambling, opium, and occasional visits to Shahr-e No. Whatever I earned, I lost in the gambling dens in the old ruins of Tehran. After many years of hanging on the edge of existence like this, I was left with nothing but my faithful opium pipe. Now here I am in this dingy room with my old wife who looks after me, and a landlord who badgers me for unpaid rent. It'll not be long before Mashallah will chuck our wretched belongings out into the lane. When that happens, I'll join the troops of junkies who roam around the holy shrines and brickworks, selling their filthy blood in order to pay for their slice of opium. Only the devil knows what'll happen to my old wife."

Grave-faced, the rest of the men listened, speechless. From one of the rooms the muffled jabbering of the women drifted out into the silent courtyard. The thick cold night breathed its icy vapour against the windowpanes. The rapid footsteps of stragglers scurrying along, mingled with the rattling of cartwheels, could be heard from the nearby streets and lanes. From time to time, the yelling of an army lieutenant warning a late passer-by to halt shattered the gathering silence that was punctuated, now and again, by the last desperate screeches of 'Shah Fled' or 'Allahu Akbar', in which the strains of an untimely melancholy music soon merged.

"Well, folks," Ghanbar Vafuri scraped the headpiece of his opium pipe with his flick-knife, "it seems at long last that we're in for some change."

"By God, I can't believe that this is happening," said Hassan Ghorazeh. "I can't go on like this any longer. I've sold so much of my blood that I look like a corpse and I can't stand on my feet any more."

"I'm sick and tired of humping loads of empty gasoline drums on my back from one market place to the next and from one shop to another in the bazaar, selling each for a few *gherans*," Mehdi Kharaki chipped in, finding an opportunity to air his woes.

"Well, don't stake your lives on the Shah's buggering off, brothers," said Ghanbar. "We still have a military government. No one knows what they're cooking up behind closed doors."

"Ghanbar's talking sense," agreed Mahmud, turning off the radio. "The military government still remains a deadly menace. But, if you ask me, the bigger and more sinister menace is those who are screaming "Allahu Akbar" in the streets and on the rooftops. We don't know who this Khomeini is and what he has up his sleeve for us. He has sprung up overnight, like the jinni in Aladdin's lamp, from nowhere, and wants to lead our nation to the devil knows where."

With their heads bent, the men listened to Mahmud, not knowing what to say. It was getting late. Each man got up and shuffled out of the room. The icy night air touched their faces, making them shiver. Once everyone was in his room, an unnatural stillness fell on the lodging house.

35

With the Shah gone, all that represented the Pahlavi Regime began to collapse like a house of cards. Day by day, the age-old system of absolute monarchy was fading into obscure corners of history, leaving behind some moaning tagalong *nouveau riches* and aristocrats who still lived in their own dream world far away from the realities of modern times and the relentless wave of events engulfing the Iranian society. A major social storm had begun and was mercilessly sweeping everything in its way.

On the bitterly cold morning of the first of February when Kazem left the lodging house to go to his kebab stall, he saw many people in the streets sweeping the pavements, tidying up their shop fronts, offering flowers to soldiers, and throwing some on the bonnets of army jeeps and trucks. People stuck their heads out of the windows of their houses congratulating the passers-by. Some had gone to the roofs, singing and dancing. This party atmosphere puzzled Kazem.

When he arrived at the square where the kebab stall was, he saw a mass of people streaming down Shahpur and Sepah Street, stampeding towards the south of Tehran, all shrieking and talking loudly. Motorbikes, on which perched up to three scruffy young men, whizzed through the crowds. Some people kept sticking their torsos out of the windows of cars choked with passengers screeching, “Imam has returned!”

“What’s going on, Ali?” Kazem asked as they set up the stall.

“Don’t you know?” Ali hefted a large sack of charcoal, emptying some into the brazier. “They say that Khomeini is returning home today.”

“Today!”

“Yes, today,” replied Ali Khalifeh. “Any minute his plane will be landing.”

“What about the army?” Kazem asked. “Is it going to stand back and do nothing?”

“I heard last night in the teahouse that the army had allowed the people to go and welcome the Ayatollah as long as they behave themselves,” explained Ali, pouring some gasoline from a tin drum on to the charcoals.

“Let’s call it a day, join the crowd, and follow them to see what’s going on,” suggested Kazem. “It’d be fun.”

“What do you mean?” Ali looked at his partner, amazed. “We haven’t even sold a single skewer of kebab and you want us to pack up and follow a mad crowd?"

"Never mind, Ali." Kazem realised that he had said something silly. "I thought maybe you'd be interested in a big event like this."

"I've had enough of big events," replied Ali with a hint of sarcasm. "What I need now more than anything else is cash. If we keep our business as usual today we'll earn some good dosh. A lot of people are going to pass this way."

He had a point. By lunchtime, they had sold out all the kebab they had. Kazem had to dash to the slaughterhouse and the bazaar to get more meat and charcoal. The bazaar was in a state of jubilation. The shopkeepers and small merchants were handing out votive dates and halva to passers-by and congratulating everyone about the return of Imam Khomeini.

It was a good day for business. Round about four o'clock in the afternoon, Ali Khalifeh decided to pack up. He took all the day's takings from the tin box, counted them loudly with the air of an unsmiling tradesman, and divvied them up between himself and Kazem. He thrust the greasy banknotes into his jacket pocket, making it bulge.

"Let's go to the Sayyed Vali's teahouse and find out what's been happening," said Ali, patting Kazem on the shoulder.

The teahouse was packed with everyday regulars from the bazaar and the neighbourhood. A lively crowd of men sat round the tables, smoking, drinking, and noisily relating to one another the events of the day. Sayyed Vali and his tea boy were run off their feet attending to the uncommonly large number of customers.

Upon entering the teahouse, Kazem scanned the room and saw Mehdi Kharaki sitting on a chair surrounded by several men, among whom were Hassan Ghorazeh, Mahmud the Scholar, and Ghanbar Vafuri. Mehdi Kharaki was holding forth in the manner of a seasoned storyteller.

"*Bah*, *bah*, Kazem Agha and Ali Agha!" shouted Hassan Ghorazeh, upon seeing them. "Come and join us!" Two of the younger men got up at once to offer their seats to the newcomers. Mehdi Kharaki, on seeing the two partners, raised himself a little, put his hand on his chest, nodded at them, and carried on with his account of what he had seen and heard.

"…anyway, folks, as I was saying, as soon as the word went round that Imam was going to give a sermon in Behesht-e Zahra, we ran and found the closest place to the makeshift stand on which he was going to sit. It was around midday that I saw a massive crowd pouring into the cemetery, screaming and yelling. It was as if doomsday had arrived. Soon I spotted a helicopter coming towards us. Once it reached over our heads, it hovered a while, making a deafening noise. To our surprise, it began to come down, lifting lots of dust and dirt, which hit our faces. The mob crouched down and scattered like fallen leaves in autumn. As soon as the Imam climbed down from the helicopter, the mob rushed to it. The bodyguards set upon them, chasing them away as hungry dogs chase off other carrion eaters. If they grabbed any persistent ones, they beat the hell out of them. Finally, they managed to settle the Imam on the stand. I was among the blessed lucky ones close enough to the stand to see the man at close range. The Imam then began to speak, giving a passionate speech about his future plans for the people. The loudspeakers relayed his voice so that everybody could hear."

"Did you actually see the Imam?" butted in a skinny young man with bulging eyes.

"As clearly I see you sitting here," confirmed Mehdi Kharaki, like a proud peasant who has seen the king for the first time in his life.

"What was his sermon about?" chipped in another young man.

"He said he would whack this regime hard on the face and, with the help of this nation he'd set up a new government," Mehdi Kharaki told him.

Kazem stayed in the teahouse a little longer and listened to the animated conversation about the significance of Khomeini's return to Iran. Half-an-hour before the start of the curfew he, Ali Khalifeh, and the other men from the lodging house left the teahouse. The streets and lanes were gradually becoming deserted. The people, weary after so much excitement, were returning to their homes, thinking no doubt that the return of the Imam would bring about some changes for the better to their lives.

36

The following morning, as Kazem was squatting on the edge of the *hauz* and splashing water from the tap to his face, he heard the womenfolk, who were coming back from the baker's and the grocer's, cackling noisily about Imam Khomeini having taken up residence in a school somewhere in uptown Tehran.

From that day on the talk in the lodging house, the neighbourhood and the bazaar was all about the Imam, his promises, the possible new government and the death throes of the Pahlavi Regime. Excitedly, people related to one another the Imam's passionate sermons about the freedom of the media, free and fair elections and so on and so forth. News circulated that the army had abandoned a planned secret *coup d'état*. People resorted to new tactics such as giving flowers to the bemused soldiers, who, being all peasant conscripts, privately sympathised with the people. Soon the news went round that thousands of army men had joined Khomeini's camp.

In a matter of days, a new reign of terror began to strike fear in people's hearts when the Imam urged them to betray anybody who was a member of the much feared SAVAK – the Shah's secret police. Stirring a cesspool of long-buried resentments and betrayals, this decree, coming from the Imam, gave free rein to the settling of all kinds of old scores against not only the real torturers among the Shah's men but also against many innocent people whose faces some people simply did not like. No one felt safe in this new form of terror in which old fears were beginning to show their ugly faces.

Once the Revolution Channel was set up on the seventh of February, the menfolk of the lodging house would huddle every evening around Kazem's radio, lugged about from one room to another, to listen to the Imam's eagerly awaited speeches. In one of his sermons given to a troop of military men assembled in the school, he had already begun to sing a different song. He openly urged the military men to come into the fold of Islam, asking them to embrace it in all aspects of their lives so that they would be protected by its life-giving warmth. He then, changing his tune suddenly, stressed the task of establishing Islam in all its glory all over Iran.

The same channel, two days later, proudly reported that thousands of military men, heeding the words of the Imam for action, had left their barracks across the city, chanting "Oh, Khomeini, we are all your soldiers," in support of the future Islamic regime. As the men listened attentively to find out more, Kazem saw Mahmud the Scholar shaking his head thoughtfully.

"Why are you shaking your head like that?" Hassan Ghorazeh asked.

"Things are already beginning to look ominous, my friends," replied Mahmud.

"Why?" asked Mehdi Kharaki.

"First Khomeini was on about a democratically-elected government," Mahmud pointed out, "now he talks of establishing Islam." After a few moments he added, "What I saw today is a bad sign, my friends. As I was coming out of the university, I saw a gang of bearded fanatics attacking a group of men and women who were demonstrating for the establishment of the constitution. The thugs then began roaming around in packs, breaking up small groups of students who were discussing the possible future government."

* * * *

The following day, when Kazem was setting up the kebab stall, he saw army trucks, jeeps, and even a few tanks roaring into the square. They were all loaded with dishevelled, bearded young men who were waving Khomeini's pictures and shouting slogans about the army having joined the revolution.

"What's going on, Ali Agha?"

"Don't you see the army trucks with no soldiers on them?" replied Ali Khalifeh. "The mob has attacked all the army and gendarmerie bases."

The same evening, as the men huddled around the radio, they heard that from the following day martial law would be brought back to four o'clock in the afternoon due to recent disturbances by political agitators.

As the next day was Friday, Kazem stayed in bed a little longer. Around nine in the morning, he heard a commotion going on in the courtyard. He rolled over in bed to see if Maryam was asleep. The bed was empty. She has probably gone out to buy bread and cheese for breakfast, Kazem thought. The samovar was whistling away. He got up, opened the casement and peeped outside. Men and women were running in and out of the courtyard gabbling loudly to one another about something happening in the streets. Kazem dressed and went out of the room, leaning against the banister. Ghanbar Vafuri, his sheepskin waistcoat thrown over his shoulders, was squatting on the edge of the *hauz*, trying to break the sheet of ice with a large pair of tongs.

"What's going on, Mash Ghanbar?" Kazem called out.

"It's real mayhem out there, Kazem Agha," Ghanbar wheezed, coughing loudly. "Everybody is out in the streets running around smashing things, breaking into government offices, army barracks, everywhere."

"How do you know?" Kazem asked, coming down the steps.

"I heard it from neighbours who had been out since cockcrow to buy supplies before the shops close early this afternoon."

Kazem looked around. The courtyard was deserted. Soon the door of the hovel in which dwelled Karim Darvish opened. With his shabby astrakhan hat pulled down to his eyebrows, his coat thrown over his head and gripping his long stick, he emerged into the courtyard. After gazing around in bewilderment, he shuffled noiselessly to the stairs and sat on the last step. He then rested his stick on his lap and gazed vacantly at the paving stones, oblivious to what was going on.

Kazem thought he had better go out and see things for himself. On the way out, he bumped into Maryam and two of the women carrying bread and cheese. He told Maryam to have breakfast with her friends while he went off to the bazaar to find out what was going on.

The first thing he did was to go and see if Ali Khalifeh was at his post. The kebab stall was not there. Kazem thought the best place to find him was Sayyed Vali's teahouse. Being Friday, the bazaar was deserted, except for some beggars and stray dogs. On entering the teahouse, Kazem saw some regulars, mainly old men from the neighbourhood, who sat around tables and on daybeds, listening to the radio with grave expressions. Kazem spotted Ali Khalifeh sitting on a daybed, drawing at a cigarette.

"Come and sit down, Kazem!" Ali cried out. "They're going to read out the army's communiqué in a minute."

Kazem walked over and sat down beside Ali. He asked the tea boy for a glass of tea and a piece of cheese with a half *sangak* bread. The newsreader began to read the communiqué:

"In view of the current upheavals in the country, the Supreme Council of the Army has unanimously decided, on this eleventh day of February 1979, to announce its impartiality concerning the present political disputes so as to prevent more chaos and bloodshed. All army units, therefore, have been ordered to withdraw at once from the streets and go back to their barracks. The army has always been and will be on the side of the decent and patriotic people of Iran and will defend the wishes of this noble nation with all its might."

All the men jumped to their feet and began to clap and yell.

"Bloody bastards," Ali muttered. "They betrayed the nation by booting out Mosaddegh and bringing back the Shah. They were trained and kept going by the Americans, and now they say that we're on the side of the nation." He looked around. "Look at these fools, jumping up and down like clowns just because the army has joined the revolution."

Kazem munched his bread and cheese, noisily washing it down with sweetened tea, nodding his agreement.

The communiqué was followed by the voice of an ayatollah urging the radio workers to put an end to their strike and return to work. The radio fell silent for what seemed an eternity. The people in the teahouse all cocked their heads towards it, anxious as to what would happen next. Maybe another plot was being cooked by British spies and the CIA to divert the people's attention in order to prepare for another *coup d'état*.

Finally, the battered radio stirred, quivering a bit and emitting some vague crackling sounds. Some mysterious noises, like scheming mischievous demons, could be heard whispering in the background. Then the voice of a newsreader, thick with emotion, came on:

"Attention, attention, this is the voice of the revolution of the people of Iran."

The men looked at each other to check if they had heard things right. They at once resumed hopping up and down, kissing and congratulating one another.

"Well, Agh Kazem," said Ali Khalifeh, tapping Kazem's shoulder, "it appears that the Pahlavi's grip on power for fifty-seven years has finally ended."

"It certainly looks like it, bro," agreed Kazem.

"Let's go out and see what's going on," Ali suggested. Kazem, having still plenty of time to kill, agreed.

People, their voices hoarse after so much screaming and having just heard the latest news, were running around like lunatics. Everybody stopped everybody else and planted a smacking kiss on his cheeks, congratulating him. Droves of scruffy young men stampeded up and down the street, yelling, "Long live the revolution!" From the shattered windows of some government buildings chairs, tables, and bundles of papers were being chucked out indiscriminately, regardless of their possibly landing on some innocent passers-by.

As it was impossible to ignore the excitement and with the curfew no longer in place, Kazem and Ali roamed the streets till late.

37

When Kazem returned home late at night, all the menfolk had gathered in Ghanbar Vafuri's room listening to the radio, talking at the tops of their voices, each relating the events of the day. The only one who had stayed at home that day was Karim Darvish, who, as usual, sat in the corner of the room, cradling his *tar*, silently intoning his poems. Everyone, looking haggard and exhausted, told their own version of events as they had witnessed the complete toppling of the Pahlavi regime in a single day.

* * * *

Kazem carried on with his work at the kebab stall as usual. Whenever he went down to the bazaar to get supplies and have tea in the teahouse all he heard was news of the confiscation of the Pahlavis' assets for the benefit of the underprivileged and of summary executions of army generals and thousands of other people who happened to work for the former regime. In the teahouse and at the lodging house he heard nothing but the braying of the mollahs about traitors, enemies of Allah and Islam.

Once the ayatollahs had accomplished their mopping-up, they announced that they had no intention of governing. They appointed a new prime minister who was a bearded little ayatollah in civilian clothes. The prime minister from the Shah's regime, Bakhtiar, went on whimpering about keeping martial law in force and the necessity of sticking faithfully to the rule of the constitution.

"Poor Bakhtiar has no idea that the hellish power of mollahs is unleashed," said Mahmud to Kazem over a glass of tea in the teahouse. "For the first time in Iranian history, the mollahs have sniffed the sweet scent of power and have already begun growling, calling other members of their pack to the lavish feast ready for them to dig their claws and snouts into."

A week after the revolution, Imam Khomeini went back to the holy city of Qom in order to devote himself to prayers, read the Koran, and live among his faithful devotees from the days of his youth. He said he had no wish to meddle with the job of the freshly appointed prime minister.

"You're all fools if you think Khomeini will sit tight in Qom and get on with his bleeding prayers," Ghanbar Vafuri said one day over an opium session." He brandished his opium pipe. "Faithful to his meddlesome nature and having long ago taken upon himself the role of a latter-day prophet, Khomeini itches to stick his snout into the affairs of the nation to push it in the righteous path of Islam handed down to him by his ancestors."

Life went on as usual in the lodging house. The only difference was that the poor had begun to have some fuzzy hopes that things would change for the better now that the Pahlavis had gone. Their hopes, however unreal, were to be fanned even more when the Imam reappeared on the social and political scene by giving a sermon in the holy city of Qom.

One chilly evening at the beginning of March, Kazem returned home to see that the men were huddled as usual around the radio waiting to listen to an important piece of news. He wanted to go to Maryam and have his supper in peace. As he passed before Ghanbar Vafuri's casement window, the men called out asking him to come in and listen. Kazem decided reluctantly to go join them.

"Imam Khomeini is going to address the nation about all the money they took from the Pahlavis," Hassan Ghorazeh cried out as if they were going to hand him some cash there and then.

After a short while, Imam Khomeini's speech was announced, given in the holy shrine of Fatimah in Qom. Then the voices of a crowd in a large hall could be heard. People were coughing and murmuring among themselves. No sooner had the Imam begun to recite some Arabic verses in praise of the Prophet and his clan than a thunderous succession of *salawats* echoed in the hall, making the worn-out radio tremble as if with the unstoppable wrath of Allah manifesting Himself through the person of the Imam. Once the commotion had died down, the Imam began his sermon in his distinctive harsh wild ass's voice about the confiscated palaces, assets and riches.

"I would personally order the government to distribute all the money we've seized from the Pahlavi regime to be distributed among the poor and the dispossessed so that they can build their own houses and live in comfort forever. *We* not only want to improve your material fortunes, but also to enrich your spiritual life with the teachings of Islam. *You* need spirituality. The Pahlavis robbed us of our dear Islam. Don't be content with just living in comfortable houses. *You*'ve got to make the mosques your second homes by visiting them every so often. *We'll* make all the means of transport, water, gas, and electricity supply free for the poor and the dispossessed. *We*'ll raise you to the level of what human beings should be."

Wave after wave of *salawats* and chants of "Oh, Khomeini, we're all your soldiers," and "Oh Allah, oh Allah, keep Khomeini alive till the coming of the Mahdi," filled the hall, sending joyful quivers through the poor old radio.

"I knew that Imam was a good man, I knew it," Mehdi Kharaki said.

"Let's see, bro," joined in Hassan Ghorazeh. "Let's see if the other mollahs and the politicians will put his words into actions."

"That's right, Hassan Agha," Ghanbar Vafuri said in the measured tones of a dignified opium junky. "We'll have to wait and see what happens next. At the moment they're too busy wiping out lots of people and that's a bad omen, bro."

"Right you are, Mash Ghanbar," Mahmud the Scholar pointed out, "Khomeini can say whatever he likes, but the signs these days are menacing. Many fanatical hoodlums have already taken it upon themselves to impose Sharia Law on women in the streets. They prowl everywhere in packs, and attack the students at the gates of the universities by threatening to beat them up if they hear the slightest voice of dissent."

"If the mollahs give me some cash, I'll do anything for them!" stated Mehdi Kharaki. The others just looked at him, knowing that Mehdi would easily cut his best friend's throat for few *gherans*.

From that day on Kazem, whether he wanted to or not, heard all the political news when he went to the bazaar, Sayyed Vali's teahouse, or at home listening to the radio. Imam Khomeini continued to poke his nose into the political life of the capital. He kept ordering decrees left, right and centre, bullying the already muddled politicians to do what he demanded.

One quiet evening when Kazem returned home, he saw Mahmud the Scholar sitting beside Karim Darvish on the bottom step of the stairs, both smoking quietly and seemingly sunk into a dark mood. Kazem approached them. When Mahmud looked up, he saw Mahmud's left eye was blood-shot and bruised.

"What happened to your eye, Mahmud Khan?" asked Kazem, planting himself before him. "Has the ceiling of your room caved in? Have the landlord's roughnecks beaten you up for your overdue rent, or…?"

"None of that, Kazem," replied Mahmud, a little amused at his friend's way of seeing things. "Had a bit of scuffle in front of the university this afternoon."

"Who with?" asked Kazem, frowning. "Tell me who did it and I'll take care of them for you so that their mothers will weep for them at their graves till doomsday!"

"Thanks for your sympathy, but no." Mahmud took a long drag at his cigarette. "You can't forever sort out people by beating them up. Anyway, all your derring-do would be futile with these creatures."

"Why not?" said Kazem defiantly. "I've taught lots of lessons to loads of bullies who thought they could get away with anything they wanted."

"Not these ones, Kazem, not these ones," Mahmud said. "These monsters are not what you, I, or anyone else can tackle. They're not just a bunch of henchmen at the service of a strongman or a knife-fighter, bullying the hardworking folk. These men and women have risen from the depths of this cesspool of a homeland we're living in. At the time of the Pahlavis their roughneck masters, who supported the regime, were only called to action if they were needed. This bearded lot you now see roaming the streets were at that time hibernating in and around the brickworks and trash heaps in the shantytowns, in the graveyards and the holy shrines, in the same way vermin lie dormant among rotting garbage, biding their time to crawl out. These ill-begotten freaks of nature born from the unholy marriage of Islam and our own corrupt culture are now out in the open; their faces look even more hideous in the daylight. You mark my word, brother. They're now on the move and no one, absolutely no one, will be able to stop them."

Kazem listened attentively, racking his brains as to how to help Mahmud. He glanced at Karim Darvish, who sat there motionless, murmuring and nodding.

Two days later Mahmud came home even more battered and bruised.

"You can't go on like this, mate," Kazem reproached his friend. "What happened today, then?"

"There was a large demonstration of women near the Tehran University," explained Mahmud, his face betraying acute unhappiness. "They were shouting slogans against the imposition of the Islamic hijab on women. My friends and I joined in to support them. The march hadn't even started when a herd of bearded heavies, followed by black-chadored women sprang up from the side-streets, fell upon the demonstrators like wild beasts, and whacked them with clubs, screeching 'Islamic hijab for all women!'"

"You said yourself we can't fight these sons-of-whores," Kazem reminded his friend. "So why are you putting your life in danger like this?"

"Because if we don't stop them now, they'll soon do much worse," Mahmud said.

Mahmud became so involved in anarchic events that Kazem only caught him for a few precious minutes to get the latest news of what was going on at the hub of the revolution – the University of Tehran. Mahmud informed Kazem that mysterious forces were at work everywhere to make sure that an Islamic Republic would be established in Iran. The Imam, as obstinate as an old mule, would not hear of any other option but the *Islamic* Republic.

38

The fateful election was set to happen on a day at the start of April. The whole nation was excited by the chance, for the first time in their history, to elect a government without a monarch riding at its back.

That day being a public holiday, Kazem stayed in bed a little longer. When he opened his eyes, he saw Maryam sitting on her haunches beside the samovar in the window recess, silently preparing the tea. A fresh spring breeze was coming in from the slightly open window.

When he stepped out on to the terrace, everyone had gone out except Ghanbar Vafuri and Karim Darvish, who were sitting on the last step of the stairs, smoking quietly.

“Where is everybody, Mash Ghanbar?” Kazem called out, walking to the steps.

“They’ve all gone to vote,” replied Ghanbar. “Have you forgotten, today’s voting day?”

“No, I haven’t,” said Kazem, sitting down beside him.

“Aren’t you going to vote?” asked Ghanbar.

“Nope,” said Kazem in his usual impassive way. “I’ve never voted in all my whole life. I don’t know what it means. No one has ever asked my opinion. I think Mahmud the Scholar’s right. They’ve left people with no choice but the Islamic Republic.”

“Mahmud’s definitely right,” agreed Ghanbar. “We have no choice. They’ve given us this sealed box that they say inside which is hidden something called the Islamic Republic for which we’ve to vote. I’ve got to know what’s in the box before I decide to accept what will happen to me in the future.”

“That’s exactly what Mahmud the Scholar says,” said Kazem.

Back in his room, Kazem sat on the floor beside the cloth to have his breakfast.

“How many people have gone out to vote?” asked Maryam, putting a glass of tea on the saucer in front of him.

“Most of them, I guess,” said Kazem, dropping a sugar lump inside his glass and stirring it with the teaspoon.

“I heard you talking to Mash Ghanbar,” said Maryam. “He didn’t want to vote, did he?”

"Nope," replied Kazem, wrapping a small piece of bread round a lump of cheese. "He says he can't vote for something he doesn't know about."

"The poor man's right," said Maryam, nibbling at a morsel of bread. "How can you vote for something that you know nothing about?" She then added after a short pause, "Especially when they keep attacking women for not wearing the Islamic hijab."

* * * *

That evening all the menfolk in the lodging-house asked Kazem to put his radio in the recess of the window so that they could listen to the outcome of the voting. They sat on kilims spread on the terrace, whiling away the time by arguing about the possible result. The women sat around the *hauz*, cracking roasted watermelon seeds, and gabbling noisily as to what their lot would be under the future government.

"The outcome of the voting is pretty much known to everyone," Ghanbar Vafuri said in his grave manner.

"Well, everyone knows that," agreed Hassan Ghorazeh.

"Why did they bother to hold an election then, I wonder?" Mahmud asked.

At that moment, the overexcited announcer gave the news that an overwhelming majority of the Iranian people had voted for the Islamic Republic to become the form of the future government. The response to the news was mixed; some of the men were happy while others looked thoughtful. Some of the women became excited, but others remained indifferent.

When Kazem left home the next day to go to the kebab stall, he noticed the air of jubilation among the bearded folk everywhere. He found Ali Khalifeh busy setting up the stall and throwing mocking glances at the rejoicing mob.

"Just look at them," he muttered. "These are going to be our new masters. Only the devil knows what will happen if they rule the land."

From that day on, Kazem and his friends, when gathered in Sayyed Vali's teahouse or listening to the radio in the evenings, kept hearing, with overwhelming astonishment, about the waves of summary executions of men and women associated with the Pahlavi regime.

In a matter of a few months, the mollahs began to take a tight grip on all aspects of life throughout Iran. As soon as Shahr-e No was razed to the ground, all the former louts, prostitutes, pimps, strongmen and knife-fighters were given power and money to enforce Sharia Law everywhere. Day and night, these creatures crept in and out of the streets and alleyways, sniffing around in search of poor folk who were not adhering to the strict rules imposed by Sharia.

Like a gigantic stormy river belching from its depths all the filth and slime of centuries, the Islamic Revolution had thrown up to the surface all the hidden detritus of Iranian society. The Revolution was like the convulsions of a nation spewing up all the hatred, suppressed wishes, deprived hopes and dead and buried animosities of long ago. Scruffy religious men and women of all types were out in the streets day after day, screeching hysterically, celebrating the second coming of the *Messiah*. The Imam, being shrewd, took advantage of their constant presence and called them "The ever-present people-on-the-stage". And they had eternally been on the *stage* all right! The Messiah who had been kicked out of Iran sixteen years before and forgotten about till he was revived from oblivion masqueraded, attired like a holy man, and was brought back to his native land to lead the nation to a long-promised, but never fulfilled, happiness and freedom. As always happened in Iranian history, he turned out to be another imposter, the worst possible kind in the tragic history of the country. It was as if the fifth man of the apocalypse had come from who knows where to lead the mob to the edge of an abyss.

Day by day, slowly but surely, the usual pattern of life was changed for Tehran's inhabitants. Their cheerful expressions during the revolution gave place to gloomy ones. Their brightly coloured clothes were replaced by black and grey outfits. Their general demeanour suggested that they had given in to absolute despair. They walked, shoulders slumped, continuously looking behind them to see if they were being followed.

Tehran changed gradually into a graveyard, amid which the citizens glided like lost souls in purgatory. When dusk came, they retreated into their dwelling places, in the vain delusion that they would be able to protect themselves against the outside world, not knowing that the ruling regime had spread its tentacles deep into every hearth and home. Woolly, bear-like men growled loudly in the media that it was the Islamic duty of all the faithful to inform the authorities of any activity against the ruling religious power. The Imam had decreed that it was the duty of everyone to report any unislamic activities everywhere. It was the duty of every Muslim to snitch on the enemies of Allah. Brother spied on brother, mothers and fathers on their children, wives on their husbands, and friends on friends.

All the simple pleasures of life began to disappear. During the day, people scurried around to earn a living. After nightfall, as there were no taverns, cabarets, cinemas, theatres, gambling dens, whorehouses or decent teahouses, they crawled back to their dwelling places. It was here that their real nature manifested itself. For the poor there was nothing but eating, quarrelling, copulating, and sleeping. For the rich there was opium, gambling, satellite TV broadcasting foreign soaps, orgies with hired prostitutes, and wild parties during which they drank smuggled or homemade alcoholic drinks.

The lodging house folk could not escape the dislocation that was rattling Tehran's society. Whatever happened in the outside world had a direct resonance in the house, making everyone react in accordance with his or her different personality and leanings. Mehdi Kharaki and Hassan Ghorazeh became staunch supporters of the mollahs by joining the paramilitary militia gang. Hassan Ghorazeh took advantage of the chaos and did not shy away from doing anything which would make him some much-needed cash. Shamsi Boshkeh and Mohtaram Torkeh, having become inflamed by love of the Imam, joined Zahra's Sisterhood – reformed former prostitutes. Ghanbar Vafuri went on cursing and swearing at the mollahs, threatening anyone who dared challenge him and reminding them of his glorious past as a wrestler. Karim Darvish remained, as always, the Silent One, unruffled as if nothing had happened, just mumbling his poems. Mahmud the Scholar kept attending political meetings and protests staged in and around the university. All his efforts to stop the relentless march of the army of Islam were rewarded by generous beatings by the thugs. Kazem, realising that fighting against these lunatics was a complete waste of time, remained as impassive as ever, quietly minding his own business to earn money and live a quiet life, if events let him, that was. Maryam occupied herself by teaching literacy to two of the women in the house, who had become quite vociferous in their views on women's rights.

The lodging house, every evening, had turned into a battlefield in which were played out loyalties to different political and religious views. Kazem and Maryam, most of the time, retreated to their room to read books and newspapers as Kazem was by now able to read some simple sentences with Maryam's help. Sometimes they listened to the radio, but that was now totally controlled by the mollahs, who carried on spouting their archaic nonsense about absolutely everything under the sun.

39

Hence, the days melted into weeks and weeks into months of misery. To add insult to injury, in February 1980, after eleven months stay in Qom, the Imam triumphantly returned to Tehran and firmly grabbed the helm of the country in his old hands. He arrogated the role of commander-in-chief of the army and nearly everything else to himself.

One bitterly cold evening, Mahmud came home battered by Sharia Law vigilantes. Kazem was sitting beside the *hauz* breaking the thin sheet of ice on the surface of the water. Mahmud went and squatted beside him.

"What happened this time, Mahmud Khan?" asked Kazem, concerned.

"Those blockheads are sticking their stinking snouts into everything," replied Mahmud, pushing a piece of ice with his hand. "They're crawling everywhere."

"You know that it's all hopeless, my friend," said Kazem. "So why are you giving yourself such a headache?"

"You may be right, Kazem," said Mahmud. "It's all pointless."

The sheets of ice glistened as they floated on the surface of the water.

"Listen, Mahmud Khan," Kazem suggested, "let's go for a drink and forget all about this filthy business of politics."

"Drink?" Mahmud let out a muffled cry of astonishment. "Where? All the taverns are shut down by these sonsofbitches."

"That's true," said Kazem, "but I know somewhere safe. If you want to forget all about it, come with me."

Mahmud didn't have to think for long. He needed a few glasses of *arrack* to cheer him up a little.

Kazem ran to his room and told Maryam that he and Mahmud were going out to Ali Khalifeh's for a few glasses.

"Be careful," said Maryam, "those mad dogs are loose everywhere."

"Don't you worry," said Kazem, "I'll be back soon, promise."

Ali Khalifeh's room was in a lodging house in the neighbourhood. Ali, being a veteran tippler, had many contacts in the black market who managed to supply him regularly with bottles of homemade *arrack*.

He cordially welcomed Kazem and Mahmud to his simple dwelling, inviting them to sit on the kilim. He shut the casement and drew the curtains so that the neighbours would not be able to spy on them. He then disappeared into the alcove and reappeared with a tin tray on which were laid out three small glasses, a bowl of yoghurt with chopped cucumber, and a bottle of *arrack*. He grabbed the bottle, pulled the cork out with his teeth, and poured some *arrack* in each glass. No sooner had the friends clinked their glasses and knocked them back, grimacing, than they offered each other a spoonful of yoghurt and cucumber. Once the *arrack* started to kick in, they became talkative and began to discuss the current events from which no one could escape.

"So, Mahmud Khan," said Ali Khalifeh, lighting up a cigarette, "Kazem tells me that things are bad these days around the university."

"Things are bad everywhere, Ali Agha," replied Mahmud, shaking his head.

"Being a *scholar*, Mahmud Khan," Ali asked with the grave face of a man who is slowly becoming drunk, "do you reckon there is any chance at all of things getting better?"

"No, Ali Agha, no," said Mahmud, knocking back another glass. "These people are positioning themselves comfortably into the packsaddles they've placed on the people's backs. Once they settle, not even the devil can shake them off!"

"But we can't stand back and let them ride on our backs," Ali said, gazing at Mahmud.

"Well, at the moment a lot of good people are screaming loudly and warning against the way things are going," Mahmud told him, "but the mollahs' ears are deaf to any voice of dissent. The Islamic Republic is established and that's that." Speaking slowly and trying to articulate, he said, "You see, Ali Agha, over the centuries, due to siding with powerful invaders and collaborating with them, the mollahs have become invincible and indestructible, rather like those corpse-washers who washed thousands of corpses during those plagues long ago in our land. The corpse-washers were the only survivors of the disease. Iranian folk came, lived a while, and perished, leaving behind only the vermin, who lived on, sucking the blood of ordinary men and women. These vermin became fatter and more adept at survival strategies. Don't lose the sight of the fact that the nastiest of insects are number-one survivors after any catastrophe. Isn't that right, Kazem?"

"You bet, mate, you bet," muttered Kazem tipsily, having only a vague idea as to what Mahmud was on about.

"So these buggers are here to stay, Mahmud Khan," Ali Khalifeh concluded, grim-faced.

"Afraid so, my friend," Mahmud agreed. "The mollahs were and are indeed nothing but a bunch of buggers and also beggars. They memorise a few verses of the Koran and always have handy a number of *hadith* in their sleeves to recite at funerals and wedding ceremonies and in the mosques and *tekiehs*. They are all sprung from remote villages infested with disease, superstition, illiteracy and all sorts of unimaginable violence. Now that they have seen their chance for the first time in our troubled history to get their share of the plunder, they've all come out of the woodwork from all over Iran, moving like an army of arachnids, wrecking everything in their path by trying to shove Sharia Law down our throats."

"*Arrack…* what?" Kazem mumbled. "Do you mean to say that they're *arrack*-drinkers?"

"They drink anything, if they get the chance!" Mahmud smiled. "Scholars call spiders, scorpions, mites and ticks 'arachnids'."

Karim laughed. "Oh, I like that," he said. "Never heard of the word. But that's exactly what they are, mate."

"And the bad news is that they trail behind them this army of mad dogs as a back-up," Ali Khalifeh said.

"That's so, Ali Agha." Mahmud nodded dozily. "Morons like these who break up meetings and bludgeon the poor folk black and blue don't stop to think. They act on instinct, like animals, convinced that the mollahs are right."

Kazem, though tipsy, listened attentively to Mahmud. He then decided to air his personal opinion on the matter.

"You're absolutely right, mate," he said. "I've never grasped what Islam is on about, despite my taking part in so many religious ceremonies and festivals. I grew up right at the bottom of this massive shithole called Tehran. Since I was a nipper larking around in the streets of Shahr-e No, I didn't like the appearance of these motherfuckers, the mollahs, that is. During Ramadan and Moharram they crawled into Shahr-e No and brayed all sorts of Arabic horse-shit, making everybody beat their chests and wail like the mongrel dogs there. The wretched whores already had a lot to lament about, so they didn't need to cry for an Arab man who got himself martyred in a desert in Karbala. Later, when I travelled around, I saw them everywhere doing exactly the same thing: making poor folk even more sad and miserable. Instinctively, I came to mistrust them. I know that once these motherfuckers grab hold of power they cling to it like fleas digging their jaws into the underbellies of cows!"

Outside, the noises in the neighbourhood were slowly dying out. From time to time, the sirens of the Revolutionary Guards Patrol and the distant baying of stray dogs shattered the silence.

Just before midnight, Kazem and Mahmud stepped out of the lodging-house where Ali Khalifeh lived. They stood in the doorway, lifted their collars up, tucked their hands into their pockets, and began to walk. Large, dark-grey snowflakes were falling, dancing gently, settling on everything, and covering them with a thin layer of snow. Though sobered up a little, they still reeled about as they sauntered in and out of the dimly lit alleyways and lanes. The silence was punctuated with the muffled, staccato crunching of the snow under the feet of late-night wanderers, who walked hurriedly, keeping close to the walls, as if in a city of lepers. From time to time, someone hurried by, teeth chattering, with his head buried in his chest and his hands thrust in his coat pockets. The night was brutally cold. Their warm breath quickly turned into a thick vapour, obscuring their vision. The closed windows and doors of the houses in which the townspeople were slumbering resembled the locked gates to silent tombs. The bare, snow-laden trees seemed like forlorn, snow-covered beggars, lifting their gnarled hands in supplication to a dark, deaf and forever silent heaven.

Once the two friends found themselves in the main street, tottering along the pavement, the glare of two strong lights hit their eyes. They shielded their eyes with their hands. The lights stopped several paces in front of them. Two figures appeared in the beams of light, striding towards them, swinging their arms.

"Mahmud Khan," muttered Kazem, nudging him in the ribs.

"What?"

"I think we've unwelcome visitors." He nodded in the direction of the shadowy forms.

As the forms came closer, they were revealed as gun-carrying men of the vice squad, wrapped in dirty-green parkas.

"Are you all right?" one of the guards called out from under his hood.

"Of course we are, officer," shouted Kazem, his teeth chattering.

"We don't think so," squawked the other guard.

"We're just shivering with cold, that's all," Mahmud said.

"We can smell the stink of alcohol in your breath from one kilometre away," said the first guard, who was obviously in charge.

"What alcohol?" Kazem cupped his hands, vigorously blowing into them. He turned to Mahmud. "Do I smell of alcohol, mate?"

"Nope," affirmed Mahmud, after sniffing his friend. "You can't find a drop of *arrack* anywhere these days."

"If you don't care about *halal* and *haraam,* you can easily find it all right," said the younger officer, obviously keen to show off his enthusiasm in upholding Sharia Law

"We're not sinners, officer." Kazem, by now a little amused, dared to disagree with the man. "We're just out to get some fresh air."

"You'll have plenty of fresh air in *monkaraat*, all right," said the commander. "Let's go." The two guards roughly grabbed their arms, pulling them towards the patrol vehicle.

The *monkaraat* was a dismal-looking building used to interrogate political activists during the Shah's era. The guards shoved Kazem and Mahmud into a dank corridor that was crammed with drunkards, pimps, prostitutes and junkies. In a quick glance, Kazem took in everything. The short corridor was littered with people picked up from all over downtown and heaped there like rubbish. They were all sitting, squatting and sprawling on the floor, or standing against the icy walls, shivering. Some of the men were wrangling noisily with the guards, reasoning pathetically with them, trying to prove that they were as sinless as holy men. The scraggy junkies, their cigarette stubs nearly burning their fingers, sat on their haunches as mute as dopey sheep and trembling like reeds. The prostitutes, having become adept at adapting themselves to the exigencies of the new life in Tehran and habitués of the *monkaraat* centre, looked calm and composed, knowing that after being reprimanded and fined they would soon go back to their usual spots on the pavements and street corners of rich districts. They were so many of them that the authorities could not even herd them into *behzisti* centres, which were all choked to capacity.

All eyes followed the new arrivals apathetically. The two friends were told to wait there until they were summoned inside to be seen by the judge. They leaned against a wall and waited. Kazem glanced at Mahmud, who looked anxious, having taken part in so many political meetings and demonstrations. He, however, kept his cool. A scruffy, middle-aged Armenian fellow, a frayed overcoat thrown over his shoulders, clung to a guard, vociferously pleading to let him go home.

"*Babam jan*, how many times I've to tell you I'm an Orthodox Christian?" he whimpered in his strong accent. "In my blessed religion alcohol is *halal*."

"I don't give a fuck what or who you are," the guard barked at the fellow. "If you've something to say, say it to the judge, not me. I'm just doing my Islamic duty."

This piece of farce, in that gloomy place, brought a smile to Kazem's face.

“Look at the poor fellow trying to reason with that blockhead,” Kazem whispered in Mahmud’s ear, nudging him.

Terror-stricken, two men, each flanked by two guards, came out of the room, being carried away to the devil knew where. The prostitutes strutted out of the room in twos and threes with their heads held high like proud peacocks whose dignity has been trampled upon but who remain noble and dignified. From time to time, they glared at the sullen-looking guards with utter contempt.

It was around the small hours when Kazem and Mahmud were called in. They had hardly entered the room than two guards pushed them down to the floor near the door. Kazem quickly scanned the room. The walls were adorned with the usual slogans of “Death to America” and “Death to Israel.” Behind a large desk sat a plump, heavily bearded mollah. Hung on the wall behind him was the stern portrait of the Imam, glowering down from under his thick eyebrows at the batch of sleep-deprived sinners sitting on their haunches on the bare floor, hugging their knees and awaiting their grim fate.

Kazem’s eyes rested briefly on the judge. Who should it be but Sayyed Hossein Mousavi, the very mollah who had married him to Maryam more than a year ago! The mollah had undergone a transformation. His chubby, coarse face was now covered with a well-combed beard the length of three handpans. His head was crowned with a clean black turban one corner of which hung over one shoulder in the manner of Imam Ali. His pot belly protruded from under his brand new camelhair *aba*. He was sitting behind the desk, his gimlet eyes fixed upon the shivering creatures on the floor. His large hands, similar to those of a professional sewer-cleaner, rested on the desk on which was laid open a copy of the Koran and a bulky record book.

“I know that mollah,” Kazem whispered to Mahmud, nudging him.

“He’s the notorious mollah whom all the *monkaraat* visitors know so well,” Mahmud whispered back.

“He must be a first-rate bastard to be able to do such a task,” Kazem said.

“He’s well-known for being a bugger, too,” said Mahmud, keeping his voice low.

“A bugger?” Kazem looked sharply at Mahmud.

“He’s known to sodomise the wretched young men luckless enough to fall into his clutches,” confirmed Mahmud.

“By looking at his face, I can tell he’s been having lots of orgies,” Kazem said.

"They all have orgies, Kazem," said Mahmud, gazing at the judge. "Once they side with the ayatollahs, they join the pack of other carrion eaters enjoying the feast. It has always been and it always will be like this."

"Come on, get up!" the young guard snapped at Kazem. "It's your turn to see Haj Agha Mousavi."

Kazem stood up lazily, strode towards Haj Agha, and planted himself in front of his desk.

"*Bah*, *bah*, Jenaab-e Kazem Khan-e Alaki," Hajji Agha Mousavi addressed Kazem in a sarcastic voice, recognising him at once. "Fancy seeing you here, son." He then threw a rapid glance at Mahmud. "You've brought along a friend, too, I see. They've told me that you've been drinking that filth."

"Come on, Haj Agha," said Kazem politely, "we were just trying to keep our balance on the snow not to fall over."

"But you've fallen already, so to speak, into sin," droned Hajji Agha Mousavi, "by drinking that filth."

"You mean *arrack*!" Kazem almost cried. "A good Muslim like me touching that filthy stuff!"

Kazem had never had any truck with the religious authorities in his life and had not the faintest clue what Sharia Law was about. So, after some reflection, he decided to confess and get it over and done with.

"All right, then," said Kazem, casting a sideways glance at Mahmud, "we only had a few tots of *arrack*, that's all."

"May Allah bless you my son," said Hajji Mousavi, sounding like a compassionate father. "Now that you've confessed to your sin, I'll reduce your chastisement from eighty lashes to forty."

"What?" yelled Kazem, not believing his ears. "What do you mean, forty lashes?"

"According to the Holy Book and the sacred *hadith* the Prophet left us," Hajji Agha said, now sounding like a preacher, "the confession to a sin is far more serious than the sin committed."

"But I didn't know about this…," Kazem was about to say *bullshit* but stopped, in case he should bring upon himself the wrath of the lackeys of Islam.

"Now you know, son," said Hajji Agha calmly, "so that in the future you'll know how to behave. You go and sit down and wait till I've heard what your friend has to say."

Mahmud's case being the same as Kazem's, was quick. The judge scribbled down some words on a piece of paper, handed it over to the commander, who, with his neophyte, grabbed Kazem and Mahmud's arms, frogmarching them out of the room.

"Where're you taking us, captain?" Kazem ventured, glancing at the stern-looking guard.

"To the *monkaraat* section in the Evin Prison to carry out the rituals, of course." The commander spoke as if they were all going to a wedding ceremony.

The guards escorted them through the now deserted corridor. Out in the street, they were bundled into the back of the patrol car.

40

The snow had stopped falling. A grey dawn was feeling its way over the rooftops, creeping down the lanes, alleyways and streets. Tehran was slowly stirring. Overcome by weariness, Kazem rested his head against the window and gazed at the shops with their closed corrugated iron shutters. In the bitterly cold, murky-grey streets some pedlars, wrapped up in threadbare coats and stooping over their carts, were trudging along gutters choked with blackened snow. On some street corners a handful of shabbily-clothed day-labourers had huddled around a fire made out of smashed wooden pallets in a tin barrel full of holes, vigorously rubbing their hands and blowing into them. Enveloped in an icy mist, they shivered silently.

The patrol car raced through the streets, splashing through the soot-covered slush. Soon the car reached the leafy uptown districts and drove towards the north-west of Tehran through unfamiliar streets. The murmur of the city faded away as the car approached the village of Evin. It then turned into a long, steep road along one side of which was stretched the most colossal wall, its end vanishing into a greyish haze. Kazem had never seen such a wall in his life. Curious, he stuck his head to the window to see the top of the wall. Constructed of concrete cement reinforced with thick iron girders, the points of which stuck out every few metres, it was far too high. Streaks of rust oozed out from beneath the tips of the girders, like blood.

Kazem looked ahead. A short distance away, two black-chadored women walked ponderously up the road at the bottom of the wall. Their movements were slow, as if they were burdened under mountains of worries. They looked like two tiny ants crawling at the feet of a reclining colossus. Across the road to his right the windows of houses were all veiled with thick curtains. As the car crawled up the road, Kazem saw a few of the curtains move aside slightly, the occupants peering out like frightened animals.

At the top of the road the car stopped in front of a huge iron gate flanked by two sentry boxes. Two guards, dressed from head to foot in heavy protective clothing and clutching machine guns, yelled for the gate to be opened. The loud clanking of the gate sliding on its rusty grooves shattered the surrounding silence. The car drove into an open space and came to a halt in the middle of it.

"Welcome to Evin University!" Mahmud whispered in Kazem's ear.

"Evin University?" Kazem repeated, gazing ahead.

"SAVAK took so many students here that they nicknamed it Evin University," Mahmud explained with a bitter smile.

"Keep your traps shut!" one of the guards barked.

In the livid light of dawn, Evin Prison, an impenetrable block of steel and cement carved into the mountain, loomed large through the fog. Agile as predatory beasts, the two guards leapt out of the car, opened the back doors, and ordered Kazem and Mahmud to get out. Stepping out, Kazem inhaled the icy air as he stretched his hands and thrust his chest out, looking around like a wolf let out of its cage. On his left stood the massive cast-iron inner gate of the prison, from the top of which powerful projectors threw a blinding light on the open space where a mass of people wandered around as mute as ghosts, casting dancing shadows on the grubby, packed-down snow. In the pale snowy light, their faces looked as if they were covered with a sickly sheen of silk. Keeping well away from each other, they were no doubt waiting for the gates to be opened so that they could find out about the fate of their lost or disappeared friends, relatives and children.

Looking towards the mist-shrouded hills down below, Kazem could barely make out the snow-covered prison wall that snaked up and down the hills like the Great Wall of China. Buried under the snow, the snarls of barbed wire on top of the wall glistened in the strong lights that punctuated the top of the wall every ten meters. Further down, stretching to the horizon like a massive graveyard, lay Tehran. A thick smog, like a gigantic greyish-black *aba*, was spread over it, smothering the quietly breathing capital whose inhabitants were struggling to tear themselves from their confused dreams before daybreak. Neon lights and street lamps gleamed, here and there, through the smog. All of a sudden a flock of crows swirled into the ashen sky. They filled the air with their deafening cawing, and soon vanished into fog beyond the mountains.

What will Maryam think if she finds out about me being here, Kazem thought.

"Move!" snapped one of the guards, shoving Kazem forward. He turned and walked heavily towards the gate, followed by Mahmud. Once inside the prison proper, Kazem heard the loud clanking of the gate behind him. The latch clicked, shutting him and Mahmud in from the outside world. Only then was he truly able to see the monumental proportions of Evin Prison.

The box-like, dismally grey buildings were clumped together. One tall, rectangular building particularly caught his attention. Carved into its slatey façade, in perfect geometrical order, were rows of windows with iron shutters. From washing lines stretched outside from one window to another hung the prisoners' uniforms, underwear, and some civilian clothes. A darkness as thick as tar reigned behind the shutters.

The guards marched the two friends to a dingy room beside a very long corridor. A stocky, bearded guard was sitting behind a long metal desk, flanked by two morose-looking ghouls attired in oversized military uniforms. One of the guards shoved Kazem towards the table.

"Empty all your pockets on the table," the seated uniformed ape ordered. Calmly, Kazem dug his hands into each of his pockets and extracted from them what he possessed: a box of matches, a half-empty squashed cigarette packet, some greasy banknotes and some change that jingled on the table and rolled around a bit before coming to rest.

A heavy silence ensued.

"Officer Ahmadi," the human ape growled, turning to the freakish creature on his left, "give him his sack of prison uniform and tell him to put it on in that corner."

The guard took a gunny sack from among many piled in a heap near the wall behind him. He thrust it at Kazem's chest and grunted, "Over there," pointing to the corner. As Kazem was taking off his clothes, he kept glancing anxiously at Mahmud, who was going through the same process.

Once changed into their uniforms, they were pushed roughly out of the room by the two guards.

"Welcome to the world of convicts, Mahmud," whispered Kazem as they were leaving the room.

"You don't seem to be troubled by being in those pyjamas, Kazem," Mahmud muttered back, half-jokingly.

"Well," said Kazem, smiling sadly, "they remind me of my good old friends in Qasr Prison."

The seemingly endless dank corridor was lit by a line of grimy neon lights in the middle of the ceiling. Along the foot of the wall a long row of young men had been forced to squat with their hands clasped behind their heads. As Kazem kept glancing at the wretches, the uniformed brute growled at him, prodding him with his rifle butt from behind. Some other brutish-looking guards snarled at the social and political agitators from Tehran's hot spots to keep their heads down. The dishevelled crew cowered under the rain of threats followed by occasional kicks to their thighs. They shivered with fear and cold, terrified out of their wits. The poor devils were, no doubt, being herded to communal cells, thought Kazem.

Halfway down the corridor, one of the guards stopped, opened the door of a cell on the right and growled at Kazem and Mahmud to get in. Once inside, the door was slammed shut with a loud bang. A foul odour of sweat, smelly feet and urine attacked Kazem's nostrils, making him grimace. In a flash the memories of that malodorous wall in Shahr-e No rushed to his mind. He peered into the gloom. The stomping of booted feet, the sound of heavy objects being dragged across the floor accompanied by the whimpering of terrified men and bellowing of guards could be heard.

Then an ominous calm reigned.

Some sprawling, shadowy forms in filthy prison rags caught Kazem's eye. What he saw shocked him to the core of his being. This was not the sort of cell he had seen in Qasr Penitentiary and the convicts were not the sort of criminals he had known there. From the only hatch-like opening near the ceiling a pallid beam of daylight streamed in like a scourge. In the patch of light, Kazem made out the bloodless faces of a handful of convicts. Some of them huddled over their knees in the manner of plague-ridden bodies; others reclined uncomfortably, resting their heads on one folded hand. Some laid their heads on the backs or bellies of others for want of space. All were sunk in an uneasy slumber. A chorus of discordant snoring, broken up here and there by mournful sighs, filled the room. Every now and then some convicts stirred in the shadowy corners, scratched themselves, muttered oaths and became quiet again.

"Over here," a gruff voice called out. "There's a bit of room for you to sit down."

Kazem threw a questioning glance at Mahmud and started to walk towards the spot where the voice was coming from. They picked their way through the grotesque-looking bodies and came to the owner of the voice. The man was sitting with his back to the wall under the hatch, hugging his knees. Kazem and Mahmud sat beside him, leaning against the wall.

"Yours truly, Kazem Alaki," said Kazem, stretching out his hand towards the man.

"They call me Hajji Jalil," said the man in his feeble voice, clutching Kazem's hand in his bony one, "but I'm not hajji. I've never set foot in Mecca in my life."

"And I'm Mahmud," said Mahmud, also stretching his hand over and shaking the man's hand.

41

Hajji Jalil was in his early forties. He had a gaunt face, dopey sunken eyes, and a boxer's nose. His hollow cheeks were covered with a thick grizzly stubble. As he spoke, slowly weighing every word, two gold-plated canine teeth glinted from among his horseshoe-shaped moustache.

All three men remained silent for a while, pondering whether to say something or not for fear of giving away too much. Drifting in through the hatch was an enormous din made by flocks of crows outside.

As Kazem's eyes became used to the dim light, he could make out the faces of the other convicts. Hearing the sounds they began to open their eyes, blinking and gazing around, bemused. They all looked gaunt with eyes almost as big as their faces and swamped by their oversized, filthy-grey pyjamas. They all stared at Kazem and Mahmud, like animals about to be slaughtered.

"What brought you to these parts, bro?" Hajji Jalil asked in the tone of a man who has seen it all before.

"Just a few glasses of *arrack*, that's all," replied Kazem calmly.

"Hmm, *arrack*," muttered Hajji Jalil. "So you're an arrack-tippler, like me. I like that. I think we'll get on well together." He nodded towards the other convicts. "Some of these poor devils have also been dragged here for drinking, others for smuggling opium, and some for not paying their debts and…"

"What's your story then, Jalil Agha?" Kazem ventured.

"*Hey, hey*," Hajji Jalil sighed. "My story is a nice one, bro. It's nowhere near any of this lot!"

"What might that be, I wonder," Kazem said, trying to prod Hajji Jalil to speak.

Hajji Jalil cast a sidelong glance at Kazem, shaking his head, as if trying to suss him out.

"You see, Kazem Agha," Hajji Jalil spoke finally, apparently finding in Kazem a kindred soul, "I know I'm a goner. Fellows like me have never managed to come out alive from Evin. This bag of skin and bones will not survive those electric cable lashes I'm going to enjoy today. Maybe it's time to put an end to this dog's life and not see these sons of whores rule supreme." He sighed. "I might just as well let you know my holiest of secrets. I was a bodyguard to the most powerful ayatollah in the land."

"A bodyguard to an ayatollah!" repeated Kazem. "Well, that's something."

"Yes, bro, a bodyguard," went on Hajji Jalil wryly. "I had everything going for me; all the privileges reserved only for the likes of me."

"So, what is someone your calibre doing here in Evin, of all places?" asked Kazem. "I always thought bodyguards were a very special lot."

"Hmm, they're very *special* all right!" Hajji Jalil's gold-plated teeth glinted. "What do you think the bodyguards, secret police, and revolutionary guards are? Do you reckon they're saints, teachers, or honest revolutionaries? No, of course not! They're just a squalid crew of good-for-nothings, sadists, gamblers, drunkards, pimps, bastards born to whores in Shahr-e No, who, like carrion eaters, swoop down on any rotting carcass, fish in the muddy waters of the Revolution, cash in on the chaos, and…"

"So how was it that you ended up in this hole?" Kazem cut into the flow.

"That's a long tale to tell, Kazem Agha." Hajji Jalil twirled his moustache as if gathering his thoughts to recount his story. "Years ago, like many uprooted peasants, I came to Tehran to find a job to earn my bread and take care of my old parents who were left back in the village. I rented a donkey from a small merchant and began selling blocks of ice to people around the Shahr-e No district. Soon I found my way into the Citadel selling ice to the prostitutes and the stallholders. Being a hot-headed youth, I found myself getting into brawls with all types of folk. Having bulging biceps and itching to do things just for kicks, one day the notorious strongman whom you might have heard of, Hossein Ramazan-Yakhi, that is…"

Kazem nodded.

"…saw me fighting with some scum. Hossein – may his soul rest in peace – liked my recklessness and sent one of his flunkeys to ask me if I'd like to join his gang. Being young and more than ready for trouble, I accepted the offer and was welcomed into Hossein's circle. From that day on we roamed in packs of threes and fours in and around the district collecting protection money from the pimps, shopkeepers and merchants to whom we offered our moral and physical support in times of need, if you get my drift. As a token of my loyalty, the merchant gave the donkey to me as a gift. I let a peasant relative, just arrived from the village, work for me by carrying the ice-blocks on the donkey around the district to earn his bread and keep an eye on people who dodged their duty to us. I soon became a full-time knife-fighter looking after my boss on his rounds to collect extortion money. Everything was going beautifully and I didn't complain; we commanded everybody's respect. Every evening we hung out in different taverns around the Citadel and café-restaurants in Lalezar, and guzzled bottle after bottle of *arrack* till we got completely pissed. We brawled over dancing girls and the strongest took the most popular dancer with him. I myself kept a mistress in every single café-restaurant."

Hajji Jalil paused and coughed noisily.

"It was all going well till one day I knifed a pimp in a brawl in the Morvarid Café- Restaurant. I had to teach him a lesson because he was not paying his share of his earnings from his *khanums*. My boss tried to save my neck by bribing the police, the judge and others, but it didn't work that time. They were too greedy and things did not turn out as good as usual. So I was arrested and sentenced to five years in jail. When the Revolution broke out the rebels tore down the prison gates and all the convicts, taking this one-off chance, bolted out of the jail and melted into the mob which was milling around all over the place shouting slogans and smashing everything. I was one of those convicts. I lay low for a while with one of my mates.

"It didn't take me long to find that almost all of the thugs I knew had joined Khomeini's camp. I said to myself, if I don't go with the flow they'll sooner or later catch me like a rat and drop me in the nick again. So I mingled with the crowd, shouting slogans at the top of my lungs. This went on till the day Khomeini and his troop of cronies were about to land at the airport. So I joined the crowds of hoi-polloi who were mobbing the airport. Pushing and shoving in the rabble, I managed to run close to the four-by-four in which Khomeini was supposed to be carried. Once a bunch of men had jostled the Imam into the vehicle, I started to run beside it, kicking, punching and pushing the mad folk, sending them reeling on the road.

"As soon as Khomeini settled in Alavi School in uptown Tehran, I began mingling among the people, egging the mob on to shout slogans and keep order. It did not take long before the person of Hadi Ghaffari noticed my zeal and asked me to join his rough-necks. Hadi Ghaffari was a young mollah who wielded a lot of power in Tehran-No Avenue and who had surrounded himself with many former knife-fighters and rogues. He paid strongmen like Hossein Farzin and his underlings, such as Abdol Bolandeh and others, who ruled in Fuziyeh Square and surrounding districts, to attack the young dissidents and knife them down. What more could I wish for? I said to myself: 'Jalil, this is a once-in-a-lifetime opportunity, don't shilly-shally and worry your head about who's right or who's wrong; go on, take it and ride the tide. These motherfuckers are getting firmly settled in the packsaddle of power. Once your lot gets better you can bugger off to greener pastures and lead a peaceful life with one of your mistresses. All you need to do is pop into the Shabdolazim Shrine, find one of those lousy mollahs who always creep around the sanctuary, ask him to pour a few bowls of repentance water on her head, mumble a few verses of the Koran, light two or three votive candles and, hey presto, she'll be as chaste as Fatima.'"

Hajji Jalil growled something beneath his breath.

"From that day on, I played the role of a devoted Muslim, praying with other revolutionary guards, fasting during Ramadan, and flagellating myself on Ashura day. I ended up seeming more Shiite than the person of Imam Ali! I also lied to everyone that I'd been to Mecca and, lo and behold, I came to be known as *Hajji* Jalil! We followed the little and large ayatollahs wherever they went, whatever they did, and whomever they met. I was now in the middle of the most powerful circle in the land. As time passed, I showed my prowess by thrashing anybody who opposed the ayatollahs in any way. One day one of the bodyguards of Ayatollah Beheshti told me that Beheshti wished me to be his personal minder. Knowing that Beheshti wielded a lot of clout in the power circle and being the one who called the shots, I accepted the offer on the spot and joined the close pack of his exclusive bodyguards."

A dark shadow passed over his haggard face.

"It didn't take me long to hear and see things that no one else had ever had a chance to witness. I'd heard before that these mollahs were a bunch of lecherous buggers, but I had not seen anything with my own eyes. For a long time I'd noticed very young women entering the room of another famous ayatollah and emerging with their faces glowing with happiness. One day, over a few glasses of *arrack*, a bodyguard friend of mine told me that the ayatollah in question takes the virginity of these young girls in his room, telling them that they will be blessed by Allah after that. Another night we had to stand guard outside a secret hideout for some influential mollahs in the cabinet. I saw with my own eyes guards lugging crates of *arrack* inside the house. Several prostitutes, all veiled in black chadors, were secretly hustled in by the pimps, most of whom I knew in my former life. The orgy went on until cockcrow. At daybreak the mollahs kicked out the whores, sat beside the *hauz*, did their ablutions and all prayed behind the imam.

"Soon I came to find out about the ruthless power struggle going on behind the scenes. I heard lots of angry exchange between Beheshti and some other ayatollahs behind the closed doors beside which I stood guard. One day I heard Beheshti growling at the person of Khomeini, calling him a motherfucker whom he, Beheshti that is, had put on the throne and saying he would drag him down by his beard if he wanted to.

"From what I've seen and heard, Beheshti was an educated mollah who had lived in England for a while and appeared to be fairly moderate," Kazem butted in.

"Let me tell you this, Kazem Agha, for the uninitiated who don't know much about him, he seemed like a decent fellow who spoke good English when being interviewed by foreign reporters, but in reality he was the mother of all motherfuckers. An educated and gentlemanly thief comes to steal things from your house with a candle in his hand. These motherfuckers are all made of the same stuff; they're nothing but a bunch of imposters. A mollah is a mollah, no matter where he was educated – England, America or Qom! He and Khomeini had only one thought inside their skulls: absolute power, do you hear me? So Khomeini, being known to the masses for a long time and enjoying a lot of popularity, wasn't able to tolerate a rival, especially after being called a motherfucker!

"After the assassination of Beheshti, I fell out of favour with the surviving mollahs, only because I knew too much. So they sent me packing, making me understand that I should keep my trap shut, otherwise they'd slit my throat in a back alley. I decided to leave the circle of power and get on with my life. I was now jobless with not so much as a *gheran* to buy even a piece of shroud for myself! Finally, I decided to become a cabby. I bought a second-hand car and started to pick up Tehran's folk from one part and dump them in another …

"I rented a small room in a lodging house in downtown Tehran to be away from all that stuff on in and around Khomeini's residence. But I knew that my days were numbered because I later heard from a reliable mate of mine that Sadegh Khalkhali – the mad dog of the regime – had one day invited all the former reformed thugs to Qasr Prison on the pretext of showing off his masterwork of annihilating anything that stood in the way of Islamic Republic, and shot them all to prevent more scandal and to pave the way for Khomeini's absolute power. Dead men tell no tales, as they say!

"In order to forget it all, I turned to opium and *arrack*. Soon my mistress left me, had bowls of repentance water poured over her by a mollah, and joined Zahra's Sisterhood, roaming the streets, harassing the decent women of Tehran to keep up with the Islamic hijab. Now the only company left to me were my opium pipe, my brazier, a few bottles of homemade *arrack* and my pair of balls, gone out of action long ago! In the evenings I sat before my brazier and poured all my sorrows into the opium pipe. I put some old cassettes in my battered tape-recorder and listened to good old songs I used to hear in taverns and café-restaurants."

Jalil fell silent, now calm, as if he had purged his soul of a deadly poison.

Suddenly, one of the convicts, a lanky middle-aged man with long hair, got up with difficulty, pulled his pyjama top over his head, stretched his hands out like a ballerina, and began to sing in his feeble voice a song sung by drunkards in the taverns:

Oh, you made my life hell by flirting with my rivals,
You didn't feel pity for my wretchedness.
What have I done to you?
You left me alone in this world,
To live only on my tears and sorrows.
I've suffered so much that
My skin has gone as yellow as turmeric.
Watching you that night in the cabaret,
Eyeing Mehti Gareh up, and
Winking at Abbas Zigil at the same time,
Pissed me off completely...

As he sang, he clicked his fingers and wiggled his bum. Some of the convicts sat up and began to accompany him, clapping their skinny hands.

"At least someone is jolly in this hellhole," Kazem remarked with a faint smile.

"Never mind about him, Kazem Agha," said Hajji Jalil. "The poor devil used to love a whore who danced in a cabaret. Since he has heard that they're going to lash him, he's cracked up. He's always sunk into gloom. Every now and then he suddenly gets up and starts singing and dancing, thinking that he's in a cabaret somewhere in Tehran and all the convicts are the customers."

"So, what happened that you ended up here?" Kazem asked, bringing Hajji Jalil back to the subject.

"In order to get rid of me in a more legal way, they planted a bundle of opium rolls in my room in a hole under the kilim," Hajji Jalil said.

"But that's diabolical, Jalil Agha!" Kazem exclaimed.

"*Aey baba*, Kazem Agha," said Hajji Jalil dejectedly. "What's not diabolical in this land of ours! Besides, who would take seriously the whimpers of an opium junky protesting his innocence?"

"But didn't you smell the strong smell of opium in your room?"

"How could I suspect anything?" said Hajji Jalil. "All my belongings smelled of opium. Its blessed aroma has gone into everything in my room like the perfume of a whore that clings to your body for days after leaving Shahr-e No!"

"No one in the house came to your help?" asked Kazem.

"*Ay zeki*, Kazem Agha, what help?" Hajji Jalil chuckled. "Those lily-livered lodgers had all crept into their rooms like mice, shut the doors, and drawn the curtains. No one dared come out, for they knew that if they did, they'd be accused of being my accomplice."

"So what did you do then?

"What do you expect a guy like me do?" Hajji Jalil replied with a sigh. "I was squatting beside my brazier when they barged into my room. One of them waved a piece of paper on which was scribbled a warrant cooked up by *monkaraat*. They then scattered around the room, sniffing everywhere like mongrel dogs. After a short token search, they lifted the kilim, and there it was: a bundle of opium rolls tightly packed in aluminium foil. When they tore the wrapping open the most heavenly sight appeared right before my eyes. For a moment I was bowled over with such ecstasy that I completely forgot where I was and what was going on. The aroma of those coffee-coloured, first-class opium rolls filled the room, sending shivers down my body! Upon this discovery, all the guards barked so loudly with joy that I tumbled down from my paradise back to this earth!

"Knowing that I was in a serious scrape, I prepared myself for the battle of my life. I said to myself: 'Let's put up a good fight.' The only useful weapon left me was my opium pipe. Looking daggers at them, I clenched my teeth and gripped my pipe with two hands like a mace, ready to do battle with them. They all looked at me mockingly. The one with the longest beard strode to my brazier and kicked it with his heavy boot, sending it somersaulting on the kilim. Embers flew off like fireworks everywhere. Another went for the pile of un-Islamic cassettes on the mantelpiece, grabbed them, pulled out the guts from inside each, hurled them to the floor, and jumped on them like a freaked-out baboon, smashing them into one hundred pieces under his boots. The third one snatched the tape-recorder, lifted it up and dashed it to the wall, wrecking it. Another went into the alcove, found my few bottles of *arrack*, and chucked them out of the window. Seeing my old companions being treated like that was decidedly the last straw. I had to defend my honour and rescue what was left of my manliness. What had a born loser like me to lose? I wasn't going to let these misbegotten motherfuckers get away with it. Oh no, not me, bro! They had no idea they were dealing with Hajji Jalil, whose name alone used to set the fear of God in people's hearts.

"So I lifted my opium pipe aloft and charged towards them. I managed to strike one of them right on the crown of his skull, splitting it a bit. The headpiece of the pipe broke and fell on the kilim, rolling about like the severed head of Hazrat Abbas. As it rolled, it broke into pieces, letting the bits of burnt opium inside it shoot out. In a jiffy I found myself spinning, threatening my adversaries with the wooden pipe without its headpiece. After a few spins I felt dizzy, my legs gave in, and I stumbled and fell. They were upon me like a pack of hyenas, punching, kicking, and hauling me around on the kilim. I still managed to stand on my feet and head-butt one of them, but no strength was left in my neck. After being tossed around like a rag doll, I felt a sharp pain at the back of my head. One of them had hit me with the butt of his pistol. Next, they charged me on the spot for pushing drugs, I was branded 'corrupter on the earth' and, after a summary trial they carted me to this kennel."

"What happened to the bundle of opium rolls?" asked Kazem.

"That's bloody obvious, isn't it?" jeered Hajji Jalil. "They no doubt sold them on the black market and pocketed the proceeds!"

Hajji Jalil's eyes hazed over. He sat with a blissful smile on his lips, as if he was inhaling the aroma emanating from those gorgeous rolls of opium.

42

The convicts were now fully awake, huddling into themselves and staring around with sleepy eyes. They looked like a dispirited shipwrecked crew in a flimsy boat about to sink in the middle of an ocean.

The door was pushed open with a screech. Two guards walked in, stood beside the door, and looked around.

"Hajji Jalil, Kazem known as Alaki, and Mahmud Farzaneh," one of them brayed, "get up and follow us to the interrogation room."

Hearing this, Kazem and Mahmud jumped to their feet. Hajji Jalil struggled up with a groan. They picked their way through the slumped convicts, who stared at them with the terrified looks of people who knew all too well the fate awaiting these new arrivals. The guards pushed them out of the door, which they shut with a loud bang behind them. The glare of the neon lights made Kazem blink.

"Straight ahead," growled one of the uniformed apes, shoving them forward with the butt of his machine gun. They were told to halt in front of a door, on which the guard in charge rapped with his knuckles.

"Enter," a coarse voice came from inside.

The guards pushed the three convicts inside.

The dank and bare room was lit by a neon light. Two iron beds parallel to one another stood in the middle of it. They were both spread over with filthy bloodstained mattresses. A middle-aged, clean-shaven man, a rare sight in that place, with an open-neck shirt and dressed in civilian clothes, was standing in the middle of the room.

"Which of you is Mahmud Farzaneh?" he asked, eyeing the three men.

"I am," replied Mahmud, raising his hand slightly.

"Take him out of the room and wait for me outside," the man ordered one of the guards, who grabbed Mahmud's arm and pushed him out. He then called out to the guard, "I've asked brother Ahmadi to put together whatever he can find from his neighbours. We want information about his past, suspicious contacts, moral corruption, specific activities against Islam."

"Where are you taking him?" Kazem cried out.

"Don't worry about your friend," said the well-dressed man. "We want to ask him a few questions, that's all."

The man walked to the guard in charge, whispered something to him and walked out of the room. After a short while another guard came in, followed by two of the most ferocious-looking men Kazem had ever seen in his life. Looking like two bears dressed up in human clothes, they stood by the door, each clutching an electric cable in his hand. The more Kazem looked at them, the fewer traces of humanity he found in them.

"Take off your shirts," one of the guards squawked, addressing Kazem and Jalil. Hesitating a little, Kazem cast a questioning glance at Jalil.

"You'd better listen to what they tell you," Jalil whispered as he started unbuttoning his shirt, "otherwise they'll kill you under more lashes."

Kazem began to unbutton his shirt in his usual calm manner, his eyes fixed on the guards.

"You lie on your belly on that mattress," the guard in charge ordered Kazem, pointing to one of the beds.

"And, you, stretch out on this one." The second guard ordered Jalil to lie on the other bed.

Kazem heard the guard in charge clicking his fingers. Upon this signal, the two creatures leapt to the sides of the beds and began tying their hands and feet to the bedposts. Kazem turned his head towards his new friend and looked at him. He'll not survive the lethal blows of these cables, Kazem thought. Once the two were tightly secured, the guard in charge growled, "*Allahu akbar*" and the ceremony began.

With the first blow, Kazem felt a searing pain on his back as if scorched by a red-hot iron rod. With each whip of the cable his body made a violent heave, arching itself as high as was possible. He clenched his teeth, closed his eyes, and did not make a sound. One should not show any sign of weakness to these motherfuckers, he thought. It was not so much the pain but the humiliation. After a few lashes Kazem's back became numb and he lay there motionless, like a carcass.

His imagination, however, was fired, with the events of his life flashing with incredible speed through his mind. One image that stood out from among the others was that of his beautiful mother. From beyond the years he remembered a day when he was sitting beside her in the hovel in Najeebkhaneh Street while she was darning a piece of clothing, humming a song. How Kazem loved it when she sang! Other images of her followed in rapid succession. He saw her wake up late every morning, give him his bread soaked in sweetened tea, do herself up by smearing her face with blusher and putting mascara on her eyelashes, before dressing in a garish blouse and a short skirt. She would then waddle out of the house with her high-heeled shoes clacking on the uneven floor tiles, to go to work in the neighbouring Shahr-e No Street as a dancer in one of the grubby cabarets. How proud I was then, Kazem thought, boasting to the other guttersnipes that my mother was an *artiste*! *Hey*, *hey*, my mother an *artiste*! When we sat in the shade of a wall in that filthy alleyway that stank of piss, I mocked the others that their mothers did nothing but sit in front of their houses, shouting at strange men to go in to talk and fool around with them.

One memory of his mother led to others. Sometimes in the middle of a game, he remembered, he'd break off and stand in front of the cabaret in which she sang and danced. He would secretly peep inside and see his mother, half-naked, heavily made up and garbed in glittering clothes, singing and dancing with some other women who screeched in shrill voices, waving their hands and wriggling their hips. Upon spotting me, she'd flutter her hands, signalling at me to run off and play with the other kids. How I liked looking at those colourful light bulbs hung on strings in the cabaret, feeling proud that my mother was dancing in such a nice place!

His mind was then filled with wailing and screeching. From beyond the mist of time, he saw himself sitting on the lap of a young woman in the courtyard. It was early morning. From inside the hovel, where his mother had given birth to his baby sister, he could hear women lamenting and shrieking. Some old hags dashed out pulling their hair, screaming and slapping their heads. Soon some people dressed in white clothes came and carried his mother away, leaving his little sister in the care of other women. He never saw his mother again. After that day he saw one of the women, who also had a baby, feeding his baby sister. He liked playing with her; her cooing and gurgling made him laugh.

One day a man and a woman, who had come from the outside world and were dressed up in nice clothes, walked into the courtyard. They whispered something to one of the old hags and took his baby sister away. No one ever mentioned the name of his sister again.

This image was soon followed by those of himself and his ragamuffin friends who played, from dawn to sundown, in Shahr-e No Street, running along the length of the foul-smelling gutters. Being a daredevil, he would goad some of his friends to brave the obstacles and sneak secretly through a dark and filthy alleyway to the forbidden territory of Shahr-e No Street to see for themselves what was going on there. Vermin-like, the boys crept and crawled in the gutters among the disparate multitude of men who had come from all over Tehran. He and his friends, both boys and girls, roamed around in the street, scampering between the legs of the teeming throng, jumping over the gutters and playing games they had invented for themselves. He and his playmates were ignored, as pests of all kinds are ignored, by the busy crowd, who scuttled here and there either to see the women, or sell their wares brought into the street from the outside world. Every day the policemen would round the urchins up and herd them back to Najeebkhaneh Street.

These images soon gave place to more recent ones, from among which he made out that of Maryam, standing at the end of an alleyway looking at him. Despite the excruciating pain, Kazem smiled peacefully. He had already made up his mind what to do with his life if he survived this barbarism. Soon his mind echoed with the heart-rending shrieks and whining of the old hags again. They all sang and danced around, wailing like gypsy women in trance. As their screeches got louder and louder, a hideous face emerged from among the other faces, dragging herself towards him, smeared with dust and dung. At close quarters, Kazem recognised the cripple in the shrine in Hosseinabaad. Her disturbing shrieks became louder and louder till they filled the whole room, becoming unbearable.

Halfway through the lashes Kazem opened his eyes and glanced at Jalil. He was snorting like a man in the clutches of death. Every now and then Kazem could make out curses and swearwords such as 'I piss in your lice-infected beards', 'I piss on your Arab God, your beliefs, everything, you motherfuckers.' With every blow his ribcage heaved up violently as if his soul were leaping up and down to free itself. His skin had turned corpse-like. He slowly became silent, with only his lips twitching under his moustache. Kazem could not bear to look at his back. Large, purplish-red streaks had appeared on his bruised skin. The whites of his eyeballs, like the glass shades of an oil lamp, had rolled back. After several spasms of his limbs, his body became lifeless, leaving an empty shell. What was the point of beating a dead body? Kazem thought.

One of the guards was counting the number of the lashes. As the beasts raised the cables high and brought them down with full force, they grunted and puffed, absorbed in their task. They no doubt had been told that whatever they did was for the glory of the Allah the Almighty and they would end up in heaven after fulfilling their Islamic tasks.

Finally the lashes stopped. The guards untied the ropes. They ordered the two 'corruptors of the earth' to get up. Kazem sat up with difficulty in bed, in great pain. But Jalil did not make a move. They shouted at him, slapped his face, and shook the bed without success.

“The motherfucker is faking death so that we should send him to hospital,” said one guard.

“I tell you what, brother,” suggested the other guard, “stick the cable up his arse and you’ll see, he’ll jump to his feet like a fucking baboon.”

Kazem knew that Jalil had given up ghost. Good for you my friend, Kazem thought, being dead in this shithole of a homeland is better than being alive.

As the guard grabbed the electric cable to do the final, most unspeakable deed to a dead man, Kazem, overcome by an uncontrollable rage, tore himself from the bed and pounced on the guard from behind, clinging to him like a wild cat and trying to throttle him with whatever strength was left in his body. Taken by surprise by this unexpected show of strength, the other guards set upon him, punching and lashing him furiously. It was precisely at that moment that Kazem heard a commanding voice ordering them to stop. Kazem, however, did not let go of the guard who was choking in his powerful clutches.

“May the Devil the Bastard be cursed,” a familiar voice rang out in the room. “If you don’t let him go, your punishment will be much worse.”

The image of Maryam appeared in front of Kazem’s eyes. The thought flashed through his mind that his love of Maryam was more life-giving than fighting with mollahs.

All Kazem’s fighting spirit recoiled from the idea of death. He did not want to die, not now, not like this. He recalled good old Mahmud saying that these mollahs lived for death, they preached it, and they did not give a hoot about life and the living. Love and laughter had no place in their religion. The real life for them started after this life. But Kazem had just found out what love was all about. By being alive, he thought, I’ll create a better life by giving my children the things that matter, things that passed me by in my meaningless former existence. The alchemy of his love for Maryam had transformed the base stone of Kazem’s life into a precious gem. He would not allow them to step into his temple of love. How could he give up all that and let himself be caught in the death snare set for him by these bearded monsters?

The voice was Mollah Hossein’s. Kazem felt something begin to well up from the depth of his being. Something unnameable and primordial, handed back to him from the age of caves. Something whispered softly to him, telling him that this was all unnatural and very wrong. He felt the rage rising from the core of his being, as lava does in a silent volcano. He began to shake all over uncontrollably. He let go of the guard’s neck, turned and began to hurl all the obscenities he had in his stock of vocabulary at Mollah Hossein.

"I piss in your beards!" he yelled. "You killed my friend, you fucking murderers, you ghouls in turbans and *aba*, you…"

He was sent sprawling on the floor by the heavy blow of a boot to his back. The guards set upon him, raining kicks and punches on him.

"Leave him," Mollah Hossein commanded. "He's raving. He's only a rogue who doesn't know what he's saying. We got the big fish. We only need to catch the educated ones. They are the real threat to our dear faith, not these good-for-nothing rascals. Let him go."

The guards stood back, breathing heavily.

"You've paid for your sin, son," Mollah Hossein drawled. "You're free to go now. May Allah go with you."

"I don't need your murderous Allah to go with me," Kazem muttered as he tried to get up. "I've managed alone so far without Him and I'll go on without Him." One of the guards disappeared and came back with his clothes, which he chucked at him. Kazem put them on with great difficulty. He was escorted to the small room at the end of the corridor and was given back his belongings. Once outside the gate, he looked up at the ashen sky and breathed in the icy air, an urban wolf, wounded in body and soul but still proud and dignified. He walked down the steep street like a man who has had a glimpse of another reality. He had been awakened to the hideous hidden realities of life in Tehran under the ayatollahs.

As he staggered down the hill along the prison wall, the real torment, far more painful than the lashes, began to gnaw at his soul.

Even if I had died for defending the dignity of my friend, Kazem thought, it would not make the tiniest bit of difference to the way the things are going. Hajji Jalil has gone and is at peace. If they had killed me, who, except Maryam, would remember me? Who would look after her? Those bastards would have chucked my corpse on to one of those vacant lots on the outskirts of Tehran, letting it rot under a heap of trash. I know my own people better than anyone else. They would soon forget all about me. If I were lucky and they made a grave for me, it would not be long that they had picnics beside it.

Would it not have been an act of sheer folly to strangle the guard, Kazem reasoned with himself. I'd slowly rot in jail even if they didn't kill me. So it was better that I swallowed my rage, got out of this hellhole, to start a new life, maybe somewhere else, in a foreign land, as many people are doing these days. Maybe all this is part of the great scheme of things, a wake-up call to tell me that I no longer belong to the land of my forefathers. But who were my forefathers? One of whose descendants happened to be my own father, who ended up being a pimp? Wasn't he a whoreson himself, who was left with no choice but procuring sexual favours for others? My poor mother, a Shahr-e No prostitute, was the grand, granddaughter of a wretched line of women who, in order to have a bread-winner for a short while, became *siegheh*s to small-time mollahs and rich land-owners. Their lust gratified, these men kicked these wretched women out into the streets. Having nowhere to go and no one to turn to, they ended up in the slums of Tehran. Soon the pimps, who prowled the lanes and alleyways in search of fresh victims, found these women, promising them a better and happier life in Shahr-e No.

Who am I? Kazem went on debating with himself. An Iranian? What does it mean to be born in a patch of land called Iran? What has Iran given me except a life of crime and misery? No education, no comfort, no money, a maternal love that lasted only five years. I've seen nothing but betrayal, treachery and back-stabbing, while constantly running after my daily bread and onion, and at the end remaining empty-handed. Wasn't I a child of rape, a child of violence, at most a son of a whore? Bastards don't belong anywhere. They are nobodies.

43

Seeing Kazem in such a terrible state, Maryam at once began dressing his wounds and looking after him. The morning after Ali Khalifeh, upon hearing the story from Hassan Ghorazeh, came to see him.

"What happened, Kazem?" he asked as he entered the room.

"When we left your home," said Kazem, "the guards took both of us to Evin's branch of *monkaraat* and lashed us forty times for drinking."

"Each band of the whoresons has their own patch and they prowl like rabid dogs everywhere these days," said Ali Khalifeh. "How about Mahmud, then?"

"They took him away without lashing."

"Who took him away and where?"

"A well-dressed and well-spoken man asked the guards to take Mahmud outside the room," said Kazem. "That was the last time I saw him."

"Did you hear anything else about him?"

"I heard the mollah in charge say they got the big fish."

"Hmm, that means that you saw the last of the poor man," said Ali, shaking his head meaningfully.

"What do you mean, the last of him?"

"That means that they've sent him to Timbuktu, from which no one has ever returned," said Ali.

"Where's that then?"

"Special section in Evin for intellectuals, writers, poets and journalists who dare question things," Ali explained.

"I'll go and find him," said Kazem defiantly.

"Are you kidding or what?" said Ali. "Primo, this is not frigging Qasr Prison where you can just walk in and say, can I see my friend, please? Secondo, it is the most secret place on this planet, guarded by the fiercest men who take special pleasure in torturing, raping and killing, be it man or woman, without the slightest remorse. Understood?"

"Still, I'll do what I can to find out what happened to my scholar friend," insisted Kazem. "I'm not going to let them kill Mahmud just like that."

"As we're sitting here and talking about Mahmud," Ali went on grimly, "they've already either killed him under torture or shot him by now."

"Even so," said Kazem, "I'll get his body and bury him myself with all the due honours for a scholar."

"Bah!" said Ali bitterly. "Haven't you heard what they do with the bodies of these good people? They pile them in trucks in the dead of night, carry them to the edge of a desert somewhere, and dump them in communal graves, or chuck them into the salt lakes in the middle of some desert, so that no one will ever find them."

Kazem became quiet, thinking of his own plans to find out about his friend who had taught him so much.

Maryam went on nursing Kazem tenderly like a kind mother. For long hours he lay on his belly, thinking about Mahmud, hoping that he was still alive somewhere. Maryam quietly bustled around the room, doing her daily chores.

As soon as Kazem's wounds had healed a bit, he joined the throng of people outside the Evin Prison who mobbed the gates day and night to find out about their disappeared friends and loved ones. Kazem pestered every guard, official or mollah available to see if they had heard about a convict called Mahmud Farzaneh. They just stared at him as if he was an escaped lunatic. Mahmud had vanished from the face of this earth as a drop of rain evaporates in the scorched soil of a barren land, leaving no trace whatever.

"You're just tiring yourself out, Kazem," said Maryam one evening, handing him a glass of tea. "Your friend Mahmud, like many others like him, is dead and only God knows where his body is now. I've heard a lot of mothers telling me about their sons and daughters who've disappeared like that without a trace."

"Maybe you're right, Maryam." Kazem sighed resignedly. "I'm becoming tired myself."

After a few more fruitless visits to Evin Prison, Kazem abandoned hope. It was as if Mahmud had never existed; no one talked about him in the lodging house, no one dared even mention his name. As the days passed Kazem was overcome by a sense of despair he had never experienced before. More and more he felt alienated and a stranger in his own homeland. He could see no hope on the horizon.

One afternoon as he was sitting on a platform in the teahouse drinking tea with Ali Khalifeh and Hassan Ghorazeh, he aired his despair to Ali.

"I feel I can't go on living here any more," he said.

"Where?" Hassan Ghorazeh asked. "The lodging house?"

"No, no," said Kazem, smiling. "I mean Iran."

"Ah, Iran." Hassan nodded.

"I've noticed that, mate," Ali butted in. "You're not yourself these days, Kazem."

"I want to breathe the air of freedom, Ali," said Kazem. "I feel I'm buried alive. I've not been created to live in the oppressive air of Islamic rules and regulations. I want to escape."

"Escape where?" Hassan Ghorazeh downed the dregs of his tea.

"Anywhere but this place," said Kazem.

"If you're serious about leaving Iran," said Hassan, after a short pause, "I know some guys who could arrange it for you for an affordable amount of cash."

"Even if I decide to go," said Kazem, looking at Hassan questioningly, "I can't go anywhere without a passport. I don't have one."

"These guys can get a forged passport for you for five thousand tomans," said Hassan, looking over his shoulder to make sure no one could hear him.

"I can knock together ten thousand," said Kazem in a low voice. "One for myself and one for Maryam."

"Once you're out of Iran, where do you want to go?" Hassan asked.

"Dunno," Kazem said. "Anywhere, I suppose."

"For that you need people to help you," Hassan said.

"What do you mean?"

"To put you in a boat to take you somewhere safe in Europe."

"I suppose they want money for that, too."

"Well, no one does anything for your pretty eyes, Agha Kazem."

"All right, to hell with it," said Kazem. "How much are they asking for that?"

"Only a grand," said Hassan. "In dollars, by the way."

"In dollars!"

"They only accept dollars."

"All right," said Kazem. "Let me see what I can do."

When Kazem left the teahouse, he had already made up his mind. At home he was thoughtful.

"What is it, Kazem?" Maryam asked. "I know there's something on your mind."

"Truth be told, Maryam," said Kazem, "the bread and food of our homeland has lost their flavour for me. I'll have to look elsewhere for my nourishment. I've been thinking lately to leave this land and go somewhere abroad together."

"Abroad?" said Maryam. "But why?"

"There's no life here for us," said Kazem. "These bastards are taking over everything. I can't live in a country when a dark cloud of suspicion hangs over my head. You hear day in day out that the Supreme Leader carries on, bullying people to grass on their family and neighbours who dare step out of line or act against the commands of Sharia Law." He sighed heavily. "You see, Maryam, repressed fear eats away at the soul worse than leprosy; it hollows a man out and takes him over. I see patrol cars snatching the innocent off the streets and dumping them in *monkaraat* centres all over Tehran and the Devil knows how many of them come out alive or still in their right minds.'

"But we don't have passports, Kazem," said Maryam.

"Don't you worry about that. I know some people who can get us passports for ten thousand tomans."

"Even if we manage to put together that amount of money," said Maryam, "what'll we do in another country if we can't stay there?"

"There are men who can arrange our safe passage to a European country if we pay them some more. Round about a thousand dollars."

"A thousand dollars!"

"That's right."

"How are we to put together that kind of money?"

"I'll work harder by doing some more jobs," said Kazem. "So what do you say?"

"If you've made up your mind," said Maryam, "I'll go along with you. I'm getting fed up myself with the way things are going. I'll give some private lessons also to earn some cash."

From that day on Kazem did odd jobs here and there, while Maryam taught some of the children and women in the neighbourhood.

* * * *

One afternoon in mid-August Kazem went to meet Hassan Ghorazeh in the teahouse to give him the money for the forged passports. Hassan was sitting with a stranger at a table, smoking and talking quietly.

"Kazem Agha," said Hassan, casting watchful eyes around, "here are your passports." He pushed a large envelope towards Kazem. "At the border try to keep cool and pretend you're a couple going for a holiday. The day you decide to depart, you pay five hundred dollars to my friend here who'll accompany you to the city of Vaan, from where you'll be handed over to another man who'll get another five hundred dollars and arrange your passage from Istanbul to Greece. In Greece someone will give you the necessary papers for you to travel to England. From then on, God be with you. Good luck."

One evening in mid-September, as Kazem was sitting in the teahouse with Ali Khalifeh, Ali asked him, "Now that you've got your passports, when are you thinking to leave?"

"Soon, mate, soon," Kazem replied. "Once I knock together the right amount of cash."

"How much more do you need?"

"Another ten thousand tomans."

Ali Khalifeh dipped his hand into his side pocket and extracted a wad of banknotes and began to count them.

"Here is ten thousand," said Ali. "Take it and run away from this shithole as soon as you can."

"No, mate," Kazem protested. "I can't possibly accept that, Ali."

"Listen, Kazem," said Ali. "You're a good man. Besides, think of your wife. There'll be no future for you both here."

"But you're in a bad way yourself, cashwise."

"Never mind about me," said Ali. "I managed to get hold of an old artefact from a Revolutionary Guard who had stolen it from a museum during the chaos of the Revolution. As they hang anyone who possesses looted artefacts, he gave it to me to liquidate it as soon as possible. I found a rich merchant friend of mine who was escaping from Iran like many others, and sold it to him for handsome cash."

Kazem hardly knew what to say. "I promise I'll do my best to pay back this kindness."

"Now get out of this country and never look back," said Ali. "The war with Iraq is sure to start any day. The war-monger mollahs are braying war cries, preparing the nation for a Holy Jihad that'll be a godsend for them to dig in as rulers for ever."

44

"We should not waste time, Maryam," said Kazem that same night over supper. "I've got the right cash now. We should start sorting out our things to get out as soon as we can. There'll soon be war and only the Devil knows what'll happen to this country."

On the twenty-second of September the war broke out and Tehran was plunged into absolute anarchy.

There was no time to lose. One mid-day around the end of the month, Kazem and Maryam, their meagre belongings packed in an old suitcase he had found in a junk shop, entered the coach station in Shams-ol Emareh. Passengers were swirling all over the station, pushing and shoving one another, stampeding over wailing children who were being tugged around by their parents.

"I bet they're trying to escape from Tehran or even Iran like rats abandoning a sinking ship," Kazem whispered to Maryam, putting his hand on her shoulders. "After all these years, they've turned us into rats!"

After handing the suitcase to the driver's mate, Kazem and Maryam settled in their seat. Kazem sat on the window side as he wanted to take a last look at Tehran. As the coach began to manoeuvre its way through the multitude, Kazem looked out of the window. They look like a terrified herd of animals trampling on each other to get away from danger, he thought. What has been done to us?

The coach left the station. As it drove through the crowded streets, Kazem looked out on the places and streets he knew so well. Everyone was in a hurry. Where were they all going? He looked up at the gigantic billboards on which were painted in harsh colours colossal images of Khomeini and his cronies, hovering over everything, making the frantic people aware, at all times, of their everlasting presence. These grizzly, bearded old men glowered down on all animate and inanimate objects.

As the coach entered into Sepah Square – now Imam Khomeini Square – Kazem looked around. The statue of Reza Khan the Cossack had disappeared. Workers were hard at work erecting another monument, even more gigantic than the one before.

Kazem surveyed the different districts of Tehran as the coach passed through them. The city seemed to him like a huge sprawling ruin. The lanes and alleyways were now deserted. The new prevailing culture of terror had cast a black *aba* over them, under which, terrified, the people suppressed their sorrows about the dead and disappeared. Shrines for young martyrs of the regime, garishly decorated with colourful light bulbs, large photos and Koranic verses, stood at the entrance of most lanes and street corners. Gathered around them were old and young women veiled in black chadors, their shoulders shaking as they wept silently, clinging to the shrines.

Kazem no longer saw a homeland but a parched wasteland. On this land, forgotten by time and the rest of the humanity, nothing grew but thorns and bracken among which crept and crawled the nastiest of creatures attired in black turbans and camelhair *abas*, resembling dung-beetles and cockroaches who crawled out of one hole, scuttled around for filth and crept into another. The loud cries of brave men and women, Kazem thought, are smothered by the ear-splitting screeches of mollahs reciting the Koran and *hadith*. Those who could not stand the howling of these hyenas in abas and turbans had already left the homeland for good.

The coach left the city and drove along beside the Behesht-e Zahra cemetery. You can't see the end of this place any more, Kazem thought. It was like an endless desert, inhabited by young souls. He looked up at the sky. The pale late afternoon sun was pouring over the tombstones like a curse from the heavens. Crows flew chaotically here and there, screeching incessantly, as if lamenting something they had lost forever.

After an hour or so, the coach stopped at the holy city of Qom. Kazem and Maryam got out and found a roadside teahouse. Kazem ordered two glasses of tea, bread and cheese. He lit up a cigarette and gazed at the golden shrine of Hazrat-e Ma'sumeh gleaming in the setting sun. Raven-like, the women veiled in black chadors scurried in and out of its vast courtyard. Young and old mollahs scuttled everywhere, their *abas* ballooning in the soft autumnal breeze.

Round about dusk the coach left the holy city. Once on its outskirts, Kazem turned and looked back at the city. Unusually for that time of the year, dark clouds like tattered pieces of black *abas* flew across the horizon in the east, obscuring the moon as it gazed down on the inhabitants of Qom. The coach drove on towards the west.

Kazem rested his head on the back of the seat and fell into musing. Everyone who came into my life has stayed with me for a short while and then left, never to appear again, he ruminated. People he had known had already begun to turn into phantoms wandering in the twilight zone of his memories. Every now and then one of them showed his or her face from behind the fog of years and was swallowed up again by the nothingness.

He turned and looked at Maryam, with her head lying on the backrest of the seat, breathing rhythmically. Kazem gently put his arm around her and rested her head on his shoulder. He remembered she had been under the weather lately. Some mornings she had been sick and looked pale. Could it be that she was . . .? As he felt her warm body against his own, he felt instinctively that another life was throbbing inside her. Who could ever have imagined that Kazem Alaki might become a father one day, he thought with a smile.

Kazem cast a last glance back. The horizon glowed from behind patches of black clouds like shreds of shrouds, torn off from the bodies of freshly-buried corpses by stormy winds.

Ahead lay the future.

Glossary

aba:	A coarse fabric of wool or hair fibre with felted finish worn over other clothing by the Islamic clergy in Iran.
abdarkhaneh:	A room in an office where hot or cool drinks are prepared.
alam:	A steel rod topped by a stylized hand used in mourning ceremonies.
alamdar:	The man who carries alam.
Aladdin:	the name of a brand for gasoline heaters used for heating and cooking
Allahu akbar:	God is great
amali:	addicted to opium
Ankahtu wa zawagto:	I ask you to be my wife. (The traditional words recited by the groom during a wedding ceremony.)
arrack:	A distilled alcoholic drink
Ashura:	The tenth day of holy month of Moharram in which Imam Hussein, the grandson of Prophet Mohammad, was martyred in the Battle of Karbala, centuries ago.
Astrakhan:	The dark curly fleece of young karakul lambs from central Asia.
Aye zeki:	an exclamation of wonder mixed with contempt and surprise
azaan:	The Islamic call to prayer (sounded usually from the minaret of a mosque)
Behzisti:	social welfare
chador:	a long veil used to cover the head and worn by women over their clothes.

chibouk:	a smoking clay pipe with a long stem
daf:	a big tambourine
dombak:	A kind of drum played with the fingers and popular in Persian music.
droshky:	a horse-drawn cab
Fatimah:	youngest daughter of the prophet Mohammad and wife of the fourth caliph Ali; revered especially by Shiite Muslims.
fehrestgardan:	a man, a note in his hand, who went round from one actor to another in a ta'zieh reminding each one of his lines.
folk ruhauzi:	A form of musical play traditionally performed on wooden planks put on top of a *hauz* in traditional Persian houses.
gheran:	A monetary unit of the Qajar period, now replaced with Rial
gheymeh khorosht:	a popular dish of minced mutton and split peas (served with fried potatoes and steamed rice)
hadith:	The body of the transmitted actions and sayings of the Prophet Mohammed and his companions.
hajji:	Muslim who has made a pilgrimage to Mecca
halal:	lawful, legitimate, permissible
halva:	A cooked paste made of flour, oil, sugar, and saffron; usually served at funeral services.
hammam:	A public bathhouse
haraam:	religiously forbidden
hauz:	An ornamental pond in the middle of courtyard in traditional Persian houses used for washing, floating fruits in them, and ablutions.
hazrat:	His Holiness
Inshallah:	God willing
Kaba:	A square building in Mecca, the site most holy to Muslims, containing a sacred black stone.

kamancheh: An Iranian musical instrument similar to the fiddle.

Karbala: A holy city for Shiite Muslims in Iraq, because it is the site of the tomb of Imam Hussein who was slain there in 680.

kashkul: an oblong bowl usually made from a coconut shell.

khanum: Honorific used for women; can be used either before a given name or surname, after a given name, or alone as a form of address. It is also a euphemistic term addressing a prostitute.

kharposhteh: A small attic-like room that opens out into a roof.

Mahdi: A spiritual and temporal leader who will rule before the end of the world and restore religion and justice.

maman: a woman who runs a brothel.

Mobarak-e inshallah: Congratulations, blessings

monkaraat: forbidden actions, sinful acts, vice

muezzin: A person who calls the Muslims to prayer (usually from the minaret of a mosque.)

naqqal: a traditional story-teller who tells stories from *Shahnameh* (The Book of Kings) in teahouses

pahlavan: a champion wrestler

piroshki: Russian dumplings, pirozhki

Qabilto: I consent. (The traditional words recited by the bride during a wedding ceremony.)

rahbar: (in Islamic Republic of Iran) the Supreme Leader

Rostam: The greatest hero of pre-Islamic Persian legend of Ferdowsi's epic poem called *Shahnameh* (the tenth-century Book of Kings).

salawat: an Arabic formula which means: Blessed be Mohammad and the House of Mohammad.

sangak bread: a type of flat Iranian bread baked on hot pebbles.

Shahnameh: Or Book of Kings is an enormous poetic opus

	written by the Persian poet Ferdowsi around 1000 AD and is the national epic of the cultural sphere of Greater Persia.
Shahmaghsood:	a pale-green precious stone mostly found in mines around the city of Mashhad
Shahr-e No:	Literally 'The Citadel of the New City'. It was the largest brothel in Iran situated in Tehran, enclosed by a wall.
siegheh:	Under Shiite Law a man may have a maximum of four wives. In addition he's allowed an unlimited number of temporary wives, who make a marriage contract for a period ranging anywhere from one hour to ninety-nine years. These *siegheh* wives have no inheritance rights and are not officially registered with the city or the mosque.
taftoon bread:	A type of round flat bread popular in central Iran
tar:	a stringed musical instrument popular in Iran.
tekieh:	A temporary mosque.
toman:	An unofficial monetary unit in Iran, equal to 10 rials.
Ta'zieh:	Persian version of Islamic opera re-enacting the death of martyrs who were killed in Karbala along with Imam Hussein during the month of Moharram
Yaa Ali madad:	Oh, help us Ali

About the Author

Feridon Rashidi was born in Iran in 1955 and came to the UK in 1977. Resident in London, for 33 years he taught in several primary schools in the city. With five degrees from two London University Colleges (B.Sc. Psychology, B.A. French Language and Literature, PGCE, M.Sc. in Child Development, and MA in Theory and Practice of Translation from French to English) he is fluent in Farsi and French. He was a trainee Educational Psychologist for one year. He is now a full-time writer and has written more than 25 short stories, 16 of which are published as a collection, Tales of Iran, including the prize-winning story, Ashura. The story is also published on writers'hub.com and Iranian.com. He has also published a mathematics scheme for Key Stage 1 children, Numeracy Lessons.

www.ingramcontent.com/pod-product-compliance
Ingram Content Group UK Ltd.
Pitfield, Milton Keynes, MK11 3LW, UK
UKHW020449200726
13857UKWH00002B/633